TOM FRANKLIN

Tom Franklin, from Dickinson, Alabama, is the author of the collection of stories titled *Poachers*, which was named as a Best First Book of Fiction by *Esquire* in 1999. The title novella won the 1999 Edgar Award for Best Short Story and was included in both *Best American Mystery Stories, 1999* and *Best American Mystery Stories of the Century*. He is the recipient of a 2001 Guggenheim Fellowship and has held the John and Renee Grisham Writer-in-Residency at Ole Miss and the Tennessee Williams Fellowship at Sewanee. He lives in Oxford, Mississippi, with his wife, poet Beth Ann Fennelly, and their young daughter Claire. *Hell at the Breech* is his first novel.

Advance praise for

HELL AT THE BREECH

'Beautifully written and potent . . . so compelling. He knows the grit, detritus and psychology of life in the rural world, is utterly convincing in his renditions of violence, yet responds to nature with a near poetry of appreciation.'
Washington Post

'Hypnotically captivating. Arguably the most extraordinary first novel to come out of the South since Charles Frazier's National Book Award-winning *Cold Mountain*. In one fell swoop, Franklin leaps to the forefront of contemporary Southern writers.'
Orlando Sentinel

'Based on a true story, *Hell at the Breech* boasts all the satisfactions of a contemporary mystery – it's as if Faulkner wrote serials, with all the pleasures and profound strangeness that that implies.'
Entertainment Weekly

'A pleasure to read for its clean, unexpected turns of phrase (in a cotton field, "each tuft [is] white as a senator's eyebrow"), the laconic humour, and vibrant, complex characters who spring from the pages.'
Publishers Weekly

From the reviews of

POACHERS

'I am amazed by Franklin's power. I'm reminded, by the evocative strength of the prose and the relentlessness of the imagination, of William Faulkner and particularly the Faulkner of *The Wild Palms*. Franklin is a vivid portraitist of these harsh human types, and his authority in depicting the natural world "along this stretch of the Alabama River" is dazzling. I can't believe he's not better known, but he will be, and soon.'   PHILIP ROTH

'I like Tom Franklin's stories the same way I like Lucinda Williams's music, and for the same reason: they're not updating an old song. They're set in the South, sure. But they're a new song for the South. They possess an inherent sweetness even when they're rough 'n' tough. And when they're funny, it's not at the world's expense. They're poignant, and their poignance comes from longing; yet not for some mossy past, but for the present, as it spirits away from in front of us just at the moment we notice it's arrived. These stories surprised me. They give valuable and unexpected depth to what I thought fiction could do.'   RICHARD FORD

'Marvellous . . . The centrepiece is the magnificent title tale where three vicious brothers make their precarious living from illicit hunting. The last paragraph will stay with you for ever; if only John Boorman's film *Deliverance* were half as scary. Franklin writes beautifully with an unsparing, detached eye.'   *The Times*

'With all these bad husbands, ne'er-do-well buddies and frayed marriages, it's as if the author kidnapped Raymond Carver's characters and set them loose in the Deep South . . . With this satisfying collection he establishes himself as one of the region's most interesting emerging voices.'
New York Times Book Review

'This is as strong a collection as any I've read in recent years. The stories in it are collectively and individually brilliant, imbued with a high sense of Southern Gothic and a dark sense of humour.'   *Chicago Tribune*

BY TOM FRANKLIN

Poachers: Stories
Hell at the Breech

HELL
AT THE
BREECH

———◆———

TOM FRANKLIN

Flamingo
An Imprint of HarperCollinsPublishers

Flamingo
An Imprint of HarperCollins*Publishers*
77–85 Fulham Palace Road,
Hammersmith, London W6 8JB

Flamingo is a registered trade mark of
HarperCollins*Publishers* Limited

www.harpercollins.co.uk/flamingo

Published by Flamingo 2004
1 3 5 7 9 8 6 4 2

First published in the USA by
William Morrow 2003

A catalogue record for this book
is available from the British Library

ISBN 0 00 226159 6

Set in Bulmer

Printed and bound in Great Britain by
Clays Limited, St Ives plc

For Beth Ann
and for Claire

And the children of Mitcham Beat were warned that if they ever heard the whinny of horses and the squeak of good leather, they had better run and hide.

—THE MITCHAM WAR OF CLARKE COUNTY, ALABAMA
Harvey H. Jackson III, in collaboration with
Joyce White Burrage and James A. Cox

AUTHOR'S NOTE

While there was a Mitcham War in Clarke County, Alabama, in the 1890s, and while the gang that called itself "Hell-at-the-Breech" did exist, and while a number of murders occurred, both by certain members of the gang and by certain men riding against it, the author has taken great liberties in the writing of this novel. Each character is fully a creation of the author's imagination and in no way represents any person, living or dead. Anyone interested in reading more about these events is directed to the excellent book *The Mitcham War of Clarke County, Alabama*, by Harvey H. Jackson, III, in collaboration with Joyce White Burrage and James A. Cox.

HELL AT THE BREECH

A SACK

OF

PUPPIES

September 1897

DAWN CREPT UP OUT OF THE TREES, defining a bole, a burl, a leaf at a time the world he'd spent the night trying to comprehend. But what would daylight offer except the illusion of understanding? At least in darkness you were spared the pretending. Behind him in the cabin where he and William had lived since the death of their parents came the morning stirring of the Widow Gates, the clatter of logs as she arranged them in a tepee in the fireplace. He should have gone and done that for her.

Her soft, clucking voice reached his ears.

Was she talking to herself? No, to the dog who'd had her puppies the evening before. Ever the midwife, the widow had aided the dog as she'd delivered, with a wet rag cleaning the pups so the bitch would be free to push and whine, the old woman stolidly taking the halfhearted nip from the dog, who was confused by the pain. He turned his head to better hear, to learn what she might confide to the dog, but her voice was too soft.

Get up and go on in there, he thought, help her get breakfast made. Act like nothing's wrong.

But he didn't. He continued to sit with his feet on the steps as the earth redefined itself around him, same as it had the day before and the day before that and as far back as his memory went, as if this dawn were no different from any other. The ground shifted and twitched with early sparrows; he studied them on their twig legs, invisible in the leaves until they moved. He remembered walking home from the meeting at the store earlier, his face to the sky, searching between branches for the white globe of the moon. How unlike itself the world seemed at night, when trees lurked dark and hulking and the birds of the day disappeared who knew where.

His head had begun to ache. He leaned forward and cupped his palms over his ears and closed his eyes, elbows on knees. He was in that position when her legs appeared beside him.

"Macky."

He turned and looked at her ankles through the bars of his fingers. "I couldn't sleep."

"Where's William?"

"I don't know."

"Still over at the store, I reckon."

She set a croaker sack on the porch by her feet. The bag was moving. From inside, behind the closed door, there came a scratching. A whine.

"How long you been up?" she asked.

He couldn't stop watching the bag. "I don't know."

"You don't know."

"That's what I said, Granny."

Her quick hand knocked his hat off. He left it where it lay.

"You'll not snap at me, boy, not after—"

"I'm sorry." His cheeks had grown hot, she had never hit him.

She reached for his head again, gently this time, but he rose and moved off and stood on the bottom step, facing away from her, gazing out at the just-born yard that lay stretched and steaming before them. The trees were nothing more than trees now and the sparrows just sparrows.

"How many did she have?" he asked.

"Six that lived. The runt died."

She stood holding the sack, then raised it for him. He took it from her; he could feel them moving, hear them crying.

"Drowning's quickest," she said.

"I know."

He heard the widow scraping back across the porch with her cane and heard the door close. Frantic toenails of the dog clicking on the floorboards. As he walked away she began to bark. He went

4

faster, having forgotten his hat, holding the bag out from his side and trying not to feel them or hear them.

At the creek he knelt on the big shale rock where he and William fished. Leaves floated past in the water. It was a deep creek, good for diving and swimming except for the moccasins and snapping turtles. Once they'd caught an alligator snapper the size of a saddle, had lugged it in thinking they'd hooked a log. Then it was sitting on the bank gaping at them, a rock come to life, its shell bony and jagged and mossy green, its head as big as a man's fist. It kept turning its snout side to side with its mouth open and trying to back up, its tongue a black wormy blob. They couldn't afford to lose their hook, but retrieving it seemed impossible with the turtle alive. After some discussion they'd overturned it and, with great care, cut its throat, dragged it far from the water and left it lying on its back. Next day they'd returned to find it somehow still alive, its horned feet kicking feebly at the sky, mouth working open and closed.

The bag lay pulsing. He put a hand over it and defined beneath the cloth a trembling body no larger than a field mouse, legs, tail, head—eyes that would still be closed, mouth seeking the warm purple teats of its mother. This dog had given birth four times in her life, and until now the old woman herself had done this deed, at first telling the boys she was giving the puppies to a colored family, until the morning they'd followed her to the creek and seen the truth. She'd explained then that while they could afford to feed one dog for the purposes it served, her litters were too much.

He looked into the creek. Another Mack Burke watched him from the water and they locked eyes and rolled up opposite sleeves and gathered the mouths of their sacks in their fists. He looked away from his reflection and submerged the bag, then loosened his grip so that cold water rushed in. He left it under for two full minutes, then let go of the sack and sought its other end, pulling it out of the water, not looking at what still things spilled from its mouth, nudged by the slow-moving creek.

5

He stood up on the rock and his reflection stood with him and rolled down its sleeve as he rolled down his and turned when he did and was lost. He wrung out the bag as he walked and at the cabin laid it out to dry on the porch. He took up his soft hat and when he opened the door the dog lurched past his thigh and flashed over the porch into the yard, scattering the sparrows. The widow came to his side, her wrists and hands white from flour, and together they watched the dog circle the yard with her nose furrowing the leaves, the circle widening until she'd left the yard entirely, headed for the creek. He didn't have to follow to know she would stop searching only when she reached the water's edge, that she would spend the day and the night there, standing in the creek to her shoulders, shivering, whining, recovering perhaps one of the drowned puppies and carrying it in her mouth to a warm secret pocket of the forest, nosing the cold soggy thing to her dribbling teat and waiting and waiting and waiting and waiting.

"HE WAS
WITH
US"

August 1898

I

THE COTTON CROP WAS LAID BY, three weeks until picking, and now were days of waiting when men saw to the maintenance of their equipment and gave their mules and wives time to rest, their bodies time to mend.

On a Friday at dusk a farmer called Floyd Norris and his three young sons were under the low roof of the porch of their cabin, the man holding an unlit pipe in his teeth and repairing a trace, the boys watching, their hands flickering here and again in unconscious imitation of the father's. Stacks of flat rocks held up the house, and underneath the porch a pair of slender black-spotted dogs lay in identical poses, their long snouts on their forepaws. Inside, Norris's wife sat on a stool nursing a baby of five months in one arm and with the other working the churn handle up and down. When a fly landed on the baby's bald head she blew it away. Presently she heard the dogs go to yapping from under the house and, stretching her neck to look through a space in the logs where a clump of mud had come out, accidentally dislodged the baby's lips from her nipple. When he began to fuss and wave his arms, she adjusted his head and her cheek twitched as he reattached himself and resumed his sucking.

What she saw through the hole was two of them in their hoods walking through the hip-high cotton. Stepping carefully, not damaging any of the plants. The baby at her breast had closed his eyes and hummed as he suckled, the fly had settled again on his forehead. She stopped churning and leaned her face closer to the wall and called, "Alvin. Alfred. Arnold."

The boys on the porch looked at their father, then at the white-hooded pair coming toward them.

9

"Go on," he said, setting aside the pliers and the trace.

The boys obeyed, rising, brushing at flies, their necks ringed with dirt. Inside, their mother told them to sit and play by the hearth but not to touch the kettle over the fire. She kept her eye against the wall.

The hooded men passed through the shadow the barn cast and paused at the edge of the houseward path between high rows of bushy cotton and faced the two snarling dogs. They held shotguns but did not move to use them. Their overalls were identical to Norris's, but neither wore a shirt beneath and their shoulders were red and scaly from the sun. One wore no socks, his white ankles showed below his cuffs. The hoods were cloth bags bearing vague blue lettering and with jagged eye and mouth holes, tied at the neck with string and darkened with sweat.

One of the dogs advanced on them, sideways, its head low and lower jaw aquiver in its growl, its hackles rippling over its back. Norris whistled a single note and the dogs snapped their heads to face him and unbowed themselves and trotted in tandem back toward the house and up the steps to the spot on the boards where he pointed. "Sit on down," he said, and they did, their tails thumping the porch but their hackles still raised. "Quiet," he said.

The hooded men crossed the yard and stood before him, their shotguns held so casually they might have been out to shoot dove.

"Sorry 'bout the disguises, Floyd," one said, teeth showing through his mouth hole.

The second one remained quiet, just the slight flutter of the hood at his nose. He kept picking at the cloth with his fingers.

"Hell," Floyd said. "No need for apologies. Y'all are carrying on in dangerous times. If I didn't have these young ones to look after, I'd be out yonder with you."

"You know why we're here."

He nodded. "What you want me to say?"

"Just say Lev and William was here with you all afternoon

tomorrow. They drunk with you a goodly amount of liquor, which they brung, and played dominoes on your porch."

"Who won?" Floyd asked.

"Lev did. You don't remember the scores."

"That might hurt your story. Lev can't play worth a shit."

The hooded men looked at each other.

"I'll have to say they brung the dominoes, too," Floyd said. "I don't own me a set."

The one who'd spoken reached into his back pocket. He came out with a box and tossed it to Floyd, who caught it one-handed.

"Don't forget," the man said.

"Naw," said Floyd. "I won't."

The hooded man nodded, then he and his silent companion turned and went back through the cotton.

Inside, the woman detached the baby with her finger and hung him over her shoulder and patted him on the back. Soon he burped. She laid him on the floor where he gaped at the ceiling and waved his arms and kicked his legs. She told his brothers to quit fighting and went out adjusting her dress.

"It was them," he said, opening the box of dominoes. In among the ivory-colored tiles, he found a silver dollar. He glanced behind him.

"You'll involve us all in their dirty work if you say what they told you to," she said.

"Be worse off if we don't, woman." He palmed the dollar and slipped it into his overalls. "Now go on get dinner going and send them young ones back out."

She shaded her eyes with a hand, watching the hooded men as they receded and grew indistinct in the far-reaching cotton. Before they entered the tree line across the field they stopped and looked back. She went cold inside. She thought of the Widow Gates, said to be able to discern ghosts from living folk and who often saw people no one else could see. The old woman would point into a field and say, There's one.

11

The hooded men had vanished now, into the woods and gone.

"Damn it," Floyd said, "I told you get on."

She looked at the back of his head. "You ain't keeping that," she said of the dominoes, and turned, went inside, and stepped over the wiggling baby on her way to the churn.

II

Joe Anderson rode his mule in the deep leafy shade of a bank of earth, the animal sinking in the loose sand with each step. It had come a good rain of late and the world seemed fresh. Grass hung off the top of the bank and sapling pines came out at an angle, you could see where children had climbed on them, swinging, a shred of rope dangling and moving in the wind. The woods were high all around, so green it felt almost cloudy, thrashers noisy in the bracken and sparrows flitting overhead, the ground slashed like paintbrush work with the shadow of pine needles.

He stopped the mule and sat still for a moment looping the rein tighter and tighter around his hand so his fingers began to turn crimson. He looked to his right and then up, to the top of the bank, where two figures were gazing down on him, their shotguns held in repose. One wore a white hood, the other seemed to be a Negro, though odd-looking in a half-finished way.

Only then did it occur to him to reach for his twelve-gauge, roped to the saddle behind him, but when his hand strayed back there the black fellow twitched the barrel of his own gun and said, "Ah."

The one in the hood rose from his squat and spread his arms for balance and scampered down the bank, bringing a small avalanche with him. He landed and stepped in the road.

"Hidy, Mr. Anderson."

Anderson glared down from his mule. "I'm not fond of having shotguns brandished at me," he said.

The hooded man looked up at his companion, who remained in his crouch. "Says he don't like having guns on him."

Without taking his eyes off Anderson, the other man leaned over the edge and let a long tendon of tobacco spit reach down off his lower lip. He jutted his chin and the spit broke loose. He said, "Tell him get down."

"You heard the man," the one in the hood said. "Get on off. And keep your paws where I can see 'em."

When Anderson stood against the bank, hands in the air, the dark-faced man took hold of one of the outcropped trees and with a rattle of branch and leaf fell more than climbed down. The mule had watched it all with an air of boredom, one eye closing and opening, its ears swiveling. It snapped viciously at a horsefly, then took a few experimental steps and looked back. Nobody moved to stop it, reins dragging the ground, so it took a few more steps at a halftrot and presently rounded a bend in the road.

The men watched it go, the gunstock wagging in the air.

The dark-faced one spat again. "Ain't real dependable, is he? First sign of trouble off he goes."

You could see the man had painted his face with ash, his eyes eerie white holes in all that black. Sweat etched down his cheeks. The lobe of one ear shiny at the edges.

Anderson squinted. "Lev James?"

The man leaned in close. "Yeah," he whispered. "I don't like wearing no hood. I get antsy."

"You'll be wearing the hangman's hood before long," Anderson said. He pointed down the road. "You're accountable for that mule and that twelve-gauge."

"Now hold that tone of yours," James said. "We could kill you right now, and nobody'd ever know it was us. Far as everbody's concerned, me and my buddy here is somewheres else, playing dominoes." He looked at the man in the hood. "How many games we play this afternoon?"

"Hard to count."

"And who won?"

"I did."

"Son, you better tell this man who really won. Joe, if I was to shoot my buddy here for a liar, would you swear I was with you? Would you be my witness? We could say we was out squirrel hunting. 'Course we might ought to shoot us a couple, just to make it look real. I could brang 'em over to your house for supper this evening. Get your wife to fry 'em up. Then me and that older girl of yours could spoon on the porch." He flapped his tongue and cackled, his coating of ash cracking at the edges of his mouth.

Anderson had gone pale. "Trash like you will never darken my table."

James stepped closer and looked him in the eyes, their noses an inch apart. "How you know I ain't gone strip you nekkid and shoot you right in your tracks here, then put on your duds and round up that mule of yours and ride over to your house and not only darken your table but darken your wife and girls, too?" He jammed the barrel of his shotgun under Anderson's chin and pushed it up so the man appeared to be looking at the sky. He forced him backward against the bank, dirt crumbling onto his shoulders, in his hair, and began rifling the older man's pants pockets, lingering around his crotch, grinning.

"Hey," he called to his partner, "you got to come here, feel this man's little biddy tallywhacker. It ain't no longer than your pinky finger. Nor no fatter neither."

The hooded man laughed, high and strange.

James pulled a watch from Anderson's pocket and snapped its fob and put it into his own pants. He found a jackknife, too, a coin purse and two metal washers which he winged down the road as if skipping rocks. Then he backed away, patting his pockets.

Overhead, clouds moved across the sun, the ground darkening, the men's shadows growing faint on the dirt then disappearing, a change so abrupt the three paused in their doings to study the sky. A flock of crows began to collect up the road in the bare branches of a dead oak tree, their voices gathering strength as they funneled down from the sky in a whorl, like a tornado in reverse, coloring the tree black.

"What is it y'all want?" Anderson said. "If you mean to kill me, then by God do it. I won't grovel."

"See," James said. "I told you. My buddy here bet me a dime you'd gravel and I said you wouldn't."

Anderson lowered his hands and clasped them together over his chest in a prayerful pose.

"Hey, Will," James said to his partner, "are you watching? First he won't gravel, next he goes and lowers his hands."

The hooded one didn't answer. He was watching the treeful of crows, stragglers filtering into the spaces where the sky showed through, an endless storm of descending birds.

"Young Burke," Anderson called to the other one, "if that's you behind that mask, I ask you to stop these insults and return me my property and let me go fetch my mule. You were raised as a Christian, so what are you doing in the company of this *trash*?"

James fired from the hip. At the same instant the crows exploded as one from the oak, dragging with them for a moment the shape of the tree. Anderson's shirt ballooned and sagged, he turned to the right, that arm raised. He looked down at his side, his arm starting to shiver. He moaned and ground his shoulders into the bank, more dirt falling on him, his shirt pocket bulging with it. The crows were whirling in the sky, their cawing impossibly loud. Anderson slid to a sitting position. Let go a breath.

It grew suddenly light underneath them, their shadows spilling out from their feet and spreading toward the east, the woods around them changing to a brighter green. James lowered his shotgun and broke it open and removed the smoking hull. He smelled it, wiggled it on his finger, and put it in his coat pocket. He reloaded, closed the gun's breech, and walked to where Anderson sat and knelt before him and gazed at the shut eyes.

"I believe he's playing possum on us."

From beside him he got a fistful of sand and underhanded it into Anderson's mouth—his lips moved, his teeth bloody.

"Hell," James said, waving his hand before the farmer's face.

Anderson's eyes came open, wet and bluer than before. He looked at the tree the crows had fled, his lips glistening with sand.

William Burke snatched his hood off and glanced down the road the way the mule had gone. "You ain't gone shoot no more, are you, Lev? We ain't too far from the next place."

"Naw." James set his gun against the bank and fished in his pockets for the jackknife. He pushed Anderson's forehead back, revealing his throat. He opened the knife one-handed—"Hope for your own comfort you kept this sticker sharp," he said to Anderson—and swiped the blade over the skin between his Adam's apple and chin, opening a bright gash that began to spout and bubble blood. In seconds Anderson's shirtfront was red. James watched his eyes, which were wide now, and the eyes watched him back, the chest twitched and a gurgling sound issued from within. One arm came up and poked feebly at him. When the eyes had gone flat he stuck the knife blade into the sand a few times to clean it before he put it away.

III

Clarke County Sheriff Billy Waite sat peeling a large green apple on his front porch, a Havana corona smoking on the rail beside him, his long sore feet propped on the rail by the cigar, his shined boot toes reflecting the bright white moon. On the other end of the porch the swing creaked pleasantly on its chains. This was the time of home-night he enjoyed, when his wife was inside asleep and he, at last, was alone. Time of year he enjoyed, too, the kind of peaceable weather you needed sleeves for but not a coat, chill in the air to make your scalp tingle but not set you to shivering.

What he'd been thinking about tonight was something he'd been pondering for a while, how his thirty-and-some years as a peace officer had so often taken him away from his family that he now felt distanced from them, the wife especially: Sue Alma could chatter straight through a day, all small talk, and not say anything of substance, or at least anything he could make sense of. How delicate the candlewicking on the coverlet. That the piecrust had too much flour. He knew, because he was a different man at home, at the head of the supper table, in bed, that she really didn't understand who he was at his core, didn't know the person who rode the trails and roads and tacked up eviction notices, who'd killed six men from behind his badge and wounded seven more and brought a dozen others to be hanged, their full names and the dates of their deaths something he could repeat backward and forward and did on occasion when the hour grew long in the saddle or when sleep seemed a young man's luxury. Sue Alma's ignorance of his true self was his own fault, though, for he'd chosen never to tell her of that other life he had lived, of blood and hurt, of exploring the dark, widening canyons that ran through some men's hearts. His own heart, too. For when was he happier? Here on the porch or there in the saddle?

Now, faced with ending his reign as sheriff, his sixty-year-old body giving out, he wondered what the two strangers in their house would say to each other once he'd handed over his badge. For what had occurred to him—stopped him as he crossed the street one morning last week—was that if Sue Alma didn't know the true him, it was entirely possible that he didn't know the true her, the self she composed behind walls and among the clink of dishes and silverware and a cranked Gramophone.

His apple peel had about reached the floorboards, one continuous curl, a feat of peeling he took pride in, took in fact more

17

enjoyment from than the eating of the apple, which was just chewing and swallowing. Same with the cigar, which he'd lit and got to burning well but now drew from but rarely, not until it was about to go out, when he'd have to pull deeply with his lungs and puff his cheeks. It kept him alert, and there was nothing to equal these little pleasures of control to Billy Waite, a peel a yard long, a cigar all the way from Havana sucked back from the dead.

Did Sue Alma know even *these* things about him? Or if asked, would she just flip her hand and say, Billy, he loves apples and cigars?

Down the road a ways a dog had gone to barking, that mongrel the dim-witted feed store clerk kept tied to his porch post. And then another couple following suit, the sibling pair of coon hounds belonging to the undertaker. Language clear as English, telling Waite someone was coming his way. On a horse.

He kept peeling, unhurried, hoping to finish before the person reached him—it was always him they came for—the peel now curling on the porch floor. He took his feet off the rail, noting that his cigar had stopped smoking, and looked behind him at the screen door. His son was grown and gone, a logger in the next county, where a fellow could make a little money if he worked hard enough and didn't drink it up or spend it on women. For a moment Waite longed for the way the boy would, on hearing the dogs, already have slipped on his boots without socks and come to stand behind his father, his black hair rumpled, a pistol concealed in the small of his back, not saying a word, just waiting.

Waite had always hoped Johnny-Earl would want to be his deputy—the position was his to appoint—the boy tough and inde- pendent and sharp of instinct and loyal and of a fair mind. It had taken Waite some time to understand, however, that what would have drawn Johnny-Earl out of bed, what would have caused him to arm himself and stand on the porch behind his father, was not a love for justice or peace, but a love for the father. A fear of losing him.

While Waite could peel his apples and watch his cigars smolder and feel a calmness, could duck behind a tree and maintain presence of mind while some crazy outlaw filled the brush around him with squirrel shot and the air with cordite, what Johnny-Earl experienced was dread. Waite had tried to tell him, dead set as the boy was on leaving, that these nerves were precisely what a deputy needed. They were a tool as tangible as a pistol or a blackjack. Recklessness would kill a lawman instantly, he'd said. The smart ones, the men who lived, were those most cautious, the fellows who handled their fear each day like they loaded a gun.

Even as he said this to Johnny-Earl, though, he'd known it to be a failing argument. And his son knew it, too. So two summers ago, at nineteen years of age, the pull of his own will finally stronger than his father's, Johnny-Earl had shrugged beyond his guilt and boarded the chuffing train in Whatley with two of his friends and a parcel of Sue Alma's almond cookies.

Now the visitor had grown close, Waite heard the horse. The dogs had fallen quiet, already bored with this event and waiting for the next thing to move through their lives and set them abark. Waite's peel fell in one piece between his boots and he rose, placed the naked apple and his pocketknife on the rail next to the dead cigar, its ash an inch long. From beneath a cloth napkin he picked up his Smith & Wesson revolver from the table and folded his arms, concealing the gun.

"You sure it ain't just a story?" Waite asked. He'd gotten his cigar going and held it between two fingers and watched its smoke drift over the rail. "Rumors fly out of Mitcham Beat like hair in a catfight."

"No," Ernest McCorquodale said, fanning his cheeks with a newspaper. He sat across the porch, his horse hobbled to the rail— he'd ridden ten miles from Coffeeville, where he ran a store. "A farmer I loan to told me. Reliable Christian fellow. He come in to pay on his bill and said everybody out there knew about it. They ambushed Anderson in broad daylight, not five miles from here. Them poor people ain't got no idea what to do."

Waite didn't care for the pious set of McCorquodale's chin, his thin pinched lips, and resented that he'd come here, tonight, to tell such news. How many ragged farmers had the storekeeper foreclosed on in the last two, three years? Dutiful Waite riding out to over half the county with a sealed piece of paper to serve, the hungry families watching him with their smutty faces, the father of each brood, nearly every damn time, asking even as he took the paper what it said because he couldn't read. McCorquodale didn't seem to give a damn that they had nowhere to go.

"This Christian have a name?" Waite asked.

McCorquodale's fan stopped. "He swore me not to use it. They'll kill him if they know."

"Well, I ain't likely to ride out yonder revealing your secrets, Ernest."

McCorquodale looked off into the yard. "I just give him my word, is all."

"He didn't say whether the justice of the peace out there had any notions of who'd of shot him? These country folk usually act pretty quick. Time I ride out yonder they'll have done took care of it."

McCorquodale snorted. "The justice is probably one of 'em."

Waite ashed his cigar. He'd heard the rumors about Mitcham Beat—a gang of outlaws, dressed in hoods, were robbing folks and burning houses and barns. Chasing off colored people. The justice of the peace, Tom Hill, hadn't been able to stop the violence and so Waite had been expecting this moment, when he'd have to do something.

"The fact is it's done got way out of hand out there," McCorquodale said. "As a tax-paying citizen, and a Christian, I aim to see something's done."

"You keep slinging that word around, don't you."

20

"What word?"

" 'Christian,' " Waite said. "In this day and age you'll get farther with 'tax-payer,' I expect."

The storekeeper stood up. "Well. I'll bid you good night, Sheriff, and hope I've had some influence on you. If not . . ." He didn't finish, just left the threat turning in the air like a smoke ring.

Waite watched him, and once McCorquodale had mounted his horse and disappeared into the darkness and the dogs had started up again, he looked at the door behind him and reached beneath his chair for his bottle and twisted off its lid and sipped, then sipped again. He would ride out in the morning.

The bluish predawn found him rising without having slept much from beside his softly snoring wife and sitting on the edge of his bed waiting for his lower back—it hurt all the way down to his heel—to loosen up. It found him standing in his socks over the commode waiting for the last of the night's urine to drizzle out. Searching for his reading glasses among Sue Alma's cluttered talcum and toilet water shelves and finally leaving without them, scratching her a quick note he could barely read himself. He had a headache from his drinking and took a powder for it.

On the porch he picked up last night's cigar—only half smoked—and tapped off its cold nub of ash and dropped it in his coat pocket and with his Marlin Model 1893 went slowly down the slick steps and through the grass of the pasture toward the stable where his eight-year-old gelding was nickering in his stall, hot white vapor blooming from his nose. Waite fed King a few old carrots and brushed his coat and combed his mane, then hung a felt blanket over his back and set about saddling and bridling him, fastening on his bedroll, a knapsack, and a russet leather gun sheath, into which he slid his rifle.

He hadn't been out in a month, not since tracking a bigamist to

Washington County, and he had to admit it felt good to be here in the dawn with the promise of heat and his boots wet with dew and the morning birds hitting their bright notes.

Passing his cousin Oscar York's large house, a few last stars overhead, he was surprised to see Oscar, the probate judge, coming down the steps between the columns, carrying a rifle. He'd obviously been waiting in the darkness of his porch.

"Morning, Billy."

Waite stopped the horse. The windows in the other houses set back along the road were lit, people stepping onto their porches to pitch last night's water into the yard, a rooster crowing from somewhere. Waite stretched his legs in the stirrups and looked down. "What gets you out here this early, Judge?"

"Just on my way to see you."

Waite looked past Oscar's shoulder and frowned. "Don't know why I even bother going to my office."

"Where you off to now?"

"Just some business. What's with the Winchester?"

Oscar looked up the road and down. He moved in close by, horse between him and the trees across the road, and rubbed King along the underside of his jaw. "With folks being assassinated, I'm just protecting myself."

"That's a long way out in the country, Osk. Them old boys ain't crazy enough to bring their doings to town."

"Ten miles ain't that far, Billy. And Anderson was a lot closer in than that. I ain't taking no chances." He looked toward the trees. "Ernest said he stopped by last evening. He's in our guest room now. You ain't never for the life of you heard such snoring."

"Yeah, he stopped by. Damn near nine-thirty."

"So I take it you're heading out there."

Waite eased back into the saddle. "I don't like being told how to do my job, Oscar. Not even from you."

"Nobody's telling you nothing you don't know already. The

truth is, them folks have been on a tear since Arch Bedsole. And everybody's saying the same thing, Billy. Voters, I mean. Saying you're too old to take on something like that bunch by yourself."

Waite folded his hands over the pommel, waiting.

"Ain't it about time you got a deputy," Oscar asked, "somebody *official* to watch your back?"

"Let me guess. You got just the candidate."

"Well. What about that Ardy Grant? He's been home damn near a month, looking for work. And talk about shooting. That knucklehead can take a skeeter's head off with a pistol."

"It's a lot more to it than being able to shoot," Waite said. "And I don't trust that boy." He gigged the horse's ribs with his spurs and Oscar stepped aside, stood in the road with his rifle.

Minutes later Waite had left behind the town and county seat of Grove Hill as it clacked and clanged to life. The yells of workers and the up-fluttering of shades along the storefronts and bump of boot heels on the wooden porches and the snorting and whinny of horses hungry in the livery and the click of wagons on the wide street—it all grew indistinct as the road steepened and narrowed and trees drew over him, twittering their leaves across his view.

Waite felt better in his bones now with the morning's rust behind him and lit the half cigar despite the early hour. King lifted his head and began to lope, splashing through a puddle. Leaving feathers of bluish smoke dissolving in the fog behind them, they passed the cotton gin with the operator already setting up the scales and two fellows wrestling with a sitting mule. A tall farmer Waite knew waved with a wrench. Half a mile farther he encountered a mule-drawn wagonload of raw cotton driven by a black man; Waite eased King out of the road and let the wagon pass, a pair of sleepy children sitting atop the cotton, one sucking his thumb. He waved to the children, then rode on.

Mitcham Beat, his destination, ten miles of bad road east of Grove Hill, was the voting district that included much outlying farmland and the hamlet of New Prospect, which was little more than a crossroads store with a rarely used blacksmith shed on one side of the building and another shed for storage on the other. There was a croquet court there, too, where the people gathered when their work allowed. All told, there were probably a couple hundred voters in the beat, mostly white, mostly cotton farmers, all poor.

Waite hadn't been out there in a year—the journey ate at his nerves and bounced his aged skeleton in his saddle; he'd frankly hoped to live the rest of his life not worrying about the place, but the currents of his blood knew he'd one day head back, for often in his dreams the land he walked was in Mitcham Beat.

The road would be tolerable for a few miles, but once you passed the covered bridge that marked the beginning of the beat, things changed: first, you had to bat your way through two miles of gnarled woodland called the Bear Thicket—this stretch of road, or shadow of road, which paralleled a creek, felt more like a cave, the trees overhead and understory below so thick at times you'd see little sky at all, the earth caught in perpetual twilight. Half-buried rocks were a hazard to your horse, and you were often off and working at moving a fallen tree from your path. To make matters worse, it was rolling land—which accounted for its not being cleared and planted—and some of the steeper hills were chancy if you were on a new horse. Waite felt good about King, though, a tall chestnut he'd raised from a foal; other than being a little knock-kneed, he was dependable and sturdy, gun-broke, fast when he needed to be, and of a mild temperament. This trip, however, could move any man or animal to foul spirits. When it came time to transport the cotton out, the farmers would take it southwest to Coffeeville.

Once out of the thicket, though, the land grew pretty to Waite's eye: field beyond field beyond field of well-kept cotton, each tuft white as a senator's eyebrow. Between the fields there were less level, unplantable spaces, lush deep wooded ravines with sprawling water oaks in the bottoms and hollows crowded with pine and other evergreens, limbs hung with Spanish moss, ivy, wisteria, and honeysuckle, creeks where cool water smoothed the surfaces of wide white rocks. Locations perfect for whiskey-making. A farmer could tend his crops and, as he passed a hollow where he kept a still, climb to the bottom and check his mash.

Which was one reason the place was an area to avoid. Waite himself didn't care to interrupt the bootleggers as he was a whiskey drinker and didn't think the tax laws fair, but there were government agents who poked about now and again. Ten years back one had supposedly disappeared out here, though nothing was ever proved, no body found. And getting these Mitcham Beat people to talk was like uprooting stumps.

Some time ago, Waite, sheriff over the entire county, had given up keeping tabs on every beat—more people arrived each season, and now without a damn army of help it was impossible. He'd had miserable luck with deputies over the years—drunks, men who were fast to be bribed or who'd lose their nerve at the first sign of a fight. So now he found it simpler just to deputize a couple of reliable fellows on a temporary basis if things got rough—that way he didn't expect too much from them and wouldn't get any back talk. Most outlying communities kept their own rough order anyway, had justices of the peace for the little matters. But some areas, like Mitcham Beat, seemed destined for trouble, and if the soil hadn't been so damned rich nobody but criminals would live there anyhow.

He drew King to a stop at the covered bridge and dismounted slowly. He adjusted his sidearm. Good and light now, the sun hot over the treetops behind him. Watchful of snakes, he led the horse down the sloping land to the creek's edge, their appearance launching a series of bullfrogs out of the grass, one after another farther and farther down the bank like archers firing. King's front fetlocks sank in the mud as he lowered his muzzle into the water and

25

drank, shaking his head at the water bugs skimming the surface. Waite took off his hat.

The woods across the creek—beginning of the Bear Thicket—were a snarled overhang of vine, tree, and bush, and for no reason Waite imagined catapulting a donkey or ox into that mess and watching it bounce off the side and land in the water. It looked even more grown up now than it had on his last trip, when he'd investigated the murder of Arch Bedsole, a storekeeper who'd surprised everyone in the county by throwing his name into the race for state representative.

Bedsole's father, a longtime resident of Mitcham Beat, had known every man, woman, child, and dog in the area and beyond the area, too, and until his legs gave out from some undiagnosed malady and his health buckled in other, less discernible ways, he and Arch with their "We're one of you" song and dance had traveled on a mule-drawn buckboard wagon from farm to farm all over the county bad-mouthing the area's prominent landowners, claiming that they only cared about middle- and upper-class folks and didn't give a damn about the so-called little man, the out-in-the-field-sunup-till-sundown cotton farmer whose product supported the whole economy. The crop lien system—where a farmer used store credit to finance his crop and paid it and the interest back based on the cotton he produced—made it impossible for the farmer to get ahead, the Bedsoles claimed, and the farmers would find themselves more deeply indebted as each season ended. They'd have been told to expect eight or nine cents a bale, say, but when the harvest came, when the cotton was brought to gin, the price would have often fallen to six or even five cents. The farmers naturally blamed merchants like McCorquodale and saw them as greedy, but Waite knew the markets were set not by lenders here in Clarke County but up in the north, in New York.

Try telling this to a farmer, though, his profit lopped off by nearly half, his young ones shoeless another winter and the shingles he wanted for his roof a dream for next year.

Waite had always thought the Bedsole clan more akin to the merchant class of town folks than they were to these rural cotton farmers, yet Ed, Arch, and the rest of them had lived out here in the country and run their store for so long that they'd gained the farmers' trust. As part of his campaign, Arch had been known to roll up his sleeves and amble out in the field and pick cotton himself—he was a good picker, at that—earning him the nickname Strut. It was said, too, that the Bedsoles knew whiskey makers (or were makers themselves) and traveled with a jug of hooch, and when they left, the farmers were often "campaigned" into a right good drunk.

Waite had no idea who would've won the election, and no one would ever know, either, because a year ago August, a mile from his own store, as the storekeeper rode home from a debate in front of the courthouse against the town candidate—a debate he'd arguably won—someone had ambushed Arch Bedsole. And to Waite's knowledge the killer still hadn't been caught.

He tugged the rein and King resisted—the horse would drink until Revelations—but then relented and allowed Waite to lead him back uphill to the road. He mounted up and they clopped into the darkness of the covered bridge and then into the darkness of the thicket. He wasn't particularly nervous—no one was expecting him and so he doubted himself in much danger—though the truth was that each time you traveled this route you might be fired upon.

By what he judged to be nine o'clock he rode through the gate of Tom Hill's place, a former plantation, a nice spread contained within a barbed-wire fence, a rarity out here—most folks cut their cross boards from trees. The place looked exactly the same as Waite remembered. Hill raised cattle and several polled Herefords stood along the fence as Waite loped past. Beyond them he could see the two-story house—painted the same shade of white as Waite's—and beyond the house a large barn and outbuildings that had once been slave quarters.

Last year, seeking Bedsole's killer, Waite had come here to see Hill, the Mitcham Beat justice of the peace, who resented the sheriff and viewed his questions as evidence that Waite thought him ineffective. Which was true. The only thing of note Hill had reported was that a cousin of Bedsole's claimed that before he died Arch had said that the ambusher or ambushers had been "from town."

After seeing Hill, Waite had ridden from one dismal homestead to the next in the hot sun, sweating through his shirt while pregnant wives with stringy hair and scurvish children peered at him as he beckoned the tobacco-spitting farmers in from their rows to ask what they knew of Bedsole's murder, listening to each man say, "Don't know," or "It was a fellow from town's what I heard," only to ride to the next place and hear the same damn thing. No surprise: these people distrusted the town law as much or more than the town people distrusted anyone from the country.

Waite eased down and tied King to a porch post and dusted off his legs with his hat. He stood bent a moment, letting his back loosen, then straightened and walked up the steps to the front door and knocked, remembering that era, forty years before, when a black servant would've admitted him. The illusion vanished as Hill's plump, unsmiling wife answered and asked him in, shushing a pair of girls in pigtails behind her. The woman held a clothbound book— she was likely the only person in the beat with the luxury to read during daylight. Waite asked if he could speak to Tom about some business. Curtly, she told him to wait and disappeared through a pair of double doors, the girls following. An octagonal cabinet clock, cased in fancy carved walnut and sitting atop a parlor table, ticked at the far end of the hall; a high window lit its glass face so Waite couldn't see what time it gave.

"Sheriff," Hill said, coming out of a room behind him.

Waite turned—neither made a move to shake hands—and

followed Hill outside and down the porch steps toward the barn, where he kept his office. In his early forties, the justice had gone completely gray, even his eyebrows, his hair nearly to his collar. He wore house slippers which made a lisping sound going over the dirt.

In the barn, horses were nickering in Dutch door stalls and a goat bleated from some dark corner. Waite folded his arms as Hill stood on the single block used for a step and unlocked the padlock, then followed him into the office, a narrow room with no ceiling above where the walls ended, just open air to the tin roof, pieces of tack hanging on pegs. Hot in summer, cold in winter, Hill conducted business here, settling disputes, witnessing official acts or, on occasion, marrying folks. Hill indicated that Waite should take one of the chairs across from his stockman's desk and then raised the window—he'd glassed it—to let in some air. He sat and opened a drawer and withdrew a logbook and wiped it on his pants leg and laid it on the desk between them.

"You can probably figure out why I'm here," Waite said. He crossed his legs and took off his hat and hung it on his boot toe. "Now I don't mean to offer insult by coming into your territory again, but folks are talking and putting the pressure on me. I'm hoping we can help each other."

Hill drummed his fingers on his desk.

Waite fished in his pocket for a notepad and pencil, then leaned up in his chair. "First off, have you found out anything else about who shot Arch Bedsole?"

"No," Hill said. "Far as I know, the same folks that killed him has still killed him and he's still dead."

"You still believe it was somebody from Grove Hill?"

"Or Coffeeville one. Ain't nothing happened to change my mind."

"Who was it said he claimed they was from town? His cousin?"

"Tooch Bedsole. Owns the store in New Prospect now."

"Store Arch had?"

29

"Only store out here. Tooch's house burned down the same night Arch died so he lives in the store now. Got a boy there too."

Waite wrote down *Tooch Bedsole* and underlined it.

"What about you?" Hill asked. "You ask all your buddies where they was that night?"

"I did. They're all accounted for. A good many of 'em was with me, in fact."

The two men sat staring at each other until Waite said, "Well. What I need to know next, then, is what you've come up with on this Anderson murder."

"What I come up with, Sheriff, is this. Nothing."

He waited, but Hill seemed to have said all he meant to say.

"You didn't go talk to nobody?"

"Sure I did. You don't think I do my job?"

"I didn't say that, Hill. Don't get your dander up yet. Just tell me what you dug up."

"Nothing. Cause there ain't nothing to be found. No witnesses, and nobody saw any strangers, so I couldn't question 'em. Anderson, he had some folks he didn't get along with, so I went to see them, but they all have alibis. Good ones, too."

"What about this gang I keep hearing about? Fellows wearing hoods?"

"I keep hearing about 'em, too."

"Well?"

Hill looked weary. "I ain't sure if there's a gang or if it's just one or two fellows. Nobody ever sees more than a couple of 'em, so if there is something organized, nobody knows who's a member and who's not." He tapped his logbook. "I've investigated a number of occurrences. Fires. Livestock shot. A real mess with the nigger church. Peddler gone missing. But ever time there's a suspect, he's always got somebody to say it couldn't of been him."

"Maybe whoever gives the alibi's part of the gang. Maybe that fellow's in a hood another night."

30

"Sheriff, them fellows that vouched is fellows I've known my whole life. Go to church. Own property. I ain't fixing to start calling 'em liars cause Joe Anderson's barn burns down or somebody messes with the niggers."

Waite looked past him through the window, where a bull swiped its tail against its flank. He rubbed the bridge of his nose, got his hat, and put it on. He stood up, boards giving beneath his weight. There was a bridle hanging on a nail on the wall and he walked over and took it down, felt its dry leather, and rolled the bit in his fingers. "Well," he said, and tossed the bridle to the justice, who caught it. "I'll see you."

He left the office and strode past the horses and mounted his own animal and rode off, glad to be done here. Though Hill would deny it, there was plenty in common with these goings-on, at least the events Waite knew about: one of the burned barns had been attached to tenant property belonging to a lawyer in Coffeeville. And a house that had been fired upon belonged to a Grove Hill banker—he'd been trying to sell it for a number of years but no one in town wanted to live so far out. Then there was the "incident" at the colored church, which had rippled back to Grove Hill chiefly because of its strangeness—somebody had carried all the furniture outside and butchered a hog and hung it over the pulpit. Lynched a colored man who came upon them.

Waite rode east through more high cotton until the land dipped and they entered a grove of water oak, Waite glad for the shade, the sky netted with vines and ivy. When King splashed through a swamp, a haze of mosquitoes enveloped them, Waite slapping half a dozen bloody splotches on his neck and the backs of his hands before he could spur King to a run. Half an hour later, in sunlight again, they flushed a covey of quail from the corner of a field, pausing to watch them scatter, then Waite turned them northwest and felt the land rising beneath them.

He looked forward to his next stop, where he'd see the old

midwife known as the Widow Gates, hers one of the nicer homesteads in the area, a small, sturdy three-room cabin built in the shade
of pecan and magnolia trees, an artesian well at the edge of her yard.
The old woman was a genius at coaxing things out of the ground and
further coaxing the plants to bloom rich, ripe squash, gigantic
cucumbers, and tomatoes. Her corn tasseled out before anyone
else's and tasted sweeter, no one knew why. Down below her property ran a creek where the two boys she'd raised swam and fished,
fine cold water that made him think of his own youth.

He looked forward to seeing her boys, too. The old woman had
reared them alone after the death of their parents. The older one,
William, had often been a burden to her, Waite knew, had gotten
into trouble from time to time, stealing a harmonica from
McCorquodale's store once, fighting at school. The younger one,
Macky, reminded Waite of himself as a boy—polite and shy, he
seemed happiest when watching his cork bob in a slow creek and
was glad to help the old woman with her garden or to wash her
birthing implements after she'd brought another baby into the
world. Waite and the widow had marveled at how different siblings
could be, Waite admitting his sorrow at having had only one son.

"Be glad you got that one," she'd said, and he'd agreed.

For the widow herself had saved the life of Johnny-Earl, and
probably the life of Sue Alma, too. Twenty-one years before, the
Grove Hill doctor had been called to aid a gunshot victim in
Coffeeville just before Sue's water had broken. This being their
fourth child—they had three older daughters—they'd felt at ease at
the outset of labor, but Sue began to double over with cramps and
when she stood up to go to the bathroom the back of her dress
was bloody.

Waite went for help and found the Widow Gates walking along
Main Street, gazing in store windows. Hardly believing his luck, he
put her behind him on his horse and rode back with her clinging to
his shirt. He remembered how his three girls had cried as Oscar

hurried them off to the drugstore for a soda, remembered praying that the screams he heard from the bedroom would stop. Finally the old woman had called him to help and he went in, rolling up his sleeves. What he saw froze his heart. He'd witnessed a world of blood in his life, seen men lose limbs in the war, seen a head and one shoulder swiped off by a cannonball once while the soldier continued to stand, still holding his musket one-handed—and then the musket had fired. He'd seen men dying from his, Waite's, gun and knife: but nothing would ever compare with the scene in his own bedroom.

Sue Alma lay covered in sweat. The bedding was red and Oscar's wife, Lucinda, was trying to hold her down. He saw that Sue had shat loose and bloody, saw the old woman had her whole hand up inside his wife's body. "He keeps moving," the widow said as Sue screamed and kicked—and only later, after several drinks, would Waite realize that the widow had known the baby's gender. Without being told, he crossed to his wife and held her shoulders against the mattress as her fists beat bruises onto his back, shoulders, face. "Push," the old woman commanded, and Sue did, thrashing, and each time she pushed, her rectum turned inside out, like a flower's face, and more blood flowed until at last the widow said she saw the crown of the baby's head. Waite felt faint with relief but still the baby didn't come. "Keeps turning," the old woman muttered, sopping up blood with a towel. "This one's active, but we need to get him on out, now." Waite and Lucinda tried to calm Sue Alma and encouraged her to push while the Widow Gates used a knife to split her open. Then Sue screamed once more and gasped and the old woman raised up the wriggling blue baby and thrust him into Waite's hands and set to work sewing up the tear.

Later, Sue cleaned, asleep, pale but alive, the baby boy nursing at her breast, Waite joined the old woman on the porch. He looked down at his shaking hands and saw dried blood underneath his nails. Oscar's and Waite's daughters were rounding the corner and

Waite's eyes suddenly blurred. "I don't know what I'd of done if I hadn't found you," he said to her. "What luck, you being in town that moment."

"Wasn't luck," she said, and though he'd questioned her about it many times after, she never spoke of it again. She'd told him, too, that this boy was the last baby they'd have, that Sue's insides were no longer capable.

When he'd asked her fee, the old woman had seemed surprised. "Most folks just give me what they can."

He'd offered her five silver dollars, which she'd stared at for quite a long time, as if puzzled by the fact of them. Then she'd taken the coins and hidden them in the folds of her dress.

Her place was one of the highest spots in the beat, the hilly land deemed of lesser value by farmers. He rode onto the shaded property and looked up into the architecture of the pecan trees where a squirrel flung itself from one limb to another, barking. He expected the boys to come out—he hadn't seen them since his last visit, when Macky had been surly and quiet. Just that age, he'd figured, as Macky and William had vanished to the barn to tend his horse. Waite and the widow had rocked in the chairs on the porch and spoke of the weather, the crops, Arch Bedsole's murder.

"I knew the second it happened," she'd said.

"Knew what?"

"The second Arch died. I can always tell when one of my babies, the ones I brought in the world, gets killed. If I'm asleep I set up in bed. Can't catch my breath."

"So you'll know when my boy dies, too?"

"I will," she'd said. "If I'm alive."

Now he dismounted, letting the horse drink from the bubbling wooden trough by the well. He took from its peg a gourd cut to be a dipper and dipped it in and drank of the sulfur-smelling water so cold it hurt his teeth. Damn, it was good, though. He got another gourdful and drank it more slowly. Below, through patches in the trees, the land was so cotton-white you'd think you stood in Kentucky or some other northern state in dead of snow-battered winter.

He looked around the homestead. A smokehouse behind the house and a barn down the sloping land laddered by the black roots of magnolias. Her old one-eared mule gazed at him from its stall. He crossed to the side yard where she kept chickens in a pen and they all ran to the edge of the wire and watched him as if he might sling them feed. He supposed that, like most everybody else, he knew almost nothing about the widow, just that she'd been here as long as he could remember, had birthed practically every baby in the beat, both white and colored. She knew the healing powers of plants, too, and had saved many of these farmers' lives.

He heard something. Without a thought he drew his sidearm and pointed it at the woods as the old woman stepped out from behind a dogwood, lowering her skirts. Had she noticed him? Waite glanced away, holstered the pistol. When he looked back she was staring at him, then at the horse. If she was embarrassed at being caught doing her business it didn't show. Her dog shot out of the woods, a fringe of wet fur along its nethers as though it'd been creek-wading, and began to bark at King.

"Hush," she said, and it did.

"Evening, Mrs. Gates." He approached her, took off his hat.

"You're back, ain't you," she said. "Hello, Billy Waite."

"Yes, ma'am. Hello."

"How's that Johnny-Earl?"

"Grown up. Out in Washington County cutting down trees, last I heard."

She smiled.

Her hair was whiter than it had been, her eyes blue and small, her face like cured leather, wrinkles so deep it looked like you could

35

stand a dime in there. Beneath her shawl and dress she wore a pair of men's pants, rolled up to her ankles.

"Where're your boys at?" he asked.

She looked past him. "Gone."

"Gone where?"

She raised her cane and pointed east. "One's working with War Haskew." Then she pointed west. "The other's working at the store." She turned toward the house, leaning on the cane. The dog turned with her. She began to labor up the three stone steps, using the post to steady herself, and limped over the porch and went in. He followed her, ducking through the low entrance, into the good-smelling room, woodsmoke, biscuits, dried herbs and sprigs of things hanging upside down from the ceiling. A monarch butterfly perched on the table on an opened Bible, its wings folding and unfolding. A piece of mirror glass sat on the ledge over a clay washbowl.

She sat with great care in a rocking chair by the far window, green pine needles outside painting the glass with quick strokes. The dog lay on the floor beside her and watched Waite, not unfriendly, its tail thumping the boards.

"Do the boys still live here?" he asked.

"They do not. William," she said, flipping her hand in the air as if to show the cavalier nature of aging, "he's nineteen."

"How old's Macky?"

"Fifteen."

"And he lives over at the store? With Tooch Bedsole?"

"Real name's Quincy. They call him Tooch. He wanted Macky to pay off our debt. Work till our account was cleared. I said go get William. He's older. Be a better worker. Tooch wanted the young one. Said you could mold a young boy better than you could a older one. Said nothing could rurn a good boy faster than years."

The old woman had stopped rocking. She looked at him, then began to rock again and he watched her profile move into the window light and out. He saw that she didn't have any teeth. She didn't seem like she'd say more, but he waited. There was a row of snuff cans stacked on the shelf over the fireplace. Leather hinges creaked on the opened windows. Drapes raised into the room by a breeze which turned the Bible pages on the table. The closed cloth bag that he assumed held her midwife's devices hanging on a nail. When he looked back at her she seemed surprised to find him there.

"I thought you'd left."

"How much was your account?"

As if in answer, she began naming things she'd bought. Dates, prices. He understood that she was going soft, and he felt bad for her. He ought to come more often. Or make sure those boys did.

"I thank you," he said, rising from the hearth, dusting ash off the seat of his trousers.

"August," she said. "The loveliest pears. Three for a penny."

Sitting his horse before the long porch of Bedsole's Dry Goods, a bench beneath one of the two windows flanking the door, Waite had to look twice before he saw any change. Then he noticed that Arch's name as proprietor had been painted out of the sign nailed over the porch and "Quincy" now replaced it. Careful, neat lettering. Other stores, like McCorquodale's in Coffeeville, were plastered with advertisements, some tin, others paper, that were replaced on a regular basis. Those porches had old men sitting on them telling lies the way old men will, drinking and smoking five-cent cigars.

Here, though, was isolation that seemed unnatural. On the right side of the store was the blacksmith shop, he could see the anvil, a bucket of black water, and the cold furnace; on the left a stall for a horse and a place to park a wagon. Fresh ruts. Behind him, across the road, lay a wide and deep cotton field and a hundred yards past that an island of pine trees beyond which lay still more cotton.

He reached into his pocket and withdrew his watch, a gift from

Sue for some long-gone holiday. A little before five. Hell. There ought to be somebody here. He dismounted and wrapped the horse's reins around the rail.

"I'll get you some sugar," he promised King, stroking his jaw and adjusting the bit in his rubbery lips.

He put his hands in the small of his back and pushed before going up the steps to the porch. He shielded his eyes with a gloved hand and peered inside. Nothing. He tried the door handle and found it unlocked.

"Hello," he called, sticking his head in. A bell clanged above him and he let it ring, hoping it might bring somebody out.

Yet the aisles remained empty, sunlight from behind him igniting the long floorboards and stretching his long shadow the length of the store. He stepped inside and slammed the door behind him, the bell ringing again.

Still no one.

He set his right hand on his sidearm, slipped the rawhide thong off the pistol's hammer and drew his Colt: something was wrong.

He went slowly down the center aisle. The shelves on either side were dusted clean and stacked neatly with merchandise; whoever stocked the place kept it well. Woodstove in the back, a door standing half opened. When he heard a board's faint screak he stopped. It seemed to be coming from the adjacent aisle. He knelt and with his pistol barrel slid several boxes of baking soda aside and moved another larger box that faced the other way.

Somebody sneaking by on hands and knees.

Waite rose and walked back toward the door in leisurely steps, as if to leave. He even whistled. When he got there, however, he sidestepped and leaned into the aisle where he saw Macky Burke kneeling.

"Damn, boy," Waite said. "What the hell's going on?"

They stared at each other as Macky stood up—he'd grown as tall as Waite, who'd held him as a baby, thrown him in the air and caught him under his tiny arms while the boy giggled, had seen him on a couple of dozen occasions over the years, taken supper with him, his brother, and the widow. Waite had made water spew out of Macky's nose with his stories, given the boys pieces of hard candy, let them ride his horse and even hold his unloaded sidearm as he instructed them in its use and dangers.

"You doing okay?" Waite pushed aside his coat flap to holster the pistol. "You look spooked."

The boy nodded. "Yes, sir, Mr. Billy."

"You're spooked?"

"No, sir." He canted a thumb at the shelf, as if to explain. "I'm okay. How about you?"

"Getting along. I was just over to see your granny. She told me you work here."

"Yes, sir."

"How long since you seen her?"

He thought. "Been a while."

"A while."

He nodded.

"Paying off your all's debt, she said."

He nodded.

"You know how much it is? She couldn't seem to recall."

"No, sir."

"Bedsole ain't told you?"

"No, sir."

"How come you ain't asked him? I don't know about you, but I don't take folks' word for much."

"I'll ask him," Macky said.

"Get him to show you. On paper."

"Yes, sir."

From outside there came the sound of a wagon. A horse whinnied.

Waite turned to see a dark-haired man walking up the steps, the

39

wagon behind him drifting backward as if the brake hadn't been set. The fellow came through the door with a quick hand silencing the bell.

He resembled Arch, but a scarred, harder version, like a brother who'd gone off to war. There were lines in his face, tracking outward from his eyes, and an assortment of freckles and moles that darkened his complexion. A bushy mustache and scruff of beard on his cheeks and a tooth gone in his bottom set. Shorter than Waite and the boy, but a man confident in his carriage, a large head that made him seem bigger than he was, though about his chest and shoulders he looked frail.

"Tooch Bedsole?" Waite asked.

"Who wants to know?"

"Billy Waite."

"Our sheriff," he said, taking off his flat-topped hat. He laid it on the counter. "I'm Quincy Bedsole." He worked off his leather gloves a finger at a time and laid them beside the hat. "What can we do for you?"

"I was talking to your helper here," Waite said, indicating the boy with a thumb. "Telling him I wanted a few nickel cigars. Some sugar cubes."

"Mack," Bedsole said, and the boy nodded and hurried to the back.

"There's something I'd like to ask you," Waite said to the store-keeper, "if you got a minute."

"I do," he replied. "Come onto the porch."

Outside, Bedsole's horse, a white mare, had backed the wagon up a few feet. He said, "Damn," and went down the steps and set the brake and came back dusting his hands. "That's a nice chestnut you got out yonder," he told Waite.

"Thank you. Raised him from a foal."

"You want to sell him?"

Waite thought this forward. Where the hell would he get that kind of cash? "No," he said. "I'm content with him."

40

They stood gazing at the cotton and the pine trees past it, a pair of buzzards smudged in the sky.

"Fine crop," Waite said. "You ever raise any cotton?"

"Once."

They stood looking.

"I was sorry to hear about your cousin," Waite said. "Called him Strut, didn't they?"

Bedsole leaned against a post. He folded his arms. "His friends did."

"I understand he told you something before he died. It's become quite a legend."

"It ain't a legend."

"Well, I've heard everybody else's version. So I'd appreciate hearing it from you."

The storekeeper took a long time to say anything. Then he told how he'd been home, reading, when he heard a commotion. Said he went out with a lantern and found his cousin nearly dead in the yard, bled plumb out, and he ran to him. Got there just before Arch breathed his last, but in that last breath he whispered something.

"What?"

"He said, 'They was from town.' "

"Who was?"

"Who you think? People that killed him."

"Did he say what town?"

"He meant Grove Hill."

"You sure about that?"

Bedsole didn't answer. Then he said, "Yeah. I'm sure."

Waite turned to Bedsole expecting him to turn, too, so they could talk eye to eye, but the storekeeper remained with his attention given to the field, showing the sheriff a profile hard as an ax.

"There's other towns," Waite said.

Bedsole said nothing.

"What about your house? I heard it burned down."

41

"That's right, it did. When I seen Arch I dropped the lantern and time I remembered it the house was burning good. Wasn't nothing to do but stand there and watch it."

Waite tapped the crossbeam of the porch over their heads. "You live here now?"

Bedsole nodded. He leaned and spat off the front of the porch. "There's a room up there," he said, indicating the attic.

"You mind if I ask how you was able to afford to buy a store?"

"You reckon it's any of your business?"

"I do. If I'm to locate your cousin's killer and the killer of Joe Anderson."

Bedsole turned then, a little. "Arch's daddy sold it to me. My uncle Ed. You can check the papers. We done it right there in Grove Hill. Lawyer and everthing."

"What about that boy in yonder?"

"What about him?"

"You own him, too?"

Bedsole stepped back and now they were face-to-face. "It's a business arrangement."

"That what you call it? I ain't so sure but I wouldn't call it something else."

The door opened and the boy came out with a handful of cigars and a small sack of sugar cubes. He offered them to Waite, who took them. "How much?" he asked Macky.

"Fifty cents."

He took out his coin purse and paid him and watched him go back inside. He opened his coat so his badge showed where it hung on his shirt and put all but one of the cigars in his pocket. Bedsole looked away again, off toward the field. Waite licked the tip of the remaining cigar and bit off its end, spat the cap into the yard and picked tobacco flecks off his tongue. He fished in his pants for a box of matches and got one and struck it on his thumbnail and lit the cigar and blew smoke across their view.

"Tell you something, Bedsole," he said. "Good sheriff has to know things, be they secret or not. Was a time back yonder in my ambitious years, when you was still chasing girls in pigtails, where I knew just about everything went on in my county, no matter how delicate, from the bowel movements of men to the ministerial cycles of women. A fly couldn't light on a stack of horse shit I didn't know about it. But then it happened I got older, as men will, and had to let some slack in my grip. You know. Now the habits of flies are unknown to me and men shit and women bleed unattended. And so there's two or three places I've let go too far. This here is one of 'em."

"That's a good little speech," Bedsole said. He took a cigar from his own shirt pocket and put it in his lips. "What's it mean?"

"Means I'm fixing to get to the bottom of some things."

"Pleased to hear it. When you find the son-of-a-bitch that killed my cousin, let me know so I can come in for the hanging."

"You'll be the first," Waite said. He went down the steps and looked back. "One more thing. That boy ought to go see the widow. It ain't right him not seeing her. Next time I come out here, I expect him to have paid her a visit or two."

Bedsole turned and went inside the store. Waite heard the door lock.

Dusk found him filling his canteen in a slow creek at the bottom of a ravine. He sat on the raised roots of a magnolia and unwrapped one of Sue Alma's biscuits and chewed thoughtfully, watching shadows he knew were small largemouth bass below the surface of the creek water. About the time of day for them to start biting. He flicked a crumb out and several of the fish rose to inspect it as it dissolved, then minnows came in like flashes of light and the bread was gone. A mosquito landed on the water in the shade of a broom of pine needles and skated across the top tethered to its reflection, then a sudden uprush and the bug was gone.

43

Waite ate three biscuits and some jerked beef. He wished he'd brought a bottle and had half a mind to poke about looking for a still. But he didn't. With King unsaddled and hobbled, nibbling at a clump of grass, he slept on the ground and woke with his back feeling better than it had in a damn month.

Let it be a lesson, he mused. You hand in that badge, get ready to stiffen up sitting on your porch peeling apples, smoking cigars, and listening to Sue Alma gab about bird feeders.

The sun reached over the horizon to find him walking the land. Around ten he shot a rabbit with his pistol and built a fire and cooked it on a spit held by forked limbs. He watched his fire burn and made coffee and drank it and ate the rabbit while listening to every sound and cataloging them: squirrels barking, a hawk's cry, wingbeat of an Indian hen, rasp of a diamondback's belly over fallen leaves.

In the afternoon Joe Anderson's widow and two daughters had little to say. Waite had finally found their house after trying two other farms and went to the opened door and saw them still dressed in funeral black and packing, a wagon half loaded in the yard, three somber-looking blond boys with enormous ears dragging a mahogany sideboard down the steps. When Waite asked Anderson's widow where they planned to go, the woman said back home.

"Where's that?"

"Wilcox County." She pointed to a table beneath the front window, iron pots and dishes full of collards, peas, corn, brought by neighbors. Flies swirled in and out of the light. "There ain't nobody left to eat it 'fore it spoils."

At his request, they sat with Waite on their porch, the mother hanging a black veil over her face before stepping outside, the plain-faced girls—ages fifteen or sixteen—sitting on the edge of the porch with their legs hanging over.

He pried gently. Had men in hoods come by?

They had, she said. Some weeks ago.

Could she tell him about it?

"Two of 'em. They come up to the porch and beat the dogs off. Stood there waiting till Joe went out. He had his gun but soon as he stepped on the porch there was another one come up behind him—"

"So there were three in all?"

She nodded.

"Could there have been more you didn't see?"

She reckoned so. Said they'd demanded he sign a paper, in blood cut from his hand. Said if he didn't, they'd get him. *Get* him, they said. But he didn't sign. Flat refused to. They'd looked at each other in their hoods. For a moment it seemed they might shoot him and come inside. She couldn't believe it—watching through the sliver between the drapes, the girls behind her clasping each other—how he stood there while they held guns on him and him reciting verses from the Bible. Proverbs, always his favorite. She hated him at that moment. What about the three of them—she wanted to know—his women, nothing but the wood of walls and the cotton of their dresses between them and these hooded things? She wanted to say the devil with your principles, Joe Anderson. Sign in your blood. Sign in what little amount it will take to write your name, for how much will you sign in later? With my blood? Your daughters' blood?

But in the end the hooded men left. Left him standing alone with the last Proverb dying on his lips as they crossed through the cotton, stopping to shoot Joe's dogs, saying he had a week to think it over.

"Go on," Waite said.

"Didn't wait no week. First they poisoned our well. Then they pulled down a fence and let our cow out, we almost never got her back. They'd come of a night and shoot in the house."

"Where was Tom Hill while this was going on?"

45

"He come over. Looked is about all he did. Looked at the dead dogs. Down the well. Looked where Joe had fixed the fence. He spent three nights waiting for 'em, but they didn't come those nights. But the next night, the barn burned."

Waite scribbled in his notebook. Did Joe have enemies they knew of? Anybody who'd want him hurt? Dead?

"Maybe that Lev James. As mean a man ever lived."

"Anybody else?"

"No one. Joe was a good churchgoing deacon. You never heard a better singing voice in your life. Bass or tenor either one."

The three big-eared boys, barefooted and filthy, stumbled out, struggling with the weight of a grandfather clock, its pendulum clacking against the glass.

Waite looked out at the fields of flourishing cotton. "Who'll harvest the crop after you go?"

"Mr. McCorquodale. He held our lien."

"Will he buy you out?"

She said she didn't know but she bet not. Probably McCorquodale would cheat them. Joe had handled such things.

They sat in silence, the women watching their belongings dragged past, not seeming to care if a bedpost got scratched on the way down the steps, not even looking up when a long, flat drawer slid out of the curtain-top desk and spilled papers over the porch and into the yard. Waite rose and hurried past the slack-jawed boys and began to collect the contents of the drawer as best he could, chasing letters and newspapers across the dirt, scattering chickens, into the cotton field.

Back on the porch he aided the farm boys with a table. As they stood at the wagon, the table secured, he asked the older boy to tell him his name.

He shrugged.

"You boys got tongues in your mouths?"

The middle one stuck his out. "We don't supposed to talk nor listen to you," he said.

46

Waite noticed that he had dull eyes. Snot crusted in his nostrils.

"Shut up, Arnold," his brother said.

"Who says you ain't supposed to talk to me?" Waite asked Arnold, holding up a finger to silence his brother.

"You the law," the youngest one said. "The law's bad."

"Who told you that?" Waite asked.

"Daddy."

"Don't y'all say nothing else," the older boy snapped. "Get on inside."

Arnold clomped up the steps after his younger brother, pausing to look at one of the daughters' ankles, which she promptly swept beneath her skirt.

"Who's your daddy?" Waite asked the oldest.

"I ain't got to tell you," he said, following his brothers.

Waite had a good mind to go inside and whip the three of them. Instead he returned to his seat on the porch and tapped his foot.

"Who're them young ones?" he asked.

"They belong to Floyd Norris, down the road a ways."

Waite knew Norris by reputation. Borrowed from McCorquodale to finance his cotton crop, one of the best growers out here, handling six or seven acres. Him and Anderson both. By all accounts decent men. He waited for the boys to come back out with the next load.

"They gone," Mrs. Anderson said.

"Gone? How you know?" He leaned and peered in the opened door straight through the house to where the back door stood ajar. He noted that three of the dishes—a plate of fried chicken among them—were gone.

You're losing your instincts, Billy, he thought.

So despite his sore back he finished loading their heavier things by himself, a large canvas-covered stateroom trunk filled—it seemed—with bricks, a rolled-up rug that he carried over his shoulder like a dead man, and finally a strange piece called a

47

Napoleon chair, the name of which he knew only because Oscar had one in his office, by the fireplace. The girls helped inside, packing away glasses in newspaper and laying them in wooden boxes while the mother stayed on the porch, rocking.

When he was done, Waite stood over her, unrolling his sleeves. He looked out at the charred remains of the barn. Curiously, a milking stool sat amidst the ashes.

I V

Floyd Norris rose from where he'd been pulling water from his well and watched the sheriff ride out of the cotton on his tall horse. A cigar poking from his mouth, Waite pulled the animal up and stretched his legs in the saddle. He said, "Good evening."

The dogs were in a fever, leaping up alongside the sheriff's legs, wetting his pants leg with their drool. He swatted at them with his hat.

Floyd whistled and pointed toward the porch and the hounds clambered up the steps and sat, their glittering eyes fixed on him, their lips smiling.

The sheriff folded his fingers over the pommel of his saddle. "Them's mighty well-behaved hounds you got there, Norris."

From inside, his wife peered through the hole in the wall, her hand upheld to keep three boys silent. When the baby fussed and wiggled his arms and legs, she undid her dress and her teat plopped out and she stuffed her nipple into his mouth to quiet him.

"Could you answer me a few questions?" the sheriff asked.

Floyd had gone back to lowering the bucket into the well. "If I can."

"Oh, you can. How many boys you got?"

Floyd drew a bucketful of water out and poured it into the washtub. "Three last time I checked," he said. "And a baby."

The sheriff was gazing out at the high cotton. "When you plan to start picking?"

"Oh—" He cast an eye skyward. "Week."

"Them boys help you?"

He nodded, dropped the bucket into the mouth of the well. A splash far below.

"Your wife help, too?"

He nodded.

"What you use for fertilizer?"

"Guano."

"You get it over at Bedsole's store?"

"Naw. I borrowed from McCorquodale's, so I got to get the goods from him, too."

"Anybody been by here? Strangers?"

He shook his head, pulling the bucket up hand over hand, blue veins rising in his forearms.

"Could you tell me what you did the day Joe Anderson was killed?"

He got the full bucket out and set it on the lip of the well and screwed his forehead, his eyeballs lolled up to the left. "Yeah," he said, "played some dominoes with Lev James and a young fellow called William Burke. Drank a little whiskey."

"Dominoes."

He nodded.

"Who won?"

"Lev."

"Where'd you get the liquor?" Waite looked around. "Don't look like you can afford the luxury."

"I can't." He emptied the bucket and dropped it into the well. "They brung it."

"If," the sheriff said, ashing the cigar, "there's something else you want to tell me, I can promise you you'll be safe. In no time at all there'd be several certain parties in the jailhouse and you'd

49

be in no danger. It could be the end of this chapter in your all's life."

Inside, his wife shook her head. What kind of ignorant fools did this lawman think they were? Did he think Floyd would turn over his friends? And even if he did, how could anybody arrest them all, when nobody was sure who they were? Or how many. There'd been a meeting at the church months ago. Joe Anderson had said, All we got to do is tell the sheriff. Then it's his problem. And someone else had said, Tell him what? We don't even know who they are. There could be some of 'em here, now. They'd all gotten quiet, then. Everybody looking at each other.

"There ain't nothing else," Floyd said.

The sheriff looked about at the well, the trough, the leaning barn, the endless white fields. He seemed at a loss.

"Your boys has got some strange notions about lawmen," he said.

Floyd didn't stop dragging the bucket up.

"Thinks the law's bad," Waite added.

Floyd paused and squinted up at him, then set back to work.

Waite watched his downturned face as he pulled at the rope, then looked at the hornet's-nest gray wall of the house. If he saw her eye centered in the space between the logs, he didn't let on.

"I'll see you," the sheriff said, and turned and rode off with a plume of dust rising into the sky. The dogs came down the steps and stood smelling the earth where the horse had stood.

"You boys get on," he said, clicking his teeth, and they disappeared beneath the house.

Inside, his wife rested her head against the wall and closed her eyes. Later she planned to take the dominoes left by the hooded men and throw them one at a time into the creek, where they could grow moldy with algae and grit and be a corruption only to the goggle-eyed bream and the whiskered catfish sucking along the bottom.

V

After visiting Norris, Waite talked to a few other farmers and learned nothing. He found War Haskew and William Burke patching Haskew's barn roof and sat aback the horse talking up at them. He told William he ought to go see about the widow and the boy spat tobacco juice and promised he would. He asked if they knew where Lev James was but they didn't. In the early evening he ran across Massey Underwood who was so drunk he fell off his mule. When Waite asked him what he knew about a group of hooded outlaws Underwood grinned and said, "I'll tell you one thing I know, Waite. I know they name."

Waite grew excited. "What is it?"

"Call they selves Hell-at-the-Breech, what I hear."

"Where you hear it from?"

He was struggling to get back on his mule, which was swatting him with its tail.

"Hear what?" Underwood asked.

And that was all he said.

Maybe I should've gone to see old Bit first, Waite thought, as he dismounted and slid his rifle from its scabbard and levered in a round and half-cocked the hammer. He felt safer now, near Coffeeville, Mitcham Beat miles behind him. He looped King's reins around a solid limb and felt in his knapsack for a carrot for the horse, then fed it into the long hot snout, the thick lips wetting his fingers.

"Good boy," he whispered. "I won't be long."

Below, he could hear the cluck of the river, smell its fishy wind, too. See its dull brown shimmer through empty spaces between the trees. He was glad to be here, eager to see his old friend, taste his whiskey, and eat whatever the old man would grill over the coals. Bit had a way with wild mushrooms—in an iron skillet with a slab of lard he could bring the holy spirit out of a deer's rump.

Carefully, Waite made his way down the incline with his rifle in one hand, clinging to limbs and tree trunks with the other. A couple of chipmunks chased each other over the face of a large flat rock, the pursuer stopping as Waite passed and standing on its hind legs with its head cocked at him. A red-tailed hawk called from atop a high tree and when Waite looked back the chipmunk had vanished.

Presently he came to the first sign, white-painted letters on a board, nailed to an oak: NO TRISPASING. There were others: FURIAS DAWGS ABOWT, LOOK BEHIND U. Waite grinned and went a few more paces, stepping over a fallen log covered in ragwort. He moved aside a fern and the river cabin's wall appeared in the distance. Because Bit wasn't expecting him, he knew it'd be better to announce himself. "Old man!" he hollered. "You got a spot of coffee for a war buddy?"

No response.

He called louder. "Got no kindness for the man saved your life?"

Still nothing.

"Don't make me regret it."

Perhaps he was on the river. Waite made a lot of intentional noise as he approached the cabin, crunching leaves, whistling, coughing. Kept his rifle down. The place looked deserted, though. He knocked, not yet alarmed, then pulled the latch that opened the door and lit the floor around his shadow.

Empty. The ceiling was low—as his name indicated, Bit was a slight man and had built the place for himself alone. Same table as always, centering the room. A dusty tin cup sitting in front of a chair, one leg mended with tightly wrapped ivy. Waite looked around, still standing in the door. The gun rack was empty. Ought to be a rifle there, or a sixteen-gauge shotgun. Bit didn't usually take both out at the same time. In one corner was the rickety homemade bed, shred of a blanket on its ticking.

Waite ducked and stepped inside. Something slithered up a corner wall, gone before he could tell what it was. Dank smell of cold ash. He cast about the room, then went to the window and with his rifle inched the shutter open. Ferns. Spanish moss.

He and Bit had met twenty years back, when a couple of fellows from Mitcham Beat had robbed a store—after shooting a young clerk in the throat—and escaped into the Bear Thicket, so thick even then it was said a snake had to grease itself up with lard to pass through and beetles just took the road. Aware of Bit's reputation as a soldier in the War, his knowledge of the thicket, and his skill as a tracker, Waite had sought him; but only after hearing the gruesome details of the shooting of the clerk, a boy fourteen years old, did Bit agree. They'd hacked their way into the thicket with his three deputies, but within a day the deputies had gone down next to a creek with a malady that left them vomiting and shitting and shivering with fever.

Waite and Bit had gone on alone. Before a campfire in a clearing, the dogs tied and pulling at a beaver carcass, Bit produced a jar and he and Waite had exchanged war stories, delighted at the discovery that they'd both fought at Nashville in '64—Bit from the 36th Regiment and Waite the 38th. After the battle, remnants of their regiments had come together and they'd known the same lieutenant, a man whose stutter only showed itself in the quiet moments between rounds of fighting. Bit did a damn good impression of the man and they laughed, then grew somber before the fire as they recalled the bullet that took the lieutenant's life, entering his face just below his right eye. Neither knew where he'd been buried, if he'd been buried. For a long time after that they'd sat in silence, little else but the night passing around them with its clicking and chirrs, the stars and moon overhead ceilinged out by the foliage. Presently they got to talking again, the jar half gone, dogs snoring, and were trying to recall the name of a tall bearded private when the two robbers rushed out of the darkness.

Waite drew his knife from his boot and got the blade between them as one of the men dove on him, the robber's own weight killing him, no sound but a squeak of air escaping his lips as he folded on top of Waite and kicked a time or two before dying. Rolling him aside, Waite hurled himself onto the other man's back and caught his arm as it raised in the firelight, a knife in its fist. Waite held him and Bit shot him in the chest, then the pair of them spent the rest of the night finishing the whiskey.

At some point, Bit had said, "You saved my neck, Waite, and I won't forget such a debt."

Over the years they'd seen each other only a dozen or so times, Bit making his home out here on the river, distilling whiskey, catching fish, existing without the need for town, or people, or law. Waite had let him alone, knowing the old man would keep to himself, visiting when business drew him near, spending a night on Bit's porch, drinking his whiskey, telling the same stories over and over—the one about the soldier from Spanish Fort who had no horse and made his tall buddy carry him on his shoulders each time they crossed a river or stream. Waite always left with a headache and a good supply of drink.

Now he went back outside, down the sloping land to the river-bank, looking for Bit's skiff. Gone.

Back in the cabin, he sat on the bed and leaned against the wall. Within minutes he'd fallen asleep.

A hand covered Waite's mouth. He jumped awake, his arms flung out, feeling for his pistol. The cabin pitch-dark.

"Billy."

A familiar, hoarse voice.

"Bit?"

The hand let go. "Yeah," he rasped, "it's me."

Waite sat up, he could smell his friend as the man backed away, giving him room. Fish and sweat. He could hear his feet on the dirt floor, though in such darkness nothing could be seen.

"How'd you know I was here?" Waite asked, blinking, pushing on his chest to quell his rabbit of a heart.

54

"Seen your horse."

Waite had found his pistol butt and now drew the gun from beneath the pillow, where he'd laid it. Quietly, he felt its cylinder to make sure it was still loaded.

"Hell," Bit said. "Billy, I'd not empty your gun."

Waite let himself breathe. "I know, Bit. You just caught me off-guard." He swung his feet to the floor and stood, careful not to bump his head on the low ceiling timbers.

"Could we get a fire going," Waite asked, "so I could see your ugly face and we could find us a drink?"

No answer. Waite strained to get a fix on where his friend had gone, discomfited by the feeling of being unmapped in such blackness. Bit's voice came from beside the window. "There's been no fire here for a month, Billy. Nor no whiskey neither."

Waite focused on the voice. Outside was less dark and now Bit's shape lay vaguely outlined, but only if he looked to the left or right of it. "What's going on?" he asked.

"I'm in a war," Bit said.

"With who?"

There came no answer, just the brush of clothing and rhythm of breath.

"Who with, Bit?"

There came the whisper of dirt as he moved, Waite couldn't tell which direction.

"Well, I wish I could tell you."

"Why can't you?"

"Cause they wear hoods on they heads."

"So you've seen 'em."

"Seen 'em? Hell, I done shot at 'em and been shot at by them. They want me to sign a damn paper swearing my loyalty to 'em. Say if I don't sign they'll get me."

"Are they the ones killed Anderson?"

"I don't know for sure, but I'd guess so. He wouldn't sign,

55

neither, I expect. Though I reckon our reasons for not is about as far apart as reasons can be."

Waite asked other questions but Bit remained silent. In the end, he only said, "Y'all from the towns ride out here on your horses or in your wagons when you get crazy enough for some whiskey, and you find me or one of the other fellows makes it. Or you come when you want a whore. But this group of fellows in they hoods is bent on taking over. They done got all the other shiners. Done scared most of the niggers off. Got help from a lot of other fellows that don't go about in hoods with 'em but feels like they do about things. I'm one of the only ones they ain't beat, yet, and they're gone keep coming, till they get me, or I get them."

"What you think they mean to do?"

But Bit said nothing else, and Waite had stood for some time longer before he realized Bit was gone. He felt his pockets for a box of matches and struck one. The lit cabin, empty except for him, seemed even smaller in the dark, which fluttered around him like curtains.

OVER

THE

DITCH

September 1897 to July 1898

MACK AND WILLIAM LAY ELBOW TO ELBOW on their bellies in the leaves beside the road, not too far from Bedsole's store, each armed with a weapon that had belonged to his dead father, William the long single-barrel sixteen-gauge and Mack the Colt revolver, a loose-feeling weapon with screws that never seemed tight enough, its wooden grips, once etched with minute checkering, as soft now as a velvet deer antler in his fist.

Clouds walled out the moon, the darkness around them a yawning, swallowing thing—as dark as the inside of a cow, the widow would say— and Mack suspected that in such overwhelming night they could have jumped in the road and waved their arms and been as hidden as they were in this noxious brush. His leg had started to tingle from disuse, but he let it alone and made a game of not moving, of lying still as long as he could, imagining he was dead, pulled apart by buzzards, melting into the ground, passing through the tubes of earthworms, then flying away in spoors on the air.

Far down in the tunnels of his bowels, there came a rumbling he knew to be a fart, which seemed appropriate, for he'd heard the dead farted, and when this one blatted out into the open air it seemed nearly as loud as a shotgun shot. Far away in the night an owl answered and Mack giggled back to life until William's elbow jabbed him in the side.

"Hell, it ain't like there's any victim to hear us," Mack said.

"Macky," William said. "Shut your pie hole."

He rolled onto his back, hands behind his head.

Her figure came to his mind's eye as it did often, from the nights the widow was gone to birth a baby, nights when they'd lit out and trotted two miles by moonlight and rowed the river in a skiff to stand at the edge of the swamp and watch her windows glow with

59

candlelight. How she moved past the glass, straight hair down her back, her neck bare and white. The room tiny and clean, her plain dress, the things that went on in there, her and a huffing man, her knees in the air, the mattress jingling.

"Will?"

"What is it?"

"You believe she'll wonder where we got the money?"

"She won't care where we get the damn money, long as we got it, Macky. Hell, half her customers probably do the same thing we're fixing to try—"

The distant clop of horse hooves silenced them. No one they knew could afford a horse, so this was it. William clutched Mack's shoulder and whispered, "Remember what I told you, Macky. I'm gone do all the talking."

They heard the chink of bridle and the squeak of saddle leather. Clip of shoe on a rock in the road.

William rose from the leaves. Mack held his breath and felt for the torch and matches. It seemed like a very long time, the hoofbeats nearly on top of him, before William's calm, disguised voice said, "Stop that goddamn nag, mister."

The rider must have been deep in thought or dozing in the saddle, for he sucked in his breath in a fashion more of awakening than fear. Later, as he lay in bed, Mack would see this as the first sign of trouble. What stranger would ride in these parts asleep, or even relaxed?

There came no sound except the horse's breathing.

Then, "Nag, you say?" It was a man's deep voice, filled with great irony, humor even, followed by the horse nickering and stamping. "Who by god is that? What's your name, boy?"

"Buck," William said.

"And Jess," Mack called from the bushes, his voice cracking.

"My country ass," the man said. "You girls go play highwaymen someplace else."

60

Mack stood up, suddenly dizzy, then buckled under a right leg fast asleep. He landed on his left knee and the big pistol fired, flaring and lurching in his hand, a world bared by lightning, then gone.

His ears rang. The crickets he'd forgotten hearing had hushed, and now the only thing larger than this ocean of night was the distant drumming of the horse escaping. An instant of relief. It was over. Failed, but done. The whore flickered in his mind, a long way away. He put his hand to his chest and felt his heart hammering at his ribs.

"*Macky?* You all right?"

He still had the pistol aimed. He dropped it to his side. "Yeah," he said. "I believe I am. I'm all right."

"Why didn't you light the torch? How come you was to shoot?"

"I didn't go to."

"Well, hell," William said. "We best scoot on to the house. Case that fellow comes back with some friends."

Mack nodded, started toward his brother's voice.

His foot caught on something heavy and he tripped, fell to all fours. He scrabbled back, hands and knees sticky and warm, and bumped into William and stopped there, his shoulders against the comforting solidity of his brother's knees.

William patted his head. "Lord-a-mighty," he said.

Then they were running.

"It could've been anybody," said William.

"Anybody killed or anybody that killed him?"

"Either one."

"What're we gone do?"

"Nothing, Macky. We ain't doing a damn thing. Just get up in the morning and finish that fence, like nothing happened. That's what we're gone do."

They lay in their beds, sheets flung back. Still no moon outside.

Nothing in the world it seemed but their two voices in the room. Mack said, "We could take off."

"You want to leave Granny?"

The answer was silence. The window was opened and the soft night chirring went on uninterrupted, ignored.

"Besides, if we run, they'll know it was you and me done it. Way I see it now, what's to lead anybody to us?"

Mack raised up on an elbow. "Who you think it was, that fellow?"

"Some stranger, probably. Nobody around here. You know anybody rides a damn horse?"

Mack lay back.

"Will?"

"What."

"Mr. Billy rides a horse."

"It wasn't him."

"How you know?"

William sighed and said what Mack had already told himself, that the sheriff didn't come out here much.

"You think we ought to tell her?" Mack said. "It *was* a accident. I didn't go to kill him."

"No, I don't think we ought to tell her. Killing's a man's business, and guess what. You just stepped across the ditch into being a full-fledged, full-growed man."

"You make it sound like it's a ditch you done been crossed."

"I believe you yanked me over with you."

A hot breeze swept the odor of sulfur water from the well in their yard and the quick thought of the whore. But just as quickly she was gone from his mind. He closed his eyes. He opened them. He saw no difference, as if he were blind. He lay for a long time, puzzling over what it meant to be dead. Was it as simple as Heaven or Hell? Gold streets like the Bible promised and church singing? Or was it high-licking flames throwing grinning devils at you until time ended? Or maybe just nothing, the conclusion to your part in the

62

world, like lying in a dark pine box forever, going to sleep and never waking.

"Will?"

"What is it."

"I killed a man."

His brother made a sound like a laugh. "You sure as hell did. Now go on to sleep."

William's breathing grew regular, but Mack stared ceilingward. How could Will go to sleep so fast? A stranger's body out there in the road draining of its blood and the killer lying here in this room, if anything more alive than ever, adrenaline surging through his body like a stampede of horses, as if in murdering a man you got the energy out of his blood. He linked his fingers behind his neck.

In his imagination he returned to the road, replaced himself with William and put the pistol in William's grip and had William do the shooting. How would that feel? To know your brother had killed a man? You would be an accomplice, nearly as guilty as the shooter, but what would your ultimate sin be? Would it be loyalty? Is that what you'd call it? You would never turn in your brother. No man could do that. For your brother you would tell lies to the sheriff and repeat those same lies on the courthouse stand, your hand resting on the Bible. Your mother would do the same, had she lived, and your father, had he. The widow too. And Sheriff Billy Waite and Justice of the Peace Tom Hill and every man in the jury and every face in the crowd would do the same, and would expect you to, too. Your only sin would be that you were your brother's keeper. Which is no sin. So now William slept the sleep of the righteous, chest swelling and sinking and swelling and eyes easily shut and mouth opened as if all that lay behind him on this night were a cleanly plowed field.

But Mack . . .

He looked across the darkness to where his brother had begun to snore lightly and knew that he and William had stepped over two different ditches at the moment of the killing. William would live the same lie as Mack, but for different reasons. William's guilt would free him while Mack's would call to him from the darkest hollows of the night—at any moment there could be composed from the darkness a torch-lit group of lawmen or kin of the dead man, and Mack could be wrestled from the house, a noose stretched over his neck and tightened, the other end looped around a limb and hands pulling him into the air, his legs kicking, face going blue, pants darkening with piss.

He sat up.

Was this the cost of killing a person? Your sleeplife? Your peace? A heart so kneaded and stretched it no longer held the shape of a heart?

Now Mack understood. He had murdered a man. Murdered. A man. And in doing so, he had condemned himself to a life of thoughtfulness.

"Will?" he whispered into the darkness.

"Will?

"Will?"

When they woke in the morning the widow was gone and they didn't see her all day, neither knew why. Neither was surprised, though, as she often disappeared on birthing missions unbidden—she would simply look up from the table and say, "Anna Bradford's due," and rise with her supper unfinished and go across the floor, pausing only to lift her midwife's bag from its nail. As boys they'd accompanied her on these trips but now, since they'd grown older, she had them stay home, saying women didn't like boys or men not their husbands to hear the wails they made as their babies split their way into the world of air.

The dog, heavy with puppies, lay in the yard in sunlight while they sat on the porch. Mack hadn't slept and the skin beneath his eyes seemed weighted with sand.

64

"You want to walk over to the store?" William asked. "See what we can see?"

Before he could answer, the dog rolled to her feet, growling. Somebody was coming.

War Haskew. Holding a shotgun aloft, he rode his mule into their yard with a croaker sack for a blanket and dismounted and as the mule wandered to the trough and drank, Haskew sat on the edge of the porch scratching the dog's head and told them Arch Bedsole had been shot dead. That Tooch, his cousin, had called for a meeting to-night, at the store.

"Who done it?" William asked casually.

"Don't nobody know." Haskew looked at his mule. "They say he burned down his house, Tooch did."

"How come?"

"Mad, I reckon." Haskew rose. "Y'all boys be there," he said. "Tooch wants ever available man."

William nodded and they watched Haskew cross the yard, climb onto his mule and wave, then ride away.

The boys waited fifteen minutes before William said, "Let's go on down to the creek. This setting here ain't doing nobody any good."

On the large rock, their lines going south with the current, William spat into the water.

"They know I did it," Mack said.

"How come? How come you, Macky? You liked Arch as much as anybody else."

"What if they ask me?"

"Just say you don't know nothing about it."

"I ain't as good a liar as you."

"Listen," William said, "the main fellow has to believe a lie is the liar hisself. Then it ain't a lie no more. It's the truth. For you and me, the God's truth from now on is that we don't know nothing about Arch Bedsole being shot."

"What about Tooch?"

65

"What about him?"

Mack's line twitched and he looked at it, surprised.

"Hold it still," his brother said.

He lowered the tip to the face of the water, his arm tense, the line slack.

"Wait'll he starts to run," William said, and no sooner had he said it than the line shot away as the fish made for the tangle of submerged limbs across the creek. When the line was taut Mack yanked it and the pole bent double. He leapt to his feet, swinging the line over William's head, and began to backpedal up the bank. William tossed his pole aside and clambered into the water to his knees, pulling the line in hand over hand. He raised the gray-blue body of a foot-long grinnel and hauled it out onto the sand, put his bare foot on its tail, and carefully picked it up behind its head.

William's line was running now, and Mack dropped his pole to grab William's and hauled forth an even bigger fish, William shaking his head and calling his little brother not just a robber of money and a killer of Bedsole but a damn grinnel-thief as well.

"Once a man goes bad he's all bad," William said, stringing the first fish and then the second. He wet his hands in the creek, flicked his fingers dry. They rebaited their hooks and sat back down, a hot breeze rippling the water and tugging at their lines, rattling branches overhead.

Something splashed in the creek and Mack jumped. The grinnel pulling at the stringer.

"Lord," he said, his breath shallow, mouth full of hot spit. Suddenly he couldn't breathe. He dropped his pole, the tip splashing in the creek. He leaned forward. Oh God, he had killed Arch Bedsole. He gagged. Something had to come out of him. He began to sob.

William lowered his head. He lay his pole across his knees and reached and raised Mack's out of the water and set it on the ground. He looked behind them, upstream, down. Mack lay back and covered his face with both forearms, his whole body shaking. He turned to his side, away from his brother, and drew his knees to his body and said, "No, no, no," and kept saying it.

William stared straight ahead. Then he said, "Go on cry. This one time. This time right here and now, and then never again. You hear me?"

At the store a number of men stood in the dirt yard and on the porch and in the croquet court. Someone had built a fire from logs beneath the shed and several of them congregated around it, hands in their pockets, their collars upturned against the wind.

Tooch Bedsole went slowly past them on the horse, not looking at them but at the store, a long narrow building made of logs and tin with a stone chimney at the back, plank steps up to the uneven porch, and glass windows in front. Twin sheds built along the sides like wilted wings, an attic window overlooking the cotton field.

On the porch Lev James, a stocky bearded man, stood from where he'd been sitting on the steps and took the horse by its bridle.

"Tooch," he said.

The man swung from the saddle and gave him the reins. "This everbody?"

"Everbody you can trust."

Tooch squinted in the fading light, looking from face to face as they amassed before him, dirt-poor farmers all but a few, some holding decrepit rifles or wired-together shotguns, one a rusted Confederate infantry officer's sword, its point snapped off. A sorry army, this.

"I count fifteen," he said. "Including you, Lev."

"Hell, you can count me twice, mad as I am."

"We'll get to that."

As Tooch stood over them, Mack saw the bloodstains on his

67

white shirt. In his pocket they saw the ivory grips of a revolver. He was no cotton farmer. He never had been.

They huddled in toward the porch.

Tooch rubbed his eyes, red from smoke and sleeplessness, with the heels of his hands. He blinked and seemed about to speak, but instead narrowed his eyes at where William and Mack stood. Both were armed, the same weapons they'd used in their robbery attempt.

"William Burke," Tooch said. "How old are you, boy?"

"Nineteen in December."

Tooch turned to Mack. "You?"

"Near—" His voice a squawk. "Near 'bout fifteen."

"You can stay," Tooch said to William. To Mack he said, "You can scat. Tonight ain't no time for children."

The boy lowered his eyes.

"Get on now," Tooch said.

William punched him in the shoulder. "You heard him, Macky."

Cheeks stinging, he left as ordered, but in the dark sandy road he stopped. He waited, holding the pistol. Then he turned and back-tracked and hid in the cotton field outside the rim of firelight on his elbows and knees and listened to what he could.

"Tooch," War Haskew said, "we got a question for you."

"Go on ask," he said.

"What do you intend to do about the killing of your cousin?"

Tooch drew deeply on his cigar and let the smoke out so slowly and for such a long time it seemed he was on fire inside and his lungs were a bellows.

"It's your place," said Huz Smith. "Whoever killed him, they got to pay. We'll help you. All we can."

"If we was to kill everbody who's guilty," Tooch said, "we'd have to slaughter the whole town of Grove Hill."

The men looked at one another.

"What the hell's that mean?" Lev James asked.

"It means the folks that killed Arch is town folks, one and all. It means they knew Arch was running for office, and it meant they thought he might just win. If we're gone level things with the folks responsible for killing my cousin, we're gone have to level the whole goddamn town of Grove Hill."

For a moment there was utter silence. Then the sounds of the night seemed to regain themselves, crickets, cicadas, whippoorwills, owls.

"How you level a whole town?" Floyd Norris asked.

"We've known each other a long time," Tooch said, looking from man to man. "I trust most of you fellows, and I hope you trust me. This here is the first time I'm going to invite anybody who ain't comfortable with certain things to leave. What I'm gone talk about, starting here, is outside the law. If any one of you is nervous about killing, I invite you to go on home right now, but I warn you: Don't speak of this to nobody."

Joe Anderson, one of the few unarmed men, lifted his hand and said that nothing would be gained by killing except more killing, and other voices were raised in both agreement and disagreement, and soon yelling had erupted. Yelling which settled down only when Anderson and four others stalked off, shaking their heads and grumbling, looking back to where Tooch stood on the porch, arms folded.

The men who stayed—William among them—gathered closer to the porch. Tooch came down the steps, and as the moon rose and the air grew cooler still a jug surfaced and someone prized out its cob stopper and they all knelt around the fire passing the whiskey, their voices low, the things they said things that Mack couldn't hear from the cotton stalks rustling around him. Flat on his belly with his pistol in one hand and his hat in the other, he tried to slide in through the rows and listen, but when he got too close Tooch paused in what he was saying and raised his head up out of the pack, his face white in the moonlight but his eye sockets dark as snakeholes. He seemed to be looking right at Mack, who began to slide back. In the trees beyond the field he pulled on his hat and got to his feet and brushed the pine straw and dirt from his overalls. Stealing a look across the field behind him, where spots of fire watched him like eyes from the cave of men over it, he stuffed the pistol into his pocket and made himself walk, not run, home.

At dawn he drowned their dog's litter.

Within two days: a man dead at his hand and six puppies as well. The puppies, had they lived, would have gone on to live as dogs do—on the porches of people or under houses or feral in the woods—and then to die as dogs die, beneath the wheel of a wagon or rabid and frothing or from a bullet to the brain.

Men were more complicated—gone now were all the repercussions of Arch Bedsole's life, all the work he would do with his hands, the things he would sell, the animals he would kill, women he would love, children he would sire and raise and beat or not beat. He was dead and there was no way to bring him back. Mack would always have that burden, would forever carry it in him, no matter how long or short he lived.

The next time he saw Tooch Bedsole was at Arch's funeral. A preacher who'd lost an arm and a leg to the War spoke of a good man smote down in his prime, of a generous heart, of the danger of other men seeking vengeance. He said he'd heard rumor of a group of men organizing with thoughts of revenge, and he said that vengeance was the Lord's and His alone, that the guilty man or men would find themselves facing the Almighty on a fateful day, Arch there at His side, and on that day would immortal justice strike with the vigor of a diamondback, fangs as long and curved as the infinite horizon. Yet until that time, the preacher warned, we must let our duly appointed lawmen perform their jobs and work to bring the men to mortal but lawful justice.

They'd started to sing "Amazing Grace" and were watching dirt spaded into the hole, over the pine box, when the Widow Gates whispered that Tooch wanted to see him. Mack looked past her pointing finger out beyond the fence into the field at the dead tree from where Tooch had watched the service in the strip of shade the tree laid across the cotton.

Tooch crooked a finger to motion him over.

He looked at the widow.

"Go on," she said. He felt her hand pushing hard against his back and remembered her giving him the sack of puppies. Far out in the field, Tooch folded his arms, waiting.

Mack pushed his hat down on his head, furrowed his hands in his pockets and stepped between a pair of graves. He could feel her watching him and wondered what she was thinking.

He opened the iron gate and closed it quietly behind him and went along the other side of the fence. It was a long walk up the sloping hill to Tooch Bedsole, a walk during which he didn't think, seemed capable of little more than containing the heart flinging itself at the bars of his ribs.

"Mack Burke," Tooch said as he drew close. He had a low, gravel voice, as if he needed to clear his throat, or didn't speak often. He resembled Arch, as people had said, but in a kind of weathered way, as two pistols of the same make and model might differ due to the use they've seen, one oiled and gleaming from a life in a glass case; but the other well-spent, carried in a belt and used as a bludgeon and thrown and dropped so that certain screws had had to be replaced, the checkering worn from the grips, a gun you knew had sent its rusty bullets into the hearts and backs of other men, a gun burdened, not blessed, with history. Tooch had the same long, down-angled face Arch had but with a cragged look and hollow, under-circled eyes and a speckled complexion. The corners of his mouth were cracked and he blinked his eyes a lot. Where Arch had been clean-shaven, Tooch's jaws held a scab of beard and he wore a mustache, as if

71

he were an inside-out version of Arch sent back on a mission of haunting from some ghost world.

Tooch turned. "Come on, son, let's you and me take us a walk. I'm sick of them graveyard vultures over yonder watching."

Mack lingered a moment, gazing toward the cluster of people who appeared to be watching only the grave being filled, the widow standing apart, her hands folded in front of her. William had removed his coat and joined the stooped group of men shoveling dirt over Arch's coffin. Nobody seemed to care a damn about Mack. When he looked back Tooch was nearly to the woods and he hurried to catch up.

As they walked, Tooch slid a cigar from his shirt pocket and ran it through the groove between his nose and upper lip. He paused to strike a match, cupping his hands against the wind. Mack stopped, too. When Tooch got it going he walked again and Mack followed; they passed under the limbs of a live oak and into the shadow of forest. The temperature changed. Cooler. Cigar smoke trailing, Tooch walked for a long time, ducking branches and sidestepping briars and avoiding puddles. Once he reached out and snapped off a twig and, as he walked, broke it into tiny pieces, scattering them.

Presently the light grew stronger and they came out of the trees and into a field of cotton, which they crossed, and ducked through the fence on the opposite side, then walked along the road for a while. From beside them a quail hen exploded and they watched her rise in the wind and pause, then crumple back to earth, only to rise again and flutter a few feet over the ground.

"She's got chicks," Tooch said. He stopped. Pointed with his cigar. "They're hid out yonder in the weeds. She's trying to draw us away from 'em."

"Where we going?" Mack asked.

"First lesson you better learn," Tooch said, resuming his pace, "is not to ask questions."

Behind them, the hen settled back into the weeds.

Half an hour of cotton fields later the wind brought the smell of something burning, or something having been burned. That odor of cooling coal. Then he knew. The house Tooch had set afire.

They walked through a gate, no fence, just the two posts and the gate that Tooch opened and held open for Mack, and there it was, a squarish pile of ashes and a leaning chimney that seemed little more than mismatched blocks stacked to the height of a house. A few strings of smoke leaked into the air from the rubble and the ground was charred where the fire had spat itself.

Tooch sat on a log with drag marks in the dirt behind it and stretched out his legs toward the ruin and crossed them at the feet, as if he'd burned the place for warmth. Mack sat at the other end of the log with his hands grasping his knees. Tooch puffed his cigar and then looked at it, just a nub now, which he ground out against the log and flicked into the ashes.

"You'll be among the first to know," he said, "that I'm in the process of purchasing Bedsole's Dry Goods. From Ed Bedsole. My uncle. Including all its assets and liabilities." He looked down along the log at Mack. "You know what that means?"

"Yes, sir."

"Good," he said. "One of the biggest liabilities of the store is the damn debts people owe. Charge accounts. First thing I aim to do is start collecting 'em. Charity's one thing I don't believe in. Nobody ever give it to me. And the biggest account on the book is your granny's. I reckon Arch was too softhearted to make her pay, an old woman with two castoffs. Arch, he run the store not as a business but as a social club. As a way of getting elected."

He looked at Mack. Then went on:

"That there's just one of the differences between me and Arch that folks is gone have to reconcile with. Now. I spoke to the widow and told her what she owed me, a debt that some of it stretched back before you was born, and together we come up with a plan to make us even. You got an idea what that plan might be?"

73

"Me."

"Yeah, you. You gone be my helper. You'll begin a week from tomorrow at seven in the morning. You'll not be late. You'll live in the back room of the store and do my bidding for two full years. At the end of that period you'll be free to return to the widow, or do whatever the hell you want. I'll feed and clothe you from the store. Our deal," he said, "ain't original. It's got a fancy name. Arch, him and his big words, would've called it indentured servitude. You know what I call it?"

He shook his head.

"I call it your hide belongs to me."

The next day, when William came outside stuffing his shirt into his pants, Mack had the ax and was chopping at a long piece of hickory he'd dragged from the woods, halving it for posts. Ten other nearly identical posts leaned against the side of the barn.

"This don't hardly seem like acting normal," William said, rubbing his eye with the heel of his hand. "Enough posts for a damn fort."

Mack ignored him.

"You get any sleep last night?" William asked.

"No."

William hooked a suspender over his left shoulder, then went into the barn and returned dragging the post spade. He scratched the back of his neck and watched Mack for a while, then picked a spot, raised the tool in his hands, and began digging.

Shortly the widow came onto the front porch. Mack had taken off his shirt and worked in his undershirt alone, his pants filthy to the knees, sweat trickling down his back, shoulders glistening. He looked up. Fog still hung in the air but had begun to burn off, the dull red sun perfectly round behind the low oak branches over the barn's tin roof.

The old woman came down the plank steps wearing her apron and stood in the yard by the washpot and watched them for several minutes—she'd been after them about getting this fence up for a week now—but if she thought anything out of sorts she didn't say. She was psychic in curious ways but had said that in regard to her two boys she couldn't see a speck of the future or the past, which often was the way with foresighted folk, that the things closest to them in the physical realm were the things farthest away in the spiritual one. Which was why she could touch a penny in a store and know the man who'd paid it was going to die within a week, or could tell what sex a baby would be just by touching its mother's belly, but if she tried to see Mack's future it just came out fuzzy, she said. Images like you remember from a dream, but ones that flicker away before you can get your mind around them. You know something is there but you don't know what.

From the corner of his eye he saw her wave a gnat from her face, then look toward the sky. Presently she climbed the steps and went inside.

Mack leaned another readied pole against the barn wall.

The forlorn dog had been watching the work with little interest, nipping at early flies and moving with the shade, until she stood and began to bark. Mack paused, a maul held at his waist, and William peered past the handle of the spade. They heard it at the same time.

A horse.

Mack moved behind his brother. "Will?"

"Hush," he said. "Don't say nothing."

The door slammed. The widow stood on the porch, a half-peeled potato in her hand. A strip of sunlight cut across her body. She descended the steps and stood at the bottom of them with her knife hand shading her eyes, the dog advancing behind her, barking.

A man on a familiar chestnut horse cantered up the hill and into the yard, and Mack felt he might faint. It was Sheriff Waite. He tipped his hat to the boys. William waved in response and Mack

75

raised his arm and moved his hand, like someone who bore some nervous disorder and whose arm would flap on its own, at the sky, a bed of ants.

The sheriff stopped his tall horse before them and dismounted slowly, the ivory grips of his pistol showing under his coat. Mack hadn't seen him in several months. His hair was grayer and he looked thinner, his face red from the heat. There were burrs in the horse's tail and the sweat-tracked coating of dust on its belly brought to mind maps in an old book he'd seen once that showed regions of the uncharted west, huge blank areas of gray, a river going in at the edge of the unknown and coming out at the opposite known, the river drawn in straight and true but everything around it in those unexplored regions empty, vast with possibility.

"How you boys getting on?" Waite asked.

"Fine, Mr. Billy," William said.

William extended his hand and Waite shook it, then did the same with Mack, who remembered, years before, the sheriff teaching them how to shake hands. "Not too firm," he'd said. "You don't want to hear bones crunch, but don't squeeze too light, neither, like you're a little girl. Just the right amount of squeeze, like you'd use to milk a cow. Fellow shakes too hard, means he's too eager. Too soft, you can't trust him."

He tried now to give Waite that handshake and made himself look him in the eye which was difficult—like opening your eyes underwater—considering that in the next second the sheriff might arrest them. Waite didn't seem angry, though, didn't seem anything other than old. But the fact that he'd come up here meant something.

He switched the rein from one hand to the other. "Cat got your tongue, Macky?"

"No, sir," he said.

"Can I water your horse?" William asked quickly.

Waite handed over the reins and said he'd appreciate it,

76

cautioned him not to let King drink too much. "He's like a damn hound."

"Can we take him for a ride after?"

Waite smiled. "Naw, I've rode him pretty hard and I got a ways to go yet. Better let him rest up while I talk to the widow."

He winked at Mack and headed to the porch, where the old woman stood waiting, arms folded, the potato now a lump in her apron. Waite took off his hat and mounted the steps slowly, a hand on his lower back, his shoulders tired, and he and the widow spoke somberly, not their usual gentle teasing. They sat side by side in the rocking chairs given as payment by Joe Anderson for his twin girls while the boys led the horse to the trough where he submerged his rubbery muzzle.

"You damn fool," William hissed from the other side of the horse.

Mack made himself look at King. He stroked the wiry mane while William drew his fingers along the gunstock protruding from the attached sheath. He glared at Mack over the saddle. "That man's gone know something's up if you keep acting guilty."

As the horse drank, they watched the old woman and sheriff talk, but could tell nothing of what they said. Presently the horse raised its head and they led him to the barn and unbridled him and let him pull tufts of hay from the mule's feeder while they sat on the dirt floor watching the adults through cracks in the barn wall. Neither the widow nor Waite smiled as they rocked and stopped rocking now and again at something the other said and then gradually started moving again. Mack rested his forehead against the hot, coarse board and tried to hear but couldn't. He picked at a splinter of wood in the wall until his finger bled and he sucked the blood. Beside him William began to snore and he stared at his brother as if he'd never seen a creature such as him before, a thing with empty air where a conscience should be.

The horse, done eating, wandered over behind him and nuzzled his neck with its hot fleshy nose. He looked up into those large yellow eyes and frowned at its earthy breath.

"Hey, boy," he said, rubbing him along the underside of his face. King nickered back, blowing his hair.

When he looked out again, Waite had stood and put his hat on. Mack got to his feet and kicked William awake. "I swear," he said, "you'd sleep through your own hanging."

His brother grinned. "Or yours."

William put the bridle back on the horse and took the reins and led the horse out as Waite descended the steps and walked over to where they stood.

"Got him ready?" he asked.

"Yes, sir, Mr. Billy," William answered. "He's good watered and we fed him, too. Got some burrs out of his mane."

Mack looked at him—another lie.

"I thank y'all." Waite took the reins from William and climbed into the saddle and looked down on them.

"I didn't bother the widow too much with this mess about Arch Bedsole getting shot," he said. "Old woman ought not to have to worry much about such business, hard a life as she's had." He looked at them, from one to the other. "But y'all are just about grown so I'll ask you, man to man. Have you heard anything might give me a head start on this business? Any idea who might've shot him? I ain't got no clue about where to start looking."

"No, sir," William said. "We don't hardly get to leave here."

"Well, I don't know if I ain't a little jealous," he said, gazing out at the scene below. He seemed lost in a trance as if recalling the long-ago days of his own boyhood. Then he blinked and looked down at Mack. "Well? What about you, Macky? You heard anything might give me a foothold in this mess?"

He shook his head. "It wasn't me," he said.

Waite's face looked strained a moment. Then he smiled. "Hell, boy. I know that. But do you know who it was?"

78

"Course he don't," William said. "This boy don't even know his own name."

Within days of that Mack had gone to the store to begin his new life there.

On his last evening at home, the widow sent him into the yard to chop wood. He'd been at the woodpile with his shirt off and the ax in his hand gazing at a horned lizard he'd just chopped in half—an accident, he hadn't seen the lizard until it flew into two pieces—when he saw her walk past the garden to the chicken pen. She bent at the gate and turned the wooden latch and stepped inside the cage and knelt as best an old woman could and spoke softly to the chickens. He liked how she called their noises talking and how she talked back, how she called them "her ladies." She must've had the one she wanted in mind for several came to her upturned palm to peck at the feed she had showing and each of these were shooed away, until finally the big white one bobbed cautiously up and she seized it by its neck and took it out fluttering, across the yard. It flew up in her hand and she seemed so small he wondered if it might not fly her away. He stood holding the ax one-handed at his thigh as she rounded the cabin. He listened as she killed it, thinking of all the death they lived amid and wondering why he wasn't more used to it.

When he finished stacking the wood alongside the cabin he came inside where she was cutting up the chicken. He carried a few sticks of wood to the stove and piled them in.

"Your last meal," William said. He had feathers on the arms of his shirt from having plucked the chicken.

"Hush," the widow said.

They ate in silence. In the morning she came to wake him but he was awake already.

"It's time to go," she said.

"Yes, ma'am." He got out of bed. William lay snoring. Mack went into the kitchen.

She made him eggs and even cooked some bacon. The smell woke William who came in without his shirt on, rubbing his eyes and stretching.

"If I'd a known the food would be this good," he said, pouring himself coffee, "I'd of sent you off a long time ago."

"Get dressed," the widow told William.

He left with his coffee and came back buttoning his shirt.

They sat eating. Through the window Mack watched the sun break over the trees.

Those first days at the store were long ones where Mack imagined scenarios, all of which ended with him getting killed. At night he lay on an old mattress ticking in the tiny storeroom in the back and listened to Tooch's footsteps above—the man never seemed to sleep—obsessed with the notion that Tooch somehow knew he had murdered Arch and had brought him to the store to keep him close until he did away with him. Mack would shut his eyes and see Tooch coming at him with a knife. With a club of firewood. Noosing him in a rope from the tack aisle and dragging him across the floor and over the jagged teeth of the porch boards and down the steps. Night after night he considered rising from the bed and escaping, but the widow's final words to him kept him there. *Whatever you do, don't get on his bad side. His or Lev's either. Do whatever they tell you to.*

Which he did. He never questioned washing Tooch's clothes, for instance, carrying the washboard down the steep hill past the mounds which were graves already and climbing back up to get the sack of laundry. He'd seen the widow wash clothes all his life and knew how, but had never imagined himself as the washer. He'd get a good fire going under the washpot and fill it with pails of creek water and add in lye and let the clothes soak, staring across the creek at the land on the other side, an easy enough jump should he choose to make it and keep going, straight for a time and then up the opposite hill and out the edge of the woods into the cotton field he knew was there. But he never jumped. Instead he rolled up his sleeves and knelt and reached into the tub and withdrew one of Tooch's wet white shirts. He laid the washboard against his knees and scrubbed the shirt, rinsed it in the creek, soap bubbles lazing downstream, then hung the shirt on a limb. Another shirt, a pair of cotton pants. Soon a dozen garments would hang in the air around him and move in the slight rustling wind, an arm of a shirt moving in the breeze as if offering advice, or pointing the way to run.

Done, he'd stand and gather the clothes and climb the hill, careful not to snag a shirt on a briar or let a pair of britches get dirty brushing against a tree trunk. At the top, out of the woods, he'd hang the things to dry on the line behind the store and return to the bottom for the washboard, rinsing the soap off in the creek. And looking once again at the opposite side, he'd clamber back uphill.

In general Tooch said little, but on the first day he told Mack, "Your job don't involve gabbing unless a customer asks you a question. Then you'll answer in as little breath as possible. I mean yesses and noes. Polite, though."

"Yes, sir."

Tooch watched him. "Ain't you gone ask 'How come?' "

Mack shook his head.

"Good. Yours ain't to question, just to do. But for your good judgment, I'll tell you the how come of it, this one time. There's fixing to be some events happening that people will talk about for a long time to come. We're fixing to embark on a mission like this county ain't ever seen. Any other counties, either. And you're gone be right here in the eye of the storm. So if you're up yonder jabbering to ever knucklehead that buys a bar of soap or a nickel cigar, something's liable to slip out. I believe a man gathers strength from one place, boy. Within. You're fixing to have you a goddamn lonely

81

spell, Mr. Mack Burke. But ever river's got a opposite side, and this lonely time'll come to a end for you, too. You mark it down, boy."

The men had their first official meeting after Mack had been at the store about a week. Those who came were the ones who'd remained the night Tooch had called them to the store after Arch's murder. Those eight—Lev and Kirk James, Floyd Norris, Massey Underwood, Huz and Buz Smith, War Haskew, and William—had begun arriving at the store just after dark. In no time a jug had come out. Tooch told Mack to go to his room and shut the door. He left it cracked, though, and on his knees he peeked out into the dark store and listened.

He saw the circle of men, shoulders and lowered heads capped with flimsy hats. He heard the soft rain outside. Pecan branches scraping the back of the store. Saw the jug passed and unstoppered and heard men sigh after raising it and letting it drain down their throats. He could imagine their eyes watering with the burn of it and their gullets constricting with pleasure and he wanted to be with them. For almost an hour they told stories about Arch and laughed, but with a tension, as if this were the wake of a man no one had liked. And finally, what had begun as a fairly loose circle closed as it grew even darker and harder for Mack to see as they knelt close to one another, speaking softly. Mack's knees hurt from the hard floor where he crouched but his ears were good. As long as the rain stayed low, he could hear.

At last Lev James shifted on his haunches. He said, "Let's get to it, Tooch."

Tooch sat opposite Mack, and between the shoulders of two men, lit yellow by stovelight, he could see most of the storekeeper as he slid a cigar from the pocket of his shirt. As he ran it through the groove between his mustache and nose. Bit off the end and struck a match on his heel and lit the cigar and sat smoking it with his forearms on his bony knees and his long chin jutted out. Even Mack's tiny room held now the smell of burning wood and tobacco juice and

82

smoke and whiskey and sweat. He shifted on his knees and opened the door wider.

Tooch extended his arm and ashed his cigar into the spittoon. "What we're gone do," he said, "is form an alliance."

"Alliance," somebody—Mack couldn't tell who—repeated.

"What kind of alliance?" Lev asked.

"A secret one."

"Alliance," Lev repeated.

"Gang, he means," Kirk said. "Like the Masons."

Lev scowled. "Secret. Who'd know about it?"

Tooch: "Just the members."

Lev shifted and spat. Mack viewed him in profile, beefy face and, his hat off, a bald head aglow in the stovelight. "What's the point of some alliance nobody knows about?" he asked. "Seems to me the whole reason to get together like you're saying is that we can do more damage. We'd be more of a threat to the town folks if everybody knew how many of us was in the alliance and knew our names."

Tooch nodded and considered. "Two things," he said. "First, if nobody knows your number, you always got the element of surprise. You got mystery. And if you got mystery, you got power. What people's most afraid of is what they don't ken. Keep folks in the dark, you control the dark."

Lev grunted.

"Next, you got a powerful tool. What they call alibis. Men backing each other up. What if we rob McCorquodale's store? What if Lev and William and Kirk and Huz did it? If somebody comes out here and tries to pin it on 'em, the rest of us will swear we was with them that night. If that damn Waite comes to arrest one of us, we'll get other fellows in the area to back us. If they don't, we'll punish 'em.

"If this is a problem to any of y'all," Tooch said, "I'm extending an invitation. Go now. Go, goddammit, right now."

Floyd Norris rose.

"Tooch," he said, "it seems like you're fixing to ask us to do something that just might get us killed."

He considered. "Yeah. It might."

Without looking at anyone, Floyd said, "Listen. Ain't none of y'all got families. Most of you is young fellows, 'cept Kirk there, and Massey, but they ain't got nothing holding 'em back. Tooch, you chose good, if you're making up some kind of army. Fellows ain't got much responsibility. But me, I got a wife. Got them four young ones. If I was to get killed, there'd be nobody to see after 'em. So I'll say good night to you all."

Mack had never heard him say that many words in his life. He and William and the widow had picked cotton with him in years past, and a quieter man you'd not find, except Buz Smith, who'd never been able to speak.

"We understand," Tooch said. "But don't speak a word of this to nobody."

Floyd nodded. "I swear I won't." He shrugged, turned, and walked the length of the aisle, opened the door and shut it behind him. They listened to his footfalls down the steps and then to nothing.

"If one of us do get jailed," Massey Underwood said, "what will become of us? Will the rest of you abandon us?"

"We will not," Tooch said. "We'll first swear to your innocence, and we'll have other men swear, too. We might send in Joe Anderson. Or some other fellow with a good reputation. We might let Floyd Norris go and say you was with him butchering a hog. So you might get put in the jailhouse, but you won't stay there long."

"You're saying you'll put up the money and do all the thinking," Lev said, "and we'll do all the damage, but won't be no way to get throwed in jail?"

"Yeah," Tooch said. "I'm saying that."

Lev popped his suspenders. "Sounds all right to me. I never did care too much for thinking. I'm in."

"I got another question," War Haskew said.

Tooch nodded.

"We all liked Arch. We all mad about what happened to him. But the truth is, this is your fight. We'll help you, but what do we get out of this club of yours, other than risk and time all used up?" He looked around. "I don't know about you fellows, but time's a thing I can't spare much of. I got a crop to tend. And William here, well, he works for me. He ain't got much time to spare, neither."

"Camaraderie's one thing you'll get," Tooch said. "And the protection I've spoke of. You think them mean sons-a-bitches from Grove Hill would of come in here if there was a gang of meaner sons-a-bitches waiting for 'em? They'll be scared to set a foot in our beat, and if they do we'll send 'em running out with a ass full of buckshot. We're gone take the law by the shoulders and shake it, boys, we're gone run this beat. Then we'll bypass them crooked bastards in the courthouse and in the capitol and set our own order.

"But them ain't the only reasons. That's just the start. We're gone split the money we get. So even if you don't care about none of the other reasons, how 'bout silver dollars? A lot of 'em."

There were other questions, and the meeting went far into the night, Mack missing some details, but by the end Tooch had convinced them all and unfolded his Case pocketknife. Mack strained to see as Tooch opened his hand and drew the blade over his right palm. He passed the knife to War Haskew, who did as Tooch had, and the knife went down the line and each man cut his hand. Tooch had a sheet of paper on which he used his finger as a pen and his blood as ink to write his name at the top of the page. When he finished he handed the paper to Lev, who, unable to write, made an X and passed it to Kirk, who made an X as well. To William. To the Smiths. War Haskew. Massey Underwood. The jug came round and each man in the circle poured a bit in his palm and closed his fist, then drank from the jug before passing it on. When all had signed, Tooch took the paper and stood and they all stood with him. He blew on the page.

He read the names aloud. He said, "Y'all have committed. This is our first step." He waited, and when the jug found its way back to his hands, he announced that the name of their alliance was to be Hell-at-the-Breech.

"Hell-at-the-Breech," War Haskew repeated.

"What the hell's a breech?" Lev asked.

"An opening," Tooch told him.

"Like a girl's cooter?" Lev asked, grinning.

"Yeah. Or like a grave," Tooch said, "or the breech of a gun."

Lev had reached behind him for his shotgun. He snapped it open and the head of a shell rose from it. "This here part," he said, tapping the hinge, "is the breech."

"That's right."

"And the breech of hell is gone be us?"

"It is," Tooch said. "We are."

Mack heard nothing else for several days. Then he learned of an attack on the property of a man called Lem Howze. His house had been set on fire and he'd been robbed of more than seventy dollars. His barn, corncrib, sheds, and privy set ablaze, too.

And thus the alliance commenced its work, groups of two or three in their white hoods going to the farms of white families, asking each man to sign their paper in blood. Most men were happy to write their name or make their mark, to participate in revenging Arch Bedsole, to secretly proclaim their anger. They were told they'd have to do nothing but possibly act as witnesses, and that they'd be paid for it. That no harm or violence would ever come to them. And if any men on their list were ever wronged by a town man, Hell-at-the-Breech would strike for them. It was their alliance, too.

Mack heard rumors of who wouldn't sign, Joe Anderson chief among them. Four or five other fellows, too. At first Tooch had others in the outer circle go and talk sense into them, which worked for everyone but Joe Anderson, a farmer named Jonesy Gray, and a bootlegger, Bit Owen.

Then Gray, a large man, came to the store one day, Mack in the blacksmith's shed hammering a horseshoe as Tooch, War Haskew, and Lev sat on the porch. Gray stalked up the steps, Lev not even getting up, and grabbed the smaller man and began shaking him, yelling that he knew it was Lev who'd burned his barn. Lev let himself be shaken and then thrown off the porch. He landed and rolled his head side to side. He stood, dusted himself off, and came up the steps. He had a pistol in his hand then and had to jump up to hit Gray, but hit him he did in the temple and hit him again and again and when Tooch and War got them separated Gray looked dead. They put on their hoods and tied him to a mule and dragged him off and Mack didn't see where they went. Later he heard that Gray had lived, and the condition for it was his having signed their paper.

By May, except for Joe Anderson and Bit Owen, the whole beat and most outlying homesteads had acquiesced, and the few black families had been frightened away—one story Mack heard found several of the Hell-at-the-Breech boys in their hoods going to the colored church and moving all the furniture outside—pews, pulpit, altar—setting it up exactly as it'd been inside. They'd captured the preacher's pig and gutted it and slung it over the pulpit. Someone had opened a hymnal to "We Shall Not Be Moved," and in pig blood crossed out the word "Not." Other black men were robbed of what money they had, and one had been hanged for saying the wrong thing, though Mack didn't know what that had been.

But still, he'd been kept distant from it, Tooch wouldn't speak of it in his presence. Since that first night, they'd had their meetings on the porch or on the croquet court, not letting him close enough to hear. There were several drunken parties, always on the occasion of a successful raid, money divided, cigars handed out, but on each of these nights Mack had been confined to his room.

And though kept from the alliance's activities, he still saw his share of violence. He'd been working for Tooch only a couple of months when a peddler came by with a jug; soon the peddler, Lev, and Tooch were drunk. They'd been swapping stories while Mack listened from inside, through the opened window. Tooch noticed him and said for him to come on out so he could hear better. The peddler gave them all five-cent cigars and fed them news of the outer world, and after a big sloppy snort of the shine, as Lev drunkenly lit his cigar, he somehow caught his beard on fire.

He didn't yell or whimper, just set his teeth and closed the eye on that half of his face and whacked himself on the cheek, Tooch and Mack watching somberly. By the time the fire was out his lip was bleeding and he was opening and shutting his mouth to see if his jaw still worked.

"It clicks a little," he said.

The peddler's mistake was laughing. "I ain't never," he said, wheezing.

"What's so goddamn funny?" Lev wanted to know.

The peddler must've sensed the danger and tried to stop laughing. But when he saw how uneven Lev's face looked with much of his beard singed off, he laughed again.

"Shit," he said, slapping his thigh. "I could of lent you a razor, friend, and spared us all the odor."

Calmly, Lev set aside his jug, stood, went down the steps to the peddler's wagon. He untwisted the wire from around a pair of iron tongs where they hung alongside many other implements, yokes, traces, scales, and such, and still opening and closing his jaw, stomped up the steps with the tongs opened like a crab's claw. The peddler lost his color and began to backpedal across the porch, ash from his cigar falling on his white shirt, but Lev snapped the tongs shut and caught the man around the neck.

Mack rolled off the porch to get out of the way and Tooch watched, holding the jug.

Lev slung the fellow in circles, the tongs fastened around his neck and the peddler clinging to the tongs, and when Lev let go the man sailed off the porch and landed in the dirt and bounced and rolled to a stop beneath his wagon. He lay there moaning. On his knees, Mack crept to the corner below the porch and had a peddler's-eye view as Lev's legs appeared on the other side of the wagon. The peddler looked right at Mack as he got dragged toward the other side. He was screaming, clawing the dirt. The wagon wheels obscured what happened next, but there was more screaming, then a gagging noise, then a moist kind of pop. Then nothing. Lev's hand reached and got the peddler's abandoned cigar from by the wheel and his legs went back around the wagon.

"You can crawl on out, boy," he said.

When Mack stood, brushing off his knees, he saw Tooch coming out of the store with a wooden crate. He tossed it to Mack and said for him to start unloading the wagon.

As he did, Mack stole glances at the dead man where he lay with his head in a puddle of blood, his eyes opened and a muddy lump lying beside him in the dirt: his tongue, which he'd bitten off.

Opening and closing his jaw and picking singed hair from his face, Lev watched as Mack passed with the box full of goods. Now and again he'd stop the boy and select an item to keep—a cinch, an awl, a galvanized washtub, a teakettle, and a railroad lantern, among others—which he had Mack pile at his feet. When the unloading was done, Tooch and Lev drank more and haggled a bit on the value of the rest of the stock, Lev claiming since he'd disposed of the peddler it was all his but Tooch arguing it belonged to them both, since he, Tooch, had occasioned the peddler's appearance and would testify if necessary that the man never stopped at the store. Finally, over still more whiskey, they agreed on a sixty-forty split, Tooch paying Lev half the cash equivalent of the stock's wholesale value, a list of which they discovered in the dead man's coat pocket. Also, Lev got the mule and Tooch the wagon.

"What about you?" Lev asked Mack as he came back outside, rolling down his sleeves, the unloading done.

"Sir?"

"Ain't you claiming a share, too? You don't want to threaten me and say if I don't pay you off you'll head right straight to the law?"

Mack shook his head. "I ain't studying the law, Mr. James."

Tooch and Lev exchanged a glance. "Give him a dollar," Tooch said. "Out of your share."

Lev reached into his pocket and flicked a coin, which Mack caught.

"This gets out to anybody," Lev said, "it'll be cause of you. You get what that means?"

Mack nodded.

"Well, then," Tooch said, "let's deal with this bleeding son-of-a-bitch before the buzzards start aswirling."

Mack dug the grave.

A life of selling dry goods agreed with Mack. Such things of wonder and color he'd seen stacked on the high shelves behind the counter while visiting the store with the widow were things he now had access to, petroleum jelly, spirits of turpentine, borax, Dr. Walter's Celebrated Eye Water, flake tar camphor, Epsom salts, a dozen flavors of hard candy. He enjoyed handling the products, reading their labels, pronouncing the strange words on the sides of boxes, bags, and cans. Tuberose snuff. Orange wine stomach bitters. Celery malt compound. He loved unscrewing lids from jars and bottles and sniffing the various powders and liquids inside, each with its own curious set of ingredients and distinct odor, this one bringing to mind green pinecones and that one cat piss or ripe persimmons, each a bona fide cure for some ailment or ailments. Each a link to the world he'd never have known otherwise. Where did these things come from? Far away, he imagined, men in aprons and leather work gloves and goggles in caves in foreign lands among barrels and copper worms with witches' pots bubbling and spitting over precise flames. Stored in the hold of a ship bucked by waves large as hills. A world outside these cotton fields and woody hollows, far beyond the brown placid river and the trees blue with distance.

Most every day during his first months, going along the high shelves, moving his stepladder a foot at a time, he discovered some oddity. He puzzled over a small box of variously sized hard rubber cups for half a day before realizing they were crutch bottoms. A curious, curled, flexible tube with a horn on one end and a small nozzle on the other was a mystery for nearly a week, until he saw an old man with the nozzle end sticking in his ear and the horn end to another man's mouth—a device against deafness! Mack had looked up the aisle and down—Tooch must have been outside—and inserted the nozzle into his ear. When he spoke into the horn he nearly fell off the ladder and spent an hour stoppering a finger into his ear to blunt the ringing.

"Get to work," Tooch would say once a day or so when he appeared from nowhere and found the boy high on the ladder gazing one-eyed and longways down the shining, jagged barbs of a hacksaw, or at the intricate stitching of a calfskin glove, but when Mack turned to look into the man's green eyes, Tooch seemed to recognize this wonder at design and execution, as if he'd been a boy here himself, atop this ladder, reaching a boy's hand far back into these shelves as if it were the past itself you could touch.

"What's that you got now?" he would sometimes say, approaching Mack, wiping his hands on a rag.

Mack would descend the ladder and offer the heavy thing he'd found.

"You've happened upon a padlock here," Tooch would say, showing how turning the attached key would release the curved metal hoop. When Mack asked what it was for, Tooch smiled and said, "What innocence, my lord. It's for locking, boy. Locking people out, or in."

"Like in jail?"

"Exactly like that."

Then he'd taken away the lock and walked back down the long aisle toward the window, calling behind him for Mack to quit daydreaming and start earning the money he wasn't being paid.

Another time Mack found a cigar box beneath the counter. Tooch was outside, talking to Floyd Norris, the two of them watching the sky for clues to the weather's disposition. Mack unwrapped a piece of string from the box, and when he opened it and saw them in their plain brown paper packages he felt his pants tighten—without ever having seen such a thing or even imagining that they existed, he knew what they were. He snapped the box shut and rewrapped it, his cheeks blazing. When Tooch appeared and saw him look up, he grinned.

"You unearthed the skins, I take it."

"The what?"

"Never mind."

He learned, too, to sneak a piece of rock candy and suck it for a few minutes before drying it and slipping it back in the bottom of the jar.

And, aside from the mysteries he'd found among the shelves and underneath the counter, Mack had discovered in himself an instinct for order—where the patient, careful counting and stacking and retrieval of boxes along an oft-dusted shelf would have driven William wild with boredom, it suited Mack to the core and out the other side. On reflection, he realized that all through his life this love of pattern had existed, though he'd not said as much to himself. How neatly he'd cut his fence posts, shaving off even the smallest stobs, always taking too long in William's snarled opinion. And how straight he'd made the rows of vegetables the widow had had him plant, weed, and pick in their small side-yard garden. The way he threaded a worm onto a fishing hook, concealing the whole of the hook, while William had stabbed the worm three or four times and plunked it out into the water. How Mack had begun to find himself whistling as he scrubbed clothes on the washboard. How neat his graves were.

The earth ticked along. Spring came, went. The dogwoods bloomed, then shed their petals and were green like any other tree. Tooch didn't kill Mack and as the days numbered on the boy started to relax somewhat; sometimes he'd realize that half an hour had passed without his having thought of being a murderer.

In early June Arch's father, Ed, died, and Mack and Tooch rode on the dead peddler's wagon, pulled by Arch's horse, to the funeral. Arch's four plump dark-headed sisters had come from wherever they lived, outside the beat, brought their earnest farmer-husbands and what seemed like two dozen children, each identical to the next. The daughters gazed with unmasked hatred at their cousin Tooch, but none of the women approached him. The members of Hell-at-the-Breech came, too, armed—though no one knew who they were—as did all the farmers who'd signed in blood. Their families were present, too, women in dresses worn only for church, men wearing what they wore for fieldwork except that the clothes had been laundered midweek and their white shirts were buttoned to the neck. Mack saw the widow—someone had given her a chair—and waved, but she seemed not to see him. He had heard she'd been living at Ed Bedsole's, tending him in his dying, and who knew what thoughts she had.

On the slow ride back to the store, Tooch elbowed Mack out of his daydream and handed him the reins.

And just under two weeks later they returned to the graveyard to bury Arch's mother, this funeral an exact replica of Ed's, same

93

people, clothes, even the weather the same, and whatever the preacher said might've been the same, too, had Mack listened.

Since buying it, Tooch hadn't changed much about the store's layout—for instance, he left the hand-lettered sign hanging above the counter, over the cash register. Arch had been a lover of bookish words, and this sign warned NO EXPECTORATING UPON THE FLOOR. Mack remembered the story. For several hours after Arch'd hung the sign, men coming in had asked what it meant.

"What what means?" Arch had said.

"That word."

" 'Floor'? Why, you're standing on it. It's composed of pine boards held together by a curious invention called 'nails,' which are long sharp fasteners—"

"The other word."

" 'No'?"

"No, not 'no,' dammit, that long one there."

Arch went on all afternoon, not telling the meaning of the word, and men kept guessing, and laughing. Someone said he'd make a good politician.

"To piss?" somebody suggested.

"No, but I'd ruther you not do that on the floor, either."

"Expect— To guess?"

"Well, if that's what it means," Arch said, winking, "then you're breaking the rules right now, ain't you?"

"To clog?"

"To lay down?"

Finally somebody got it right, "To spit," and the community had itself a new ten-dollar word, and for a spell you could hear it used whenever possible:

"You reckon it might expectorate on us today?"

"I expectorate so."

Tooch's visible changes to the store, when they came, came slowly. In fact, he'd owned the place for two months before the quiet spring afternoon when he climbed the stepladder and went to work on the sign nailed up over the porch. It said BEDSOLE'S DRY GOODS in large, ornate letters. Beneath those, in smaller, plainer letters, it read ARCHIE BEDSOLE, PROPRIETOR. Tooch simply painted over Arch's name and replaced it with QUINCY. Mack had been raking the yard and watching. He asked, "How come you ain't changed that sign before?"

Tooch climbed down the ladder and stepped back to inspect the sign. "Cause whenever you come into a place, it's best to come slow so you're dug in before anybody gets wise to you. Remember that. Nothing alerts people more than things that move fast. Now get back to work."

One Sunday a month or so later he was raking the dirt in the croquet court when an acorn fell out of the air and hit him on top of the head. Mack dropped his rake and looked up, a perfect gray-blue sky with a smudge of late-afternoon sun in one corner and a parchment moon in another. He looked between his feet and saw the acorn, and saw others, too, all around where he'd been working. He took off his hat and one rolled out of its brim and he caught it in midair. He frowned at the woods twenty yards to his right, no wind able to carry acorns this far.

Then, from the patchwork of trees, he saw his brother's face peering out between the wishbone of a mimosa trunk.

Retrieving his rake, Mack idled over, aware of Tooch behind him in the store, and shouldered into the cross-stitch of briar and vine.

"Hell," William said. "I been throwing acorns at you for ten minutes. What the hell you studying so hard?"

"What you think?"

William looked behind them, down the inclining hill to where the creek chuckled below.

"I done told you, Macky. Don't ever mention that."

"It's easy for you to say. You ain't gotta walk around knowing you killed him, knowing he ain't gone ever come back."

William got up from the stump he'd been sitting on and with his jug started downhill, up to his ankles in dead leaves.

"Wait."

When he stopped, the paper leaves stopped rustling. Not looking back, he said, "If you mention that one more time, I'm going down this here hollow and up the other side and you won't see me no more. There's things I need to tell you and things you need to hear. But I ain't gone waste my time if you're still the same goddamn baby you was five months ago. I'd have hoped Tooch would've worked some sense into you, after all this time."

Mack squatted on his haunches, holding the rake like a banjo. "He has. Come on back. I done said the last of all that."

"Cross your heart."

He crossed it.

William returned and squatted beside Mack. His brother looked older, his hair longer and stringy around his face, his cheeks mossy with a red stubble. He smiled and reached across the distance between them and grasped Mack's shoulder and squeezed it hard and shook it.

"He ain't killed you, I see."

"Not yet."

William held up the jug. "You want to try a little? Put some hair on your tallywhacker?"

He nodded. Drank and spat it back out, a fine mist that landed on William's face.

His brother laughed. "You better learn to hold your liquor. Try again. Go slow, though. Just take little sips at first. And go on swallow it. Don't try to hold it too long in your jaw or you'll taste it and won't never get it down."

96

He did, then opened his mouth to cool his tongue. His eyes were moist.

"That's the boy." William took back the jug and drank from it as if he'd been doing it all his life. "It tasted like shit when I started it, but if you're faithful it'll grow on you."

"That ain't gone ever grow on me," Mack said. "Gimme some more."

"Naw, you go back in the store drunk and Tooch'll skin us both." William leaned back against a tree, and Mack's chest and the muscles that stretched up into his neck ached with longing for how things used to be, the two of them fishing in the creek or playing croquet with the widow watching and Arch alive and up on the porch giving one of his speeches.

"You ever see the widow?" William asked.

"He won't let me. Do you?"

"Yeah. I go have supper with her on Sunday evenings."

"How's she doing?"

"Fine."

"She ever mention me?"

William shook his head. "I believe she's trying to put you out of her mind. How's Tooch treat you?"

"Okay, I reckon."

"You reckon."

He shrugged.

"He hit you?"

"No."

"What's the worst thing he does?"

He thought. "Makes me count buttons."

"Do what?"

"He has this box full of about a thousand buttons. Whenever he leaves he takes some of the buttons with him in his pocket. I have to count the ones left and tell him how many's gone. He says it keeps me from going out and getting into mischief."

"Well, good luck to him."

William drank again and laughed.

"Sometimes I dream about him," Mack said. " 'Bout him coming after me. Using a ax, or a knot of kindling wood. This one time it was a shovel."

"Hell, boy. You always did have a active mind. I remember them dreams you used to have. Bears chasing you, and you ain't ever even seen a damn bear. All that reading you do. You read in his books any?"

"Sometimes."

"There's your problem. You let them words in and you're in a peck of trouble. Best to keep your mind occupied with other things."

"Like what?"

"Work." He smiled. "Whores."

"You seen her?" *Annie.*

"Seen her? Macky boy, I done screwed her."

"You ain't."

"Oh, I have. More'n once, too."

"Is it like we used to talk about?"

"You wanna find out?"

He nodded.

"Then you best forget this Arch business and keep your mind on your work. I been trying to talk 'em into letting you join up."

Mack said, "I don't know that I want to."

"Boy," William said, "you ain't got the sense God give a toad-stool. You so worried 'bout Arch you ain't thinking clear. If there's a storm, where's the safest place to be?"

"In the house?"

"No, not in the damn house. And not in the barn, neither, Macky. Safest place is in the eye of the storm. Now Tooch is got some big ideas, and we gone need some new blood to do all the things he's talking about doing."

"What things?"

"Hell, I can't tell you, boy. We took a vow. All of us. And if anybody breaks it, they gets killed."

As August drew near, Mack sensed something big in the gang's workings; the laying-by season gave those who grew cotton a few weeks of respite from their normal tedious days and so the men congregated almost daily at the store. They'd sit along the bench and on the edge of the porch and tell stories and laugh, eating venison or beef and passing a jug. Mack went about his chores but noticed in them all a change, and not just that their clothes had improved, the usual threadbare overalls more patch than original material now strangely gone, replaced by wool britches and chambray shirts, new hats, their brogans new and shiny except for Lev, who couldn't find a pair to fit his large feet. Many had upgraded their firearms, too, William no longer toting their dead daddy's old shotgun but a new Parker twelve-gauge double barrel with twin hammers and a blue sheen about its metal.

The gun had come in the mail, packed in straw and paper in a long wooden box. Sorting through the letters and packages, Mack had seen his brother's name on the box. Later in the day William came to the store and found Mack in the shed shoveling horse shit.

"I get any mail?" he asked.

"A long box," Mack replied, not looking up.

William had already gone, though, clomping up the stairs and slamming the door.

He and Tooch came out later and stood in the road examining the shotgun, Tooch pointing out its excellent features and congratulating William on such a fine choice of firepower. With Mack kneeling and watching through the slats of the parked wagon, William unbreeched his new gun and accepted from Tooch two shells from a new box. He snapped it closed, a sound so quiet Mack

99

barely heard it, and raised it to his shoulder. He aimed for a long time, Mack peering to see what he'd shoot.

There was a blue jay thirty or so yards away on a fence, and when William shot, the bird exploded in a mist of blue and white feathers as the gun's echo died out in the oak trees.

Mack had finished mucking out the horse's stall when William snuck up behind him and poked the gun in his back. "Surrender," he said. He let Mack hold the twelve-gauge and break it open, two brass-capped red shells rising an inch out of its breech. It had intricate checkering on its pistol grip stock and two triggers. Mack raised it to his shoulder and eyed down the barrels.

His brother moved in close behind him, as if offering instruction. "I been chose," he whispered.

"For what?" At the other end of the shotgun Mack sighted a mockingbird that had just landed in a pine tree, then lowered the gun.

"A raid," William said.

He turned up the following Sunday and whistled for Mack where he was feeding the horse in the shed; a glance behind him, Mack hurried over the croquet court brushing hay from his arms. They sat in the line of shadow a tall pine cast, William holding the jug he never seemed without, his head hung. He took a long swig and looked up at Mack through his hair. There was something different about his eyes. "I was there," he said.

"Where?"

"Joe Anderson."

Mack glanced toward the store. "You killed him?"

"Hell, no, I didn't kill him." He brushed at something on his pants leg. "Lev did."

He began to tell how Lev had shot Anderson, then cut his throat with the man's own Barlow knife, and how after he died Lev sat down beside the body poking its foot, which gave at the ankle. How Lev asked, "What you reckon it's like, being dead?" How he said, "Seeing his eyes? It give me a thought. You reckon somebody's blood is where they life is stored? I mean, you can take off a fellow's arm at the shoulder and he might live two dozen year or more with a stump, long as you stop the blood. Same with a leg. I knew a old fellow lost his leg just above the kneecap in the War, used to hobble about with a crutch under his arm. Said he woke up one night and got outta bed, plumb forgot he didn't have but one leg, and fell right over. Said he wished they'd a kept it when they sawed it off so he could be buried all in one piece. You can pack such a thing in salt. The leg I believe he said was in Georgia."

How Lev had taken the dead man's booted toe between his fingers and shaken it almost tenderly, the way you'd wake a sleeping friend. Then how he blinked, his trance over, and said, "Hey, them's nice boots, ain't they? God dog," and began tugging them off.

The boys sat on the ground with sunlight through the leaves dappling their arms and legs. Both looked up when a hummingbird buzzed past and Mack remembered that William had once told him how after they're cast from the nest hummingbirds never land, that they spend their entire lives darting through the air. When Mack had asked the widow if this were true, she'd laughed and said, Nonsense, how could a thing never stop moving?

"It had to be done," William said, tracing a finger around the mouth hole on the jug. "We give him ever chance to join with us. He was a stubborn old jackass."

Mack nodded. Then looked up. "I been thinking I'd best join up, too, if they ask me."

"I been telling you," William said.

DIRTY
WORK

August to October 1898

I

WAITE SAT AT THE DINNER TABLE enduring his wife's silence, which said much more to him than her usual chatter. The clock struck noon in the next room and he listened as its metal cogs and wheels realigned, a sound he'd come to think of as the sound of time itself. He always heard the old clock if he was home; no matter if he was on the porch or even asleep, he'd hear the sliding noises of metal on metal and the pendulum clicking and feel a comfort at things working in the order they were supposed to.

Sue leaned over him now and ladled beans onto his plate and poured a stream of thin gravy onto his mashed potatoes. He raised his fork and mixed it in, tines ringing on the plate. The consistency of the gravy irritated him—she knew he liked it thick—but bringing it up would prompt her to air the thing she was mad about, whatever it was. So he kept quiet, hoping he'd get out of the house before she spoke up; then he could work late and come home after she'd gone to bed and, if he played it right, get up and be gone before she rose the next day. Get breakfast at the hotel where they never cared about things more weighty than the weather.

He'd spent the previous night in Bit's cabin hoping his friend would return with a jug, hearing each sound outside as the sound of a foot snapping a twig, crackling over leaves. An hour before dawn he was in a nervous froth and had left and found King as jittery as he was, probably wild dogs in the area. The ride home was long and jarring, a jumpy horse beneath a jumpy rider. He'd arrived at midmorning to find a letter from Johnny-Earl. Addressed to him but Sue had already opened it. He slammed his gunbelt on the rolltop desk and the cat had sprung away and regarded him from

105

the back of the sofa as if he were a man who didn't belong in a parlor.

After a bath and a change of clothes—Sue hovering around him silently, bringing in more heated water and frowning at how his shirt smelled of smoke and sweat—he sat in the parlor and read and reread Johnny-Earl's letter while she made dinner. The boy had broken his arm felling a water oak and had met a nice nurse at the doctor's office where they'd taken him to have it set. Waite wondered about the idea of more grandchildren—he had five by his three daughters—and in his mind had been composing a return letter to him.

But it would be a while before he got the luxury of writing back. He had two days' business to attend and half a day to do it in. If only—Sue sat down across from him, not making eye contact—he could get away before she got into it. She put her napkin in her lap, folded her hands, and waited. He waited for a moment until he remembered to say grace, which he cleared his throat and said, same prayer he'd given for forty years, blessing the food and his wife and children and grandchildren each by name.

He ate quickly while she forked a single bean at a time into her mouth. He was almost done, had decided not to get seconds or dessert though he wasn't yet full, when she said, "The judge came by."

Waite had been reaching for his glass of tea and stopped, then reached on. She'd always called Oscar by his title and Oscar's wife called Waite by his—both women proud of their husbands' positions and each indulging the other. *Would the judge like some more pie? Did the sheriff's new coat fit?* Here, though, him and Sue alone, he found it annoying.

"You mean Oscar?"

"Yes, Oscar. Of course Oscar."

Waite drank and put his glass back. "I'll see him uptown, I expect."

But now he knew the problem, at least. Oscar had been by and obviously mentioned Waite's going out to Mitcham Beat alone. His cousin had used this tack before, getting at Waite through her. Oscar knew he was thinking of retiring and wanted that damn Ardy Grant to be his deputy until he did, then take over as sheriff.

He stood up and thanked Sue for the meal and crossed the room and bent to kiss her forehead as she sat stiffly.

"Don't wait up," he said before he shut the kitchen door.

He went by the courthouse and checked the papers on the sale of Bedsole's store from Ed Bedsole to Tooch and then walked to the office of the lawyer who'd written the transaction up. His name was Harry Drake. He and Waite had played horseshoes as partners in a few county fairs together and beaten Oscar and his partner for the trophy, a thing his cousin sorely hated and Waite sorely enjoyed. He kept the trophies in his office and pretended to polish them when Oscar stopped by.

The sale of Bedsole's store was all straight, according to Drake. He said he hadn't talked to Ed Bedsole himself—the old man been too sick to travel—but had written up the forms for Tooch.

"So Ed sold it to him, all legal?"

"Legal yeah, but you could barely call it a sale."

"What's that mean?"

Drake tapped the paper on his desk. "Tooch Bedsole paid the sum of one dollar for the whole business, building, inventory, all money owed to it from people's credit accounts. Even got a horse in the deal."

"A dollar?"

"It's not that unusual," Drake said, handing the paper to Waite, "for sales between family members."

"How do you know Tooch didn't force Ed to sign the paper? Was there a witness?"

107

"In fact, there was," Drake said. "That old midwife."

"The Widow Gates?" Waite put his glasses on and scanned the page to find her signature—the first time he'd ever seen it.

"That's right. She come with Tooch Bedsole."

Waite felt betrayed and insulted at once. He wondered why she hadn't stopped by to speak to him, as she usually did on her infrequent trips to Grove Hill. More than once he'd extended an invitation to her, if she ever needed a bed while in town. And why didn't she tell him about this when they'd talked yesterday?

"I thank you for your time, Harry," he said.

The lawyer stood behind his desk and slung his arm out like he'd thrown a horseshoe. "You ready?"

Waite grinned. "The judge is still looking for a new partner. We might be playing ourselves."

He found Oscar on the porch of the store with several fellows, including Ardy Grant, telling one of his travel stories. Grant was just into his thirties and a good-looking fellow who took a little too much pride in his appearance. Wore a bowler hat and red armbands on his white shirt. White oxford shoes. Couldn't pass a window glass without pausing to check the set of his hat on his head.

Now six or seven men sat along the benches listening to Grant, some smoking cigars or pipes, Grant a cigarette, and many an elbow tilting glasses of Coca-Cola back—the store had just installed the town's first soda fountain. Most of the men wore sidearms, and a couple had rifles against their legs, a trend Waite had noticed since Anderson's murder. Just asking for somebody to get shot, is all it was doing.

Waite climbed the steps and folded his arms and leaned on a post to await a chance to get Oscar alone. The men all nodded to him and Grant even paused in his story to tip his hat. Waite nodded back.

"It was a Chinaman," Grant continued. "This is in north

California," he added for Waite's benefit, "couple years back. Now most of these little yellow chinks shave their heads bald but keep these here little biddy ponytails of hair down their backs."

Oscar broke in. "Chinese law requires it," he said, "if they ever mean to return home."

"How in the Sam Hill do you know that?" a banker and war veteran named Claudius Thompson asked.

"I got me one of those things," Oscar said. "You might of heard of it. An education?"

Thompson thumbed his nose and several men laughed.

Grant paused until they'd quieted down, then went on:

"Well, this little fellow I'm talking about, he wasn't going home no time soon, I'll tell you, cause me and one of my buddies got corned on the Fourth of July in a saloon room, and my buddy snipped that rattail off him. Chinaman was a shoeshiner, little runt named Chang. He got mad as hell at what my buddy done, but he couldn't do nothing about it. See, Chinamen are maybe a notch above the niggers and the Indians, so all he could do was just wait for it to grow again."

He paused and drank from his Coca-Cola and ashed his cigarette. "Now this Chang had him a pet bird, though, a crow he'd trained to say things in Chinese—"

"You can't train no crow to talk," Oscar said.

"You can a California crow. They call 'em ravens out there. Maybe it's a different kind, hell. But this one used to perch on Chang's little yellow head and recite cusswords it heard in the bar. It was real quick to skedaddle, though, cause ever once in a while somebody would get drunk and take a shot at it."

Waite listened idly and gazed across the street to the barbershop, the stairs beside it leading to the dentist's office.

Grant was saying he and his buddy had sobered up a day or two after cutting Chang's hair, and were soon off on a scouting trip—their job was to survey new tracts of government land for the

L & N—when one night, out of the dark autumn sky, a rattlesnake drops into their camp. Nearly bites Ardy on his foot before he kicks it in the fire, where they let it cook and then eat the better part of the meat. They'd been drinking some and didn't get to questioning the snake's heavenly origins until the next day when Ardy's buddy says, "Say, where do you reckon that dang rattler come from last evening?" Ardy stops and puzzles over it a bit. Perhaps it fell from a tree, he says. Perhaps some trickster threw it.

It remained a mystery to them, but since they'd both seen stranger happenings they continued on up toward Oregon. That night, though they'd camped far away from any tree, another snake dropped down between them, this time a fat black cottonmouth. Mad as hell, too. They shot it to pieces, a little spooked, and to get shed of the willies they opened a bottle of bourbon. Soon they'd forgotten about the snake and were swapping tales, and they proceeded to get even drunker. Then, boom, another snake drops. It lands on Ardy's buddy's hat, right in the brim, starts rattling its tail. They were too wary to try anything for fear of triggering the snake, which went to buzzing every time Ardy's buddy moved. Ardy peeps in and sees that it's a big long timber rattler, so there's nothing to do but wait.

Finally, hours later, Ardy's pal goes a little crazy and says he'll by god put a stop to it. He unholsters his six-shooter and points it at his hat. He's crying and his hand is shaking and, being generally a poor aim, he shoots himself through the forehead.

Ardy sits there, stunned. His buddy topples over and the snake slides off the hat brim and crawls away.

Then, from the sky, there occurred some strange words, words he couldn't understand. At first he thought it was a demon speaking in tongues, but finally he realized it was Chinese he'd been hearing, that that damn Chinaman's bird was up there, zigging and zagging in the dark. Ardy starts to hop about and point and yell how it was the other guy, the dead fellow, who'd cut off Chang's little ponytail.

Then he gets on his knees and apologizes to the sky for a solid hour. Once in a while something else sails down out of the air: a bullfrog, a big rat, four or five moles, a gopher turtle, a tarantula. About dawn, as he's yelled himself hoarse and is about half loony from dodging falling creatures, one more thing drops out of the sky. It's the shape of a snake, and Ardy sees it hurtling toward him. Coming right for his head. He just closes his eyes, stretches out his arms, and hollers, "O take me, Lord Jesus!"

"The thing lands right across the bridge of my nose," Grant said, touching his nose, "and stays there. I shut my eyes and wait for the fangs to go in, holding my breath, but nothing happens. The snake just lays there. It's a little biddy one, so I figure it's a coral snake this time, or a ground rattler. Finally, I get up the nerve to open one eye. What I see, though, don't resemble a snake at all, it's real fuzzy. Then I open up the other eye—"

"It's the dern ponytail," Oscar said.

Several of the men started to laugh.

"True story," Grant said.

Everyone declared the tale a hoax, until Grant hopped up from his chair and excused himself past Waite and bobbed down the steps to where his good-looking mare was tied. He got something from his saddle purse and came back. They all saw it was a small weave of gray, brittle hair. He tossed it to Oscar.

"It's horsehair," the judge proclaimed, bringing it to his nose, and the hair was handed man to man and its authenticity debated until Waite caught Oscar's eye and motioned him across the street.

"Ain't that young fellow something?" Oscar said, still chuckling, as they walked toward his office. He carried his Winchester as before.

"He is," Waite agreed, "something."

They stepped around a pile of horse shit and Waite glanced up the street for the boy from the livery whose responsibility it was to clean up such messes.

"You thought any more about giving him a job?" Oscar asked as they turned the corner.

"Not really. I been a little on the busy side."

"That's exactly why you need him."

They walked east on Court Street, past the watering trough, to the courthouse, a small white building with green shutters and a covered porch; a fence surrounded it to keep pigs out, and King stood inside beneath a large sugarberry with his neck stretched through the rails grazing on what grass he could reach. The shutters were opened, which meant the county solicitor was in. Part of the building had burned a few years ago and some of the wood was still black. They mounted the steps of the stile and descended on the other side of the fence, crossed the yard, and went up the porch steps. Oscar held the front door for Waite and followed him into the hall. The circuit judge's office was shut—he was fifteen miles south, in the town of Jackson— but the county solicitor, an owlish man in his early thirties with his glasses pushed up on his forehead, sat behind his desk frowning at a writ and wanted Oscar's opinion. The judge said, "Later," and he and Waite went into his office and Oscar shut the door.

Leaning his rifle beside the tall coatrack, he motioned for Waite to sit and walked behind his desk and sat in his ornate office chair. It had come on a steamboat from Mobile and before that on a ship from Paris, France. On the underside of its seat a French wood-worker had carved in his name and the date. If you knew what to look for you might catch Oscar's left hand straying down and fondling the wood beside his thigh, running his fingers over the craftsman's name as if he were reading Braille. Oscar indulged in the finest objects for his office—the house was his wife's domain, but here, this room was his. He glanced at the cherrywood clock against the wall and folded his pink hands. He crossed his legs. Behind him stood a shelf of large, leather-bound volumes of law, gold lettering on their spines that Waite, without his glasses, couldn't read.

"Well, first off," Waite said, "I wish you'd not put ideas in Sue

112

Alma's head. All your meddling's doing is slowing things down and making it awful quiet over at the house."

Oscar tilted back his chair. "I just worry about you, is all, cousin. You get killed out on one of your jaunts, it might be a week before we figure it out and send somebody to get you. By then they'll have buried you in some godforsaken hole and I'll have to go to the trouble of finding a new sheriff."

"Ain't that what you want anyway? Get your man Grant in my office so he can tell stories?"

Oscar smiled. "Maybe. It'd sure be nice to have a fellow I could boss some."

"Also," Waite said. "Since I'm fussing at you, I wish you'd leave that Winchester at home. You ain't setting a good example around here. It's starting to look like the Yankees is fixing to invade, way everbody's toting a damn cannon."

"Billy, I'm just protecting myself. We all are."

"You gone get yourself shot, is all." He jerked a thumb behind him. "For one thing, you can't hit nothing, never could. For another, you don't bring a rifle into a place with you and leave it halfway across the room. You're supposed to keep it nearby, in case a country fellow comes in shooting."

"I take your point." Oscar got up and fetched the Winchester and stood it beside his chair. "Happy?" He sat back down.

"Yeah. I'll sleep better now."

"So if you're done chiding me, maybe you can tell me what you dug up in the wilderness."

Waite recounted what he'd found in Mitcham Beat, in effect nothing, and concluded with his trip to Lawyer Drake's office and the old woman witnessing the sale.

"Heck," Oscar said. "They all sound guilty, even the Gates woman. Not talking to you, that's obstruction of justice right there."

"You're gone need a bigger jail if you want me to bring in the whole beat."

"This Tooch character," Oscar said. "What you make of him?"

"I think he's neck deep in it, is what I think."

"Why don't you start by running him in?"

"There ain't enough to go on, Osk. He's smart. Made it all good and legal. But I do believe the Widow Gates knows a lot more than she's letting on."

"How come? You and her's always got along. Why ain't she confiding to you?"

"Well, if it come down to it, I think she'd choose her country friends over me, but my guess is Tooch is threatening her in some way. He's got that poor boy working there like a damn slave and scared out of his wits. And the old lady, well, I believe she may be going a little daft."

Oscar stood up, walked around his desk, and looked out the window. "Billy, your one problem's always been that you just too slow. Thinking too much. Sometimes you got to strike first." He clapped his hands, loud in the hot, still room. "I'll get whatever papers you need and you can bring in this Bedsole and keep him locked up. If he's out of the picture maybe that old woman and the boy will talk."

Waite stood up, too. "Oscar, I've already said—"

"—don't tell you how to do your job. I know. But it ain't gone be long before somebody else gets killed. Them fellows may think they've got it rigged so they're above the law, Billy. But they ain't. If they're playing this way, we got to play this way, too. This ain't something I say often, and I wouldn't say it to anybody but you, but it might be time to step around the law a little bit."

II

A row of ripe apples lay along a section of the polished counter that ran the length of Bedsole's store. Early sunlight from the pair of tall unshuttered glass windows lit the floorboards and

114

shadowed the cracks between them, glint of nail heads in their immaculate lines.

Bent over the apple barrel and pleasantly dizzy from the aroma, Mack fished out the remaining fruit and laid them at the end of the row on the countertop. As usual, these from the bottom had gone mealy, flattened on one side, like the soft spot on a baby's head, and he placed them in a straight line in a separate row. Then he went backward along the counter, lifting and turning each apple, checking for cuts, bruises, wormholes. Half a dozen failed the inspection and he cradled these in his arms and carried them all to the wooden box by the back door. He set them down gently, not wanting to damage them further. There were other "nigger boxes" here, too—stale bread, uneven cakes of cheese that were more mold than cheese, bags of flour the cockroaches had burrowed into—but because there hadn't been a black person at the store in months, the only person eating from the boxes had been Mack himself.

He rolled up his sleeves and paused at the water barrel he filled each morning, removed its lid, and dipped himself a cupful, drank, then poured the rest down the neck of his shirt. He hung the cup back on its nail and walked to the rear of the store and ducked through the low door into the small storage room where his bed was—sheet and blanket tucked at the corners—and took the can of leather oil from a shelf. On a rack across from the bed stood a dozen shotguns and rifles, boxes of cartridges and shells beneath on a narrow shelf and a jumble of pistols in a drawer covered by an oiled cloth.

He pulled the door shut and walked to where the tack hung. Hooking a short milking stool with his foot, he settled down and crossed his legs at the ankles. An hour passed, the sun as it set filling the window, illuminating the boards leading to the back door. Tooch would close the shutters, but Mack liked the way the light revealed how full of tiny spinning particles the air was, like water swirling with sediment. You could sneeze into the air and see the sneeze diffuse. You could shake pollen from the shoulders of your jacket and watch it hover.

He'd oiled all the bridles and most of the harnesses when the cowbell over the front door clanked. He looked up to see the Widow Gates walk in, her thin hair in a bonnet.

He was stunned to see her, she hadn't come to the store in a year.

Beneath her long gray skirt and the men's pants, she wore a pair of men's brogans, given to her from a small-footed farmer as payment for a baby she'd delivered. People paid her in everything from work on her house to skinned rabbits to fresh eggs and milk. The only thing she didn't get was money. It suited her fine.

"Hey, Granny," Mack said, setting the oil down next to a bridle and wiping his fingers on a rag from his back pocket. He stood.

"I didn't see his wagon," she said.

"He's out at Lev's."

"Getting whiskey, I imagine."

He looked away. "No, ma'am. Just delivering some fertilizer."

"Macky Burke," she said, coming toward him with her cane, "when you lie to protect women from the things other men do, it means you're deep in the ruts of turning into a man yourself."

"Yes, ma'am," he said. "I thank you."

"It ain't a compliment."

She tapped his elbow with the end of her cane and inspected him. In the months he'd been working for Tooch, he'd grown to nearly six feet in his socks. At night his bones hurt, which Tooch said meant he was still growing. He had long rangy arms and legs, a huge Adam's apple and a dusting of reddish freckles over his cheekbones.

Embarrassed in her lingering gaze, he looked out the window at the tall cotton plants, the bolls long out of their green shells. A flock of grackles flew out of the low sun, turned in the sky, and descended on the huge live oak at the far edge of the field.

"Lord," she said, poking his ribs with her cane, "he ain't giving you enough to eat, not to keep up with your sprouting, is he?"

116

"I believe he thinks I'm growing to spite him."

"At least he gives you these nice things to wear." She rubbed the sleeve of his shirt between her fingers. Then let go and opened her knapsack. "I brought you something."

She took out four hard-boiled eggs, already peeled, wrapped in waxed paper. He ate them as quickly as she offered them, barely chewing.

"Slow down. You don't want no salt?"

He swallowed. "He counts the grains."

After the eggs she produced for him half a dozen buttermilk biscuits smeared with her homemade muscadine jam, and after that a piece of dewberry pie. When he finished—they'd sat by now, in the two rocking chairs by the windows—she gathered the hem of her skirt in her fingers and dabbed his cheeks and lips.

She hadn't taken her eyes off him. "You seen your brother?"

He belched. "He come by the other day."

"How'd he look? He ain't come by the house in pert near a month. Living like a goat in that man's barn."

"Same as always. He bought him a new gun."

She turned to the window.

He didn't know what to say. He'd lived with her most of his life, three miles from here, his world her tiny yard and the hollows and ridges beyond, the slow creek behind the house at the bottom of the gully. He'd seen few other places—Coffeeville half a dozen times and Grove Hill once—but mostly just the widow's yard and the woods around it and the houses they'd visited when she went to deliver a baby. This store and the croquet court outside.

He remembered it all fondly. In those days the children played first, and then the young men, and finally the adult men, who'd competed in teams of two, matches likely to take three hours apiece, before each shot a discussion of strategy, the men in pairs whispering behind their hands as if life and death existed in the lay of the balls. Those days had usually ended with Arch donning his church coat

117

and mounting the porch to a scattering of applause and giving a speech. Mack remembered the crowd sitting or standing before the porch and Arch up there, wiping the back of his neck with a handkerchief, shifting from foot to foot as if the porch were hot, while below him the sharecroppers listened, the men sipping the whiskey Arch had supplied, the women knitting or tending babies, Mack and William and other boys back on the court, playing their own invented version of croquet which involved knocking the balls as far away as possible—even beyond the mallet's length boundary around the court, sometimes under the store, other times across the road into the cotton or into the woods, down the hollow to the creek. Then the long walk home, tired, full, the widow singing softly and holding Mack's hand in one of hers and William's in the other, her happiness something he could feel humming on his skin.

Then—and even now—he had little notion of other places. He had never seen mountains or the sea, and while the widow had mentioned to him and William in passing the Smoky Mountains she'd grown up ignoring—to her, mountains were nothing but things that blocked the sky—she'd spoken differently of the ocean, which she had visited only once, as a child after a long rail trip, spoken of the water's wide curving vista and its eternity of beaches: this sixty years after seeing it, as she rocked on the porch, a mess of unshelled butter beans in her apron, Mack and William squatting beside the bottom step playing mumbly-peg in the dirt with their dead father's jackknife, early bats twittering in the last red rags of sky, lightning bugs blinking at the edge of twilight. Those had been hot, still nights when there had descended upon the little yard a disquiet, something Mack felt in his nerves but thought the old woman sensed, too, for after she had described the way the unending foamy waves of the Gulf of Mexico came lapping in and wet your feet, dispensing all manner of alien things—pulsing jellyfish and translucent stiff-legged crabs and tiny white clamshells that burrowed within seconds into sand wet and reflective as glass—she would fall into a silence heavy with meaning and edged with sad yearning, the kind of mood a child recognizes and is thrilled by, the first ginger tug of your older self, a kind of undertow.

The widow was gazing at him, sun through the window lighting her skin so she seemed almost to glow.

"I recall that rainy night y'all come to me," she said. "William just a knee-baby and you—" She touched his cheek. "You wasn't no bigger than a kitten. 'Bout half dead. Couldn't hardly kick your little legs, just about couldn't find you in that natty blanket."

A story he'd heard often, growing up. Their father dying in a fire and the mother, badly burned, getting them outside. The smoke had alerted a neighbor who brought the boys to the widow.

Now, with each telling of the tale the widow would say how she nearly cried at finally—after delivering two hundred babies—having two of her own. Joy quickly gone, though, when she saw how near death Mack was: her mad footrace to a nearby farm where there was a milk cow, the white-haired Negro man looking down at Mack and saying, That thing ain't gone live the night.

"But you did," the widow would conclude each time she repeated the story. "Thank the Lord, you did."

They sat awhile longer.

"I reckon I'll get a few things," she said, "since I done walked all this way on my tired old legs."

"Yes, ma'am." He stood.

She held her hand out and for a moment he didn't know what she wanted. Then took her fingers and she let him pull her gently up, her weight no more than lifting a coat from a chair. She began padding along the aisles as he followed, collecting in the nest of his long arms the things she handed behind her without looking at him, a bag of coffee, a pound of sugar, a box of matches, he felt the bitter tug of nostalgia and wondered if she did, too, and then understood by the way she focused so intently on each item, inspecting each package as if for clues to some puzzle, her squint perhaps the thinnest shield for tears, that yes, indeed, she felt it. She passed him back two pounds of flour, a box of salt, four tins of snuff, a half-gallon jug of molasses. He wondered where she'd done her shopping in the past year, if she'd gone all the way to Coffeeville, how she'd gotten there, if she caught a ride or had someone else pick up her things; he knew he could ask her but speaking seemed inappropriate now, he couldn't quite say why.

Not until he was wrapping her things and silently toting the prices did he realize he'd have to charge her—Tooch didn't allow credit. As she watched his nimble hands tie string around the brown paper, he knew she was doing her own mental addition, as she had when Arch had been here behind the counter and Mack and William stood on the other side with her, licking the peppermint sticks the storekeeper would have given them. *Arch never charged her.* The enormity of Mack's crime of murder settled on him again—again he understood that in killing Arch Bedsole he had killed a part of each life the man had affected.

"Macky?"

His hands paused. "Yes, ma'am?"

"I'll keep one of those snuffs out. For the walk home."

He didn't know what to say except, "It's a dollar eighteen, Granny."

For the longest time she looked up at him, past the mound of her goods, wrapped in brown paper and tied in coarse string. He'd become so proficient at packing things, salt in with flour, coffee with sugar. The paper folded precisely. The string so tight no grain could fall out.

She said nothing. She turned and began walking down the aisle toward the door. The goods she'd picked left there before him.

"Granny," he said.

Without looking at him the widow went out the door and over the porch as the bell hardly jingled. She carefully descended the steps and walked with her cane into the muddy road.

Then Mack was fumbling, his arms full, running over the floor-boards and dropping and going back for a package, grabbing from a wooden box an empty flour sack saved for a hood and dumping her groceries into it, bursting through the door with the bell ringing out over the cotton. The old woman turned, her cane upraised as if he'd attack her. He foisted the bag upon her, not even looking to see what might or might not have been in her eyes.

Back inside, he watched her drag the flour sack away, through the dirt, his forehead against the window, breath misting the glass, until the cotton closed around her.

Half an hour later he heard Tooch trundle up in the wagon. He looked out the window and saw him hop down from the seat.

"Boy," Tooch called as he came in the door, the bell ringing. "How's business?"

Mack had been at the button box. "Slow," he said, not looking up.

"Anybody come in?"

"Just Granny."

Tooch pulled off his gloves and laid them on the counter. "What she buy?"

"Few groceries. Nothing much."

He took the money box from underneath the counter, opened it. "We'll just tack another week to your time here," he said. "What you think of that."

His boots creaking over the boards, Tooch walked to the post office nook at the front end of the counter, went behind the partition, and squinted at Mack through the letter slots.

The boy reached for another handful of buttons.

"Go on out yonder and unload that wagon," Tooch said. "I don't pay you to count buttons."

You don't pay me at all, he thought.

"I heard that," Tooch said.

They kept the whiskey in a deep rectangular hole in the ground under several removable floorboards in the back of the store—a hiding place Tooch had devised and Mack had dug. Now Mack used a knife to prize up the board ends and set them carefully along the wall. He pulled the tarp off and struck a match and peered down into the darkness: often a rat, possum, or other creature would have crawled beneath the store and fallen into the hole, which was about the size of a grave, and been unable to get out. Nothing there today but a spiderweb in the corner. Black widow. He hopped in and used a match to shrivel it up like a raisin, then climbed out brushing off his hands. He made several trips outside and returned each time carrying four jugs. By the time he'd gotten the two dozen stored, thrown a tarp over them, and replaced the boards, Tooch was already into the jug he'd kept out.

The hour of dusk—what the widow used to call candle-lighting— was the worst time at the store for Mack. Days would be filled with chores and tasks, hurrying here and there and merchandise forever in his hands, conversations with whoever came to the store, and children dashing up the aisles and more often than not three or four men on the porch trading lies. But then at five Tooch would collect his ledgers and climb the ladder into his loft room, and Mack, alone, would go out to the porch.

Tonight the sun had fallen behind the trees across the field and the land beyond it seemed afire, light flickering in the folds. Mack sat on the edge of the porch and swatted at mosquitoes and watched the night's advance and whittled on a knot of wood. Now and again he'd hang his head and spit between his knees into the same spot in the dirt, a kind of project of his, the ground there concave and forever wet-looking, as in ghost stories the widow had told of murder sites where blood could never be scrubbed away, blood that would come back even after you removed the stained boards and replaced them with new ones, or dug up the bloodied dirt and refilled it with dirt altogether different. He leaned again and spat and thought how much blood this land had seen and how much more it was yet to see. Wondered how much it could take before it had had enough and started giving blood back.

These were lonely nights but tonight was especially so as it was a year since Arch's death. To rid himself of the memory Mack cast about for another thought and settled on one of the times he and William had risen from their bed, already dressed and with their plot in mind, kicked the sheets aside, and swung their feet onto the floor, tunneling their socked toes into their shoes and struggling with the laces in the dark. Soon they were on the road, the dog ordered back. It was two miles to the river and they ran all the way, scarcely a word passing between them.

I love her, Mack had thought those many, many nights ago as his feet pounded the road beneath him, and he wondered now as the horizon grew orange if he did love her, if you *could* love somebody you'd never spoken to, love a woman you'd seen only by spying through her window at night. He thought you must be able to, surely this thing lodged in his chest even now had to have a name.

The boys would stop at the soft muddy edge of the river and cling to vines to catch their breath and wait, listening to the dark murmuring water dragging its ageless fingers along the banks and its belly over the gauzy bottom, the *sploop* of a fish stabbing the surface, cry of some night bird. In the glowing strand of river and the sky itself they could see stars and their constellations. The Big Dipper. The little one.

It would take a few minutes to locate the old canoe they'd hidden, to tear it from its mooring of vine and shrub and flip it over—both of them stopping once as something large and very close slurped from the bank to their right—but soon they would be kneeling in the boat's wet bottom and paddling in long practiced strokes, Mack watching the shape of his brother as he bent with the work of propelling them toward the other side, where her lamplit windows were visible as they pulled the canoe ashore.

She never slept, it seemed like. Annie. Each of the times they'd gone to spy her windows were lit, her shadow passing. Sometimes they'd stay till near dawn, dozing and waking in the chill air and then a frantic dash home. Sometimes there would be men inside Annie's cabin, their large silhouettes alongside her smaller one. Or sometimes two or three fellows on the porch, drinking and cursing and kicking the wall to hurry the occupied one.

Only once had William and Mack seen her refuse a man, who'd begun to yell and threaten her and pound the door until she opened it and backed him across the porch and down the steps with a sawed-off shotgun. They'd elbowed themselves deeper in the weeds as the thwarted man grumbled and stalked around the house, cursing at her and throwing rocks onto her tin roof, once passing within a yard of where Mack lay, a smell of immense body odor and woodsmoke and whiskey. The fellow had finally given up and left, but only after he'd done a thing that shocked them both, dropping his trousers and, his white buttocks shining in the light of the moon, working his arm and shuddering and spending himself right on the side of the house.

Another night a chair leg had come through her window, and a man's loud voice had roared, then smacks of someone being hit and her shouting. Then a gunshot. Mack followed William through the tall wet weeds to the porch, but when the door burst open they dove sideways—William left, Mack right—and rolled beneath the porch and watched a shirtless man tumble down the steps bawling, his hands over his crotch. He got to his feet and fell again, the blood on his hands and thighs black in the moonlight. "You've done me!" he yelled. Overhead, the boys heard her weight on the boards as she came to the edge of the porch. "Get on home, dog," she said, and they heard a shotgun snap shut, heard its hammer click back. The

124

man scrabbled away while Mack and William watched, and after a few long minutes Annie had gone back inside.

They'd never found out what had happened to the man, but Annie had been back in business a month later when they'd gone again and crouched in the tall weeds with the river gurgling behind them and the sky spitting its stars overhead.

Now Annie worked for Tooch, though Mack didn't know if Annie owed him money, too, or if Tooch had simply made an agreement with her. These days, if you wanted to be with her, you had to come see Tooch, get the password. Otherwise, Annie wouldn't let you in, and everyone had heard about her sawed-off sixteen-gauge.

Mack looked down. He'd whittled his knot nearly away.

Behind him the door opened and Tooch came out. He stood holding his jug and put his right hand in the small of his back and stretched.

"You get them bridles oiled?" he asked.

"Yes, sir."

"Tomorrow first thing get going on washing them clothes."

"Yes, sir."

Tooch stood a moment longer, then turned and sat on the bench and uncorked his jug. He hooked his thumb in the thumbhole and hefted the whiskey in the crook of his bent arm and drank, his throat pumping, then rested the jug on his knee. For a time they sat watching softly burning fireflies and the wicks of stars, the only other light a glow from the lantern behind them in the store. After a while, Tooch said, "Did you know me and Arch was the same age?"

Mack didn't know whether to answer, so he waited.

"Same age," Tooch went on, "grew up in the same house, went to school together. But time we turned twenty, Arch was running the store. He was a landlord, postmaster, beat supervisor, and fixing to be a politician. And me, I wasn't nothing but a sharecropper."

They sat, then Mack asked, "How come?"

Tooch paused and took another drink, and Mack feared he'd

asked the wrong thing, but abruptly Tooch began to tell how his mother had died delivering him, how the Widow Gates couldn't stop the bleeding, and by the time the Coffeeville doctor came in his wagon blood had soaked through the mattress to the ground under the bed. But Tooch—his given name was Quincy, after his father— had lived. He was taken by the widow to his father's brother's house where he stayed for three years. Perhaps those times were good, Tooch said he couldn't remember now. His uncle Ed and aunt Clarabel had their own children, three girls and the new baby boy, Arch, who'd been delivered by the Widow Gates four months before Tooch had, without a hitch.

"Without a hitch," Tooch repeated.

He and Arch had slept together in the same crib, nursed at the same mother's breast. When he turned three, Ed and Clarabel Bedsole decided little Quincy should return to his own father's house. Quincy Senior had had enough time to recover from his sadness, they felt, though the blue of loss about him could color a room.

Of living at home with his father, Tooch said he remembered only the day his father left. The father rising that morning from his sagging bed as he always did, shirtless, his black hair hanging long off the front of his head, hiding his eyes, giving the impression to the boy of a crow's tail feathers. The father dressed without speaking that day, without looking at his son, fastened each button of his sweat-yellowed shirt, rolled the sleeves to his biceps, pulled on a pair of things so soft from use and age that they seemed little more than piles of dirty cloth until his feet and ankles gave them the upright shape of boots. He took from a peg in one of the wall logs his shapeless hat, and clutching it in his fist walked over the dirt floor, got his rifle from the corner and lifted the piece of rawhide that let up the latch and filled the room with morning, then closed the door behind him, pushing in the rawhide strap so it fell along the inside of the door, locking himself out.

Having gone with the widow to the poorest sharecroppers' shacks to deliver their babies, Mack, as he whittled, could imagine filthy little Quincy on his pallet on the floor. Could imagine him scratching the lice in his hair, the ringworm on his cheek, the one under his arm. Imagine him thin from worms. Sores on his elbows and knees and flies landing in them until he wipes them away, then they land again.

Mister? Tooch says.

All day he moves around the room waiting for his father to return. He watches the limp rawhide strap and cries softly, then loudly, his cheeks burning from the salt in his tears, his voice going hoarse, until he gags and vomits on his naked legs. He marks the sun's progress by where the light is strongest between the cracks in the walls. He sleeps on his pallet. When the light is gone he rises, his thighs and ballsack burning from his piss, his bottom pasted with shit. He moves across the dirt, not even bothering to flick at the flies on his head, in his sores, wiping at them only when they get too close to his eyes.

Mack listened and imagined. Tooch peering through the hole over the rawhide strap. A bright night outside, brighter than in the cabin, and the wild dogs he has been hearing have massed in the front yard. Now one leaves the pack and side-walks toward the door, head down, hackles up, eyes gleaming. He sees the black rubbery skin casing its yellow teeth. He hears himself crying and knows this is what has brought these things. He claps a sour hand over his mouth, scattering the flies. There is quiet scratching on the door now, and quick breathing. This goes on for a long time. The dogs begin to howl and yap, circling the cabin, raising their muzzles to the moon as it bores through the clouds and across the map of stars.

That's all, Tooch said, he remembered of being four years old. He was told that the dogs did not get in. Told that Ed stopped by a day—or was it two days?—later, finding him hiding under the bed, malnourished, in shock. That he didn't speak for almost a month after Ed and Clarabel took him back in and got the Widow Gates over to doctor him to good health, purge the worms, give him her bitter, leafy medicines and dab at him with poultices to kill the lice and cure the sores. They started calling him Tooch as a nickname. He was told that this came about because in play he would make a pistol of his hand and cock back his thumb and aim it at Arch and say, "I gone tooch you." The name stuck.

What Tooch remembered after the wild dogs were things that seemed random, chasing lightning bugs with Arch—they are six years old—catching the drifting bugs between clapped hands and shrieking at their glowing skin, chasing more and smearing the jelly on their faces, necks, bare chests, sticky with light. Catching garter snakes, toad frogs, box turtles. Fishing with Uncle Ed and Arch in the pond while water bugs glide over the surface, joined at the feet to their reflections—underbugs, something hovering beneath the sunlit earth like a dark-sided bad dream, forgotten in the light of day but not gone, never gone. Then memories of nights in bed beside deep-sleeping Arch when a dog would howl far away, on a hill in the woods, and Uncle Ed would find Tooch beneath the bed in the morning, his thighs wet from his own piss, and there would follow the jolted trip through the kitchen, his nightshirt clinging to his bottom, out over the rough dirt, steered by Uncle Ed's hand on his neck, a limb snatched from a passed tree, his legs laced with red welts.

Uncle Ed owned the store then, had felled the trees with a crosscut saw twenty years before, and aided by Quincy Senior had muled them out and fitted the staggered corner logs and mortared them with mud and raw cotton, had stacked and mortared the flat chimney stones and nailed up the store-bought shingles and laid the milled floorboards perfectly level. He had borrowed two hundred dollars from a man in Coffeeville to finance his stock and had struggled but survived, had gotten along well with the peddlers who clanged up in their wagons.

Good days to be a nephew, better days to be a son. While Tooch always felt loved by his aunt and uncle and secure enough in their care, there were differences between the way he and Arch were treated. There was Christmas, when Tooch's stocking was mismatched with the other children's, crocheted from different, cheaper yarn, his name not stitched in red letters like Arch's and the girls'. And Arch's harmonica would be fancier than Tooch's, Arch's apple bigger, his orange softer. When the boys were twelve and the encyclopedia set came in the mail, Arch got to crowbar open the heavy wooden box, Arch got to lift out the first book and unwrap the brown paper, to page through the S volume, to trace his finger over the drawings of a cobra, of an anaconda, a python. Somehow, whenever he wanted to read one, Tooch felt compelled to ask if he might take a volume from the cherrywood rack by the mantel.

When the boys stole a plug of tobacco from the store Tooch got his licks first, behind the barn, Ed holding his head down and slinging the leather strap so hard his hat flew off. Dismissed, Tooch limped dry-eyed around the corner past the spikes of a harrow and nodded to Arch, who nodded back in passing and went to get his own whipping. Crouching in the barn, peering between the slits in the boards, Tooch counted each lick Arch got, unsurprised when his cousin got half the stripes he did, delivered with half the fury.

Perhaps, added to other minor and boyish mischiefs, it was the stolen tobacco that convinced Ed to split the pair up, not let them come together to the store where they'd both been working. Now they were fifteen, done with school, and Ed sat Tooch down on a March evening after supper when everybody else had gone to a church meeting where there was supposed to be fried chicken and baseball. "Boy," Uncle Ed said, "it's come time for you to earn your keep in our family. We do consider you a part of us, like a son," he said, "but there ain't enough to keep a pair of young ones busy in the store and that's how come I've decided to lend you out to Isom Walker. He needs a hand with his crop, and he'll pay you a good wage, which I expect you'll be glad to contribute to the family that raised you."

Tooch agreed. Like a son.

"You're a good boy," Ed said. "Your aunt and me know it—there ain't a speck of your daddy in you."

For four years after that, Tooch was a cotton farmer's hired hand. Because the Walker place was four miles away, Walker and Uncle Ed had agreed that Tooch should bunk in the tack room in Walker's barn or, if it were cold, on the floor beside the fireplace in the house. He would spend weekends at home, and never see a dime of the money he earned.

Those were days, Tooch said, to be forgotten, meals with Walker and his pious wife, Bible readings around the table; the path he wore in the grass from the back door to the barn; the udders he pulled in the morning; the shit-speckled eggs he gathered; the earth he plowed and fertilizer he slung and seeds he planted, staring at the fly-ridden haunches of Walker's cantankerous mule; learning to watch the sky for signs of its disposition; entering a cotton field at first light and leaving at dark; bent over hoeing, bent over picking; the too-quick days at home with his uncle, aunt, and cousins; borrowing one encyclopedia volume a week and reading it by candlelight in the barn, exploring the world a letter at a time. Isom Walker was a man who called boys "Son" and Tooch hated this, had begun to imagine that he was no one's son, not Walker's, not Ed Bedsole's, not even his own father's. One evening he heard Mrs. Walker read from the Bible of the prodigal. Tooch was no prodigal, for if he left there would be no father to regret his absence.

By the time the boys were nineteen, Arch was managing the store while his father oversaw the four or five farms he owned or had a stake in, and soon the Bedsole Mercantile sign over the porch saw added, in neat white letters, MR. R. ARCHIE "ARCH" BEDSOLE, MANAGER. He had a knack for dealing with people, could remember their names and the names of their children, names of their mules, whether they'd want a nip of the busthead whiskey he kept in the back. He knew without being asked when to palm a fellow the brown-wrapped contraceptive devices he kept under the counter, or a woman a can of tuberose snuff. He even treated black folks with respect, understanding that to thrive his store had to serve them, too, and though they knew to come to the back door to place their orders, he extended them the same credit as he did his white customers, and knew each of their names as well.

Soon, with his father's blessing, he'd opened the post office in the store, a small cubicle he built just inside the door, and he'd read letters—the mail was delivered from Coffeeville twice a week—to those who couldn't read; people trusted him because he wouldn't speak of the content of their letters, be it good news or bad. In the post office he also had a stack of the thick, richly illustrated catalogs of Sears Roebuck and Company, J. H. Whitney, E. Butterick, Montgomery Ward. You could page through and order from these, so Bedsole's Mercantile became everyone's link to the larger world.

Arch served cheese and crackers for a nickel, oysters and crackers for a dime. To foster goodwill in the community, he ordered from Sears Roebuck the croquet set that the hamlet would embrace for the next decade.

"And me?" Tooch said, setting his jug on his knee. "I quit working for Walker to work my own place. Sharecropping for Uncle Ed first, and then for Arch. Ten years of it," he said. Then he said, "You know where I was the night Arch got killed?"

Mack did, but asked, "Where?"

"Sitting in that same damn shack, same one my momma had died in. Reading the R encyclopedia. Reading about them redwood trees they got out in California. You ever heard of 'em?"

He said he hadn't.

"Wasn't nothing in that shack but a half-ass bed that'd give your back the cramps. Not even a table for my lamp. Had to go out fetch me a piece of pinewood for a table, saw off the ends. And ever night

I'd sit there on the bed and read. Arch would lend me them encyclopedias, one at a time. They was still his books. Only difference was we was grown up.

"Night he died I'd been looking at that picture of them redwoods, and at my little wood table. Thinking how some trees out in California is so big a man can stand in the roots and get his picture drawn, and then there's little loblolly pines in Mitcham Beat gets cut up and used as furniture. You know what I mean?"

"I reckon."

"All my life, boy, I envied Arch." He looked at Mack. "This ain't general knowledge. Fact is, what I'm telling you is something nobody knows but two people, one of 'em's me, and the other one—Arch—is in the ground." He got up from the bench and stood weaving, the boards groaning beneath his weight. The lantern inside had gone out and the cotton before them, washed in starlight, looked blue. Tooch stepped unevenly over the porch and leaned on a corner post and let it guide him to sitting. In the dark his shoulder brushed Mack's. Tooch's hot whiskey breath burned over him. "If you're gone work for me, Mack," he said, "I'm gone have to trust you. Can I trust you, boy?"

"Yes, sir."

"Yes sir, what?"

"You can trust me. I won't tell nobody what you're saying."

"If you do, you know what will happen, don't you?"

The skin on the back of his neck tingled. "You'll kill me."

"There you go. I wouldn't want to. But if you betray me, you ain't giving me no choice, are you? You got to be as honest with me as a preacher is with God or Jesus or whoever. You got that?"

"Yes, sir."

"It can't be no secrets between us. I mean I don't want to know if you have a dirty thought or shit your britches, but if it's something big comes up, you damn well better let me hear of it even before you put it in a prayer and aim it at Glory. You got me, boy?"

132

"Yes, sir."

For a time neither spoke and Mack thought Tooch might've passed out. His breath came even and deep. But then he said, "Part of me was glad when Arch died. You know why?"

Mack thought. "It gave you a shot."

"It did, didn't it."

Mack looked at Tooch. "That set of books has one missing. The R one."

Tooch nodded. "Burned up with the cabin. Night Arch died. Redwood tree picture and all."

They sat. Tooch took another drink from his jug. "You never did know your daddy, either, did you?"

"No, sir. This knife," he said, holding it where Tooch could see its blade glowing in the starlight, "used to be his. The widow, she give me it and his old pistol and give William his shotgun."

Tooch sat holding his jug on his knee. A far-off dog's bark cut through the air. Tooch waited for it to drift away. "You tell me one," he said.

"Sir?"

"A story. You tell one."

"I don't know any."

"What about growing up. With the widow. That old woman's gotta be worth a thousand stories. She was the one drawed us all from our momma's wounds. Reckon she's seen us all nekkid, ain't she. Gives a woman a certain advantage."

Mack looked up at the stars. He did know a story.

"I used to have the asthma," he said. "Real bad. The widow told me when I was a baby I like to died from it about twice a week. I'd turn all blue. My face. Lips. Couldn't breathe a lick. She had to tote me around the room, holding me just about upside down, she said. Said she got no sleep at all first year of my life.

"When I was older it was better. During the day it'd be okay. Long as I didn't run or get too hot or breathe too much dust. We used to play mumbly-peg, me and William. By the steps. But at dark it always come. The widow said the night air did it. Just about time the moon came up I'd start a wheezing. And I'd sit up all night, wouldn't lay down cause I couldn't breathe. Couldn't go to sleep. Just sat there wheezing.

"But the widow, she'd stay up with me, all night. Said she was glad to, said she felt like she'd slept near 'bout her whole life away before she got us. She'd let me sip sugared whiskey, and she'd sip it, too, sometimes. And we'd talk. She'd tell me all sorts of things, about being a little girl in Tennessee. About the ocean, which she seen one time. What all the things in the woods are. Mushrooms and what leaves you can use for curing sick people. Told about her husband, who got killed in the War. Said they hung him from a trestle near Pea Ridge, Arkansas.

"Thing is, I didn't half listen, I was just trying to breathe. But her voice, it helped me. Something I could ride on, get me from one breath to the next. I remember how we used to listen outside. Birds. Bugs. She'd say, 'You hear that one?' and I'd say, 'Yes ma'am,' and she'd say, 'That's a katydid. And that one?' and I'd say I did, and she'd say, 'That's a whippoorwill.' All the time rubbing this hot stuff she made into my chest and wiping my head with a warm rag and feeding me that sugared whiskey."

He had stopped whittling. He said, "There was this bantam rooster this old colored fellow had. Lived about a mile off, to the east. At night we'd always listen for the rooster to crow. When we heard it, the widow would say, 'It's almost morning. You can breathe now, child.' And I knew I'd be able to sleep."

"What happened?" Tooch asked. He belched. "You breathe fine now. Don't need me in there all night, babying you."

"Well, it's the strange part of the story," he said. "It was Arch. One day when me and her and William went to the store, Arch told her he'd read how this little biddy special kind of dog from Mexico would take the asthma out of a person's body. You got one of the

134

dogs and let it sleep with whoever had the asthma, and after a spell the asthma would be gone."

Tooch snorted.

"About a month later, when we went to the store, Arch said he had a surprise for us. He put a box up on the counter there. We looked in and it was the ugliest little rat of a dog you ever saw. He said it was a Chihuahua. A yellow thing with big eyes and ears. The widow started crying. Might've been the only time we ever saw her cry. She hugged Arch. We went on home and she held the dog to my chest all night. I remember I could feel his heart beating. Smell his breath, smelled like fish.

"I hated to do it," Mack said. "Hated to give my sickness to this little innocent dog, but if you'd spent so many nights drowning—not able to get no air, you'd do it, too. She wouldn't let us name him. Said no use getting fond of him. This went on for weeks, I guess, until the dog started getting sick."

"You lying."

"No I ain't. It started getting all jittery. You'd hear it cough, too. These little coughs. And it quit eating, and if you wasn't careful it'd bite you. Then one morning I woke up and it was dead. Stiff. Little spot of blood on my shirt. The widow made me face north and cough into some green tobacco leaves and bury the dog wrapped in the leaves."

A whippoorwill called, one answered.

Tooch said, "You expect me to believe that?"

Mack took a deep, deep breath. Held it. Let it go.

Tooch smiled but Mack had grown silent. Gazing at the moon just cresting the tree line over the field, he wondered if it was the same moon from those breathless nights or a different moon traveling the same path. Perhaps a new moon passed each night, launched from an endless supply, or—he frowned—a limited one, like a boy throwing rock after rock after rock across a pond. Soon the rocks would run out or his arm would tire or suppertime would call him away and the pond would see no more rocks overhead. Or some highwayman might come out of the edge of the woods with a knife and steal behind the boy and pull his head back by the hair until the skin of his neck grew taut and slice open his throat and let him fall, the rocks dribbling from his fist.

"That old woman babying you all night made you soft," Tooch said.

"I reckon."

Mack kept watching the moon.

"That Arch," Tooch said, "he always give too much charity."

"I can breathe, cause of that charity."

Tooch took another drink from his jug. "Well, it's a goddamn shame somebody shot him, ain't it, boy."

Then, using the post, he clambered up and staggered inside.

III

A buckboard wagon clanked over the knoll, sunlight glinting from a hundred hanging tools, pans, pots, funnels, dippers, buckets, the peddler hunched in the seat beneath a yellow umbrella, shucking a piece of charred corn and then peeling off the dry silk a strand at a time and flicking it from his fingers. Once he'd nibbled the kernels away he dropped the cob around his feet where several others lay in the dust, for use later when his liquid bowels let go, as they did several times a day, usually with the damn corn kernels still intact. More than once he'd leapt from the wagon fumbling with his pants—which he'd begun wearing unfastened—just getting them down in time. Done, he'd swirl a cob among his chapped nether regions, grinding what few teeth there were left in his gums, then he'd rise and pull up his britches as he hurried after the wagon, the mule never having stopped walking, the peddler imagining clusters of cornstalks springing up irregularly behind him, a fertilized trail all over Southwest Alabama.

Because he trusted men on good horses, he never thought to pick up the sawed-off shotgun, charged and propped beside his seat, when he saw the stranger coming from the other way on the fine-looking dun. He swiped a hand across his beard to free it of corn pellets and pushed his derby hat back on his head. You never knew when you'd make a sale, and this wagon beneath him had in its stores about everything a human being could use, an inventory he could name from adze to yoke. There wasn't an item on the wagon including the wagon or the mule pulling it or the new plow shoes on the peddler's feet—a gift from his sister—he wouldn't sell for the right price, including the wooden box on the seat beside him, a gift from a rounder out of New Orleans. Inside the box a pretty woman reclined on an ornate chaise longue—a naked woman, everything bared. The peddler had been calling her Matilda.

He had departed McCorquodale's store in Coffeeville two days prior, and though he'd stopped at a number of farms and shown the box to the skinny men, none had had the cent it cost to have a gander. The last person to view it had been stodgy old McCorquodale. Frowning, the storekeep had held it up to the window light in his store, as the peddler had instructed, and gazed in for a reasonable amount of time, and then lowered the box.

"Let that boy get him a eyeful," the peddler had suggested, noticing the boy called Carlos where he stood at the end of an aisle in his store apron.

"He don't need to poison his brainpan with such as this," McCorquodale said. "I'd seen that when I was his age, I would've become warped in a way no man could unwarp."

"Do him good," the peddler said. "Education. It's among the things you can't take from a fellow. Heritage, blood, common sense—" He had several more in his list, but McCorquodale interrupted.

"I'll educate my son my own way," he said. "We'll not be needing this viewing device and I'll thank you to put it out of my sight."

"Your gentleman customers might pay a good penny to see such as she," the peddler said.

"Their pennies go elsewhere."

In your pocket, the peddler had thought. He'd taken the rest of McCorquodale's order and left, heading toward Bedsole's store in New Prospect, which he was more than a little concerned about—the peddler who usually ran this route had disappeared, inventory, wagon, mule, and all, a few months ago. One of this peddler's assignments— his boss had said—was to see what he could dig up about the mystery. The local justice of the peace—a Mr. Hill—had been informed by letter and he'd written back saying the fellow hadn't come through there at all—he'd asked around and no one had seen hide nor hair. The peddler wasn't surprised. The whole damn area had itself a reputation of being lawless, so more likely than not the peddler's predecessor had fallen prey to highwaymen, his inventory scattered to the four winds.

But now the fellow on the good horse had drawn close. The peddler raised a hand in greeting, the fellow raised one back.

They stopped, facing each other in the road, then the man moved his horse aside in what the peddler took as a show of manners and came alongside the wagon. He was handsome, early thirties, in possession of all his teeth. He had a good smile and a haircut that looked paid for. A shaved face. He wore a sturdy green denim shirt with fine gold stitching and silver buttons, the kind of detail the peddler always noticed. Fine leather boots, a matching leather belt. His saddle had been well-oiled, too, the stock of the rifle in its scabbard unnicked. A well-tended firearm. Here sat a gentleman who might covet a box wherein a naked Matilda reclined on a chaise longue.

"Afternoon, friend," the peddler said, doffing his hat.

"Afternoon yourself," the fellow replied, his hands folded over the pommel of his saddle, fine calfskin gloves on his hands.

"Lovely today," the peddler said, glancing up to give the sky its cursory credit.

"Lovely," the man agreed. "How's it feel under that umbrella there?"

"The sun bringeth up the cotton," he said, "but also redness of the skin. I prefer it under here." If the fellow wanted an umbrella, there were half a dozen boxed ones back there beneath a crate of shovels. For eighty extra cents the peddler could even rig an attachment to a saddle.

The man's horse shivered and lifted its tail and large cubes of green-black shit began to tumble out. The peddler envied such solidity. If the well-dressed man noticed what occupied his horse, however, he had the manners not to show it. The turds hit the road in dull thuds.

"Say," the peddler said, casting a glance behind him, "would you be interested in a . . . shall we say . . . exotic item? Mister . . . ?"

The man didn't say his name. "What sort of item?"

The peddler tapped the box on the seat beside him. "Inside this peculiar-looking paraphernalia resides something of exquisite beauty and rare charm. A lady, shall we say, of the evening. I call her Matilda but you can call her anything you'd like."

"Say there's a picture of a lady in there?"

"You're a careful listener, I can tell."

With such good manners, such good clothes and such neat hair and upon that fine horse, the man would have money in his pockets. The peddler envisioned him riding away in his finery, face upturned and the box to his eyes, the naked woman reclining for him forever, or until he traded the box to another peddler for another exotic item. Such was the world that made sense to this peddler, good men purchasing quality merchandise and him making a fair percentage.

His bowels churgled, the horse turned its head.

The man's face changed. "Was that you?"

139

Which disappointed the peddler. The polite thing to do was ignore it.

"My stomach," the peddler admitted, "is not well. Please excuse me."

Burning with shame and the sale in jeopardy, he hopped down from the wagon, palming a corncob. In his haste he forgot the shotgun and the little strongbox under the seat. He stepped around the horse and slipped into a grove of pine trees with his pants half down and shat what felt like hot water. When he came back onto the road, the man was sitting in the wagon seat beneath the umbrella with the box held to his face, his features in shadow. He was grinning.

"Normally," the peddler said from the road, "I charge a penny for a look. Which is, of course, deducted from the price."

"How much?" he asked, still looking into the box.

The peddler's favorite question. "For you? One silver dollar."

"Since we're gone be partners," the fellow said, "I should know such things."

"Partners?"

"Ardy Grant," he said, lowering the box. "Pleased to meet you."

IV

Mack had spent the day digging a grave, it lay at the foot of the hollow behind the store, an inch of water accumulated among the white roots snaking its bottom. He'd been in it to his shoulders, spading dirt out, when Tooch's shadow fell over him. For a moment he expected the impact of a bullet but kept digging.

"That's fine, Mack," Tooch said, and offered down a hand to help him out. They stood looking at the square sides. "Damn, but you're a hard worker, boy. Go on up there and take a rest."

Now, exhausted, he sat on the porch watching a crow bury a

pecan in the croquet court. Nobody had shown much interest in the game lately. Mack missed playing, pictured, as he watched the crow, different shots he'd made. He'd always heard crows were canny, but now, seeing this one peck at the dirt, he doubted it. This fool bird had not only chosen the hardest ground in the county—the court pressed flat and smooth by years of feet and shoes, people chasing their croquet balls from arch to arch, post to post—but had elected to do its hiding in plain sight of Mack.

The crow paused and looked sideways toward the north road and jerked its head and looked again through the other eye, then took a few running steps and sprang into the air without the pecan, climbing quickly, circling the store and giving its hoarse, nasal calls before alighting in the oak tree in the back corner of the yard. Mack squinted down the road. Someone was coming.

He saw Lev James first, the long black beard he braided into a pair of pigtails hanging down along his once-blue shirt that was so sweaty it had gone black and seemed as attached to his body as a second skin. He was leading a mule, and in his right hand held his twelve-gauge shotgun by its twin barrels with the stock on his shoulder, a deceptive fashion of toting the gun designed to look as if he weren't ready for a fight. But Lev James was always ready for a fight.

Mack recalled the longest croquet game ever played in the beat. Several years before, during the laying-out period, the weather good and everyone's spirits high, there'd been a gathering at the store. A Saturday evening. The game began with six of the men who'd been drinking freely from the whiskey Arch had provided. There were three teams, Tooch and Lev James, who were first cousins; the Smith brothers, Huz and Buz; and a pair of Scottish fellows from across the river—five of them, all brothers, had come in looking for whiskey and been invited to stay.

The game began with the men lagging for the order of play, shooting their different-colored balls at the end post. People

141

gathered at the boundary to watch, including Arch's father, Ed. He'd have played himself but his legs were already failing—he sat in his rolling chair and smoked his pipe and sipped from his jug. The teammates consulted one another and Ed before every shot, often taking ten, fifteen minutes to decide on the best strategy, another few minutes to discuss the lay of the land and where to hit the ball, and so on. With six players, the game stretched into the evening and the night, Arch bringing lanterns from the store, boys—including Mack and William—recruited to hold the lanterns to light the court.

In the game's sixth hour, just after nine o'clock, one of the Stewart brothers hit Lev James's red ball in a long, curving, lucky shot. The Scot let out a cock-a-doodle-doo, his cry of victory, which Lev had heard a few times too often. Wagers had been made on the game's outcome, and Lev had bet one of them ten dollars. "You want to go on pay me now," the fellow asked Lev, who brooded and whispered something to Tooch.

The Stewart who'd hit Lev's ball hurried to it, placed his own green ball next to it, put his boot over his ball and knocked Lev's red one clear across the court, out of bounds, just missing Ed's chair wheel, and into the shed beside the store where the ball rolled underneath the building. Stewart crowed again and did a little dance, the whiskey working. Arch had stepped in by now, whispering to one of the brothers that it wasn't prudent to anger a drunk Lev James, or even a sober one. But the Stewarts were Scots and didn't listen.

Lev sent Mack under the store after his ball, and by the time he'd found it and come back out covered in dirt and spiderweb, the fight had started. Men where cheering as Lev and the Scot rolled in the dust, upsetting a table on which sat a half-eaten pound cake, rolling beneath a wagon and upsetting the mule team so that they dragged the wagon, its brake set, into the cotton field.

Mack held his lantern high, and presently he and the others

became aware that it wasn't a fight so much as a massacre, that it had been a while since the Stewart fellow had landed a punch or even given any indication that he was still breathing. What remained was Lev James hitting, kicking, elbowing, kneeing, choking, eye-gouging, hair-pulling, scratching and biting the other, finally using a croquet post to beat him. All this within two or three minutes. A pair of Stewart brothers fled to their mules to fetch pistols but Tooch had already fetched his and held them back, said let the winner be decided fair.

What's fair about this? one of the Scots cried, but the fight was let to continue.

No one doubted that Lev would have killed him, and that Tooch would have watched it happen, but Arch said it had gone far enough. So Tooch told the Stewarts they were welcome to break it up, but that if they used guns or knives he'd shoot them. Two of the Scots grabbed Lev by the legs and two under his arms and the fight came apart. Lev flung himself loose and began to laugh; his opponent lay unmoving. The Stewarts hoisted their brother across his mule and left.

The game continued with the Stewarts' balls removed, and Lev and Tooch beat Huz and Buz Smith just after midnight.

The story didn't end there, though. There was a ferry at the time that carried news—in addition to people, horses, wagons, and goods—over the river. Several weeks later the ferryman bore the news that one of the Stewart brothers had turned up dead from a broken neck. Thrown from his horse. A couple of months after the funeral another died when his house burned. The kerosine lamp must've exploded, one theory went. Half a year later the third got it, snakebite, twice—they found him in a bedroll with the pair of copper-heads curled around his cold feet. A few months after that another drowned when his skiff capsized. But now people had begun to view it differently; they waited for news of another deceased Stewart the way one might wait to hear who the next governor would be.

The last brother, the one who'd fought Lev, had grown scared. He'd been said to have lost an eye to one of Lev's thumbs and, because of a badly set break, limped with his right leg. The end of a finger was missing, bitten off. He had scars on his face and a perpetual tremble in his hands from the blows to his head—the list went on and on, growing each time the story was told. He'd holed up in his house, the ferryman reported, armed with all the guns of his dead brothers. He was waiting for Lev and Tooch. But they never came. He waited some more. They still didn't show up. So, unable to sleep, he became mad with fear. His wife took the children and fled, left him peering out the windows, firing at anything that moved.

Now the procession coming to the store had grown close and Mack noticed who sat with his wrists bound behind Lev on the mule's back—Bit Owen, a bootlegger. The man for whom the grave lay waiting.

Following the mule, War Haskew was limping, his pants leg bloody below the left knee. War was a good-looking man, straight white teeth, clean-shaven, good head of yellow hair. Kirk James walked along beside him, carrying both men's shotguns. Kirk, older than Lev by a few years, looked nothing like his brother. Where Lev was a thick root of a man, corded and gnarled, Kirk was a tiny wisp of a fellow. Scant. Five feet, three inches. Thin arms and legs and a thin trunk. Humped-over shoulders and large ears and an ax blade of a nose—as boys, William and Mack had called him the Buzzard. Kirk and Lev were sons of a prostitute, most of her children fathered by different men. One had left her with Lev in her womb, another with Kirk. They had other brothers and sisters, too, some nearby, some they'd never see again. Rumor held that Lev and Kirk had hanged her for being a whore.

Finally, behind everyone else, walked Mack's brother, William, dragging a dirty blanket on which lay several gallon jugs of bootleg whiskey. He looked up and saw Mack on the porch and grinned and lifted a hand.

The procession of mule and men stopped in front of Mack where he stood, Bit Owen's cut-up face down, his shoulders pulled back by his bound hands. The men lined up facing the porch.

"Boy," Lev ordered, "fetch us Tooch."

"Yes, sir," he said, turning for the door.

Tooch stood there already, looking at his men through the rusty screen. He came out. "Here he sits," Tooch said, flicking a dismissive hand at Owen, "the man who would refuse our offer. Who would rather be friendly with the high sheriff than with his own kind."

Mack edged along the wall toward the side of the porch.

Tooch had turned his attention to War Haskew, who favored his bloody leg. "He get you, War?"

"Just a skritch," Haskew said. "It ain't much."

"You should've came over with us, Bit," Tooch said. "Now you'll never again taste your own whiskey."

"You won't neither," Owen said. "I got a powerful recipe, not written down nowhere."

"I believe we can work a goddamn still," Lev said. He came up the steps and stood beside Tooch, then sat on the edge of the porch and laid his shotgun aside. He had his face painted with ash. "William," he said, "bring me one of them." William untied the jugs and carried one to Lev, who unstoppered it and sniffed its mouth. He closed his eyes and his countenance relaxed.

"Corn base," he said.

"Hell, everbody knows that," Owen said. "I ain't used taters for years now."

Lev closed his eyes, tilted the jug back, and took a mighty swig. He sloshed it in his mouth, held his head back, and let it slide down his throat.

"You use sugar, don't you?" Lev said, once he could breathe again. When he opened his eyes they were moist. "Would that be your secret, Bit?"

Owen looked flustered. "Hell, no," he said. "They's more to it than that."

Even Mack could tell he was lying.

"I believe," Tooch announced, "that we got us a whiskey artist here among us, boys. Hand me that splo, Lev."

Lev, meanwhile, began fashioning his rope into a noose, doing it in plain sight of Owen. It had grown darker, the sun dragging its final light over the edge of the fields.

"The truth," Owen said, looking at Tooch, "is that I've had me a change of heart. Yes, I reckon I have. I've decided just now to take up your offer. My gun is yours. My two stills, too. Let us declare battle upon the courthouse, or whoever it is who's irksome to you."

"Your *three* stills is mine, all right," Tooch said, "and your gun, too, and so is everthing else we find out in your shack. Your mule there is mine. Your skiff is. Your chickens and the eggs they shit out. If you'd of ever took a wife, she'd be mine to concubine, as the Good Book calls it, and I'd of made her a whore to go along with that other one."

"Well, it seems fair," Owen said. "You bested me, and I'm in your service."

"Lev," Tooch said, and Lev came forward with the noose.

Mack pressed himself into the wall, not making a sound. This was far more than he had been allowed to witness. His heart convulsed in a strange way—he was fixing to see Bit Owen strung up in the huge oak tree where the crow still sat, eyeing its half-buried pecan.

"Mack," Tooch said. Lev paused. Even Bit Owen looked upon him, for a moment.

Mack's ribs constricted with relief and disappointment. He ducked his head as he came forward. "Sir?"

"Inside with you, boy."

He turned, and—glancing one last time at the crow where it sat in the tree—opened the screen door and closed it behind him. He didn't look back. He went down the aisle to his room. He closed that door, too, and sat down on his bed ticking. Across from him the rifles stood in their rack. He reached for a Winchester Model 94 and took it from its place. He worked its lever, the ratchet sound it made. He aimed it at the ceiling timbers and snapped the hammer, *click*. Then he flounced back onto his blanket, the gun clutched at his chest.

Not much later he heard Tooch's footsteps. He came to the door and opened it without knocking.

Mack stood up.

"Here," he said. "Got a job for you."

He felt small following Tooch through the store, over the porch, and down the steps. The men stood around Bit Owen's body where it lay in its filthy long underwear, his clothes a mucky pile beside the corpse. Lev had taken his shoes, though they were too small, and was unnoosing his neck and others were drinking and passing the jug among them. Mack looked at the dead man, his throat red, the underwear wet and soiled. He pushed his hands into his pockets.

"Find your spade," Tooch said, flipping a casual hand at the body. "You know what to do."

He nodded and ran to get the shovel from its nail in the shed by the stall where the horse stood back in the shadows. It heard him and came forward, pushing its snout through the boards, showing cubes of yellow teeth.

At the edge of the hollow Mack slid the shovel headfirst down the ravine, through the dead leaves, where it clattered at the stones along the bottom of the gully. He came back for the body, which lay alone now—the men had gone to the porch and were sitting, drinking, War Haskew telling Tooch the story of the raid and gunfight and Owen's surrender.

The dead man lay unmoved on his belly. Mack took him by one

loose ankle and lifted the leg, surprisingly heavy, and began to drag him over the court. By the time he'd gotten to the edge of the woods he felt faint and realized he'd been holding his breath. He let the foot fall and turned away from Owen and bent, hands on his knees, light-headed. Before anyone from the porch could see him he recovered and took the same foot and pulled the man into the bushes. On the porch the men had broken out cigars and were lighting them with a piece of kindling.

Mack set to rolling Owen down the sharp ravine, an easier job than pulling him overland. Twice the old man became wedged on trunks, but Mack dislodged him with his foot and soon Owen lay beside his grave.

Here was the time to say words over the dead body. Mack had only had a couple of dealings with Bit Owen but had found him pleasant enough—once years ago at this very store on a croquet Saturday he'd given Mack a four-point buck horn he'd found on the riverbed, and when Mack had asked about the tiny craters eaten in its side the old man had explained how mice and other small varmints got nourishment from the horn, how if left alone in the leaves where he'd found it it would've soon been gone entirely, eaten away.

Mack tried to recall an appropriate Bible verse to recite but could only remember the one about how everything had its time. A time to gather stones. To throw them away. To die. He repeated what he could remember of the list quietly, worrying that his voice might drift uphill, but the sentiments seemed empty and unfit for quoting over a body. A time for everything. What did that mean? He tried to think of something else.

No words came, though, so he picked up the shovel and wedged it beneath Owen and levered him into the hole, muddy at the bottom. He landed faceup, one arm flopping over, his mouth open but his eyes shut. Glad for that, Mack peered at him. He didn't look dead in the near dark, he might've been asleep. You could even see a slight movement there on his chest. Tooch had said that often dead men move. Their tallywhackers get hard. A foot might twitch, a finger curl.

As he shoveled dirt into the grave the green clouds of evergreen trees and the gray poles of sycamore trunks began to recede, night accruing around his feet like floodwaters and seeping up the hill. He always felt trapped by darkness when it came. Before it grew to where he couldn't see he climbed the bank and went through the croquet court and to the porch and between the laughing, drunk men and into the store for a lantern.

"You ain't buried him yet?" Lev said. "You must've had a little romp with him first, eh?"

They all laughed, William the hardest.

As Mack filled the lantern with oil he could hear Lev telling one about a man he knew who used to like to corpulate with dead girls. Couldn't ever get him a live one, this fellow was so ugly. Not even a whore, there wasn't enough money minted. There was even a couple of dead girls that had tried to get up and crawl off in the middle of it, Lev said, and the men laughed. Encouraged, Lev said the fellow used to attend funerals of girls and when the mourners left he'd go after the dirt while it was still manageable, and when the girl was, too. "Once they legs freeze up," he said, "you got a hell of a time spreading 'em."

"You ought to know," War Haskew said, and they all laughed.

Back at the bottom by the grave, something was wrong. A hand had come unburied. Mack watched it, his bowels going cold as if Owen's ghost had passed through him. He looked back up toward the top where trees silhouetted against the last dying glow of the sky had assumed ghoulish forms, outreached arms, bony fingers. Laughter trickled down. He looked back into the grave, holding the lantern over it, and saw that the hand had moved again.

Its fingers opened. They closed.

He caught his breath as the arm rose, bending at the elbow, and

149

the other one unearthed itself, too, and soon both were clawing at the mud covering Bit Owen's face, which emerged thick-lipped and black with muck. He coughed and spat. Rubbed his eyes with the heels of both hands and sat up, flinging mud from his fingers.

"Lord," Mack whispered, feeling for the handle of the shovel where he'd stood it.

Owen opened and closed his mouth. He turned his head and put both hands to his throat as if to choke himself. Then he saw Mack and recognition dawned in his eyes.

"Boy," he croaked. "Help me on up out of here."

Mack slowly shook his head. He felt tethered between the lantern and the spade, his ability to hold things aloft his only reason for being.

"Just pass me down the handle of your shovel, then, and I'll pull myself out." Owen held his arms up. "Ain't nobody got to know. I'll hightail it out of here. The county, I mean. You won't ever have to tell a soul. You can go on cover up the hole. Hell, I'll even help you, soon's I catch my breath."

He tried to get to his feet but collapsed onto his knees. "Lord, that were a close call," he said. "Them old boys up yonder so drunk they can't even hang a fellow. You figure it'd be second nature to 'em."

He tried again to get to his hands and knees and looked up, a pained glaze in his eyes. "Reckon I shat myself," he said. "Ain't right a boy to smell a man like this. I was in the War and fought brave, captured two Yanks once. Hand me that shovel, now, will you?"

Mack looked to the top of the hollow. Their laughter floated down. From where he stood he could see the shape of the hanging tree. He had buried others down here, too—another bootlegger, the peddler Lev had killed. Sometimes, digging, he would uncover the hand or face of a previous corpse.

"Come on, honey," Bit Owen croaked from the bottom of the grave. "Pull me out. I'm fixing to catch my death." He bent over and retched. He threw up. His underwear was black with mud. "I'm a vile creature today," he said, wiping a string of vomit from his chin. "Yet I reckon a man spared the fires of hell ought not yammer on about the terms of his salvation, eh?" He smiled. Rose to a kneeling position, hands on his thighs. "Why, I declare if I ain't feeling some better now. Being near 'bout dead ain't so different than a regular old hangover, I reckon."

The lantern had grown heavy. Mack lowered his arm and the sphere of light around them shrank. Below, Owen had gone to coughing again. Mack looked to the top of the ridge. Someone belched enormously and it echoed. When he looked back, the image of Owen trying to stand, using the pale elbows of root protruding from the side of the grave for leverage brought to mind a knee-baby pulling itself up on anything it could cling to. He'd seen so many babies, going as he had in his childhood with the widow to deliver them, babies born alive, babies born dead.

Finally Owen gained his feet, steadied himself against the sides of the hole.

"You made it a deep one, didn't you, boy?" He ran a finger along the edge. "This here's prime workmanship. You got you a future as a gravedigger, I'll tell you that. As a man fixing to be raised up from the dead I can vouchsafe for the work you do, boy."

Mack's legs lost their sand and he knelt, still clinging to the shovel handle and the lantern.

Owen was trying to climb out, holding up his hand for Mack to help him.

"I can't," Mack said. "If I let you go, you'll come back. You'll come back and they'll know."

The old man coughed and rubbed his throat, his elbows on the side of the grave. "Naw, boy, I ain't coming back. Hell. Who'd show they face after this?"

Mack looked to the top of the ridge. No one was coming. He looked back down at the old man. Then reached and took Bit

Owen's hands in his and bracing his feet against the ridges of magnolia roots, nearly getting pulled in himself, wrenched the man up out of the mud in a foul embrace. For a moment the two of them lay side by side, panting.

Owen sat up. "I'd like my shoes back," he said. "I can't fathom this harsh ground without 'em."

Mack shook his head. "Go on. Now. Else they'll kill us both."

Bit nodded, a hand at his throat. "I see your point, boy. I done been hanged once today. That ought to 'bout do it."

Mack looked to the top of the hill, figuring to see Tooch's silhouette there. But he saw nothing, and when he looked back toward Bit, the old man had vanished. Mack bent and began to shovel furiously, watching the top of the hollow.

V

With the locals deep in their harvest and the peddler acting as guide, Ardy Grant spent a few days learning the landscape of Mitcham Beat and hearing its gossip, the biggest news of which was, of course, the night riders operating hereabouts.

He heard of buildings burned, people threatened, dogs killed. Shots fired into windows, wells poisoned, fences pulled down. Heard what they'd done to the colored folks' church. How they'd ambushed Joe Anderson.

He was told lesser tales, too, and he found it odd how the people unburdened themselves of these details to him and the peddler, for he knew how secretive these country folks were. He knew because his mother and father had themselves been from the country—not from out here in Mitcham Beat, not from anywhere, really, just itinerant farmers, a couple who traveled year by year until they found a spot and a well-off man who'd front them money and supplies—a mule, seeds, fertilizer, tools, and a place to live—in exchange for their labor, clearing, plowing, planting, cutting, picking, carting to market. They might stay one season or two but always his father would run astray of the landowner or the law and they'd leave in the middle of the night owing money.

They'd fled one spring to a place near Grove Hill when Ardy was three years old, a time of which he had no memory, the family arriving on foot with nothing except the clothes they wore and a few belongings his father carried while his mother carried Ardy. They stopped at the edge of a field beside a shack with wide gaping spaces between the planks that made up its walls, most of the shingles blown away. His father, the story went, had left, gone to find food or work or both. They never saw him alive again. The owner of the shack and the land around it brought him back, dead, that evening. The man had shot him for a thief, having surprised him at his, the landowner's, smokehouse, where Ardy's father was trying—the landowner claimed—to steal a ham.

Ardy's mother was an attractive woman, with a good figure and eyes so green people would pause when they saw her. Who knew what thoughts she'd had and in what order they'd come, or how she had reordered them, to allow her to marry—six months later—the very man who'd killed her husband. So Ardy had grown up in this father-killer's house, though he didn't know it then. He called the man Mr. Carter, as did his mother, and the two of them wore finer clothes and had enough food and slept in the flickering heat of Mr. Carter's fireplaces, one in each large, high-ceilinged room of his two-story house. Picture molding along the ceilings and portraits of his father and mother and gray-haired uncles hanging on the walls.

Mr. Carter was a perfectly decent man, though distant. He might go a week without giving Ardy a look, or a month without speaking to him. He often would give instructions through his wife to her son—"Tell the boy to bring in wood"—and Ardy would rise without having to hear them again, from his mother. At meals they'd eat quietly, no one speaking save Mr. Carter saying grace, always asking

God's blessings on himself, his land, his tenants, and finally his wife, but never on Ardy, who as a child began to imagine himself ignored by God, for how could a being as large and faraway as God see him if Mr. Carter did not?

Yet each night, after each omission, when Carter had gone to one of his farms to talk with his tenants, Ardy's mother would be in the boy's room an hour, two, and he came to understand her affections as intercessions to God, for each night she would clutch him and pray on her knees by his bed, ask in a panicked whisper for God to *please please please* watch over her little Ardy, her hands squeezing the skin of his forearms so hard they'd leave marks, her eyes shut so tightly she seemed in pain. He watched her during these hissed prayers—her face lost its beauty in concentration—and he divined that she must suspect God of not listening to her; similarly, he understood from Carter's quiet confidence as he prayed at the supper table that it was him whom God heard.

What to think, then, of a boy brought up outside the circumference of God's vision? He didn't know that this was not the way other families lived until, older, he befriended a boy who not only informed him of how strange the Carter household was, but also told him what everyone else knew: that Mr. Carter had killed Ardy's real daddy. When he asked his mother about this after one of her prayers, she'd grabbed his arm and scratched blood from it in her fervor. "Don't you ever mention that again. *Ever*." And so he hadn't.

And if he wasn't able to satisfy his wonder at why his mother had married her husband's murderer, he never wondered why he, Ardy, at age sixteen, killed Mr. Carter. Why he walked up behind his stepfather as he bent down into their well, trying to untangle the bucket Ardy had secretly tangled, and knelt and grasped the man's ankles and tumped him in. Carter fell headlong with a girl's cry and landed in the water far below. But once there, he never moved. When they pulled him out they found his neck broken.

Sheriff Waite came. He led Ardy down the back path and out of sight of the house and they stood facing each other in the dim shadows of white oak branches and Waite set his right hand on the butt of his pistol and said, "Son, did you kill your stepfather?"

Ardy said, "No. I did not." He said, "Why would I kill him?"

Waite studied him. Peered into his eyes, green as his mother's. "Do you know how your real daddy died?"

"Mr. Carter shot him."

Again Waite studied him. "How'd you find that out?"

"Everbody knows it."

The sheriff looked at him and he looked back, and Ardy knew then that Waite had guessed the truth, but that he could never prove it. Which meant Ardy had won. After a while he said, "Can I go?"

His mother and he inherited everything, and she began to sell plots of Carter's land and the houses on the land. She kept the money in the Grove Hill bank. One night Ardy came in from riding Carter's horse, which he'd claimed as his own, and found her beside the fire, rocking. She looked at him in the half-light. She'd taken to drinking a glass of buttermilk before bed and was now turning the glass in her hands. He couldn't see her face and didn't think she could see his. "Did you push him in?" she asked.

"Yes, ma'am," he said.

"Why?"

"Because he killed my daddy."

"You didn't even know your daddy." Her voice stayed even. "And there wasn't anything that I put into you that would make you do such a thing. Your doing such a thing was something else. Something you got on your own."

"Maybe I got it from him."

"From who?"

"Daddy."

"Yes," she said. "Maybe you did."

And they'd never spoken of Carter again. His mother lived in comfort and didn't remarry and took rail trips to New York and the

Gulf Coast, and Ardy left at age twenty with a pocketful of money to see the west from the back of his horse. When he learned she'd died he came home. Ten years had gone by and here he was, a different man altogether. Riding a new horse, he'd looked over the Carter land, what little she hadn't sold, and understood that he felt nothing about her passing. He rode into Grove Hill to see how much money there was and found she'd spent most of it or given it away to the Methodist church, left only the house and enough for her own funeral. He didn't care.

Billy Waite had grown thinner in his absence, tiny red veins over his cheekbones and his nose larger, redder, and when Ardy encountered the sheriff on the millinery porch his fourth or fifth day back he saw in the old man's eyes that Waite still believed Ardy had killed Carter.

"Well," Waite said. He folded his arms, a buggy rattled past on the street behind him. "You're back."

"Yep."

"What you plan to do?"

"Ain't got no plans, really."

The old man exhaled, his breath stank. "Would you do me the favor, then, of leaving? Take what time you need to settle whatever needs to be settled, but then go. Go."

Ardy smiled. "I ain't yet sure what I'll do, Sheriff. But I thank you for your opinion."

The old man walked off, porch boards sighing under his weight.

A week later Ardy ran into Judge Oscar York in the barbershop, a towel over his face and the tall bespectacled barber drawing his straight razor over the leather strop.

"Judge," Ardy said.

Oscar reached and took away the steaming rag, his cheeks red from the heat. He looked puzzled for a moment, then his face changed.

"Why, Ardy Grant," he said. "You're back."

"Yes, sir."

"Son," the judge said, now getting up out of the chair but still wearing the barber's smock. "I was so sorry about your mother's passing. We always loved to hear her tales of the great white north. Did you know I gave the eulogy? She and my Lucinda were like peas in a pod. Two of 'em drunk so much tea the Chinese should've put up statues of 'em."

"I was sad not to have been here," Ardy said, wondering briefly what his mother would have told them to explain his absence. "Bit by the travel bug myself, I reckon," he said, then relaxed as the kind-eyed judge nodded. He should have known she'd never air any ugly family business. That she'd only speak well of him.

"Well, a fellow needs to do that," said the judge. "Travel. Broaden his horizons. Myself, I went up to Tuscaloosa for college. Left a boy and come back a man." He winked.

"Yes, sir."

"How old are you now, Ardy?"

"Thirty, sir."

They chatted as Oscar sat back into the chair and got his shave, the judge asking if he thought he might stay in Grove Hill and Ardy deciding the moment he said it that yes, he would. The idea of Waite's suspicions excited him. A moment later he'd accepted an invitation to the York house for supper, and by the time the crickets had warmed up their singing and the cicadas theirs, he and the judge were sipping lemonade on the judge's porch with a small wicker table between them, Ardy telling stories from California and Idaho. Montana. As he talked he heard himself telling how he'd worked as a deputy in Wyoming, making up stories of captured outlaws or putting himself into the roles of others. He even pretended great sadness at the "only man" he'd had to kill, a younger fellow than he, he said, but (lowering his voice) a rapist and therefore not fit to live.

"It's a wretched place," the judge said, "this world. I see it myself,

157

all too often. Those country fellows are such ruffians. It's a harsh life, judging others."

"It don't have to be so, sir," Ardy said. "We just need the right men in office. That's our only chance."

"May I inquire," the judge said, leaning closer, "as to your plans, now that you're home?"

"Home," he repeated. "Well, being as my experience is with the law, I was hoping Sheriff Waite might need a hand somehow. I could clean up in the jailhouse, or be a clerk . . ."

"We can do better than that," Oscar said. "Let me see what I can do. I have a little influence with our sturdy sheriff." He winked. "We're first cousins, you know."

During supper Ardy charmed Mrs. York and endured stories about his mother, and when he left at just past nine he was whistling. He rode back to Mr. Carter's dusty house and sat amid cobwebs on the upper balcony drinking from a bottle of good sour mash whiskey and marveling at the strands of fate, where they began and where they ended. He recalled Waite asking if he'd killed his stepfather. Recalled his mother's handwriting. A black girl he'd raped in Minnesota and the little accountant he'd shot in the throat in Memphis. Recalled a good cut of beef he'd had in New Orleans, recalled a book he'd read and how he'd cheated a Dallas lawyer out of the fine Colt Peacemaker heavy now in its holster against his ribs. He recalled a hotel burning and a magic show, recalled and recalled and recalled and recalled, all beneath a dark-speckled sky where just before he passed out drunk he saw a star falling and told himself that not too far from now he'd be sheriff of Clarke County.

Oscar York found Ardy at the Cunningham Hotel dining room a week later and asked to speak to him in private; in the judge's office, the door shut, he listened to Oscar say how Billy Waite didn't want a deputy. Waite was getting older, though, and he needed help worse than ever.

"For some reason," the judge said, "he's biased against you. Do you know why?"

"No, sir."

"Well. He won't say why or why not, he just ain't receptive to the idea. Or heck, maybe it ain't even you. He don't want anybody, really. Figures he can handle it all."

Then the judge stood, poured them coffee, and began to tell him about the goings-on in the place called Mitcham Beat. How everyone out there had an alibi. "Heck," the judge said, "if this bunch had been in the Garden of Eden, the woman would've had 'em testify she'd never even seen the serpent and we'd all still be nekkid and the Good Book would've ended in Genesis." He drummed his fingers on his desktop. "How would you handle that bunch, if you were sheriff?"

"Well, I wouldn't want to say too much about that," he said. "It might sound disrespectful. To Sheriff Waite. If I was to question his methods. But let me offer you a deal, Judge." He took out his tobacco and papers and began to construct a cigarette, giving himself a moment to think. "Suppose," he said, "I ride out yonder wearing another of my hats. As a private detective. I did some of that work in Billings, Montana. Learned from the best there, fellow named Chip Hurdle. You ever hear of him, Judge? Well, it don't matter. Point is, he taught me all he knew about detective work." Ardy struggled not to grin—the true Chip Hurdle had been a man whose wife had died while he was on a trip to buy goats; when the women of the community went to prepare her for burial and removed her dress and underthings they'd found her to be a man. Hurdle, on his return to Billings, had been hanged.

The judge tapped his chin. "What would you do, as a detective?"

"Nothing illegal, of course. Just ride out there and sniff around. Don't none of 'em know me, and so I might be able to dig up the facts that the sheriff ain't been able to find."

159

"They're pretty tight-lipped. Clannish. Plus they're dangerous."

"Well, Judge, I've got some experience in getting people to betray their selves. Trapping 'em in their own deceit. And not to brag," he said, pulling back his lapel to reveal the butt of his pistol, "but I ain't too worried about a little danger."

On his first two nights in Mitcham Beat, near the end of August, he and the peddler had parked the wagon in someone's yard along about sundown; they'd be waiting as the family trudged in from a day's cotton picking. The farmers spent the evening listening to Ardy's stories and then he asked gently into the goings-on of the region, learning all he could about it, its people. He never pried, just let the details collect and a picture form.

On the fourth night they parked the wagon by an empty corncrib at the edge of a field, no house in sight. Ardy told the peddler to hobble the horse and mule and he sat back and raised the box and peered in—but because it was dark he couldn't see her and tossed the box aside.

Later he watched while the peddler entered the cornfield and stripped ears right from the stalks and peeled, desilked, and skewered them with a sharpened stick and roasted them over a fire. It smelled good so he did the same. The peddler had a case of bourbon out of which Ardy took a bottle and drank from while listening to whippoorwills and owls.

"Them's a dollar," the peddler said, pointing to the whiskey.

"Put it on my account."

They sat.

"What the hell you expect to find out here, anyway?" the peddler asked.

"None of your business," Ardy said.

"I thought we was partners."

"Consider me a silent partner." Ardy stretched his boots toward the coals and put his hands behind his neck. "Tell you this, hoss. Sooner I find out what I'm looking for, sooner our partnership will be dissolved."

The peddler thought about that one. "We should go speak to a man called Massey Underwood," he said. "This here's his corn."

Ardy repeated the name. "What makes you think he'll tell us anything new?"

"Well, he's said to drink to excess, a great topic among the churches. You take one of those bottles and give him a few swigs . . ."

"We'll go see him tomorrow."

The peddler rose so suddenly Ardy's reflexes pulled his pistol. Then he lowered it, seeing the man's pale face.

"Your bowels?"

He nodded.

Ardy flicked his hand toward the trees at the edge of the field. "Go on."

The peddler dashed off, unfastening his pants.

A few moments later his voice called from the darkness. "You reckon you could toss me a couple of them gnawed-over cobs?"

The next day the two of them found Massey Underwood forking hay from his barn floor into a wagon. His house, visible through a sparse vegetable patch, was little more than a hodgepodge of leaning boards held up by stacks of rocks and roofed by rusty tin. Underwood came out with his hay fork in one hand and a long-barreled pistol in the other. He wore a pair of wretched overalls and no shirt underneath. A droopy thing on his long narrow head that once might've been a hat.

Side by side on the wagon's seat, the peddler and Ardy Grant waved, Ardy's horse tied behind the wagon. Underwood lifted the fork in return to their greeting and walked out to meet them, stuffing the pistol into the back of his britches.

"What's the news of the outer world, friend?" he asked the peddler.

"Ask this here fellow," the peddler said.

Underwood's skin exuded alcohol, you could get drunk just standing downwind of him. Ardy reached between his legs and when he came up with the bottle he was facing the barrel of Underwood's pistol.

"I ain't that drunk," he said.

"Whoa, hoss," Ardy said, raising his hands, the whiskey in the left. "Just a little busthead here."

Underwood smiled and put the gun away. "Sorry, boys. I'm a little jumpy these days." He stabbed the hay fork into the ground.

"It is hard times," Ardy said. He tossed the bottle down.

Underwood caught it in both hands. "Who's this generous young fellow?" he asked, leaning against the peddler's wagon, prizing the cork out.

"My partner," the surly peddler said.

"You don't say." Underwood screwed off the cap and sniffed the top, his eyes watering. "That's some sweet-smelling shit." He licked his lips and smacked them and drank.

"Fact is," Ardy said, "the company both him and me represents is sending one of us supervisors out with each of our representatives. Just to get a sense of the country."

Underwood finished his swig. "A mighty good idea," he said, catching his breath. He took another deep belt and recapped the bottle and returned it to the peddler.

Ardy said, "Would you mind if we took a little of your time, asked you a few questions?"

"Got a lot of work to get done. Will that bottle be a part of the deal?"

"No," the peddler said.

"What he means," Ardy said, opening his coat in a way that Underwood didn't notice, flashing his pistol butt to the peddler, "is

162

that while you and me conduct our interview, he'll go and take a inventory." He took the whiskey, gave it to Underwood, and hopped out of the wagon. "Give me that box," he ordered.

Underwood collected the fork and walked across the dirt into the shade of the barn.

The peddler handed down the box with the lady in it. "How much longer we gone be 'partners'?"

"I'll let you know."

He watched the young man walk to the barn, looking into the box. He climbed down and started poking at things, clanking metal, opening and closing wooden boxes.

It was cooler in the barn.

"What you got yonder?" Underwood asked, already squatting in the style of poor country men, knees up by his ears and his arms between them, the bottle on the ground before him. Ardy noticed he'd kept his back to the hay wagon, though, and so he sat down beside him, both facing outward.

"Have a look." Ardy pitched the box over.

Underwood caught it and turned it in his hands.

"You put your eye against that hole there, and hold the other end up towards the light."

Underwood took another swallow and set the bottle in the dirt beside a lantern. Behind him a threadbare mule looked out of an improvised stall, boards nailed together haphazardly. There came on the breeze the odor of pigs. Underwood raised the box with both hands and with his mouth hanging open looked into it for a very long time. When he lowered the box he was grinning.

"How much you asking for this thing?"

"It's a prize," Ardy said. "To the person who gives us the most helpful information. You consider yourself helpful?"

"That's what I've been called on more than one occasion," Underwood said, raising the box again.

"Then this just might be your lucky day. Now," Ardy said. "I'm fixing to reach into my coat here, just so you'll know. Don't want you pulling that shooter on me again. My bowels can't take another scare like that one you give me while ago."

"Out here you get used to being aimed at," Underwood's mouth said under the box.

Ardy brought out a pair of the peddler's nickel cigars, put one in his own lips, and offered the other.

"I will," Underwood said, lowering the box. "Obliged." He took the match Ardy offered, too, and struck it on his thumb and soon, smoking, they were talking and swapping the box and whiskey. Each time the bottle came by him, Underwood would say, "Don't mind if I do," and he would. Then he'd exchange it for the box and lift it to his eyes and whistle. When the whiskey came to Ardy, he'd fill his mouth but let most of it trickle back into the bottle.

He began with mundane questions, what all Underwood grew— corn, mainly, he had no head for cotton—what kind of fertilizer he used—gee-ayner—whether or not he owned his place—he did but had a lease on his crop, the only way a farmer could survive in these strangling times.

"Enough shop talk now," Ardy said finally. "Go on tell me about this beat of yours. It's got itself a reputation, you know."

"I reckon it does."

"A place that swallers up peddlers. There's been one of our kind rolled in here never to be seen again. They very nearly didn't let me come out here. They said I'd be endangering my life."

"That what they said?"

"Them very words."

Underwood considered this. He looked in the box as if there were answers there. "How come you was to come, then?"

Ardy shrugged. "Myself, I kind of admire those old boys. It ain't a popular opinion where I come from. You can imagine. But I grew up in the country. I know how them damn town folks treat the common farmer. I seen it growing up and I see it in my job. I'm out here fifty weeks of the year, talking to good hardworking people. I ain't in no office, pulling no strings. Fixing no ballots." He looked coyly about. "Don't tell nobody, but if it was up to me, I'd be buying them old boys a drink."

Underwood had the bottle turned up. He lowered it. "Tell you what, cowboy. You is."

Ardy said, "What you mean?"

Underwood winked. "You won't ever get me to repeat it, and if you was to ever squeal it to anybody, I'd kill you. But I trust you, friend, and I'll tell you this. I'm in Hell-at-the-Breech."

"In what?"

"That's our name. It ain't many folks knows it, neither."

Ardy let a moment pass. He said, "I believe you've just won yourself that there box, Mr. Underwood."

"Go on call me Massey."

But when Ardy came out of the barn an hour later he held the box under his arm as he pulled on his gloves. In his back pocket he had Underwood's pistol. The farmer lay passed out half beneath the wagon, his flat belly expanding and falling, expanding, falling. The bottle beside his head all but empty. Ardy looked out the door—the peddler's wagon and mule were gone, tracks going east.

"Why, he ought not to left without saying good-bye," he said.

He caught up with the peddler in less than an hour. The firefight was brief and he found a pond green with algae and weighted the body down with a flour sack full of rocks and watched the algae close around the peddler. A hand came back up out of the water as if to make a final point and Ardy worried he might have to wade in and push it down—he entertained the idea of shooting the fingers off one at a time, but abruptly the hand went under, too. For a spell he stayed and watched, air bubbling now and again.

Just after dark Ardy and his mule, wagon, and horse returned to

Underwood's place and took a set of chains and locks he'd found in the peddler's stock and fastened them to the snoring man and loaded him, still unconscious, onto the wagon.

Then he clanked off into the night.

VI

On the morning of August twenty-fifth, when there were pools of shadow still on the ground, as if the woods hated to let go of night, Mack was down at the creek stoking the fire under the washpot. Tooch appeared at the top of the hollow and called down for him to come to the store.

He climbed the hill, rubbing his hands together to clean them of ash, and crossed the croquet court and went up the steps and into the store. He was surprised to find Floyd Norris there with Tooch.

"Mack," Tooch said, "much as I hate to, I'm putting you on loan."

Mack looked at Floyd who was appraising him, probably remembering the time he'd picked cotton for him before. Mack remembered it, too, as the longest two weeks of his life.

"Floyd here needs a hand with his harvest," Tooch said, "and since you're experienced, as he tells me, you're elected."

Suddenly the wash seemed the work of paradise. But Mack knew better than to complain. "Yes, sir. When do I start?"

"Now," Floyd said. He turned to Tooch. "I thank you."

"If he don't work up to your satisfaction," Tooch said, "just let me know."

Floyd nodded and put his hat back on and headed down the aisle toward the door. Tooch was already going up his ladder. Mack looked at his boots disappearing into the ceiling and then at Floyd's back as it crossed the porch and hurried outside.

It was a two-mile walk to Floyd Norris's place and they walked it without talking. Mack dreaded the work. For a cotton farmer it was work most all the time, work that began in late February when you raised the scythe, the mornings still frosty, and destroyed the scuttle of last year's crop, grimly hacking and raking away the dried scraggle, like shaving a dead man's cheek. Then, when the March days lengthened, the one- or two-muled breaking of ground, the gut-jarring plowing, bound at the shoulders with traces and following the animal in a circle the shape of the field, laboring toward the center, like being sucked down a drain. After what you hoped was the last frost came the bedding, the funneling of fertilizer down the horn into the dark raised rows, a precise amount measured by eye and eye alone, and then days and days with a hoe, turning the earth back over, the harrowing and planting in conjunction.

Next the first waiting, perhaps the hardest time of all, maybe five days or maybe two weeks, as allowed by God and the soil and the weather. If a late freeze came, you began again. If not, when an inch of plant showed, came weeks and weeks of cultivating, of barring off, chopping, more hoeing and the repeated, tender sweepings as the plants unfolded delicate as lace handkerchiefs out of the dirt and grew taller as you chopped the weeds away and waited and chopped and waited.

And then, at last, the laying by, that long six weeks with nothing to do but worry and watch and wait and keep the rows clean, repair tools, roofs, fences. And then the harvest.

Here, in years before, was when Mack and William had joined him. The widow, too. They'd needed money and Floyd had promised them a penny for each two pounds they picked. So they'd all worked, the boys lolling in the heat, slapping at bugs, tearing loose the damnable cotton and bagging it, the widow keeping a close eye on them, saying, "Don't get too hot, go rest in the shade," but never a minute's rest for her, or for Floyd's wife, or for Floyd either, small and lost in the haze of the field, directly below the sun, picking and picking and picking and picking his cotton. The fingers of his two quick hands darting among the leaves, two quick hands the color and feel of a reptile's belly, quick-striking fingers with blunt black nails and big knuckles.

The eyes under the strip of shade from Floyd's hat were a marvel to Mack for the emotion that wasn't shown there, as if those eyes were twin puddles reflecting a blank sky. Or no sky. Floyd Norris bent and creeping along the rows of his field, fingers opening and closing, feeding and feeding and feeding and feeding the long heavy dirty sack clinging to his left shoulder, growing thicker and thicker in increments as small as seconds but as quick as seconds, too, which become minutes which become hours, then days, weeks, months: bolls of cotton accruing as surely as time ticked on, time not felt as it passed him by but which he must have sensed only after it was gone and left was nothing but repercussion and consequence and the memory of possibility. The hope of money.

Floyd Norris was said to be able to pick nearly three hundred pounds of cotton by himself, three hundred pounds from when he stepped into the field at dawn to when he stepped out long after the sun had scalded the western sky and vanished. He went into a kind of trance, ignored his wife when she called for him to kill a copperhead or whip one of the straying boys. When she led the three of them from the field at blistering noon for dinner, Floyd alone remained, fingers picking and eyes dead, his bag round and rounder and leaving in its wake a smooth, deepening smear of dirt. Then his hunched shoulders would rise and he walked stiffly, stretching his back, to the wagon, pouring out the contents of his bag with no sense of pride or achievement, just flapping the bag empty and hopping down, rolling his head side to side, uncapping the water barrel and lowering his blank face in and drinking like a dog. Chewing a cold biscuit. Then back, where he would be when his family came hurrying out, the mother carrying the baby and chattering to the boys who cast slant-eyed looks at each other, plots taking root in their brains, dirt clods to be thrown, big caterpillars to be put down a shirt collar as the mother scolded them and implored Floyd to take a switch to one boy or the whole brood, but Floyd's eyes registering nothing, his fingers reaching and picking.

When they neared Floyd's easternmost field he slipped into the woods and Mack followed silently. They slowed and went very quietly, Mack understanding they were sneaking up on someone. He knew Floyd hadn't joined the core group of the alliance because of his family. Now Mack wondered who they were fixing to ambush and wondered where Floyd's gun was.

At the edge of the woods they looked out over a half-picked field, the wagon on the far side tiny in the shimmering heat. Floyd strained to see and Mack followed his eyes. Finally they both saw the three blond-headed boys.

"Goddammit," Floyd growled.

The boys weren't picking. They were bent in the field doing something else. Keeping low, Floyd left the woods—snapping a branch the size of his thumb from an oak sapling—and crept along an unpicked row, through it and then into another. After a moment, Mack followed, dread kindling in his belly. Soon he and Floyd had reached the boys, who appeared to be torturing an injured rabbit.

One of them looked up when Floyd rose from the cotton. The others followed his gaze. They stood in unison, the youngest already crying, unhitching their identical tattered overalls. They turned and let the clothes fall, revealing their red backs, their naked bottoms.

Floyd looked at Mack.

"Get you a bag off that wagon," he said, pointing with the switch. "Start over yonder."

Mack obeyed, hurrying so as not to hear the whipping, the boys' cries.

*　　*　　*

He'd never been more tired when he emptied his last bag, the moon yellowing its low corner of the sky and a few early dull stars showing. His arms were so tired they felt numb, and his fingers were bloody, they ached when he flexed them. Still, he helped Floyd's boys empty their bags, too, as they slogged in, none speaking or looking at him, switch stripes on their shoulders, necks.

Floyd brought his last bag to the wagon and set it down. He hitched his mule to the wagon and they followed it as he drove it to the cotton house two fields over. They weighed the cotton as they stored it, the boys asleep standing up.

"You can go on back to Tooch's," Floyd said to Mack when they'd finished. "Be here just 'fore light tomorrow."

Tooch was waiting on the porch smoking a cigar when he dragged up. "How was it?"

Mack told him about the boys and the rabbit, the whipping they'd gotten.

"Floyd's in a bad way these days," Tooch said, pointing to the step.

Mack sat. "How come?"

"His wife died yesterday. That's how come he needs another hand."

Mack was too tired to be shocked. He remembered her, though, a shapeless woman with enormous breasts. Remembered the story of her third-oldest baby being born. The widow had told him, said Floyd's wife was in labor for more than a day, seemed the baby would never come, as if it knew what kind of life lay waiting and wanted no part of it. It was harvest time and Floyd had picked the whole day and come home expecting the baby to be swaddled and suckling, but when he found the woman still sweating in the bed inside her mosquito netting he just glared at her. It's a slow one, Floyd, the widow had said. I reckon, he'd answered. That whole night, too, the labor lingered, and in the morning as Floyd came in from the porch where he and the other two boys had slept to avoid her moans he gave her a savage look. What the hell, he said, and the widow said, You can't never tell what calendar a baby will keep. Go on out, Floyd said, and get you a sup of water. She did, casting a look at the woman who had her eyes now on Floyd, and in a minute Floyd came back outside without looking at her and walked on to the field to start his day of picking. The widow went inside and, she swore, within half an hour the baby was crowning.

"How'd she die?" Mack asked.

"Just keeled over in the field," Tooch said.

Mack leaned his head against the porch post. He couldn't move his arms. In seconds he was asleep.

Some time later, Tooch's voice woke him. "You'd best get something to eat and sleep in your bed. You got another day tomorrow, and another one after that."

August ended slowly and September began slowly. Alfred told Mack how their mother had collapsed mid-row, how Floyd had noticed her not working and stalked over and stared down at her and knelt, placing a hand on her chest, then lowered his ear to her lips as if she might tell him the secret of how to leave. Then he'd put his flat hands against the ground and crouched there for a time as bugs shot around his face and crows quarked and cawed in the sky and gathered in the trees along the limbs, watching like they knew what had happened, knew it all along. Then Floyd had pushed himself upright, and without looking at her again, he'd left her lying where she'd fallen while the three boys sat around her, plucking at her dress, picking bugs off her tongue, the baby at the end of its row wailing until Alfred sent Arnold after it. Floyd told the youngest boy to watch the baby and the others to keep picking and he himself picked, too. When dark fell and Floyd had emptied his bag the final time and helped the boys with theirs he went to her at last and lifted her in his arms and carried her into their house (the boys following, Alfred trying to shush the screaming baby) and dressed her in her other dress, the white one she'd got married in, and washed the dirt from her face, hands, elbows, feet. He'd gone outside and dug a hole behind the house and climbed down in it with her for a long time. The boys dared one another to go have a look, but none would, and then a hand appeared at the lip of the grave and another and their father's red eyes appeared. He'd told them to go to sleep—their momma was gone—and he'd carried the baby off. They hadn't seen it since.

"Where you reckon he took it?" Mack asked. They'd met at the wagon and were emptying their bags, keeping an eye on Floyd's bobbing hat in a distant row.

"Reckon he killed it," Alfred said.

He looked at the blond boy. "Killed it," he repeated.

Alfred cast an eye toward the field. "He's watching."

Mack had thought loneliness meant working in Tooch's store, but true loneliness seemed to grow alongside the cotton here as he crept from plant to plant on his knees, pulling one boll and then another, the sun so hot the dirt seemed like ash taken from a glowing fireplace. His fingers had been torn at the nails at first by the cotton shells but now they'd callused over and his hands seemed new to him, tough as the bottoms of his feet in summer, when no child in Mitcham Beat wore shoes.

In the evening, at Tooch's, it occurred to him.

"That baby," he said, "it's at the widow's."

Tooch grinned at him. "You been replaced."

While picking cotton, he might go two hours without seeing Floyd or one of the boys, or he might empty his bag alongside Arnold or Alvin or Alfred, or Floyd himself, might wait for Floyd to dunk his head in the water barrel on the back of the wagon or might dunk his head alone. The boys got a whipping or two a week, usually for playing when they should be working, and the cracks of Floyd's switch and the yelps that followed became another sound to ignore, nothing more or less than the buzz of a grasshopper, the nervous dry-rattling tail of a garter snake against leaves, the constant trill of birds. The days melted together and the nights were forgotten as he walked to the store in a trance to find Tooch waiting alone on the porch or with Lev or War Haskew and William or Huz and Buz. Tooch had begun having a meal waiting for him on the counter, beans in a tin plate or biscuits smeared with jelly, oyster crackers, and sardines from cans. At night his sleep was that of the dead, or the unborn.

Except for a curious and disturbing event that occurred on an afternoon when Floyd was picking in a field around the bend and the boys were hidden in their rows, penitent after yet another whipping, little happened to remember those days of work.

Mack had just reached the end of a row, his bag nearly full, cutting into his shoulder, when he looked up and saw a man standing in the shade watching him. In a land of overalls, brogans, and dirt-black straw hats, here was a fellow in good trousers and leather chaps, a fine chambray shirt and a new-looking fedora. He wore a strange rig for his gun, a holster around his body, and held folded over his forearm a duster jacket. His face was hidden in shadow.

"Hidy," he said.

"Hidy," Mack answered. He unlooped the sack from his neck and stood up, enjoying the stretch.

"What's your name?" the man asked.

He said it. Then thought he shouldn't have.

"You the boy works over at the store?"

He nodded.

"How come he's got you doing this nigger work?"

Mack shrugged and came closer so he could see his face. While

173

the man was nice-looking and clean-shaven, something in his green eyes seemed worrisome. Mack knew revenue agents came occasionally to look for stills.

"I wouldn't work out here," the man said.

"Everybody picks this time of year," Mack replied.

"What about your boss? Toochie?"

It was funny hearing his name in that variation. Mack nearly grinned.

The man saw it. "Toochie Coochie," he sang.

Mack tried not to smile. He looked away.

"You wanna see something?" the man whispered. He looked around as if the bolls wore ears. He took the coat off his forearm where a wooden box had been hidden. He beckoned Mack close and let him look in a black hole. Inside he saw a picture of a woman with no clothes. Having gone on many of the widow's midwife's trips, Mack had seen breasts and even the hairy spot from which babies entered the world, but this, now, this was something altogether different. It was like she was there *for him*. In a dark room, she lay upon a frilly couch of some sort, with her right knee upraised and her hips tilted slightly toward the front so you could see the dark patch under her little belly. You could see both breasts, too, large and with perfect round nipples. Flowers around her. She—

The man snatched it away and sunlight filled Mack's eyes. He squinted.

"You tell me what I want to know," the man said, "and you can look again."

He wanted to look again. Worse than anything. "What you want?"

"I want to know when your little gang's meeting next. I want you to tell me what Toochie Coochie's planning."

Mack said, "Who are you? You a revenue man?"

He grinned. "I'm the devil, boy. And you better tell me what I

174

want, else I'll snatch you down to hell." And with that he grabbed Mack's crotch and squeezed. He gasped and collapsed in the dirt. The man fell on top of him and took Mack by the throat and began to strangle him. Mack grappled with his wrists but the other's grip was iron-hard. He tried to knee the fellow in the balls as William had once taught him but couldn't move his legs for his opponent's leg, which was pinning them. All the while he was being choked harder and harder and felt himself beginning to grow faint. Then, suddenly, he could breathe. The man was gone as if whipped away on a wind. Mack opened his eyes.

Arnold walked out of the cotton and watched Mack struggling to get up. The pain had gone to a dull ache in the bowl of his belly, trickled down his thighs.

"I'm gone tell Daddy you taking a nap," the boy said.

Mack coughed and his eyes watered. He felt his sore neck and thought of Bit Owen. He sucked air down his burned throat and looked at the ragged child before him. "You tell him," he wheezed, "and I'll break your little neck."

Afterward he would watch the ends of rows and the dark spaces between trees, but it would be several weeks before he saw the devil again.

One night when he walked back to the store all of them were on the porch, except Massey Underwood, who no one had seen in weeks. As Mack approached, they fell silent and watched him. A few gun barrels inching his way. He felt a blush liven his cheeks and forgot his fatigue. For the first time since the man showed him the box and choked him his brain seemed there for a reason.

He climbed the steps.

Kirk looked at him, amusement in his eyes.

"Tooch give you a promotion?" he asked, and the men laughed.

Mack made his way through the cigar smoke and the odor of

whiskey. Before he could go in the store, Tooch said, "Get your victuals, boy, and bring 'em out here."

He was too thrilled to eat the food on his plate as he sat down beside William, who elbowed him and winked, then plucked a sardine off the plate and swallowed it and soon had finished them all. When the jug came round, Mack took it and drank. William was right, it had grown on him.

They were discussing Underwood's strange disappearance. The Smith brothers and War Haskew had borrowed Floyd Norris's hounds and let them get a snootful of one of Massey's shirts. "Damn thing was so ripe," War said, "*I* could've tracked him by it." The dogs had gone to an old barn and circled around inside it, then headed out toward a pond over on the back part of Massey's property and bounded off into the water to their shoulders and stood howling. The men couldn't see into the pond because of its thick coat of algae. They tried wading in but it got real deep real quick.

Then the talk turned to a bullfrog they'd encountered on the bank. "Big as a damn washpot," War Haskew said. "Buz here stobbed at him with a stick and, I swear, the frog bit the stick."

"It didn't," William said.

"Tell 'em," War said.

"Damnedest thing I ever seen," Huz said.

"Let's finish talking about Massey," Tooch said, "before we start discussing the size of frogs."

"You think he got so corned he stumbled off in that pond?" War asked. "The damn goop's so thick he'd have to dig down in it to drown."

"He could just be off on another one of his drunks," Huz said. "It won't be the first time. When he gets a notion to drink hard he likes to be off in the woods, nobody around to interrupt him."

Buz was shaking his head. He looked at his brother and wiggled his shoulders, moved his hands as if he were pulling in an invisible

176

rope and then flattened them out and lowered them slowly down along his belly, hips, thighs. Raised his eyebrows.

"What's he saying?" Tooch asked.

"Says old Massey's at the bottom of that pond, all right. Says them hound dogs of Norris's is smarter than any of y'all."

They looked at one another.

"The widow says if you fire a cannon over a body of water, a corpse will rise," William said.

Huz said, "Where you keep your cannons, Tooch?"

"Hell," War Haskew said. "Maybe that damn frog et him."

The jug came Mack's way and he took a drink and passed it on.

The next order of business, Tooch said, if they were done talking about Massey, was that some imported niggers were picking Joe Anderson's field and two white fellows were overseeing it on horseback—guards armed with rifles. Lev thought they should ambush the horsemen and scare the niggers off. Send a message back to town.

"Be hard to ambush 'em," Tooch said. "That's what they'll be expecting. I done been over there watching 'em. No matter how hot it gets, they stay out in the middle of the field. Don't sit on their horses, neither. Just huddle in the middle of the niggers, like it's the niggers doing the protecting. Be a hard shot to make, and once you miss, the jig's up."

"Then we won't miss," Lev said.

"What if we get 'em on the way to gin," War Haskew asked. "Bide our time."

They decided to discuss it later, though Lev hated to wait. He said he hadn't killed anybody in a long time.

Mack, Floyd, and the three Norris boys drew to the end of the harvest in late October. At midday on the last day of the month Mack stood at the full wagon, a thing like pride filling his lungs.

"You can go on back," Floyd told him. "We'll get the short rows."

Mack lingered. Not knowing why. "Good-bye," he said.

But Floyd had walked off, toward his house. From where he stood, Mack could see the mound where the man's wife was buried. The cross stuck at its head a simple limb, two little branches trimmed into arms. He took off his hat in respect and saw he'd sweated the band through. He looked toward where the fellow with the naked lady box had appeared. He looked down at his hands, changed now to the hands of a man, a killer's hands but also the hands of a pardoner, Bit Owen alive and out in the world somewhere. In a week he would be sixteen years old. He put the hat back on and turned toward the store.

INTO
THE
BREECH

November 1898

I

ON BUSINESS IN COFFEEVILLE, Waite went up the steps at McCorquodale's. The storeowner's son, Carlos, stood a few feet inside the door with a broom over a little circle of dust, ash, and other debris he'd swept up. When Waite opened the door the wind came in past his legs and again when he closed it.

"Sorry," Waite said, nodding at the dust. "But it sure is a blustery one today. Reckon it's fixing to come a rain."

Carlos wore a pristine white apron. "It's okay," he said, corralling the dust again.

Waite paused. "When you leave for college?"

"After the busy season," the boy answered. "I was supposed to go in August but Daddy needed me here."

Waite nodded but thought it odd. McCorquodale insisted on overseeing every operation of his store and his tenant farms as closely as possible. He had Obbie, a colored man, working here in the store with him and another few fellows on the payroll. Didn't seem like he needed Carlos at all, not enough to keep him out of school, anyhow. All Waite had ever seen the boy do was sweep.

"Your daddy," Waite asked him. "He here?"

"He's in the office."

Waite went down the length of the aisle to the glass door, where he could see McCorquodale, bent over his desk and swatting at a fly. He knocked on the door and McCorquodale glanced up and waved him in. He sat behind a rolltop desk with its pigeonholes bulging with papers and receipts. Waite's office was neat, in fact it had become a joke with him and Oscar: "Where you keep the possum turds?" Oscar would ask, popping his head in. "Filed under O,"

181

Waite would respond. "O?" Oscar would say. "For what?" "For Oscar."

Waite stepped into the office and closed the door behind him and then leaned against it and folded his arms and waited. McCorquodale was listing figures in his long green ledger and held up a finger so Waite wouldn't speak and lose him his place. It looked like a hell of a lot of numbers. Must equal a hell of a lot of money. When the storekeeper came to the end of a column, he put down his pencil, took off his glasses, and gave Waite his attention. "Afternoon, Sheriff."

"McCorquodale," Waite said. "I won't keep you, just wanted to see what you mean to do about Joe Anderson's widow."

"Do about her."

"Yeah. Their cotton was just about ready to pick, way I understood it, before the women left. Ought to be about finished now. Gone to market."

"Just about all picked, all right." McCorquodale noticed a slip of paper on the floor by his chair and reached for it. He put his glasses back on and frowned as if trying to place it. The fly flew across his desk and he flipped a backhanded hand at it.

"Well?" Waite leaned against the door. "I reckon what I'm asking you is whether or not they'll get their share of the money, now that it's all picked. Looked like a pretty good crop."

McCorquodale was bothered by the paper. Then he seemed to remember that Waite was there. "What? Oh, no, Sheriff. The way I structure my contracts with liens is if the borrower or his beneficiaries leave in the middle of the season they forfeit their part of the gross. It's standard."

"These seem like nonstandard circumstances, though," Waite said. "Anderson being killed and all."

McCorquodale looked up. He leaned back thoughtfully in his chair. "Well, I reckon if there was a fellow that, say, killed somebody, shot 'em in the head, say, but he had him a real, real good

182

reason, you'd let him go. Sort of bend the rules?" He paused. Then said, "No, you wouldn't, and I can't either. Fact is, I had to find me some colored folks to pick that crop. Last minute. Had to leave here and deal with a mess I ought not to have had to deal with. Pay a bunch of folks I ought not have to. And pay 'em higher wages than usual, too, cause they had me over a barrel and was afraid to go out there near where that thing happened to the colored church. Wound up sending two of my overseers to guard 'em with rifles. Got 'em out there right now. Where you think all that money's coming from?"

"It just seems like you could deduct them costs out of their end. Give 'em something, at least. That woman lost her husband. Them girls their daddy."

"Way I see it, Sheriff, if you'd done your job in the first place and run that gang off, then Anderson never would've been killed, and we wouldn't even be having this discussion."

Waite came off the door. "Okay," he said. "But since you feel so doggone ready to tell me how to do my job, let me tell you how you might ought to start doing yours. You might ought to go a little easy on folks, especially with the times being so tight."

"Is that right? Is that how I ought to comport myself?"

"Just some advice, Ernest." He turned to go.

"Wait," the storeowner said. "I got one for you, since you're here. Floyd Norris. He's delinquent. I've already swore out the papers, they'll be in your office tomorrow or the next day."

Waite couldn't believe it. For a moment he didn't know what to say. Then he said, "Sure thing. Yeah, I'll go foreclose on him. Run another family off. Fellow lost his wife and had to farm his baby out. Yeah, I'll go out there and boot him off his property."

McCorquodale took off his glasses again. "Sheriff," he said, "you might think I'm the villain here, but I'm not. I'm just a businessman, trying to get by. Working within the boundaries of the laws you're supposed to protect. I got my own debts—"

But Waite had gone, slamming the door so hard the glass in it shook.

He sat half drunk on his porch holding his pistol in one hand and a dead cigar in the other. A bottle of bourbon beside his chair leg. Sue Alma came out for the third time and stood looking down on him.

"Billy.

"Billy."

She stood a moment longer. He knew she was worried past her anger. She didn't allow drinking in her house or on her porch or even, hell, within her sight, and here he was doing it right out where the neighbors could see. She'd always known he did it on occasion but they'd had a quiet understanding that he'd keep it hidden and she'd pretend not to know. Some men had women they visited, he had his liquor.

"Billy."

He looked at the small table beside his chair, at the sealed paper smudged from his pocket that he should have already delivered to Floyd Norris but had put off now for two days. Put off. A thing he'd never before done all the years he'd been pinned to his badge. His goddamn badge. Its weight inside his coat was a thing he'd grown accustomed to, a thing he wasn't aware of—like some internal organ going about its silent duty. And like some dutiful organ it operated a part of him, did for him certain things he'd not have otherwise done. As if his conscience had become grown about the badge and shaped around it like trees he'd seen with bark grown over metal signs nailed to their trunks, the sign as much a part of the tree as leaf or root.

"Billy," she said.

He put the cigar in his pocket and reached down beside him and picked up the bottle and drank from it. Sue Alma put her hand over her mouth and made a noise not among her regular noises, a sort of hurt gasp, and turned and went inside. She didn't slam the door. Was that the first time he'd raised a bottle directly in front of her? He looked back at the door. He supposed so. You'd think a man would care about such a milestone, when you insult your wife perhaps to the point of never being able to uninsult her. The truth was he could have raised his hand and slapped her across the face and she'd have been hurt less than she was by his brazen whiskey drinking. Yet he didn't give a good goddamn anymore. His coat hung by the door with the badge pinned inside it, and now, for the first time in his career as a sheriff, he could feel the metal as an organ gone bad, liver mossy or kidneys hardened, heart flattened out and its rivers of blood dammed off.

He took another drink.

He didn't know what time he'd passed out in the chair, but when he woke dawn was breaking and his pistol lay in the yard. His neck ached and his head, when he moved it, throbbed. He got up slowly, ignoring the empty bottle, and retrieved the gun and went inside. Sue had slept in her clothes on the couch by the window. First time for that, too. Her face gray and etched with the lines from the rough damask upholstery. The very least he could do was go back outside and pick up the bottle and carry it across the road and throw it in the bushes.

This Saturday, most of the cotton picked, was a big ginning day and a day when the rural folks rode into Grove Hill, wagons clogging intersections and the streets growing foul with horse and mule shit. Rain had made it worse, muddying everything, and industrious merchants had lain boards across the side roads in an attempt to keep the mud contained. A failing effort. One clerk had unscrewed the head from a push broom and affixed it upside down to his porch

185

floor so folks could kick the stiff bristles to get the mud out of their soles before entering his store.

With his coat collar turned up, Waite walked his horse along the street, nodding to men and touching the brim of his hat to ladies. At the south end of town there was a long line of wagons backed up with farmers white and black standing and talking and occasionally bending to spit as the gin ginned. For a long while there was a halt while a belt was replaced with several white farmers observing and offering advice to the black man who went about his work politely, stopping to consider each nugget of advice and even to try a thing suggested, only, in the end, to go back to his own way of doing what he'd done dozens of times before, the gin soon back to work and the wagon line advancing slowly in the light rain.

Two fellows approached Waite where he sat looking down from the saddle. He thought he knew them but couldn't place their names.

"Sheriff," the first said. He kept popping his suspenders. They looked new.

"Morning, gentlemen," Waite said.

"That son-of-a-bitch," the second man said. "You better go check his scales."

"The scales is fine," Waite said.

The men looked at each other and then turned and went back through the mud to their wagons. They said something to another farmer who looked at Waite and shook his head. He knew he smelled like whiskey. He wished he could just sit on a porch with Bit not talking and waiting for noon when he could drink again.

It thundered and he looked up.

After a few minutes he judged everything in order and worked his way back through the maze of wagons to the hotel. He dismounted, held on to a post, and tried to scrape his boots clean one at a time. A buggy went past behind him, too fast, and flung water onto his shoulders. He turned in a rage to dress down the person but they'd gone by already, a man with a woman at his side, both looking happy. Waite's rage left him, taking with it his energy, and he sagged against the post. His head continued to throb but the fact of it was he wanted another drink. He looked at his pocket watch. Ten-thirty. He had a bottle in his locked drawer back at his office and headed that way.

Halfway down the sidewalk he came face-to-face with Floyd Norris, his three boys in tow. They were barefooted, high-stepping in the mud, their feet enormous clay molds. Norris looked away from Waite's eyes and would have gone on past but the sheriff said, "Norris. You got a minute?"

He stopped and waited, looking off down the street. Each boy held a peppermint stick, their points licked sharp as ice picks.

"I got a paper for you," Waite said, glad he'd thought to bring it this morning. Give it to him now, make sure he understood it, and go to his office and get that drink. He handed it to the farmer who took it and folded it and placed it in his pocket.

"Can you read?" he asked Norris.

The farmer looked down at his boys. "Y'all go on to the corner yonder and wait."

They slurped on down the sidewalk. The littlest one looked back at Waite with his peppermint stick in his mouth and waved. Waite thought, quite simply, that the world was a terrible place.

"Can you read, Norris?" Waite asked again.

"Just go on tell me what it says," the farmer said. He was looking across the street at a window display of toy wooden blocks with letters on them.

"Says you're to appear in court for not paying McCorquodale his lien money."

The farmer blinked. "I paid him once," he said. "He wants me to pay again?"

"Well. I don't know the fine print, but it says you ain't paid. He swore it out."

Norris gritted his teeth. "He's a goddamn liar."

Waite nodded down the sidewalk so that Norris would see the black family, six children holding a rope along behind their daddy, coming up. Norris ignored them and they passed him and went on.

"Morning, Sheriff," the man said.

"Good morning," Waite answered.

"A goddamn lie," Norris snapped.

Some of the children looked back.

"Well, it ain't for me to decide," Waite said. "But if I was you, I'd be there. Else they'll swear out a warrant for your arrest."

Without ever having looked at Waite, Norris walked off. Waite hurried after him and stepped in front of him. Now Norris looked up.

"Give me your pistol," Waite said.

Norris stared at him. "You reckon I'm fixing to ride over to Coffeeville and shoot him?"

"It's a damn good possibility," Waite said, thinking I wouldn't blame you either. He held out his hand. "Give it to me. You can get it back later. I'll keep it safe."

Norris made a move to step around him and Waite grabbed his shoulder. There was a tussle and they fell together in the street, both facedown in the mud. They struggled briefly while a crowd gathered, no one eager to step in and help and get muddy himself. Waite aware of rolling in shit. Then someone pulled Norris away by his collar. Waite pushed to his feet, hardly able to catch his breath. He slipped and fell again. He got to his knees, heaving. Down the block Norris's three boys stood watching. Somebody asked Waite was he okay and he nodded, still unable to speak. He held the pistol, by now nothing but a shapeless slug of mud. Norris was furious. He tore from the interloper's grip and leapt to his feet and flung mud from his fingers. He yelled swearwords at them all. Waite let him.

"You can," he panted, "pick this up, later."

Waite left them and walked away, not bothering to avoid the mud, his vision darkening at the edges. He thought he might vomit.

He saw Oscar standing with Harry Drake beside the livery watching him, their mouths agape. He ignored them.

The hearing was a week later, at the courthouse. Oscar had recused himself and the circuit judge presided. Waite sat in the second row brooding over the week he'd had, not a word from Oscar, more silence from Sue Alma, and three more good drunks. Somebody had taken a few shots at McCorquodale's overseers and the black folks picking cotton but nobody had been hurt; McCorquodale had sent more men out and started a petition to get Waite fired.

Twice since then Sue had said she was going to her sister's and packed, but both times she'd unpacked, crying, and made dinner for him and they'd eaten in silence. He kept waiting for a visit from Oscar, but, thankfully, it hadn't yet come.

He sank now in his seat in the courtroom hoping no one would talk to him. An hour ago, Floyd Norris had come to his office and asked, "Can I get my gun back?"

Waite hadn't risen from behind his desk. "You can after the hearing's over."

Norris turned as if this were the answer he'd expected and started to walk out.

Waite said, "Norris."

He stopped but didn't look back.

"Do yourself a favor in there today," Waite told him. "Behave. I know you don't give a damn for the process, but—"

Now Norris did turn. His eyes were small. "How you know what I give my damns for, Billy Waite? I'm here, ain't I? Didn't I come all the way back over here? If I didn't give a damn for your courtroom do you think I'd be here now?"

"Well," Waite said. "I'm sorry if I misjudged you."

"You and me both know it won't be the only misjudging of today, don't we?"

After Norris left, Waite got the man's pistol out of his locked drawer. He'd already cleaned the mud off and oiled its cylinders. Just a plain cheap six-shooter with one of the wooden grips missing.

The courtroom was crowded and hot but with the chill outside it felt good. Soon the judge came in, a fat man with muttonchops and wearing a hunting coat and hat. The fact was, Waite liked him a lot, had deer hunted with him on occasion. He sat down and removed the hat and took a pair of eyeglasses from his pocket and laid them on the table before him and things commenced. In the witness chair McCorquodale simply said that though Norris had always been a reasonably reliable farmer when it came to business, he hadn't paid him the money due by the date on the contract. In fact, he was five days late when the papers were filed. He was a lot later now. McCorquodale's lawyer, Harry Drake, asked a few more questions and McCorquodale answered them. As Norris had no lawyer, the storeowner was excused.

Drake asked Norris to proceed to the chair. He rose. He wore patched overalls and had to be told to remove his hat. After he'd been sworn in Drake asked him if he knew Ernest McCorquodale.

Norris folded his thin arms, slouching in the chair.

From the bench, the judge said, "Answer the question, Mr. Norris."

"Y'all know goddamn well I know him."

The judge slammed his gavel and the pair of eyeglasses he'd set on the desk rattled. "You'll not blaspheme in this court, Mr. Norris. One more cussword and I'll hold you in contempt."

"You'll hold *me* in contempt."

Waite lowered his head and rubbed the bridge of his nose. He had Norris's pistol in his pocket and very quietly removed it and ejected the cylinder and shook the cartridges (there were only four) into his fist.

The judge was glaring at Norris, then looked over at Oscar, who shook his head.

"Just proceed then, Mr. Drake," the judge said.

"Thank you, Your Honor." To Norris: "Did you borrow money from Mr. McCorquodale to finance your cotton crop?"

"Yeah."

"You heard Mr. McCorquodale's testimony, did you not?"

"I heard his lies."

"Hold on, Your Honor. I'm not interested in this man's accusations. If lies were told, this proceeding will find them out."

"Right," the judge said. "Mr. Norris, you'll answer the questions without casting aspersions on Mr. McCorquodale's honor."

"*Aspersions,*" Norris spat. He looked over at McCorquodale.

"Do you know what 'aspersions' means?" Drake asked.

"I can figure it out."

"What His Honor means is that—"

"I said I can figure it out."

"Then I'll just repeat my question from before. You heard Mr. McCorquodale's testimony, didn't you?"

"I done said I did."

"You heard him state, under oath, Mr. Norris, that you never paid him the lien on your cotton crop."

"I heard it."

"Heard him say that whenever he takes a payment of any kind, from anybody, he always writes them a receipt, and his employees— one of which is willing to testify, if we need him—are instructed to write receipts, too. Can you, then, produce a receipt as evidence of your claim?"

"No."

"Why not?"

"Cause he never give me one."

"Never give you one, you say?" Drake turned dramatically to the gallery of faces who'd come to watch the hearing. "Most of us in this room have done business with Ernest McCorquodale, walked in his store out in Coffeeville and bought some groceries

191

or a bridle or"—he winked—"a pinch of snuff. So let me ask y'all a question: Have any y'all ever had a business transaction with Ernest or any of his hired help, large or small, when you did not receive a receipt?"

The people exchanged glances. But nobody said they hadn't.

"I've got an exhibit here," the lawyer said, going to his table and opening a satchel and emptying forth dozens of slips of paper. He took a handful from the pile and raised them toward the ceiling, two or three floating from the bunch and landing on the floor. "I'm something of a pack rat," he said. "Never throw anything away, as you can see. Drives the little lady crazy."

Laughter.

"But all these here are receipts from Ernest McCorquodale's store. Here's one, let's see, pair of brogans, August 4, 1889, half a dollar. Half a dollar?" He feigned indignation. "Well, nobody ever said old Ernest's merchandise was cheap."

More laughter, even McCorquodale's chin moved in a subdued grin.

"Here's another one, dated last March, for five pounds of flour and a bag of sugar. That must've been when my luscious Darlene was making me a red velvet birthday cake." He patted his suspendered belly. "Probably a lot of receipts in here for sugar and flour."

Even the judge chuckled this time. In the back of the room, Waite watched Norris. It had crossed his mind the man might bring in another pistol.

"But," Drake said to Norris, holding the slips of paper before his face, "you claim you never got a receipt from Mr. McCorquodale."

Norris, seemingly unperturbed, said, "Would it be okay, Judge, if I was to say my side of the story? Or is this slick here gone keep on pulling his fancy parlor tricks?"

The judge nodded. "Go ahead, Mr. Norris. Let's hear what you have to say. Is this okay with you, Counsel?"

"Absolutely, Your Honor, by all means." He waved his handful of paper slips at the audience and shook his head comically and got another, smaller laugh. Crossed the room and sat down, dabbing his forehead with a handkerchief.

Norris waited until the room had grown very quiet before he began to talk. Outside, a dog barked.

"I come up to McCorquodale's to pay him. It was raining. Cold. I give him his wad of money and watched him count it. He said he'd write me up a paper the next day and have a nigger run it out to me. Well, I never seen no nigger, all I seen was that sheriff yonder saying they's gone foreclose on me if I didn't pay up."

The judge took five minutes to find in favor of McCorquodale. Norris stood up and was told to sit back down. He did. He was told he had thirty days from the date of the original court order to either pay McCorquodale his money or to vacate his farm.

"And when I say 'vacate,' " the judge said, "I'd advise you to vacate the county as well."

Norris turned before the judge had completed this statement and found Waite's eyes and stared into them until the sheriff glanced away. The cartridges in his hand had grown so hot he wondered if they might not discharge.

II

On his birthday, Mack lay on his back on a burlap bag underneath the wagon, greasing its axle, surely God's nastiest work. He could see the mare's legs at the front, she would lift a hoof now and then and stamp and nicker, the air vivid and strangely lit around them with the energy of a coming storm. He lay on his side looking out at how the color of things seemed a shade wrong, as if light had somehow come too quickly at dawn and caught the earth unawares. Leaves not yet stripped by the late-fall chill rasped on their limbs and fallen ones scraped over the croquet court, through or around the wickets and over the road into the picked field which seemed in the strange light a place where thousands of men had bled and died. He'd heard if you stood on certain battlefields you could sense the deaths that had occurred there, the way the widow could feel a ghost in a room. Perhaps in killing a man you began to see this other-worldly light on a more regular basis, perhaps the soles of your feet became conductors of supernatural energy and you drew the death upward through your bones.

Around the corner someone walked up the steps. He heard footsteps over the porch. Then he heard the door open and simultaneously the bell. But it wasn't somebody going in; Tooch had come out.

"Howdy, Floyd," Tooch said. "You want to come in or just stand out here on the porch."

Floyd said, "Well."

The door opened again as they went inside. Mack slid out from under the wagon and pulled himself up using its sideboards.

Finished, he wiped his hands and sealed the grease keg, rolled it to its spot by the anvil. He used the horse to back the wagon into its place and unharnessed her, led her to the stall at the rear of the shed. He brushed her down, trying to calm her, her hair bristling as the first invisible rain side-wound its way under the shed and wet his cheeks and the backs of his hands. He told the mare she'd be fine and scratched her withers and set a bucket of oats before her and closed the stall door.

He paused on the porch before going in. Earlier in the afternoon Tooch had handed Mack his pocketknife and instructed him to sharpen both blades without saying why, though Mack had suspected the reason. As the storm gathered out beyond the trees across the field, he'd spent an hour on the porch steps oiling the knife and cleaning it with a chamois, and then with a new flintrock from the box under the counter he'd given it an edge like no knife

194

had ever seen, had held it against the graying sky and imagined it could slice a rock like a potato, cut a rifle barrel into washers.

Inside he saw Floyd talking quietly to Tooch in the back. Both men looked at him as the bell rang but he'd learned to go about his work as if unaware of the presence of other people. He strained to hear what they were saying but heard nothing except the breath of their whispers.

Half an hour later, though he hadn't been told to, he started counting buttons in the corner where the mail desk was. The rain fell hard now, a steady patter with intermittent gusts against the window like water slung from a bucket. The store had grown dark as the storm and night both came on, the only light the dull throb from the stove and the yellow cast of a lantern on the counter. As he counted, Mack looked out where trees and the road and the field of stalks bared by lightning seemed yet another shade of unnaturalness, a glimpse into some nether place or the setting of a dream. When he saw a soaked Lev James dismounting his waterlogged mule in such a glimpse, both Lev and the mule seemed to belong in that place, and when a second burst caught him ascending the stairs holding his coat closed at his throat, Lev looked up and saw Mack watching him, and the boy's nape hair rose electrically as if he'd been touched by a ghost.

Lev stomped inside in a swirl of wind, unloosing his overall straps, water puddling beneath him. Without even looking at Mack he unbuttoned his coat and peeled it off, hung it on the coatrack to dry.

"I swear," he said, "it's done run out of cats and dogs and now it's raining jackasses and bulls."

The others, all equally wet, arrived soon after, except for Massey Underwood, who was still missing. What early talk there was concerned the storm. Mack stayed at his post by the door.

Within half an hour it was time. William sat on a sugar crate by the apple barrel, trying to get a cigarette built from his wet papers and tobacco. War Haskew was beside him drying his Remington lever action with an oiled rag, whistling "The Rose of Alabama," and tapping his foot—he seemed the only man whose temper hadn't been fouled by the weather. Huz Smith sat in a chair by the stove and his brother leaned against the counter, smoking a cigarette. Lev paced the aisles. Tooch came from behind the counter, lifting the movable section and ducking a little, holding the clay jug marked with a crude drawing of a cottonmouth. He tossed it to Kirk who unplugged the cork and took a goodly snort and passed it along to William with the cork dangling from its string.

Tooch passed the stove and bent to stoke the coals with the Yankee sword he kept for that purpose, a tradition begun long ago by Arch. He returned the sword to its corner, straightening in time to catch the jug William pitched to him. He hefted the weight of it, then got a cup from a peg on the wall and poured a shot. He sipped it, turned.

"We got us a guest tonight," he said. "As y'all have noticed. Welcome back, Floyd."

All eyes went to the back of the room, following Tooch's gaze. Floyd, his hat in his hands before him, came forward. Lev scowled at him as if the man's dry clothes were an insult. Someone tossed Floyd the jug and he set it atop his bent arm with his thumb hooked in the thumbhole and raised it and drank.

"Obliged," he said.

"Get you another drink," Tooch told him, and he did.

Chairs and stools were scooted back so Floyd could join the circle around the woodstove.

"Floyd's told me a tale tonight," Tooch said, "that I want y'all to hear. And then I want us to decide what we ought to do." He nodded to the small farmer.

Floyd took another mighty swig and in a quiet voice began telling how they all knew he'd had a good and longstanding business relationship with Ernest McCorquodale—going on five years—and though there'd been ups and downs, it had more or less been a good arrangement. But now, he said, looking at the floor, something had happened.

McCorquodale, he said, was using the law to cast him off the land. Evict him.

"It was a week ago," he said. He reached into his overalls pocket and withdrew a corncob pipe and placed the empty stem in his mouth, began to chew on it. "Was a rainy night. Nothing like this here one, though. But my lien was due and I figured if I didn't go on in and pay the son-of-a-bitch, he'd start compounding my damn interest. I walked over to Coffeeville and went to his door and knocked and he opened it and said, 'You go to the back,' and slammed the door in my face."

"He sent you to the back?" War Haskew asked.

"Course he did," said Lev. "Like a goddamn nigger."

"Finish your story," Tooch said.

Mack listened as Floyd told how he kicked through the mud around the house and waited by the back door for a minute, two, three, his coat heavy with rain and a rivulet falling off the brim of his hat, Floyd at the back steps, waiting until McCorquodale finally opens the door and without even saying Good evening just sticks out his hand. Floyd offers up the sheaf of soaked bills, the whole of the debt, and McCorquodale takes it and steps back out of the weather and closes the screen door. He licks his thumb and counts the notes and counts them again, Floyd waiting in the rain all the while. Satisfied it's all there, McCorquodale says through the screen how he doesn't have any receipts here, they're at the store, and he'll get Floyd one as soon as he can. Then he shuts the door. Floyd stands for a moment, waiting, then gathers the folds of his coat at his neck and turns and walks home.

And then, a week later, no sign of anything wrong, when Floyd has taken his boys to town to fit them for shoes, the sheriff stops him and gives him a paper.

The storm had settled some, the thunder gone, and now the room seemed very quiet. Just a smattering of rain over the roof.

"How come you didn't come to us first?" War Haskew asked.

"I wanted it legal," Floyd said. "Didn't want to involve y'all in my business."

"But you are now," Lev said.

Tooch had lit a cigar. "His business is our business, Lev. He signed our paper, didn't he? In blood." He looked at Floyd. "You're one of us, even though you've been on the outside. Till now."

"I've had it," Floyd said. "They mean to put me out of my house. Off my land, where I buried—" He stopped and looked toward the front of the store. "Mean to put them young ones out, too. I been on that place near ten years. Done just about broke even. And now—"

"You're a hard worker, Floyd," Tooch said. "Hardest worker in this room. Nobody here will deny that." He left his stool and stepped between the dark smoky bodies of the grumbling men and went up front behind the counter. When he returned he had a tin of Bull Durham pipe tobacco. He offered it to Floyd.

"No," he said. "I thank you, though."

Tooch took the man's wrist, turned his hand over, and set the tin in his hand.

"I can't pay for it," Floyd said, not raising his eyes.

"You ain't got to," Tooch told him.

Floyd turned the package in his hands. He looked up. "I want to pull the trigger," he said, his eyes bright in the stovelight. "And then you'll have somebody else on that list say I was with him. Say we was playing dominoes. Say I won."

Tooch narrowed his eyes and pondered it. "No," he said. "When McCorquodale dies, they're gone put it on you, so you'll need a damn solid story. We'll decide who kills McCorquodale."

"I'll do it," Lev said. "I hate that son-of-a-bitch."

"Is there a fellow from town you don't hate, Lev?" Huz asked.

The jug made another round. Floyd loaded the bowl of his pipe and someone handed him a match. He struck it on the side of the stove and got the tobacco glowing, smoke framing his face.

The rain had paused now and the room was absolutely quiet.

"We began this organization," Tooch said, "as a tool to get some revenge for Arch. To get those fat-cat sons-of-bitches in Grove Hill. Well, we been going slow. Been gathering our wealth. But I propose, fellows, that it's time we make a big move. A bold one. Announce our intentions."

A mumble of assent.

"We're gone need some more men, though, ain't we," War Haskew said. "If we mean to do that? Especially with Massey gone."

"We've got two here tonight," Tooch said, "who're ready to join us."

They all turned to Floyd, who nodded. "I'm ready," he said. "I ought to done joined up. Y'all knowed my reasons for not but my reasons is changed."

"Who's the other fellow?" Lev asked, and then he and the rest looked to where Mack sat, his hands full of buttons, one by one dropping back into the box.

"Boy," Tooch said. "Come here."

Mack came over the creaking boards.

"How old are you, boy?" Tooch asked.

"I'm sixteen."

"As of when?" Lev asked.

"Just today."

War Haskew began to whistle "Happy Birthday," but no one laughed.

Lev didn't look too happy but said nothing further.

"Your brother's made a solid case for you," Tooch said. "He says you'll behave as you ought to, and from what I've seen of your work this past year I believe you're a sturdy, dependable fellow. Are you prepared to join us?"

"Yes, sir," he said.

"Then it's time for the swearing-in," Tooch said.

The men surrounded Mack and Floyd. Mack felt a hand touch his back, kindly. William. Someone blew out the lantern. Tooch stepped into the circle and faced them. He set down his cup and unfolded the longer blade of the Case pocketknife he kept in his watch pocket and presented it to Mack. He took it without hesitation, would have known it blind among a thousand similar knives. He touched the blade to the tip of the pointing finger of his right hand, not having decided whether a horizontal or vertical cut would be best. A thing he hadn't even considered.

"Slow down, boy," Tooch told him.

Mack wanted to look at them, their darkened forms, but he couldn't raise his eyes from the knife, his finger.

"This here is a commitment you won't be able to get out of once you sign up," Tooch went on. He placed a fatherly hand on his shoulder and squeezed it until Mack looked at him. "Are you willing to own up to the responsibility we're fixing to yoke upon you?"

"Yes, sir," he said.

Tooch looked at Floyd.

"Yeah," he said.

"Are you willing to kill, if given the order?"

"Yes, sir."

"Hell, yeah."

"Willing to die, if it comes to that?"

"Yes, sir."

"I reckon."

"In return, you'll get the protection of this inner circle, and of the larger circle without. Since Arch was murdered, we've all bunched together in this alliance, with the goal to set things right, and if we all get rich in the meantime, well, that's okay, too.

"If you ever tell any of what you'll learn, you'll forfeit your life. We'll all kill you. Do you understand that, Mack?"

"Yes, sir."

"Floyd?"

"I hear it."

Mack looked down. He felt William's gaze on his back. Suddenly he and his brother are sitting together on the sandy edge of the creek beneath the widow's house, their feet submerged, their lines stretching out toward the middle, bending with the slow current going south. William is fourteen, Mack ten. They've caught a mess of bream which pulls at the stringer stuck into the bank and they're happy because the widow will praise them when they go up for supper. When she calls them just before dark, when the shadows are stretching downhill, Mack is already looking forward to scaling the fish, he likes how when you scrape against the grain the scales fly off in tiny transparent chips that stick to your face, lodge in your hair. He and William always try to flick them into each other's mouths and laugh and the widow, watching, laughs, too. Yet when they bend to pull up the stringer it's heavier than it should be. A cottonmouth has attached itself to the fish, has swallowed one and half swallowed another. Delighted and terrified, they pull the stringer onto the bank and begin throwing stones at the snake as it tries to divest itself of the fish and find the water again. The brothers digging up stones and hurling them and laughing as the cottonmouth hisses and strikes.

"Swear your loyalty," Tooch said.

Mack raised his head. "I swear it." The knife sweat-slick in his fingers.

Floyd did likewise.

The men mumbled their assent, faces vivid for a second with lightning. Thunder drumming in the distance, like horses.

"Okay, then," Tooch said. "You know what comes next."

Mack held his breath. He touched the blade against his finger.

"Boy," War Haskew advised, "we found it's best to make your cut in your palm. Fingers don't yield enough blood, less you can't write and just gone mark you a X there."

"What's wrong with a goddamn X?" Lev asked.

201

War Haskew didn't answer but underhanded Lev the jug, which he caught and unstoppered and tilted back. He swirled the whiskey in his mouth and swallowed, belched.

"Ah, God," he said.

Now the jug came Mack's way as he readied the knife.

"Have you some of that inside lightning first, boy," Kirk said.

Mack nodded his thanks and set aside the knife and worked the cork out and hooked his thumb through the thumbhole and turned up the jug in the fashion he'd seen the other men do. He drank and swallowed. His eyes watered, his chest burned. His supper rose in a hot ball in his throat but he choked it down, his teeth gritty as though the whiskey had dredged up long-settled sand. Maybe it had. Maybe that was what it was for.

"Easy, now," Tooch said.

Someone relieved him of the whiskey. Taking the knife, he opened his right hand as wide as he could, the skin taut, and with the tip of the blade traced one of the lines in his palm. He felt no pain, as when you fire at a deer you hear no shot, feel no recoil from the gun.

"That's enough," Tooch said. "You get gangrene and you ain't gone do none of us any good." He reached into his shirt pocket for the folded paper, opened it with care and set it on the counter between them. "Go on."

It was half an old newspaper page—the one with the brief story of Arch's murder—men's names written in their own blood in two large, irregular columns. It also bore several cross or X marks of men unable to spell their names.

Mack stirred his left pointer finger in his cupped palm which had filled like an inkwell and wrote his first and then his last name on the vacant, corner spot Tooch indicated. As he dipped his finger in his blood again to finish, he felt Tooch's hand steady his shoulder. He was glad to pass the knife along to Floyd, who cut open his palm with no hesitation and scratched an X on the page. The others clapped the two of them on the back, laughter was general. There were stars popping in Mack's vision as the jug found its way into his good hand.

"Welcome," Tooch said to them both, "to Hell-at-the-Breech."

Mack sat and listened to the men talk. When they'd decided on the night of McCorquodale's assassination—the Yankee holiday of Thanksgiving, which the storeowner insisted on celebrating—it came time to decide who would go. Tooch went to his attic and returned with a sack full of heavy things. Croquet balls, Mack realized. Tooch had said that because Lev volunteered to kill McCorquodale, he would captain the raid. They'd decided two more men were needed, one to go with Lev and one to cover the back.

Tooch said, "There are six balls here. Lev is accounted for. Floyd can't go. Which leaves Huz, who'll be green. Buz is red. War, you're blue. William, orange. Kirk is black. Mack, our newest and still unproven, will be the yellow one." Tooch held the bag up, jostled the balls, then lowered it and submerged his arm into the folds and came out with two, orange and yellow.

"The Burke brothers," War Haskew declared. "By God, a family affair," and Mack felt his back slapped.

Later in the evening the store had grown stuffy with the odor of smoke and sweat so they'd gone out to the porch where the world seemed fresh and cool, washed. Overhead the moon shone so brightly it came through the smoke of a cloud. The men kept talking, planning the raid on McCorquodale. Mack was told he'd cover the back, the easier job, as it was his first time.

After a while he got up and went down the steps, reeling with a head full of drink, and as he was unbuttoning his trousers Tooch appeared beside him, unfastened his own pants, and began to piss.

"You've joined us now," he said, the sound of his water on the leaves, "and that's a sacred vow, boy. You've signed in blood and that's as hard a promise as you'll ever make. You believe that?"

He said he did.

"Good. Now I want you to be real honest with me, Mack. You're holding your pecker in your hand, and so that'll be the thing you swear upon."

"Yes, sir," he said, though suddenly the urge to piss had vanished.

"Supposed Oscar York comes out the back," Tooch said. "Will you shoot him?"

He thought.

"I'm glad you didn't answer fast," Tooch said. "The man that answers too fast is the man that don't consider things."

"I'll shoot him," he said.

"You sure."

"Yes, sir."

"How is it you're so sure?"

Mack gave up and buttoned his trousers. "Because if I don't, Lev will kill me."

Tooch was still pissing. "That's a fact. But fear's as good a reason as any for what we do, ain't it? And guess what. Even though that's your reason this time, next time you won't need that to be the reason. Cause ever time you do something, no matter what it is, if it's whacking a croquet ball or catching a fish, ever time you do a thing, the next time it's a mite easier. And finally you get to be good at catching fish, or playing croquet, or even killing. You get to where you can do it without thinking."

"Yes, sir," Mack said.

"And now," Tooch told him, shaking himself dry, fastening his own pants, "I got a mission for you."

"Who is it?" she called.

He said his name. Behind him, Tooch's horse nickered where he'd tied it. He'd ridden all the way over barely aware of the fine white mare between his legs, not even dismounting on the ferry.

"Who sent you?"

Lowering his voice, "Tooch did."

There was movement inside, her shadow under the door. "Tell me the word."

"Breech," he said.

The door opened. She was smoking a pipe. The dog looked him over, then returned to the corner by the hot stove and, circling several times, lay down.

"How old are you?" She was looking at him funny, into his eyes.

"Sixteen."

Her hair was more blond than he'd thought, her eyes blue. She wore a yellow dress with green and blue embroidered flowers on the bosom. Pleats below the waist. She was barefoot with small, dirty feet, a bandage around one toe.

"You know the arrangement, I expect," she said.

He had the dollar ready, it had sweated in his hand all the way over. He held the coin out and she took it and rubbed it between her thumb and forefinger.

"Well, then." She knelt before him, her legs disappearing beneath her dress, and undid his pants. His eyes rolled back in his head, he had no idea where the coin had gone. He thought his knees might give over. She had his pecker out, handling him roughly. He understood it was an examination, but, Lord, it felt *good*.

"This your first time, darling?"

"I don't remember." He felt dizzy.

"Alrighty." She stood and peered frankly into his eyes and looked his face over. Then she crossed the room pulling the dress over her head. Beneath it she was naked, her wide bottom bruised in the shape of hands and her thick calves shadowed with dark hair. She crawled onto the bed and slipped under the covers, but not before he'd seen her enormous, drooping titties and the black thatch of hair between her legs. He looked down and saw he'd refastened his pants. She moved her legs under the quilt. A tiny black speck—a flea—landed on the back of his hand and sprang away.

"Come on over here," she said, "Mack."

"How you know my name?"

"I know some things."

He took off his coat and hung it over a chair back, undid his suspenders and let them dangle along his thighs, began battling the buttons of his shirt.

"Slow down," she said. "It's only a boy's first time once."

He made his fingers undo the buttons at a reasonable rate. He told himself to remember every detail to think about later. He imagined telling it to William. Then knew he never would.

He had his shirt off, but suddenly a pang of shyness clapped around him. As if she understood, Annie turned away, blew out the bedside lamp, and let him undress in the dim light the stove gave.

He unlaced his shoes and stepped out of each, slid his pants down and left them crumpled atop the shoes, as if he'd been nabbed by the spirit world, snatched right down through the soles of his old brogans. Naked but for his hat and socks, he crawled onto the bed, the mattress soft under his knuckles but sandy, too. She put her hand on the back of his neck, pulled him close. Just the touch of her knees on his shoulders and the sweet-musty tang of a thing he'd never smelled before but recognized instantly sent him into ecstasy and without touching her he wet the sheets between her legs.

"Shit," he said, grabbing himself too late. His hand came away sticky. He was sick to his stomach in a sweet kind of way. His foot had a cramp.

She giggled. "It's okay, sugar. If I was made the way you was I'd a sprayed them sheets myself." Her knees bumped against him. "Just come set up here beside me. Let's talk a spell. In about fifteen minutes you'll be ready to go again. You got another dollar, ain't you?"

He lay stiffly beside her while she kindled her pipe. "Don't you sull up on me, now," she said. "I don't get too many good-looking boys in here with such nice clean peckers." She moved and lay against him. A fire-yellowed room with dull edges. "Dern, you stiff as a board." Her fingers touched his thigh and rubbed it up and down. "Relax, sugar. Close your eyes and breathe in and out." The thick smell of her pipe.

"Take off your hat."

He did.

"Hang it on the post yonder."

He hung it.

"Now pull off them old socks."

He pulled them off.

She had been stroking him and now, suddenly, he stiffened in her grip.

"Well goodness," she said. "That's the quickest one I ever laid a hand to. You been saving up, ain't you?"

She kept her pipe in her lips and rolled over, straddling him. Smoke had filled the dark corner where the bed was, making him dizzy. He nearly gagged. Her tongue appeared at the corner of her mouth as she reached between her legs and guided him inside with deft fingers and slipped all the way down atop him with a slurp. He'd imagined it might be a more snug fit but no matter. Warmth had kindled in his pelvis and he forgot to breathe. The bedsprings jingled beneath them as she wiggled and bucked and did a thing where she tightened around his pecker and he felt his insides rally and gather, heard her quick breathing, the smoke burning his eyes.

"You like it?"

"Yes, ma'am."

Later he lay beneath her, he could feel her paunch of belly touch his flat one as she breathed. He'd grown soft, still embedded inside her, but didn't want to leave her yet. She seemed to sense this, not moving. He gazed up at her, she was facing the stove. Here he lay and here she was on top of him, breathing with her mouth open and her false teeth out.

"I love you," he said.

She giggled.

Then she lay back onto the fronts of his thighs and put her ankles on his shoulders. It felt as if his whole middle—and hers—were a puddle of warm water.

"I love you," he repeated.

"Lord, if you ain't the sweetest thing," she said, giggling again.

Suddenly he was angry, gathering his legs to push her off. Then the dog began to bark.

"Damn it to hell," she said, rolling off him. His bare middle was very cold. He sat up and began groping for the covers.

A pounding on the door.

"What is it?" she called, feeling for the dress with her feet. The dog lay back down.

Laughter. "Tooch, he sent me." William's voice was full of whiskey. "Hell-at-the-Breech, woman."

"Hell's breech," Lev's voice added, "has done sent us all."

There followed a loud argument about who was going first, and then a scuffle, then William saying, "Okay, okay, let go, let go."

"Relax, sugar," Annie said to Mack, who was trying to pull his pants over his boots. "Let 'em whoop up on each other for a spell."

When Mack stepped out with his hair ruffled they cheered. William handed him the whiskey jug and slapped him on the cheek. Lev fired his shotgun into the air. Buz Smith was pissing off the edge of the porch and grinning toothlessly and wagging his bushy eyebrows. Annie at the door looked out—she was mopping the space between her legs with a rag—and said, "My lord. Look at the mob of you."

*   *   *

He walked uphill in the pine-scented air scratching at the fleabites on his arms, the weather cold on his cheeks. They'd all fallen asleep on her floor and he'd awakened in the afternoon. His privates were sore and chapped so he walked a tad bowlegged, something William had teased him about as he'd left. Come with me, he'd asked his brother, but William had said no, he was going with Lev, get more to drink.

How long since you seen her? he'd asked his brother.

She don't want to see us, William had said.

Do what?

But William wouldn't say why and Mack had gone on alone, leaving William the horse.

Not too much longer now before dark. The widow would be putting supper on, piling her logs in the fireplace, maybe a crock of collards stewing. Or did she even make supper anymore? What was her life like now that her boys were gone? An image came to him, her rising in the morning and putting on water for the tea leaves she liked but forgetting to drink it. Going to the porch and sitting in her rocking chair, gazing out over the valley below her house, the dog already gone, left because she'd stopped feeding it and herself, nothing underneath her dress and men's pants but bones now, the loose cloth and nothing else keeping her from blowing away.

He walked faster. But when he smelled the sulfur breeze he stopped. How long since he'd been here, to the house where he'd grown up, to the old woman who'd given herself to raising them? How many nights had she carried him in his babyhood, how many nights staying up with him as he couldn't breathe, talking to him, telling him stories, describing the ocean? And how had he repaid her? By killing a good man. He tried to recall Arch Bedsole's face and couldn't, could only picture Tooch, as if he were standing in front of Arch, blocking Mack's view.

The dog leapt from the porch when he came into sight, recognizing his walk or smell perhaps, and bounded toward him. He knelt and let her lick his cheeks and neck, unable to stop the laughter he barely recognized, the laughter of a boy.

When he at last pushed her away, marveling at how she'd forgotten that here with her was the murderer of her six pups just a year before, he saw the old woman standing on the porch, holding something in her arms.

"Granny," he called.

He walked so as to appear grown up, though he wanted to run to her and spring into her arms. And then he saw what she held.

The baby. He'd forgotten it.

"Macky," she said.

"Granny."

"You're back."

"Yes, ma'am. Guess I am."

They looked at each other and he felt a hole open within his chest, one he knew would never fully close.

"Tooch let me off," he began, "and I figured—"

"It's hard times," she said.

"What you mean, Granny?"

"The baby's sick." She looked down into its eyes. "Did you bring any food? Did you bring money for food?"

His cheeks grew hot. He'd spent the two dollars Tooch had given him on Annie.

"I ain't got any money," he admitted.

"You have a good time with that whore?"

He looked up, surprised. Ashamed. Then he looked off at the familiar trees—which ones hadn't he climbed? The dog nosed his thigh and he petted her head absently, unable to look up at the old woman. He felt he didn't know anything, that in the world he'd killed himself into there were no certainties, nothing you could count on. He was a thoughtless rotten thing.

She jiggled the baby. Its arm rose from the blanket and poked at her nose.

210

"I have something to tell you," he said, gazing into the dog's eyes, his reflection looking back out at him, upside down and as tiny as the face on a coin.

"Macky Burke," she said, "it's past this baby's feeding time. I've got to tend to him."

"This is important."

"So is feeding a baby."

"Yes, ma'am."

"You go on back to the store. If you ever come back you bring something."

"Yes, ma'am."

He turned to go, his eyes burning, his throat tight like he was being choked from the inside. As he walked, the dog trotting alongside him, he felt certain the widow would call for him to stop, that he would turn and hurry back and they'd look in each other's eyes and her face would warm to a forgiving smile.

The weather had turned, the week's worth of rain finally blown south, and the temperature had dropped slowly and steadily all day, settling now before dusk in the midthirties. Along the high ridges to the west a line of dead live oaks stood bare and black like splintered bones against the sunset, the bottom of the sky streaked with dark, red-edged clouds.

Last up the incline behind Lev and William, Mack noticed a fox squirrel on a high limb, how it rippled its tail and scratched itself with a hind leg, doglike, then, seeing them, vanished. He paused with his shotgun cradled in the crook of his left arm and blew into his cupped hands and rubbed some heat back into them. Swallowed more air into his dry throat and blinked at the old landscape made new, snugged his hat brim lower over his eyes and followed the others, cresting the ridge. Except for wind feathering through the higher branches this was a silent earth, the leaves underfoot slick and plastered to his shoes. He scraped the sole of one against a flat rock and then the other, his breath smoking in the blueing dark that seemed to edge down from the clouds and up from the ground, trapping a bleak red line of horizon in the middle, the eye of the world shutting.

He caught up with William and Lev where they'd stopped at the bottom of the next hollow, beside a pool of floating leaves. William knelt, resting his gun butt on the ground, and touched a track the shape of a flower.

"Y'all Burkes can shoot bobcats tomorrow," Lev growled. He fished around in the pockets of his loose-fitting knit pants and came out empty-handed. "Got some chew?"

William reached his fingers inside his jacket and found a plug of tobacco. He handed it over.

Lev produced the knife he'd taken from Joe Anderson and cut himself a large mouthful and stuffed it into his cheek. He worked his tongue slowly, folding the knife blade away, settling his gaze on Mack.

William got the tobacco back from Lev and bit himself a chunk and tossed Mack the rest. He took what was left, balled it up, and pushed it into his jaw with his thumb. It unfurled against the wall of his teeth and burned pleasantly.

"Remember what to do, boy?" Lev asked.

Mack nodded, not looking at him.

"Dammit. Tell me."

His breath misting, Mack repeated his part of the raid again, how he was to go silently upwind, around the McCorquodale house, hide, cover the back door, and give the signal when ready. Once the shooting began in the front, he was to drop any man who came out. He was not to shoot a white woman or child.

"When I hear y'all's call," he concluded, "I'm to hightail it to the creek behind Tooch's."

"You mess up, boy," Lev said, "and I'm the one you'll be

answering to. Not God nor your big brother nor even Tooch'll be able to keep me off you. Understand?"

"Yeah."

William leaned and spat into the pool. "He'll be fine, Lev. This knucklehead's a born killer."

Lev exhaled and unhooked a cloth bag from his belt. He loosened the drawstrings and dipped two fingers in and started to smear ashes on his cheeks. Mack and William took some, too, dabbing at themselves, faces, throats, backs of hands. Normally William wore a hood, and Mack had been curious to try his out, too, but Lev said when he captained a raid those in his command did as he did.

When they'd finished, Lev closed the bag and they surveyed one another, pointing at a speck of white on a nose, an ear. William turned Mack so his neck under his hairline could be touched up. Lev grunted in approval and spat, then shrugged and with his sleeve rubbed dry the double barrels of his Remington. He snapped it open for the third time in half an hour and fingered the red-colored loads, his knuckles black against the metal, then closed the shotgun quietly and rested it in the bend of his arm. He pulled the long Colt pistol from where he wore it concealed behind his back and ejected the cylinder one-handed and spun it with his thumb. The quick, minute clicking seemed loud and wrong in this fog-shrouded hollow. He had six bullets chambered, no slot left empty for safety. Satisfied, he replaced the revolver and watched William break open his new Parker twelve-gauge and Mack their dead father's sixteen.

Then they went on.

Single file, down another ridge and up the other side, the terrain softening to shadow as darkness leached what variations of gray remained, tree, ridge, and sky joined by tether of night, the two silent silhouettes in front of Mack swaying and bobbing like some movable, detached element of the landscape, a primitive force jarred into motion by aeons of erosion, or gravity, or the rising waters of a flood, yet a deliberate thing, too, a part of the earth but apart as well, as if a river, or falling rock, could form malice.

The creek at West Bend was swollen from all the rain, its old clay banks gone and loose new ones formed, as though the trees had taken a step back, giving these woods a quality Mack didn't trust. Lev went up and down along the water's edge, stomping his feet and muttering. At places the old creek had been easy to cross, get a good running start and leap. Now it was either wade through the fast chest-high water or find another crossing point. Lev, who wasn't fond of water since a childhood near-drowning incident, headed upstream, William trailing him and Mack trailing William.

On and on like that for too long. The water fast-moving and full of nasty-looking bubbles and dead leaves, turning in the current, sticks going past, the creek black in the near dusk, its bottom hidden.

Soon, as Mack followed the two men around a bend, a horizontal tree unmurked in the dusk, smoothly cut and perfectly felled over the water by some industrious creek-crosser, a good-size green loblolly pine, bowed a tad but no stobs to mar your passage, the rough bark good for traction, just a dozen quick steps over to the far side.

Lev paused, stroked his chin with his blackened fingers.

William stopped beside him. "I hereby declare this the Lev James Natural Bridge," he said, tapping it with the barrel of his gun.

The big man cocked his head and studied the tree. "Naw," he said. "We'll keep on alooking. One of us tumps over and falls in our disguises'll get rurned."

"We should of wore hoods," William said.

"Hell with your hood," Lev said. "Let's go on find some other way over."

"There ain't no time, Lev," William said. He leaned his shotgun against his shoulder like a soldier. "We got to get on, got to cross. We gone be late as it is."

"Goddamn weather," Lev mumbled, glaring at the ever-darker sky through the triangles and trapezoids the limbs made.

With no idea why he did it, Mack ambled past William and stepped gamely onto the tree. Arms out for balance, he tightroped across and soon regarded the blackened versions of his brother and Lev James from the north bank of the creek. Then, with a flourish, William was halfway over the tree, tottering a little, regaining his balance, taking the black hand Mack offered, and gaining land.

Now both faced Lev, in the deepening night already harder to see, tilting his broad head and eyeing the log like a man might a cottonmouth.

"Come on, Lev," William called, pointing west with his gun. "We got to skedaddle."

"No way in devil's hell," Lev growled, looking upstream and down, even glancing into the air overhead as if he might scale a tree and swing across on a vine. He took off his hat and the white bald spot shone pale as the moon.

"Old McCorquodale ain't gone wait," William called. "Maybe me and Macky ought to go on do the job and meet you back here."

"The hell," Lev said. He replaced his hat. Took a deep breath, as if he meant to duck underwater, and felt for the log with his foot like a blind man. Then pulled the foot back and seemed to be reconsidering. Mack's mind flashed other instances of airborne Lev James, sailing out of a skiff, off a bluff, headfirst from a hayloft. What bone other than his neck hadn't he broke?

William elbowed Mack in the ribs, as if to say, You know he's gone fall, and I know he's gone fall, and *he* knows he's gone fall. It's just a matter of not laughing when he does.

Mack glanced downstream, and when he looked back Lev was testing the log. He glowered over as if he might shoot them both, then came forward in an apelike crouch, clutching his shotgun. Mack remembered the peddler Lev had killed, the man facedown in his grave, dirt over his neck, hands, torso. Lev took a step. Good so far. Another. He still hadn't breathed.

Then it happened. His left foot came down askew and skidded a little, and when he fell he fell quickly, a mirror image of every other fall he'd taken in a lifetime of cruel gravity, a serene surrender, perhaps the only grace allowed him, to plunge without fighting his own awry existence, his arms and legs unflailing, body relaxed, his lips pinched shut in an angry line and his white narrow eyes watching for the laughter Mack and William didn't dare show.

He went under and immediately came up, holding his hat in place, standing in water to his chest. The shotgun was dry, and, impressed, Mack realized it had never gone under. Lev began to struggle against the current, and the brothers reached to pull him out. Mack nearly laughed when, at last ashore, Lev shook like a dog, his blackened makeup running down his throat and onto his blue shirt collar. He unholstered his Colt and water leaked from its sides.

"Slipped," he muttered.

Straight-faced, William handed him a cloth. Lev snatched it and thrust his shotgun at Mack, cursing, wiping the ash from his eyes, leaving white smudges down his cheeks. From the kerchief he fashioned a bandit's mask and tied it behind his head. Took his gun back and lurched off, and soon the three were making good time through the slick gray beards of Spanish moss.

William glanced back once, eyes shaded by his hat, his face barely perceptible but reassuring, then looked forward again, moving smoothly, the rounded shape of his shoulders and neck and his slightly pigeon-toed walk familiar as he climbed the hill, careful not to pull a vine or brush a limb for fear of setting off the water each tree held. In his brother's movements Mack saw shadows of himself, recalling the afternoon in a Coffeeville dry goods store when he'd seen his profile revealed by the reflection of one mirror in another, the two hung at a precise angle on different walls. This disconcerted him, not only seeing his vaguely unfamiliar half-face for the first time, but the idea of the arranged reflections: that a person might be so consumed with appearance as to need not one mirror but two. In the widow's cabin, half a mirror stood propped on a narrow shelf over the wash pail. Growing up, Mack had seldom viewed himself. What need was there? What could a boy see in his own eyes that would surprise him?

He spat and wiped the back of his hand over his dry lips. They'd left the woods behind now, were crossing a field of tall wet dead cornstalks, walking bent, staying out of sight of the distant road or the edge of the woods, Mack holding his shotgun low, keeping the round eye of its barrel dry. And then downhill, cover of woods again. Level ground soon enough and their backs straight. Fewer trees in this better acreage, their own community behind. The sky darker still, stars for the first time in days. A barbed-wire fence that Lev held apart for the brothers, then squeezed through as William spread it for him. Lev gave them a look—"Come on, you sons-a-bitches," he said from under the mask—before they crossed a muddy logging trail, William stepping in Lev's tracks and Mack in William's—into an orchard of loblolly pines. Soft brown needles underfoot. Nailed near the bases of the trees were wooden boxes for collection of resin, one of McCorquodale's side businesses. The pines, their bark gashed, bled sap slowly. On Mondays he sent a couple of Negroes to empty them.

Not Monday next: Lev stopped at the first box. He looked up the length of the tree as if to take revenge on its cousin that had bucked him into the creek. Seeing the box nearly full, he circled the loblolly and raised his foot, kicked the box to pieces and watched the thick resin ooze into the brown wet straw, nothing left but two nails curling out of the tree. He veered to the next pine and did the same, then the next and down the line, missing now and again and nearly falling twice and falling flat out once but back on his feet right away and kicking, his boot gumming up, bark and wood chips and nails sticking to the sole and the boot growing larger and Lev beginning to limp, dragging nearly a clubfoot to the next tree, sweating white lines in his forehead, as if he intended to smash every box. Mack looked at his brother, concerned about the noise, but William seemed

217

blessed with a calm most people would never own. Still, there was a job to do and finally even he had had enough. He went up to Lev and grabbed his shoulder.

"Let's get on," William said, peering into Lev's eyes. Then he turned and walked in the direction of McCorquodale's.

After a moment Mack followed, giving Lev a wide berth as he scraped at his boot with a stick.

By the time Mack was out of the orchard Lev had passed him, muttering. He overtook William in time for the three to huddle together, the stink of resin enough to gag over. Lev's forehead was striped, like war paint. His reddening eyes fixed on Mack, voice muffled.

"Okay, boy," he said. "Remember. Aim for the gut. Don't try to be no marksman with a head shot." He poked him in the belly. "The *gut,* god damn it."

"Gut," Mack said in a breathless voice, and William gave him a nod and squeezed his shoulder. Then Mack was off through the trees at a trot, quiet as dusk.

It took nearly half an hour to work into position behind the house, going quietly and downwind to keep from alerting McCorquodale's dog, and by the time he'd settled in behind the soft wet tendrils of a weeping willow fifty feet from the back door it was dark. He could outline the shape of the two-story house by its well-lit downstairs windows and the ceiling, a shade darker than the sky. Kneeling, he propped the shotgun across his knees and pulled back its hammer, heard the tiny, delicate spring of metal as it caught. The smell of smoke passed on the air, some kind of cooking meat, too. He'd never been inside this house, never would, probably. They said it had indoor plumbing. Lead-lined water tanks in the attic and a rain catcher on the roof. In the parlor a piano. Mack imagined the piano playing its rolling notes, a sound he'd heard only twice in his life, both times when they'd gone to the church in town. He cocked his head. A figure passed in one of the windows, a girl's shape, hair tied in a bun. She passed again, carrying something. McCorquodale had four daughters and a son, Carlos, who'd never spoken to him. Fancy children with no use for country folk.

He looked up at the sky through the trees and the smoky haze of the chimney. Suddenly he knew it had been too long. *Shit.* He cupped his hands and did his owl, but the call was too shrill. If any man in the house was of a careful or suspicious mind he would have paused halfway to his mouth, other hand reaching for a pistol.

Mack waited, listening.

Nothing.

After a moment, from the woods beyond the house, William's owl hooted back.

Mack waited, heart slamming in his chest. Leaned and let tobacco spit drop from his bottom lip without taking his eyes from the window. Shifted positions, putting one knee to the wet ground and using the other as a prop for his elbow, aiming the shotgun at the back door. Blackened as he was and covered in the willow, he tried to calm himself by imagining that he blended into the night, relaxing into his invisibility, at the wood end of a gun and invincible, sprayer of lead-fire, messenger of death. When the girl's shape appeared again to turn up the lamp's flame, he settled on her with the squat bead at the end of the sixteen-gauge's barrel. His finger touched the trigger, testing its exquisite resistance. *I am the angel.* His left eye closed.

Lesser angel, the one sent to guard the back.

From the front of the house the dog began to yap. McCorquo-dale's fabled watchhound. Mack remembered her from his few trips to Coffeeville, how she'd stand when they approached the store, her hackles up, and growl. People said she went each day with McCorquodale to his store, trotting alongside his horse, obedient, trained. Waiting outside all day under shade of the porch, chin on her paws, then going back home with him after dark.

Now there came a man's voice: "Who the *hell* is that?"

Now a woman's.

When the shotgun blast answered it felt too close and Mack nearly pulled his own trigger. He closed his left eye and bit his bottom lip and aimed at the door. Clamped his teeth together to quiet them. *Don't nobody come out now. Nobody better not come out here.*

No one did. No one did.

The dog was barking. A woman was screaming, girls screaming, too.

A door slammed.

Another shot. The dog stopped barking.

Mack rose, still aiming. He'd swallowed his tobacco and nausea surged in his chest, his mouth full of hot spit, eyes burning wet. Overhead, the chimney belched a spray of embers that circled in the night. He took two steps back, blinking, lowering the gun, couldn't catch his breath. Then William's hoot-owl call echoed in the trees and Mack turned, uncocking the sixteen-gauge, gagging, keeping low, holding his arm up and puking under it while he ran.

Later he wouldn't remember getting there, but when he finally caught up with Lev and William they were at the meeting point, squatting by the creek in the bottom of a hollow a mile south of Tooch's store, a respectable fire going despite the weather, washing the ash off their faces and laughing. The resin on Lev's boot bubbled with heat, a smell of burning sugar.

His face, scrubbed clean, looked orange in the firelight when he stood to meet Mack. "The hell took you so long to hollow, boy? We'd about decided you lost your nerve and run home to the widow."

"Just going quiet and careful," he said, trying to catch his breath, "like Tooch told me to." He dug out his handkerchief and bent and wet it in the creek and began to rub the ashes from his cheeks.

Lev glared at him. "My goddamn legs near went to cramping from waiting," he said.

William, hatless, hair slick with sweat, wiped the back of his neck with a cloth. "Hell, Lev, you got the son-of-a-bitch, plus half his damn tar collector boxes. Let Macky alone."

Lev stared at William, but finally he started to laugh. "Shit," he said, underhanding Mack a jug of whiskey, "after I got old McCorquodale your damn big brother here takes it on hisself to perform some justice on that old loudmouth hound dog."

William was smiling. "Couldn't let you do all the shooting, could I?"

Mack hefted the jug and unstoppered it, and later, at Tooch's, drunk, he'd listen as Lev told the story over and over, how he waited until Ernest McCorquodale, clutching a cloth dinner napkin in his hand, stepped onto his front porch before he fired the first time, how McCorquodale's wife, who'd followed him out holding a lantern, got winged, too, how that first spray of shot got McCorquodale in the chest, gut, and neck, and burst the lantern, how its flames set his shirt on fire. His wife fled inside clutching her arm. McCorquodale, still standing, stepped back to the left and leaned against the wall of the house, patting at his sleeve. Lev fired again and McCorquodale spun around, slinging sparks, before toppling. He lay burning. Then William shot. The dog fell, crawled in a circle, lay still.

III

Half drunk, and with Carlos McCorquodale sitting on the horse behind him, Waite trotted at a good clip down Court Street, yellow lamplights flaring in the windows, silhouettes of heads looking out, the people indoors catching on that something was amiss. Carlos, gulping for air and clutching at the cramp in his side, had said his daddy got shot on the porch. That somebody just pulled the trigger and ran off and now his daddy was dead. He'd jumped onto one of their horses and ridden after Waite but the horse had thrown him a mile from Grove Hill and he'd run the rest of the way.

Behind him the boy shuddered like he was cold and Waite realized that Carlos was crying.

They rode past the blacksmith's shop and Simmons's dry goods store with its green shutters pulled to and a holly wreath on the door. It had rained earlier and King kicked up crescents of mud and slid a little, then caught his footing and nickered softly in protest. Waite leaned forward and patted the horse's neck and tried to think of some comfort to offer the boy behind him, that maybe his daddy wasn't dead after all, that the doctor could perhaps mend his wounds, often a lot of blood meant nothing, looked worse than it was. But the boy had said Oscar sent for him, and if Oscar said McCorquodale was dead, he was dead.

When they were half a mile from McCorquodale's, slowing at a turn in the road, Carlos slipped off King's back and stood in the dirt. Waite reined the horse up and turned in the saddle. The boy watched him.

"Carlos?"

"I'll walk on up in a bit."

Waite looked toward the tall dark shroud of trees to the left of them, to the right. "Might still be chancy out here."

"Go on ahead, Sheriff," the boy said. "Please?"

"You'll follow me?"

"Yessir. I'll be on."

Waite nodded and jobbed the horse's ribs and left Carlos in the moonlit road.

Oscar stood on the steps waiting for him, holding that big gold pocket watch of his in one hand, as if marking how long it took Waite to arrive. In his other hand he had a Colt pistol. His sleeves were rolled up and his white shirtfront had blood on it. His graying hair, normally combed back very carefully, hung over his forehead. He descended the steps into the yard, breath smoking in the chill air, and held Waite's horse by the bridle while his cousin dismounted. Waite took the reins and, businesslike, tied them to the post. He looked around, light cast from the windows of the big house lay flickering, elongated squares over the yard. When he faced his cousin, Oscar wore a determined look. "I told you," he said.

Waite let this go. "What we got?"

"You need some coffee? Sober you up?"

"Don't push me, Oscar."

"A goddern bushwhacking's what we got, Billy." He motioned with his head and stalked along the front of the porch and around the corner. Waite followed him through the high wet grass out past the pear tree, into a dark pocket of night. There was something white on the ground and Waite stared at it for a moment before realizing it was a dog. He knelt and touched its cold throat with his knuckles.

"They shot the *dog*?"

"Yeah. I drug him over here, get him outta the way."

Waite looked off into the night. "Why in the hell would they do that?"

"They probably hit it by accident. I'm more concerned, Billy, with the fact that they shot Ernest."

Waite had blood on his fingers, he wiped his hand front and back on the grass before standing.

"I swear," Oscar said. "On his own porch. With his wife standing right beside him. My *sister*, Billy." Oscar looked down at the gun in his hand and scratched his head. He cast his eyes toward the darkness masking the trees across the road. "They were right over yonder," he said, pointing with the pistol. "Just waiting. Goddern bushwhackers."

"You were here," Waite said, "right? When it happened?"

Oscar nodded.

"Tell me about it."

They'd been eating supper. Oscar sat at one end of the table, Ernest at the other, going on about that bunch out in New Prospect, how it wasn't safe for anybody since they shot Joe Anderson, when the dog started to bark. The girls chattering about a dance coming up. Dog keeps barking. Ernest says, "Damn," and slams down his fork and gets up out of his chair and goes to see what the racket means, pulling his napkin from his collar. Been in a foul mood all night, even forgot to say the blessing. Ulrica had to remind him. Ernest goes on out through the front door and stands on the porch for a minute, yells, "Who's out here?," then Ulrica gets up and follows him out, bringing a kerosine lamp, saying, "What is it, Ernest?"

"I swear to God," Oscar said, "I just thought it was a dang fox or coon or something. Why I didn't go with him. I should've known, though. It was bound to happen."

"Go on," Waite said.

When Oscar heard the first shot, he jumped up from the table and ordered everyone to the floor. The girls hollering, covering their ears with their hands. Colored maid yelps and disappears. Oscar's wife, Lucinda, faints. Ulrica comes running back inside, clutching her forearm, blood on her dress, spurting between her fingers. Screaming bloody murder. Oscar scoots over the floor on his knees and elbows and pulls her down, puts his hand over her mouth to hush her up. His pistol is in his coat in the foyer by the front door, and he crawls that way, yelling for everybody to stay down. Another shot, and quickly another, and now it's quiet. He reaches the foyer and pulls down his coat, rack and all, gets his gun out. Raises up over the windowsill and sees Ernest lying there in the dark, shirtsleeve on fire. Puddle of black spreading under him.

"What time?"

He considered. "Hadn't been dark too long. Half hour?"

After a few moments, Oscar sighed. "You going to get him, right?"

Waite folded his arms. It was colder now, a little fog in the air. A whippoorwill cried from the tree overhead and Waite looked up at the stars, breeze on his cheeks, remembering when he and Oscar were young and Oscar's daddy had told him to shoot a little stray dog that had taken up under their house, mangy gray mongrel that shivered all the time and bared its teeth, but out of what seemed to young Waite something other than meanness. Fear, maybe. But Oscar's daddy (he was a lawyer) thought it might have the rabies, besides it was wild, he said. He handed Oscar a giant dragoon pistol and told him to lead the dog off and shoot it. Waite went with him, remembered now how they got to their knees and called the dog. How old was Oscar? Nine? Ten? He'd stuck the gun in his belt like a sword—nearly pulled his pants down it was so heavy; the barrel fell even with his calf—and they coaxed the dog in sweet chirping voices but finally had to get a big hambone from the house and use it to entice the stray from where it hid trembling under the back steps. When it came out it pissed on itself, and soon, with drool strung from its chittering lips, it was following them out beyond the livery and past a pen of mares and one bluish jackass that brayed at them and showed its yellow teeth and flexed the skin of its hips against the giant black horseflies.

Oscar said, "Well?"

"I guess I am."

"You want me to roust some fellows, go with you?"

Waite shook his head. "No, a mob's the last thing we need now. We go riding in there showing force and we'll have a damn shooting war on our hands, in their territory."

Oscar watched him. "We got that already."

A noise to their left and Oscar's gun arm flew up.

"It's just me," said Carlos.

He rode hard through the fields. Angling for secrecy, he veered off the road and found a back trail he'd discovered on the previous trip, let King follow it while he dozed in the saddle. There were dreams, unusual for him. A house burning. His own? His father, dead thirty years, off to the side on a bicycle, watching.

When he woke, the horse had stopped and was rubbing its head against the mossy side of a sweet gum, the land slanting sharply down. Trickle of a creek in the bottom of the hollow.

Didn't take long to realize he was lost—for him a rarity—and soon he'd wasted an hour prodding King along a series of steep slippery slopes, ducking low branches, breaking sodden spiderwebs with his chin. "Last time I trust a horse," he muttered, swatting King gently on the mane. With each misstep of the animal he felt each of his years in his lower back, and twice he dismounted to piss but when he stood waiting he couldn't.

Lord, but he could use a drink.

After another hour he still hadn't found his landmark, a large fallen oak tree which some yokels tried to saw in two and from which you could now see half the crosscut saw protruding, the handle long ago snapped off for its wood or the screws in it or just yanked off out of frustration. Were it his own mistake, he'd have hammered the saw into oblivion, not showing anyone his own failure, a log unhalved. He'd begun to think someone had done exactly that, though, or moved the whole log, and he dismounted and stood on the spongy ground with his hands on his hips. He could see his breath and King's. Finally he began to lead the horse, pull him, more than once tripping on a rock and nearly losing his grip and fighting to keep the animal calm, King blowing and fretting and rolling his eyes, as if there were rattlesnakes clicking about. Waite, now very cross, stumbled into bushes, nicking his cheeks and throat, and soon his boots were caked with mud and his coat soaked from rain pelting him from trees, as if each damn pine limb cupped a jawful of cold spit just for him.

"Crazy," he muttered, and King whinnied in agreement.

The stray dog young Oscar had shot all those years ago haunted

226

Waite as he walked, how it just followed them ignorantly to its appointment with death, patches of scratched-bloody skin showing, the way its hide looked like it had shrunk and could no longer hold the dog inside it, ribs you could count, the way it trembled like it couldn't get warm, the way its tail wagged as it followed them, the dog with no idea of what was coming. Boys with no idea either. Waite could tell that Oscar felt important, like a grown-up, a man in charge of shooting a dog, carrying a pistol nearly as big as he was. Despite himself, Waite had had to admit there was something to it. Can I carry the gun? he'd finally asked.

Nope, Oscar said, Daddy give it to me. I'm the boss.

Where you gone shoot it? Waite asked.

Just round that bend yonder.

I meant which part of the dog.

In the head, Oscar said. Gone pop it right 'tween the eyes.

Why don't you aim for the heart? Waite asked.

Where's the dang heart at?

Shoulder, stupid.

The dragoon had been too heavy for Oscar's arm, so he'd used both hands, and when he'd fired at the stray dog, aiming, Waite supposed, for its heart, he hit its hip instead. The dog's back half collapsed as if something below had snatched it down. It barked, almost a girl's scream, and began to scramble in circles, dragging its limp hind legs, leaving a jagged design of blood in the dirt, bloody dirt caking on its skin. Oscar shot again one-handed and in a panic and missed by a yard, the gun recoiling nearly straight up, then he fired again and missed again, the dog righting its course and dragging its nonworking half under a fence and into a cotton field in full brilliant bloom. Mute, the cousins marked the stray's progress through the field by the movement of the bolls and the shrieking of the dog. Their halfhearted attempt at tracking—bright red splotches on the white cotton—had lasted only a few minutes, to the other side of the field, the edge of the woods, and they'd given up and never

227

seen the dog again. Oscar had made Waite promise never to tell, and he never had.

He finally fell upon some luck and found himself on a narrow wagon trail, grass growing calf-high in the middle of deep muddy ruts. Then the oak, the saw, which he approached and touched, grateful. His thumb came away gritty with rust. For a time he waited to catch his breath, then climbed back into the saddle, leaning forward to whisper to the horse, stroking his long wet cheek. Such a good sport, King. Should've brought some sugar cubes or carrots. And why didn't he bring a damn bottle? What a comfort it would be now. But he'd be crazy to drink out here. He took off his hat and slung the water from it and replaced it and rode on with his hand on the stock of the Marlin in its saddle sock.

The land was more familiar now, even by moonlight, and soon two barking dogs pricked the horse's ears and Waite clucked his tongue and in a short while they were loping through field upon field of harvested cotton, wind rattling through the stalks, then topping a rise and in the middle of yet another field was the darkened hulk of Norris's cabin. The stars and the moon were high and white, casting the homestead in a dim, surreal glow. A pair of outbuildings to the west, places to hide. Waite slid the rifle out and levered a round into the chamber.

In front of the porch now, blocking the sheds with the house, he called, "Floyd Norris! Come on out here."

It wasn't Norris who appeared from underneath the house but two dogs, silently, racing out and leaping at him on the horse. Waite kicked at them and fired in the air, driving them back beneath the porch.

Only now did he form into word and image what he was about to do, though he'd known it since Carlos came panting to his porch. As soon as Floyd Norris stepped out the door, Waite would raise his rifle and aim at the man's chest and pull the trigger. Then he'd ratchet the lever with the gun still at his shoulder and before the ejected casing hit the ground he'd shoot again, and he would repeat the process until the gun was empty if that was what it took to drop him.

He waited, the dogs howling.

There was always a chance it would be a fair kill, that Norris might come out shooting, proving his guilt, or that he might take off running, but Waite reckoned that chance a slim one. To use his office in this way, as he had once before, as that of official assassin, troubled him, but Oscar was right. At times you had to step around the law.

But nothing happened. Floyd Norris didn't walk out peaceful or charge out firing or come sailing off the roof Indian-like with a knife.

Waite said *Hell* quietly. He dismounted, one-handing the Marlin, and stood with his fingers in the horse's mane. "Easy," he whispered to King. To himself. He didn't dare light his lantern and give Norris a clear shot at him, thinking it as likely as not that the farmer was laid up with a jug in the bracken behind him. Or in one of the sheds. Couldn't blame the man for that, you could smell the place clear out here. He'd heard about Norris's wife, dying in the field, but couldn't recall if he'd ever laid eyes on her.

Waite rocked from one foot to the other, back aching, the rifle in his left hand, and listened. He walked the length of the house, the dogs pacing him under the porch, he could hear them growling.

He was about to circle to the rear to bust in the back when a door creaked. Waite swung the rifle over as a small hand appeared, fingers splayed.

"Daddy ain't here," a boy's voice said.

Waite kept his rifle on the hand. "Come on out," he called. He wouldn't put it past Floyd Norris to use his children as a diversion.

"Daddy said us weren't to leave the house."

"If you don't, I'll come in and get you."

One of the boys appeared, his face brown with dirt, followed by the other two, each a little shorter than the one before him, probably all less than a year apart. All thin. The oldest two wore identical filthy pairs of overalls. Ratty shirts, no shoes. The youngest wore only a long shirt, he was grinding his fists into his eyes, half asleep.

"Where's your daddy?" Waite demanded.

"I ain't got to talk to you."

"You don't, boy, and I'll take you to the jailhouse."

"Over the river," the slow one said. Waite couldn't remember their names.

When the oldest turned and pushed his brother, Waite saw the enormous bowie knife, nearly a sword, hanging from his overalls.

"Son," Waite said, "you better start talking to me, or you're all under arrest. Where over the river?"

It was the slow one again. "Said he was fixing to go get hisself a present."

"What's that mean?"

For a time none of them spoke. Then the oldest relented. "Means he's going over to the cathouse."

Annie.

The youngest boy began to whimper, the oldest turned and socked him in the shoulder.

"You boys go on out in the yard," said Waite. "Over by that well yonder. And you," he said to the oldest. "Lay that pigsticker down and call these damn dogs out."

The boy knelt and raised the knife and jabbed it into the porch boards. He whistled and the dogs slunk out and waited as he and his brothers filed down the steps, going around the giant knife. The dogs followed them out to the well. There, the boys peered at him from behind the trough, their faces glowing in the starlight.

Waite crept to the edge of the house farthest from the well, and with his breath held, he moved along the wall, only the rasp of his overcoat against the wood of the shack. Dead cotton under his feet.

He came to a shuttered window and ducked beneath it, turning and looking up. He smelled urine, as if they used the window to piss from. He removed his hat, dropping it crown-down onto the rags of cotton. With the rifle barrel he opened one half of the shutter, then the other half. He looked in. He saw a fireplace glowing with a bed of embers. No Floyd Norris. Just squat hunks of firewood, arranged in the floor in a square, a fort the boys had built.

He retrieved his hat, eased to the rear of the house.

When he touched the back door, it fell inward, onto the floor. Waite's stubborn bladder nearly let go. He poked the barrel of his rifle into the room, followed it in, stepping on the door, just a few boards nailed together. He lit a match and looked around. A table. A sagging, filthy bed. The log fort.

Their fire had nearly gone out. He picked up a log and tossed it on the coals, shifted it with his rifle barrel.

He went back out without fixing the door and stood in the dead cotton looking at the stars. His boots were heavy with water. His back throbbed. Something was moving through the field, low and fast, and he pointed the rifle at it. Just the dogs, circling the house.

Waite called for Floyd Norris's boys to come back but heard nothing. The well stood alone.

On the porch, the knife was gone.

Before he left he got on his hands and knees and looked under the house and searched both outbuildings, rooting out nothing but a sleepy hog and a flying cat that almost gave him a heart seizure. Finally he mounted up, shaking his head, thinking himself crazy to come out here, alone, at night. It's a doggone wonder you're still breathing, Billy Waite.

Something hit him back of his shoulder, and a cold, slimy thing smacked his cheek. He aimed, then stopped himself and regained his head. Mud balls. From behind the porch the boys were firing them silently, throwing, ducking out of sight, throwing again.

"Dammit!" he yelled as one clobbered him on the back of the

neck. He hunched in the saddle, making himself a smaller target, and spurred the horse on, still holding the Model 1893, heading for the river, mud flying past his ears like bullets.

The boys laughing.

He couldn't get the ferry until dawn, and when he finally led the skittish horse off the boat, over the bowing plank, pulling at the animal and trying to calm him, he was in a fouler mood still. On the boat King had tried to bite him and he'd balled his fist and cocked back his arm before he caught himself. What damn fool punches his own horse? His clothes were wet, heavy, caked in mud, and he was dying for a drink.

Aland, he somehow got turned around looking for the whore's cabin, took confusing directions from a stuttering old colored man chewing a huge wad of sugarcane and driving a decrepit mule with a switch, and the sun had traveled well up over the treetops by the time he stepped down in the mud yard and looped King's rein to the porch rail and mounted the two warped board steps onto her porch. He looked at the yard—mule tracks. Recent ones.

From inside, her dog started to bark.

"Who is it?" she called before his knock.

"Sheriff."

Behind him, over the dirt road, were thick woods. The ground steaming as the dew burned. Like a spring morning, not the heart of winter. Waite removed his waterlogged hat and rubbed his scalp. Felt his cheeks with his fingers, the stub of whisker there. His back aching.

"Ain't nobody here," she called.

Waite pulled the leather strap used as a handle and stepped into the room well lit with morning, windows open, curtains drawn. She sat in a caneback chair by a table, wearing a housedress, breaking snap beans into small pieces and dropping them into a pail between her feet. A pipe on the table. Behind her, against the wall, stood her short shotgun. He raised an eyebrow at her, but she kept breaking the beans. Her dress was spread at her knees over the pail, showing her white skin, blue veins. How old must she be now? Fifty? Her hair as blond as ever, though.

"Well," he said.

"Was they something you wanted?" Annie asked, not looking at him, just snapping the beans. "We closed."

The dog lay in the corner by the popping woodstove, head up.

Waite circled the table and pulled out the other chair and sat in it, put his hat on the table. Crossed his legs.

"Set yourself down," she said.

He rubbed the bridge of his nose. "What would you charge to whip me up some fried eggs and sausage?"

"This ain't no boardinghouse."

"You'll take a dollar to bed a man you don't know but not a quarter for some breakfast for a public servant?"

The beans hit the bottom of the pail harder. "Go to hell," she said. "Do me a good deed there and just go straight to hell, Billy High Sheriff Waite."

"You got anything to drink, then?"

She looked at him. "No. I ain't got a thing."

"Listen," he said. "I ain't here to mess with you, and I won't arrest you for anything you tell me. But I need to find out something from you. It's real important." He watched her. "Well?"

"Well, what."

He looked past her out the open back window, then back at her. Her eyes. "You have any visitors last night?"

"Visitors."

"Customers."

She stopped snapping the beans. She wiped her hands on her apron and hooked a stray shuck of hair back behind her ear. "Why you want to know?"

233

"Just answer me first."

"You come seen me once," she said. "As a *customer*."

"I don't recollect that."

"Lord, just as green a rich town boy ever got lost in the woods. Come in here with your ding-dong about to bust out of your britches, you and your cousin Oscar York both."

Waite supposed a man's past was like an apple peel with him at the knife: you never did get cut loose from it, it just curled round and round. "I reckon ever boy within ten miles has been here," he said. "Only thing I care about today is if somebody come by last night."

"They was somebody."

"What was his name, Annie?"

She looked at him.

"You can trust me. You know that. I ain't ever done wrong by you."

"You ain't never done right by me, either."

He sat back. "Well, I expect I'm fixing to start doing real wrong by you, if you don't tell me what I'm asking you. And I ain't paying for no answer, either."

"Threats," she said to the dog.

He took the blackjack off his belt and put it on the table.

"Jubal," she said.

The dog's ear twitched. One eye opened.

"Kill."

The dog closed its eye.

"Annie," he said quietly. "I'm usually as good-humored a fellow as you'll find in this county, but today, I'm just flat ornery. I've had me a hell of a night." He touched the blackjack. The heavy sand inside.

"It was Floyd Norris," she said at last.

"What time did he get here?"

"Just 'fore dark."

"How long did he stay?"

234

"All night."

"That something he does regular?"

"Naw. It was his first time. His wife got lucky and died on him."

"I need to know, Annie. Did he leave at any time? Go out and come back? Or talk to anybody?"

"Just went to the porch to take a piss or fart. I don't allow no farting in here."

"I'll try to control myself. Did anybody else come by? Did he talk to anybody?"

"Naw. He stayed pretty much on top of me the whole night. Damn near chapped me raw."

Waite raised his eyebrows. "Did he say anything unusual? Anything might lead you to believe there was some crooked business going on?"

She shook her head. "Some fellows chatter on while they do their business. Not him. He forget I was even here. One of you fellows just in it for yourselves. Your cousin Oscar's another one."

Waite let this go. "What time'd he leave?"

"Oscar?"

"Norris."

"Just 'fore you got here. Not more'n half a hour 'fore you knocked on the door." She waved a hand in front of her face. "You can probably still smell him."

"How much did he pay you?"

"Usual. For the whole night."

"A dollar?"

"For a whole night? How cheap you think I am, Billy Waite?"

"That ain't for me to say. How much, then?"

"Four and two bits."

He lifted his eyebrows again. "Would you be prepared to state what you just told me to a judge?"

"Which one?"

"Whichever one," he said. "To any one."

235

"I guess I would. If you twisted my arm. But not that Oscar York. He's been out here other times," she said. "Not just that first time he come with you."

"I just have one more question, and I'll go," he said. He watched her carefully. "You know anything about Tooch Bedsole? That gang of his? Their night doings? What he's up to now?"

"Tooch?"

"That's right."

She shook her head. "I don't know nothing about him."

He couldn't tell if she was lying or not. "Did Norris mention him?"

"Yeah. Lying on top of me going 'Tooch, Tooch, oooh Tooch.' " She giggled like a young girl, slapped her knee.

He stood, put on his hat, and crossed the room. At the door he stopped, fitting the blackjack into his belt.

She stared boldly back at him, her knees apart a good three inches.

Too old to be tempted, he thought, but couldn't stop himself from remembering their night together, so long ago. Right before he got married. Oscar had brought him here, drunk, on a gelding called Spot. The truth was, it had never again been so sweet.

Maybe she sensed his memory, or maybe she was just a woman. "Tell me something, Billy," she said, giving him a tiny smile. "What you think? Have I aged well, or poorly?"

He put on his hat. "We all age poorly, Annie." He went out and closed the door behind him.

"Lotta good you was," he heard her tell the dog.

Oscar's phaeton was in front of Waite's house.

"Hell's bells," Waite said, sitting astride the horse for a moment, rubbing his tired eyes, then he climbed off and took his time tying the reins to the post. Something irregular on the saddle caught his eye— someone had nicked the leather, knifed out a fingernail-size piece.

Inside, Oscar sat stiffly on the sofa, both feet planted on the floor, a cup of coffee on the doily on the small polished side table, Waite and Sue Alma's daguerreotype hanging above him. He wore his overcoat, even though the room was warm, and his legs were crossed. His Winchester was propped against the sofa and there was a sidearm on his belt.

Sue Alma sat not rocking in the rocking chair. She seemed relieved to see him but finished her sentence, something about new hymnals for the church. She held a coffee cup, too, one of the china ones. Always bring out the best for Oscar.

Waite closed the door and wiped his feet and removed his coat and hat, hung them on the deer antler rack Sue's father had given them as an anniversary gift. Unbuckled his gunbelt and tossed it heavily onto the sofa, next to the cat, which sprang away with a yawl.

"How dare you go without leaving me a note," Sue said.

One-handed, he unfastened the top button on his shirt. "Nothing to be worried about. Routine foray."

Oscar was watching him. He looked at Sue impatiently and back at Waite, who said, "Sue, would you go in and fix me 'bout six eggs and get some ham to frying?"

She looked like she might tell him to go to hell, but in the end she just turned to Oscar. "You want some, too, Judge?"

"No, thank you, Sue, darling." He tapped his chest. "I got a touch of the indigestion this morning. This coffee do me fine."

She passed between them. The kitchen door rocked on its hinges, angry clank of pans.

Oscar stood up holding the rifle. A hunting knife sheathed on his belt.

Waite raised his hand. "Oscar, I didn't find him."

"Dang it," he hissed.

"Hell, I rode over ever damn inch of the place looking for him."

"Then let's saddle up now, go find his ass 'fore the sun goes down. You and me and whoever else we can round up."

"I don't think we ought to do that."

"How come?"

Waite picked at the dried mud on his pants leg. "He has himself an alibi."

"An alibi." Oscar raised his hands and wiggled his fingers. "Well, there's a surprise."

"This one's a little different." Waite lowered his voice and told him about Annie.

Oscar lowered his voice, too. "You're taking some goddern dollar whore's word for it? Hell, Billy. She's probably in it with 'em."

"You been out there to see her quite a bit, sounds like," Waite said quietly. "I wouldn't take her for a liar, and I'd rather not start questioning her integrity, if you catch my meaning. You with your spotless reputation to think of. She don't care for Norris no more than she does you nor me. And it'd take quite a plan to cook up all this, get her in on something she wouldn't be likely to agree to in the first place. I think we missed our chance."

Oscar sat back down. "You mean you missed. If you wasn't half drunk you'd of probably got him easy. You reek like a still, Billy. You think folks ain't talking? You think the whole town's blind?"

Waite drew a deep breath and held it as Sue came through the door with a cup of black coffee for him. He took it.

"How's Mrs. McCorquodale?" he asked Oscar.

"How you think? Just about out of her mind. We got her sedated. Doc Moore's with her. Says her wounds won't be no trouble, unless they get infected."

"That poor thing," Sue said. "I'll make some soup for her right this second." She disappeared back past the swinging door.

"Why don't we run over there to her house," Waite said, "see what we can find."

*　　*　　*

238

They took Oscar's phaeton to Coffeeville. The day was warm for November, and just past the old Sikes bridge Waite leaned forward and shrugged out of his coat and hung it over his knees. On the way Oscar told how he'd spent an hour that morning at the telegrapher's office, trying to notify McCorquodale's relatives from up near Birmingham. Pell City. Said he paid for it out of his own pocket.

At McCorquodale's they found Carlos on the porch, staring at his feet. Looked like he hadn't slept in a week.

"Hey, boy," Waite said.

Oscar patted him on the back. "You okay, Carlos?"

"Yes, sir."

"Don't you worry, son," Oscar said. "We'll get the fellows that did this. I promise you that."

"Yes, sir."

"Well, I'm gone go in, see about your momma." Oscar took a look toward the trees across the road, then disappeared inside, carrying his rifle.

Waite remained on the porch. He looked at the floor, the blood-stain like thick paint. It had run down between the boards and would be hard to get out. A lot of blood. Hell of a lot. Oscar'd said Ernest was dead when he got to him and beat out the fire on his arm. Said you could still smell him burning.

As Carlos watched from the steps, Waite examined the wall, a few lead pellets embedded in the wood. He let himself inside the house, grateful not to see anybody—he heard low voices from upstairs—and got an old-looking paring knife from a drawer in the kitchen. He saw a closed door and figured that was where the body lay. He knocked softly and when nobody answered he went in.

McCorquodale was on the floor, underneath a sheet red with blood. Waite knelt by the body. Pulled the sheet back. Where the hell is the undertaker? He rolled up his sleeves and began to unbutton McCorquodale's shirt. Marked where the shot went in, the angle, then carefully took the body by its shoulder and lifted it, saw an old tablecloth beneath, also stained red. No exit wounds. Which said a lot about the distance of the shooters—they'd have been across the road, just inside the trees, probably. Where he would have felt rage ten, even five years ago, now he felt tired. He put his hands on his knees and stood.

Outside, Carlos watched him as he dug out the pieces of lead shot from the wall and held each misshapen piece between his finger and thumb before dropping it in his shirt pocket. Already he could see some were buckshot and others lesser: eights or, more likely, sixes. Two shotguns. So they were dealing with a pair of killers here. At least two.

Waite took off his glasses and put them in his pocket. He exhaled deeply and sat beside Carlos.

"You making it all right?" he asked.

"Yes, sir."

"How old are you, Carlos?"

"Seventeen."

"Seventeen." Waite rubbed his chin, the stiff whiskers. "My daddy got killed when I was fourteen," he said. "Threw from a mule's back at the blacksmith's. Hit his head on an anvil. Just went to sleep and kept sleeping."

Carlos didn't say anything.

"I sure wanted to kill that damn mule," Waite said. "Tell you that."

"Did you? Kill it?"

Waite bent and picked up a smooth pebble from the step. "No, no. Wouldn't have been practical. I remembered something, though, 'bout that mule, during Daddy's wake. When I was in bed one night that old sack of bones got outta the barn, trotted over to the house and poked her fool head in me and my brother's window and brayed to high heaven. My brother, name was Butch, he come off the mattress 'bout four feet, and I just about wet the bed. Butchy, he had a short fuse on him, he rolled straight outta bed, went to the rack and grabbed Daddy's twelve-gauge shotgun. Runs down the hall." Waite was smiling at the memory. "Momma run out and stopped him, said, 'What you gone do with that shotgun, boy?' and Butchy says to her, says, 'I'm gone shoot that damn mule's what.' Momma turns around and yells at Daddy, 'Do something!' and Daddy, he's still laying in bed, says, 'Hell no. Let him shoot the son-of-a-bitch.' "

Carlos smiled, too.

"If Butch had shot him that night, Daddy'd lived a lot longer. But you can't do that." He thumped the pebble into the yard. "Can't think if I'd a done this or that, something else might've happened. You'll drive yourself crazy like that. Fact is, things happen and nobody knows why."

They sat, looking out at the road. The doctor's wagon had left tracks in the mud.

"Carlos," he said, "did you see or hear anything that might give me an edge on this business?"

The boy shook his head. "It was that Floyd Norris, Sheriff," he said.

"That seems to be the going opinion," Waite admitted. He folded his hands on his knees. "And one thing I've learned after being a sheriff for this long is that usually the man who seems guilty is. Usually, but not every time. Sometimes, just every once in a while, the things that seem obvious are too obvious. Now we all know why Norris might've had reason to pull the trigger. Your daddy fore-closing on him. Putting him and his family out. What I need you to do for me, though, is to try and think of anybody else might've had a strong reason to shoot your daddy."

"I been trying," the boy said. "Daddy, he keeps, used to keep, his business quiet. Didn't ever let none of us have much to do with it."

"Not even you?"

"I guess I was the one he said the most to. Which wasn't much.

241 .

Or maybe Uncle Oscar. Never told Momma a thing. Always said the Lord God intended the world for them that wears pants."

"It's a fact you can get places faster in a pair of britches," Waite said. "Tell you what. Why don't you and me go on over to your daddy's store and take us a look at his records and papers. Might be something we can use over yonder."

Oscar came out, rifle in his hand. He eased the door shut behind him. "I believe I'll go with y'all, if that's okay."

"How is she?"

"Asleep. Poor thing."

When they arrived at the store, Obbie, the middle-aged black man who clerked for McCorquodale stood on the steps waiting, holding a lunch pail. He was the only black man Waite knew who wore glasses.

"Morning, Sheriff," he said. "Good morning, Mr. Carlos, Judge York, sir."

"Morning," Waite said. Carlos nodded to him.

Oscar climbed down from the wagon. "You doing okay, Obbie?"

"Yessir, thank you, sure am."

Oscar nodded and went up the steps and searched his pockets for the key and found one and tried it and unlocked the door. He went in and Carlos followed, his head lowered.

"How you today, Sheriff?" The clerk came down the steps and took the horse's bridle and held it as Waite climbed down from the buggy, moving his gunbelt so it wouldn't catch on the brake lever.

"Listen," Waite said, looking down the street, "Mr. McCorquodale's been shot."

"Shot? What you mean, Sheriff?"

"He's dead."

The black man's eyes grew wide and he shook his head. "It's bad, bad times," he said.

242

Waite nodded. "Well. You can go on about your normal chores, I guess," he said. "Open up, business as usual. From what I knew of McCorquodale, it's what he'd a wanted."

Waite went in, down the length of the counter, to the glassed office in back, where Oscar was seated behind a desk, going through the ledger, Carlos watching him.

Passing a barrel, Waite picked up a big red apple and looked it over for bruises or wormholes and polished it against his shirtsleeve. He stopped in the office door and leaned against the wall and kept polishing the apple. Behind him the black man was opening the front door, already talking to a customer, repeating the news of McCorquodale's death. *Bad, bad times.*

"Son of a gun," Oscar said.

Waite was about to bite into the apple. "Find something?"

A cry from the back room brought them all running. The black man was staring at a place in the wall where several boards had been removed. Someone had broken in.

Waite's head hurt. It was the day following McCorquodale's funeral and he'd drunk too much and not slept well. Now he watched his cousin behind his office desk and the drained-looking boy facing him.

"There's no easy way to tell your mother what must be said," Oscar told Carlos. "Your family is broke. Your daddy's business has been in some serious jeopardy for a number of years now, and now that he's gone his debtors are about to rush his estate like a pack of starved hound dogs. We don't even know how much cash was taken from the safe, though we can harbor a guess it was substantial, since it held a lot of cotton money. Your daddy, he never did trust banks."

Oscar didn't look at Waite, who leaned against the window ledge, the sunlight warm on his shoulders. The judge had a way of doing that, of making you feel like you weren't in a room.

243

Waite glanced behind him, out the window to the street. A pair of black men moved off the sidewalk for a white lady to pass. She ignored them, they her, a simple and daily transaction. Waite rubbed his temples. Life went on beyond the glass, didn't it? No matter how devastating a blow a boy is dealt, like Carlos's daddy getting shot and the news of the family's finances, the clock keeps ticking and the world outside the window is the same world it was before you lost everything.

"I've been puzzling over this," Oscar went on, watching Carlos. "And it seems to me the only solution is to sell your house. You can auction off some of the things inside—that piano, for one—and with the store's inventory, that should about even things up. Leave y'all enough to get a smaller place. I'm willing, if you and your mother want me, to come in as a partner on the store."

The boy sat in the chair across from his uncle, dressed in a suit and a bow tie, a hat in his lap.

Grow on up, Carlos, Waite thought. Your childhood's ended.

The office was too warm with the fire going. Waite pushed off the ledge and crossed the room to the rack by the door and removed his coat, cartridges clicking in the pocket, and hung it up by Oscar's and went back to the ledge.

"But that's not the only reason I asked you here today," Oscar told Carlos. The judge rose and went to the window and looked out past Waite's shoulder, Carlos behind him. "I've been thinking on what we're gone do about your daddy's murder. Been talking to Billy about it, too."

Waite rubbed the bridge of his nose. He and Oscar had gone over McCorquodale's ledgers carefully, looking for a sum that might reflect the money Norris had paid. They'd found nothing. Which Oscar said proved it. Waite said it proved no such thing. He said how much of his—Oscar's—dealings did Oscar record on paper and Oscar said every blessed one. Then you're rare, Waite had said.

Oscar turned and faced the boy. "Your daddy, he did foreclose on a few farms in the past. He believed, as I do, that there's a certain order to how men should be regarded. Men like your father and I, we have a responsibility to the working landholders. We have to keep a grip on what little was left to us by the northerners. We have to cling to it, to *cleave*, as the Good Book says. And these country fellows, they have to be watched and treated a certain way. You can't give them charity or they'll come to depend on it. And those who lose their farms due to bad business choices, or bad luck, or just general sorriness, well, your father and I both believe that they're better off going someplace else."

Oscar returned to his chair. "See, Carlos, the thing about it is this. Sometimes the law gets bogged down in itself. What the Britishers call red tape. Bureaucracy. And at those times, it's the responsibility of good citizens like you and me to follow their conscience. Now since Billy feels like his hands are tied in this business, I've gone past him. I've had a fellow, what you call a private detective, out in Mitcham Beat for a good while now. At my own expense. He's gone get us the proof we need to convict not only Floyd Norris but all them night riders."

Waite had had enough. He snatched his coat off the rack and left. The hell with Judge York.

I V

A gang of schoolboys lay pillowed in their folded arms watching the crowd from under the boards of McCorquodale's store's porch.

"Now give me your attention," the auctioneer said. "This next item will be of particular interest to you ladies out yonder." He stood with his sleeves rolled up behind a desk pushed out of the store, its drawers with their heavy brass knobs removed to make it lighter, a claw hammer with the price tag still on it in his left hand so he could bang it like a gavel and declare items sold. After he'd pounded the desk a time or two, Judge Oscar York, grinning at the crowd, had slipped up onto the porch and slid a piece of lumber under the hammer so as not to further damage the desk. The auctioneer nodded and two colored men carried a hall tree out from the store. They set it beside the desk and stepped back and stood side by side, shuffling their large feet.

"Thank you, boys. Now," the auctioneer went on, "this here is a genuine hall tree from Ulrica McCorquodale's own parlor. The upstairs parlor, it says here. And it also says, let's see, that it come from a gallery down in Mobile. Fine creation, ain't it?" He paused and rocked back on his heels, gazing at the towering piece. "Now some of y'all might've seen it in the McCorquodale house during parties," he continued, "but I myself never was invited to no parties there, which don't depreciate the piece none."

Laughter.

The judge, off to the side, seemed frozen in his smile. Billy Waite, behind the crowd, sitting on the back of a wagon peeling an apple, seemed more interested in the apple than the auction. He had a rifle propped beside him.

"I'm gone open the bidding here at, well, fifteen dollars."

York flashed all ten fingers twice.

"Judge says no, we got to ask twenty for it."

"I'll bid ten," somebody called from the back and everyone laughed.

"No, no, it's twenty, like the judge here says."

It went on, the ten-dollar bid stood.

"The next item on the docket some of y'all have been eyeing for a spell," the auctioneer said. He left his desk and with the hammer held loosely in his right hand walked to the other side of the porch to the piano, which was covered by a sheet. He pulled the sheet off slowly, then handed it to one of the colored men who didn't seem sure what to do with it. The piano, highly varnished, shone in the sun.

"She's a beaut, ain't she?" the auctioneer said, and the murmuring crowd agreed. The auctioneer slid the hammer in his back pocket and raised the lid and propped it up. He punched a few of the keys to show they worked.

"I'm gone ask the Reverend Washington Ethridge to come on up here for a moment, if he will," the auctioneer said, and the crowd parted to permit a very thin man in work clothes to the front. "Come on up to the porch, Reverend," the auctioneer said.

He waved, no, thanks.

"Well, folks, he's just gone stay down yonder. Reckon this ain't his kind of audience, is it? Fact is, was he to come up here, he'd probably get to preaching, wouldn't he? And I myself find once a week's enough for me."

Ethridge shook a finger at him, grinning.

"Well, the good reverend wants this piano for his church, and so at the judge's discretion, we're gone start the bidding here on this piano at twenty-seven dollars and a half. That's a bargain, and I happen to know the reverend here's gone start the bidding. Am I right?"

"Twenty-seven and six bits," Ethridge called.

"Do I hear twenty-eight?" the auctioneer said, putting a dramatic hand to his ear. "No? Going once, going—"

"Twenty-eight," somebody yelled. From back of the crowd.

All looked around. Judge York came up on the lowest step for a better vantage point. Waite had paused in his peeling.

It was Lev James. He sat aback his mule with one foot tucked under him, a natty blanket for a saddle and a saddlebag behind him. A pistol handle sticking out of his trousers.

"Twenty-eight and two bits?" Ethridge said, looking at Oscar as if he'd been double-crossed.

"Twenty-nine," Lev James yelled. He leaned and spat. "Hell, thirty."

The judge flung up his hands and turned his back on the crowd. He glared up at the auctioneer, who shrugged.

"Do I hear thirty-one?"

"No, you don't," the sheriff said. Rifle in hand, he slid down off the wagon, his apple left gleaming on the rail. If he saw the child's hand reach up and take the apple he didn't acknowledge it, choosing instead to lock eyes with Lev James, who'd turned on the mule to watch Waite's approach.

"Thirty-one," Lev James said. He smiled at Waite, three yellow teeth showing out of the mass of his dark twin-braided beard.

"You expect us to take your bid serious, James?" the sheriff said.

"Not no more seriouser than you expect me to take you."

"Oh, believe me, James," Waite said. "I take you very serious." He had been holding the rifle one-handed at his side. Now he moved its forearm to his left hand. "You got the money you bidding with," he said, "or you just here to mess up a nice event?"

He cast his slanted eyes about, women covering their children, herding them away, men gathering and looking sidelong at one another, mustering courage. "Nice event," James sneered.

"So far. Now you go on get out of here."

"I got me plenty of money, Billy Waite. And don't you forget it."

Waite raised his rifle, calmly, aiming it at James's right shoulder. "There's about fifty witnesses watching," he said quietly, "and if you go for that gun I'll drop you here in the mud your goddamn mule's standing in."

James's eyes flickered over the crowd. His smile had never faded. He held up his hands, slowly. "Won't let me bid, folks," he called. "Seems if you from the country and you ride into the big old grand town of Coffeeville, the sheriff here'll try and run you out." He reached slowly into his pocket and brought forth a sheaf of paper money. "Looky here, Billy Waite. More than you'll make in a goddamn month."

Waite lowered the rifle.

James grinned. He looked back toward the auctioneer. "Thirty-five dollars," he called. "That pianer's gone look good on my porch."

The street Lev rode was fairly deserted, a few parked wagons and buggies, smoke from steamboats on the river visible over the tops of trees. He leaned and spat off the mule's back and smiled at a chubby lady coming out of a store. She recoiled and went back into the building. He rode dead center down the road, pausing to spit on the wooden sidewalk. He watched his and the mule's slow-walking reflection in a storefront window and adjusted his hat, then turned the mule and walked it down the street, past the hotel, its balcony empty. A sign swinging on its chains, what it said he didn't know.

He drew the mule to a stop and threw his leg over to dismount. As he landed, though, his foot seemed to buckle beneath him and he collapsed. He sat in the street beneath the mule and looked around for somebody to have seen. No one there.

He drew his foot to him and examined his boot, the heel that had come off and which lay cupped in the big dirty palm of his hand.

Limping, he led the mule to the side of the street and looped the reins over a post. He looked up and down the street until he spotted a hanging sign with the picture of a lady's shoe burned in wood.

The cobbler, a man named Wilkins, was polishing a pair of brogans when Lev came in. There were racks and racks of shoes and a wall with pairs of socks displayed.

"Can I do something for you, sir?" Wilkins asked, smiling and setting the shoe on the counter before him. He wore a pair of round spectacles and had a long nose.

Lev tromped through the store, rising and falling with the uneven height of his shoes. He stopped before the owner and looked down at him, then sat the tattered heel of his boot on the counter between them.

"I'll need shoeing," he said.

"Of course, Mr. . . . ?"

"You don't need my name."

"Fine. Can I have, er, the rest of this boot?"

Lev stared for a moment, unsure if he was being teased. He decided not, and bent and removed the muddy boot and set it beside its heel. It all but collapsed from how worn it was, more like cloth than leather.

"Well, this one's seen some use," Wilkins said, looking as if Lev had set a dead possum there.

"What's that mean?"

"It means you've got yourself a dedicated piece of footwear."

"Can you fix her or not?"

"I can give it a try. I'm a cobbler appreciates a challenge."

He lifted the boot and took it through a curtain to a back room. In a moment he returned with a pair of pliers and got the heel in their jaws. "It'll likely be a few minutes." Back through the curtains.

Lev placed his hands on the counter, on each side of the mud print his boot had left. His hip had a kink in it from being uneven or from the fall so he limped over to a chair beside a box of wooden shoe lasts and sat, removed his other boot. His socks had bunched around his toes and he pulled them higher and frowned at the holes in the heels.

"Goddamn," he said. Hardly the footwear of a piano owner. He gazed over at the selection of new, shiny shoes and then back at his own deflated one, he stood and walked to the door, looked out where the mule stood tied, the jug hung from its flank. He started out the door, then stopped and looked to his left.

They were beautiful, a pair of black oil crain Dom Pedro plow shoes on a wooden rack, all by themselves. Beneath them the price written on a small chalkboard was $1.35. The numbers $1.42 were Xed off. He lifted the left shoe and pressed his face into it, its new leather smell. Without even a look at the curtains where the cobbler had gone, he placed the shoe on the floor beside his foot. It seemed a match, even in its wide width. He'd gotten out the wooden last and started working his toes into the shoe when it occurred to him such new footwear shouldn't suffer such old socks.

When the owner came out with the old boot upside down on a stick, cleaned, shined, the heel nailed back on and filed a bit for a more even walk, the store was empty. He cast his eyes about and saw that the plow shoes, which had been on the bargain platform, had been replaced by the muddy twin of the decrepit boot he held before him. Stuffed in the mouth of the boot were a pair of socks that looked as if they'd been unearthed from a mud pit. The two wooden shoe lasts from the Dom Pedros were on the floor.

He found the thief standing by his mule and drinking from a jug, the plow shoes, impossibly shiny beneath the man's drab overall cuffs.

"I see you've decided to trade up," he said to Lev's back.

"Do what?" he asked, not turning.

"The shoes you're wearing. A fine choice, and you'll not find a better price in the vicinity. I trust they fit. We've got just about ever size a man could need. Some are in the back, though. Boxed up."

Lev unlooped the mule's rope from the post and climbed on.

"It'll be, oh, let's say a dollar eighty-five in all," the cobbler said.

Lev worked at turning the mule parallel to the porch.

"That's for the plow shoes you're wearing now, the socks, and the repair," Wilkins said.

"I already paid." Lev clucked his tongue and the mule began to walk.

"Sir," the cobbler called, "I'll fetch the sheriff."

He stopped the mule and looked back, down over his shoulder. "For what?"

"You've not paid, sir."

He rolled off the mule and snatched the decrepit boot out of Wilkins's hand so quickly that he'd beat him unconscious with it before the cobbler fell. Yet when the man was down Lev continued to

251

hit him in the head, face, and neck with the limp old boot. When the heel flew off it set him in a rage anew, as if sloppy craftsmanship were one more kind of fuel for the furnace of his heart.

V

Ardy had been waiting for nearly half an hour at the edge of the field. Had Oscar gone somewhere else? He'd heard about the judge's bad sense of direction, so it was possible he was in the wrong place, but he'd also gathered that Oscar liked to make you wait a spell. But he paid well, in cash, and on time. Now Ardy sat in the shade of a large poplar with the woods to his back, breaking twigs into tiny pieces, going over Oscar's instructions, replaying their meeting of two days ago in his mind. Oscar had said, "She could go someplace else."

And then he'd said, "I ain't saying do anything *to* her."

And then, "I just can't have her around here anymore. You understand what I'm saying?"

They sat across from each other at a small fire Ardy had built. He'd brewed a pot of coffee, too. He'd said, "You want me to run her off."

"Yeah. Just as long as she don't come back. Ever. Not even for a visit or for a whores' convention where they give her a medal. She comes back it means you ain't done your job."

Ardy said, "What you figure to do for her, to get her to cooperate? Pay her off or scare her off?"

"Those are my choices?" Oscar tapped his chin. He looked into the tin cup Ardy had given him, the black coffee there. He'd taken one sip and not another. "Well," he said, "I surely don't want any harm to come to her. Do you expect she'd go for twenty-five dollars?"

"No sir, I don't. She'd be leaving that house. That property. The place she's lived all her life. Friends. You don't want your coffee?"

Oscar looked at the cup. "She ain't got no friends. The women won't mention her name and the men look down at her from on top of her." He sipped from the coffee.

"You ask me," Ardy said, "I don't think you're gone get her outta here for less than fifty dollars. And a train ticket."

"Train ticket."

"Yeah. To New Orleans. She'll be able to ply her trade real good there. They got old ones, young ones, virgins, niggers, octoroons, whatever you want."

Oscar drummed his fingers on his knee. "Virgins?" He looked past Ardy into the woods. He looked up at the sky. "I don't get out enough," he said.

Ardy said, "Well?"

Oscar leaned forward and poured the rest of his coffee into the coals. "I won't be a part of any harm coming to her. Is that clear? I want you to pay her," he said.

Then they'd agreed to meet here, today, where Oscar was to give him the money.

Ardy rose from his crouch, looking along the ground at a line of deer tracks. You could tell a doe's from a buck's because the buck's front hoofprints were deeper due to the extra weight he carried, bulky shoulders and the antlers they supported. A doe would often follow a buck, stepping in his tracks.

Back in the trees his horse nickered at something. He looked through the leaves, wondering if there was a buck in the vicinity. Riding in, he'd passed a spot on the ground a piece back, the leaves and grass scratched away, what deer hunters called a scrape, where a rutting buck had pawed the dirt and pissed, a love note for a doe. Ardy took the sugar bag from his jacket pocket and unfolded it. Bucks did another thing in their amorous rutting season, they rubbed their antlers against low trees, stripping the bark away, leaving raw places in the trunks.

A quail burst from the dead cornstalks across the field: Oscar in the distance, driving his phaeton.

Ardy folded the bag in half, then in half again. He put it in his jacket pocket and stood and raised a hand in greeting.

"Evening," Oscar said as he drew close.

Ardy nodded. "Evening, Judge." He looked over the dead field before him at the line of evergreens beyond.

Oscar stopped the horses and sat holding the reins in the shade of the canopy, the cushions, plush velvet-red material, warm-looking. The kind of rig you'd take a woman out in. A pair of lanterns on both sides of the seat and fancy, polished fenders. The big wheels had red mud on the spokes. Oscar set the reins down and withdrew from his inside coat pocket a railroad ticket folded around several bills and handed it to Ardy, who took it without looking at it.

He unbuttoned the top button of his coat and stuck the ticket and money down his collar. He refastened the button.

"Where's your horse?" Oscar asked.

He pointed to the woods. "I seen a scrape back in there."

Oscar peered under some low limbs, obviously wondering what the hell a scrape was. "Well," he said. "Like always, this here meeting never took place. I'm on my way out to see about Ulrica. We just had the auction and it would break your heart. One of them Mitcham Beat thugs outbid a church for a piano. You ever hear the like?"

"Outbid a church, say?" Ardy was impressed. "What was the fellow's name?"

"Lev James. You know him?"

"Know of him. And I've seen him from a good piece off. But I ain't ever had the pleasure of meeting him face-to-face."

Oscar shifted in his seat. "What is it you're finding out there?" he asked. "Why won't you fill me in?"

Ardy glanced out past the buggy. "Judge, the reason you hired

254

me is to keep you clear of the muck. Mitcham Beat's got as much muck as any place I ever set a foot in. And the more you don't know, the better. I'll have you some news, soon."

Oscar took the reins. He looked like he wanted to add something but couldn't phrase it. Finally he goaded the horses, and the phaeton jerked and clicked away on its big wheels.

Ardy stepped back into the shade of the woods. He took out the railroad ticket. Counted the money. Fifty dollars. He recounted it and then began stuffing it into various pockets.

On the ride out, as he passed the scrape, he reined up the horse and dismounted and pissed in the wet patch in the raw spot of earth.

The whore lay panting underneath him, her soft belly rising and falling as he moved over her, her breath distant through the heavy cloth of his hood.

After he was done, their stomachs sticky with sweat, she whispered, "Boy, it ain't nobody give it to me like that since I was a little girl." She reached up and took the frayed neck of his hood between two fingers. To fasten it securely he wore a section of hanging rope noosed around his throat like a necktie.

"Well," she said, "do I get to see which of you it is under here?"

He turned his head in the hood. "Guess," he said.

She giggled. "Alrighty." She ran her hands up and down his back, riding over the ridges of his spine and up the incline of his rump. She cupped its two cheeks, squeezing them, then slid her fingers back up and rested them on his shoulders. "You ain't that William," she said. "He's taller than you. That other boy, too.

"And you ain't War Haskew neither."

He put his lips to her ear, he could feel her through the heavy cloth. "How you know?"

"A girl knows."

"My pecker's bigger."

She popped him playfully on the bottom. "Mind your manners, Mr. Hell-at-the-Breech."

"Well, you're right," he said, moving his hips, "I ain't none of them. Keep guessing."

"You couldn't be Buz cause he don't talk, and besides, you smell better than either one of them Smiths. But"—looking over his shoulder—"you ain't got no scars, either. Them two's covered up with 'em."

He shook his head. "No, not them, neither."

"Not Lev. You too skinny. And he don't let me talk, just makes me lay there like a dead girl."

"Do what?"

"When he comes over I'm to be lying here with my eyes open, wearing a dress. He comes up to the window and peeks in and watches me for a spell. Then he climbs in the window and pulls up my dress and does it pretending like I just died or something."

Ardy lay over her, breathing in the hood.

She looked down. "Why, you're ready all over again, ain't you."

"Shhhhh," he said, and took her arms from around his neck and held them against the pillow behind her. Through his eyeholes he could see that a darkness had fallen on her face.

"This ain't funny no more," she said. "Go on tell me. Who are you?"

He pushed up and left her lying in the bed. She looked more closely at his body.

"You ain't none of 'em," she said, sitting up, gathering the quilt and covering her chest.

He turned and walked across the floor and went outside, naked but for the sugar bag and his socks, and stood on the porch with his flesh tingling with cold, his breath a hot mist around his eyes, his nipples rigid, his erection pointing straight up. Trembling, he turned and went to the wall and pulled from its nail the set of six-point antlers that hung as decoration between the front windows and hurried back inside, pushed the door to behind him to see it was closed tight.

She was still in the bed, she'd gone pale. The quilt covering her. "Who are you?" she asked. "How'd you get that password?"

He came forward, raising the antlers.

"What are them for?" she asked.

He stopped at the foot of her bed and began to scrape the high posts with the antlers, scratching the wood.

"Stop it," she said. "This bed was my momma's."

"Was she a whore, too?"

She reached into the covers beside her and withdrew a stunted shotgun, its barrel sawed so short it resembled a long pistol. She raised it. "Now go on take that hood off."

He watched her, then shrugged and unnoosed the rope as if he were loosing a necktie and dropped it to the floor and took hold of the hood at the crown of his head and pulled it off. His erection was wilting.

"Who in the hell are you?" she asked.

The quilt fell, revealing one of her breasts, and she let go the gun's forearm to reinstate the cover. He threw the hood at her face and dropped to the ground. She fired both barrels high, into the wall. The dog was barking. Ardy rose up in front of her on the bed still holding the antlers and snatched the gun from her and flung it aside and raised the antlers to her neck and pinned her back against the headboard with them.

He rode from there directly to Carter's house. He unsaddled his mare and fed and watered her, then built a fire in the upstairs bedroom where his mother and Carter had slept. He drew himself a bath and sat smoking in the tub, gazing at the sawed-off shotgun where he'd laid it across the mantel. He lathered his face and neck and shaved, stared at his clean cheeks in the mirror. He washed

257

his hair, then went to bed and slept for fifteen hours. The next morning he rode into Grove Hill. After a breakfast of ham, eggs, and grits in the hotel dining room, he crossed the street, tipping his hat to a woman in a long green dress, and went into the courthouse.

Oscar listened to Ardy tell how he'd tricked Massey Underwood into revealing his membership in a secret society called Hell-at-the-Breech. Then, as he listed the members of the gang, Oscar wrote them down.

"What about the situation with the whore?"

"Took the money and left."

Oscar's eyes fell to his desktop. His hands were flat on the polished wood. When he moved them, their heated impression remained for a moment before disappearing. He let out a long breath. "Good work, Ardy. Will this Massey Underwood testify, if we go get him?"

Ardy shook his head. "No. I believe he's left the county."

"He has?"

"To be honest, I advised him to. Said after he'd sang like a little bird his buddies wouldn't take kindly to him."

Oscar looked at the clock. Then out the window. "You sure you can't go find him, bring him in—Billy can lock him up and we'll get the same confession out of him."

"He's in Mississippi by now, I expect. Or Louisiana."

"You should've brought him in."

Ardy didn't answer. He didn't like the judge's tone. He considered that he could shoot him right here. Then he said, "I'm sorry I didn't, Judge. You're right, Judge."

"Well. I got another job for you."

"Kill Floyd Norris."

The judge looked at him for a long time. "Yes," he said. "But I want you to take my nephew with you."

"Do what?"

258

"He's soft, which would've been fine if he'd gone off to college like his daddy planned. Now he'll have to stay here. I want you to toughen him up some."

"Judge," Ardy said.

But Oscar had called for the boy to come in.

Footsteps, and the office door opened. Oscar's nephew stood in a corduroy jacket, jeans, and boots. Carlos was a tender-looking fellow, long sensitive fingers and long eyelashes. Thin wrists. Ardy had disliked him from the first time he'd seen him.

"Judge," he said again.

But Oscar shook his head. "Not negotiable," he said. "The only thing I want you to guarantee me is that you'll keep him safe."

Ardy looked from the boy to his uncle. "Safe," he repeated.

They loped their horses over hills and through clean-picked cotton fields and back into woods with their breath sucked away behind them. Ardy had unshod the horses to silence them and several times he gave a signal with his hand and the two of them faded off of the road, ducking into the wall of woods, and dismounted in tandem, the boy taking the horses by their reins and slipping back farther in the shadows while Ardy crouched just inside the blanket of the trees. The boy would come lie beside him and they'd watch the road. Ardy called it drilling. "Comes to fighting," he said, "you can't afford no mistakes. Else your enemy will be the one laid up in the bushes with his sights on your head."

Before dark they reached Mitcham Beat and made camp back in the woods a hundred yards from the road. Ardy watched the boy water the horses at a blackwater slough and hobble them and remove their saddles and brush them down.

An hour later they were picking their way through a cotton field on foot, downwind of Floyd Norris's house. Moon high overhead, and bright. Soon as they'd drawn to within a hundred yards of the house, they dropped to their bellies and slid in in that fashion, holding their guns before them.

"He's got a couple dogs," Ardy whispered.

"Wait," Carlos said. "What are we gone do?"

"Why, kill the man killed your daddy. The hell you think?"

Ardy had crawled a few yards before he noticed the boy wasn't alongside him. He stopped and then crawled in reverse to where Carlos lay.

"What the hell, boy?"

"I don't know if Uncle Oscar wants this."

"He does. He said it."

"He didn't to me."

Ardy snaked his hand over and took Carlos by the throat. He closed his thumbs around the boy's windpipe and felt him struggle. He closed harder and said, "Don't never question me, boy."

Carlos's fingers were opening and closing in the cotton wreckage like moth wings in a spiderweb. With a gust of hatred so hot it surprised even him, Ardy realized the boy was so afraid, right down to the level of instinct, that his own hands wouldn't move to defend him, would only writhe there. He let go.

"You about a sorry little girl, ain't you?"

Carlos lay gasping.

"Carla. That's gone be your name from now on, till you earn you a man's name. Now you want to come with me, little girl, and settle this feud, or you want to lay here in the mud and cry?"

He didn't answer.

"Suit yourself."

Ardy crawled off.

Keeping the wind in his face, he veered right. The hounds were dark lumps on the porch. He went quietly, glad Carlos wasn't there to stir things up and wake the dogs, and arrived at the rear of the house unseen, unheard. He looked through a crack in the shutter and saw a pile of shadowy children sleeping by the fire and, through another crack, a man's shape in a chair rocking forward and back with his head straight up, gazing it seemed right at Ardy. He continued to rock, though, and did even as Ardy eased two soundless steps back and creaked open the shutter with one hand while pushing the rifle barrel in with the other. Before Norris could move Ardy squeezed the trigger. Norris's head snapped back and the chair tipped over, his feet flying up. Ardy stuck his head in the window, ignoring the scramble of the boys by the fire, and studied the man where he lay on his belly. He reached inside his coat and took the pistol and stuck his arm in and fired six shots into the body, which jerked with the first bullet but took the others as if resigned to it. When Ardy withdrew his arm he did it too quickly and his coat sleeve snagged on a nail, tearing the material and his shirt underneath and gigging his biceps. "Shit," he said, hung up. He'd set his rifle aside so that with his other hand he could dislodge himself when he heard the dogs and understood they were very close. He grabbed for the rifle but it fell, then they were on him. Oh, Carla, he thought, are you in for an ass whipping when I get back to you, little girly.

The next morning they headed back to town. Ardy's legs had been torn up by the dogs, one of which he'd eventually shot dead, though the other had escaped. He'd ripped an extra shirt into bandages and stopped the bleeding but rode in a gloom over his shredded pants.

Carlos was flung across his horse with a bullet hole between his eyes, one in his right shoulder and another in his belly, the horse covered in blood. They were a quiet duo now, so Ardy heard the approach of the other rider—who was singing—in plenty of time to guide the horses into the edge of the woods. He swung from his saddle and dumped Carlos and led the horses into a grove of pine trees where he hobbled them quickly. The rider's song still rising and falling in the air, Ardy hurried back toward the road and dragged the dead boy behind a rotten log and lay down beside him. In front of them, beyond the log, he could see a low spot in the road with a trickle of water cutting it.

"Half a dollar says his mule or horse will stop at that little crick yonder," Ardy said, pointing with his Winchester barrel. He worked his tobacco in his jaw and spat and glanced at Carlos where he lay on his belly just inside the shadows of a pair of young pin oaks. "Well?"

He waited, then, "I don't bet," he answered for the boy, in a falsetto voice.

"You what?"

Same girl's voice: "We don't believe in it."

He looked at Carlos. "How the hell am I supposed to mold you into a man if you act like a church lady?" He held out his hand. "Here. Shake my goddamn hand."

The boy lay dead.

Ardy reached and grabbed his cold hand and squeezed hard before he let go, the fingers mashed together and yellowing.

"There. We've shook on it. That mule stops in the crick, you owe me a dollar."

He looked off down the road. Birds crossed and recrossed, chasing one another, the air busy with their whistles. A shadow on the dirt and he looked up to see a large crow veer its course and light in the top of a leafless pin oak, watching them.

"Your more superstitious folk might take that for a bad sign," Ardy said. He shifted his rifle on the log and lowered his shoulder so his sights centered the crow. "Look at that," he said. "That peckerhead knows I ain't gone shoot, don't he?"

He watched the crow, its white breath borne away on the breeze.

Then he saw the man, on a mule riding in the middle of the dirt road, passing in and out of shadows. Heard his warbling voice.

"Quiet," he told Carlos.

The man sang, "She'll be driving six white horses when she comes, when she comes, she'll be driving six white horses when she comes, when she comes, she'll be driving six white horses she'll be driving six white horses she'll be driving six white horses when she comes."

"Look how he's sitting on that mule," Ardy whispered. "He's drunker than shit. This is gone be a cakewalk, boy. Go on cock your gun."

"We will all have chicken and dumplings when she comes, when she comes . . ."

Carlos didn't move.

"Cock it, dammit."

The boy remained frozen, so Ardy with his eyes on the faraway figure reached across and clicked the hammer of Carlos's shotgun slowly back.

"We will kill the old red rooster when she comes, chop chop . . ."

He saw now that it was Lev James on the mule, chop-chopping with his hand as if it were an ax with the actions of the song, and Ardy's insides seemed to fill with bright warm light. This would be three of the gang dead, their number cut almost in half. He clutched Carlos's shoulder whispering, "Wait, wait, wait . . ." as James drew closer, was nearly in range, fifty yards, his mule raising its muzzle at the smell of water and swishing its tail.

"Come on," Ardy whispered, "come on, you jackass, lower on down in there and go to dranking."

The mule approached the creek and stopped. James paused in his song.

Ardy bit his bottom lip. "Drank up."

The mule lowered its head and began to lap the water.

"A dollar," Ardy said to Carlos, "but you can pay me later. You can go on shoot whenever you ready."

"I can't do it," he whispered for the boy in a sissy's voice. "Oh, I'm a little girl I'm so *scared*, Mister Ardy."

Lev James may have sensed them then, as buck deer are said to be able to do, or maybe he heard something unnatural to his ears, or

263

perhaps he'd made a deal with the devil—which might have accounted for the crow's watchfulness—for without the smug expression on his face altering and without panic or even seeming to hurry—the only change you could see was a lock of hair falling across his eyes—he dropped his jug to the sand while reaching right-handed behind his back and withdrawing from his waistband a long-barreled pistol. As it passed his right hip he cocked it with his other hand like a trickshooter Ardy had paid a dime to see once in Hatties-burg, Mississippi, and then in a movement gauzy with speed he'd switched the gun to his left hand and raised his right forearm flat before his eyes for a prop and steadied the barrel over the forearm and sighted down the length of the gun.

He seemed smaller now. He'd hunched behind the mule's head and curled his shoulders inward. The jug had just stopped its roll in the road.

Ardy didn't hurry his first shot. He planted the squat bead at the end of his Winchester at James's breastbone. James hadn't fired, was still searching the brush for movement, when Ardy squeezed his trigger. James would have died quickly, except the mule raised its head into the bullet's path and was suddenly vomiting blood and teeth.

Flung back and off, James held on to his pistol as he flew and landed and lay flat in the dirt while the mule buckled to its knees squealing and panting, rolled onto its side, clambered back on its feet. Then it fell again, kicking. James scrabbled to his right to avoid the mule's thrashing, but kept it between them. He fired once, clipping a leaf above Ardy's head, and Ardy knew he would be a good one on your side in a fight. Carlos of course hadn't moved the whole time.

James fired twice more, both shots high, and Ardy held off, not wanting to give his position away.

"Who the hell's shooting at me?" James bellowed.

The mule had settled on its side and lay kicking and squealing

264

through its ruined snout, blood soaking the dust and creeping in its pool nearer and nearer to James's elbow. Ardy saw the outlaw's rump rise a bit and knew he meant to move forward, use the mule for cover, which is what Ardy himself would've done.

He came on all fours, but when Ardy shot, James's right sleeve puffed and he yelled an animal sound and grabbed his shoulder. Still he came, a flurry of knees and elbows. Ardy ratcheted in another round and fired, hitting James in the left foot. The outlaw yelled again and fell behind the mule, which continued to squeal and struggle to rise.

Until James shot it in the head and it lay still.

"Hey!" Ardy called. "You dead yet?"

James peeked over the mule's flank. "I'll be doing the killing today," he said. Then he did a surprising thing. He stood up. His shirt and pants were entirely red, though were it mule blood or his own Ardy couldn't tell. He walked with a limp, directly toward them with his pistol aimed. He'd reloaded and made their position. He fired once, twice. Ardy kept his head down. A bullet sprayed him with dirt. Another hit a tree. One smacked Carlos in his white face, destroying his nose and turning his head toward Ardy.

Good shot.

Then nothing. Ardy raised his head. James continued toward them, aiming, clicking, his gun empty. He kept walking, twenty feet from the edge of the woods, fifteen. He threw his gun at them—it landed just in front of Carlos's frozen face—and fell to his knees.

First Ardy thought he'd gone down at last, then saw he was digging at rocks in the road. He stood up with his right hand full and began throwing them with his left. Running. Ardy raised up on one knee over the log and aimed at the man's gut. A rock hit him in the shoulder and it hurt but not bad and he was glad it wasn't a bullet. He fired. James hadn't stopped running and Ardy fired again, and then the man was crashing between them, falling over the log with the iron odor of blood. When he landed he was still.

"That's one tough son-of-a-whore," Ardy declared.

To be sure he was dead, Ardy reached the barrel of Carlos's shotgun to the man's hair and pushed it up under the base of his skull. He pulled the trigger and the head burst like a melon. Then he stood and listened. What a silent world. He looked up into it. He felt like the center of something. The crow had flown or he would have shot it, too.

VI

Waite sat thinking in his office, sun coming in through the window and igniting the crystal figurine Sue Alma had given him to use as a paperweight. He never did stack papers under it, preferred to keep things neat, filed and locked away, but he did like to heft the thing— shape of an ocean fish, a porpoise—and he liked its weight, its smoothness. When he blew on it it misted up, he liked to watch it unmist in his hand. He'd enjoyed fishing as a younger man, taking his daughters in a little rowboat he'd made himself and named the *Clara Nell* after his two oldest. Now he smiled. Several years back Johnny-Earl had lobbied for a boat of his own, the *John Earl,* and Waite had got him the lumber as a Christmas gift that year and the boy had labored for nearly a week, refusing Waite's help, not even letting him come into the stables to view it on its sawhorses. When he'd finished, he ceremoniously led Waite, Sue Alma, and the three girls to the barn and with a flourish snatched off a bedsheet to reveal the boat. Instead of the *John Earl* he'd named it the *Sue Alma,* causing his mother to cry and Waite to flush with pride.

He shook his head, as if to clear it. Beside the paperweight lay a shapeless lump, the heel of Lev James's boot, with which he'd beaten poor Clarence Wilkins half to death. Waite had no doubt it had been Lev, who'd been at the auction and kept the Methodist church from getting itself a new piano. Lev had paid a couple of fellows to haul it

266

out to Mitcham Beat by way of Coffeeville—you'd never lug a piano through that damn thicket. Now Waite knew he'd have to go out there and pick him up for the assault on Wilkins, a thing he dreaded, knowing the man wouldn't come in peacefully. Which meant Waite was faced with riding out to Mitcham Beat and killing Lev James.

As he thought, he picked up the heel of the boot and held it. Something in the treads. He idly scratched at whatever it was with his fingernail, hoping it wasn't a year's worth of compressed horse shit. He unfolded his glasses and put them on and frowned at the gunk. It was of a certain viscosity that was familiar to him and he raised it to his nose aware even as he was doing so that if anyone happened to walk in or peer through his window they'd see him sniffing the bottom of Lev James's boot.

Pine tar.

He did the paperwork to arrest James for McCorquodale's murder and sat waiting for Oscar to return so he could get a signature. In the meantime he opened a drawer in his desk and removed a list of men who'd served as deputies in the past. One had died so he scratched his name off and pondered the rest.

Presently he heard soft footsteps down the hall, heard them stop as whoever it was looked at the four doors. He set his list aside and took his feet off the top drawer where they'd been propped, butt of a pistol within grasp. When he saw who came in his door, he closed the drawer.

"Hello, Bit," he said.

His friend looked haggard beyond reason, like a man who'd been dumped by a typhoon on an island: he wore pants much too large for him and a woman's lacy blouse with elaborate daisies stitched into the sleeves. His beard was caked in mud and the skin of his face was mottled red, covered in scratches and sores, red welts on his neck. Waite stood to see the rest of him. His pants were frayed at the bottoms, and for shoes he'd tied rags around his feet, the yellow-nailed big toe of one foot visible like the head of a turtle. By now the office had filled with the rank odor of something dead.

"I could arrest you for your smell alone," Waite said.

"Billy," Bit said. He raised a hand to his head as if he might take a hat off, but he wore nothing on his mud-flattened mat of hair and dropped his hand back along his side.

"This one I've got to hear." Waite pointed at his neck, the welts there. "What happened?"

"Just about got hung."

"By who?"

Bit was still looking out the window. "I'm fixing to tell you some things, Billy, that I ought to told you when you come see me last time. I had what they call misplaced loyalty. Well, here I stand in a ragged state, sucked back from Hades, ready to repent."

Waite put his handkerchief to his nose. "First let's get you cleaned up and get you outta that woman's smock. If any children see you, they'll have nightmares for a year."

In a tub in a hotel room Waite had charged the county for, and with the things Bit'd been wearing in a sour pile on the floor, the bootlegger looked just about human again, though against cleaner, whiter skin his wounds seemed more severe, especially the infected ones covering his neck. Waite had sent for the doctor and expected the man any moment.

"Did you sign their paper?" Waite asked.

Bit sat up in the tub—the water just about black—and ashed his cigar into the soap dish. "I didn't, Billy, but they was three of 'em come to my house. They said they was a organization that meant to attack the courthouse and get some new blood in there. They figured if they killed all the town fellows they could get their hands on, some good men would have to fill in." Bit inspected his cigar. "I ain't so sure they're gone find 'em, Billy."

"You mean there ain't enough decent town men to reconstruct the government once the good decent country fellows murder all the current folks in office?"

Bit raised a peeling yellow foot out of the water, then submerged it again. "You reckon that fellow'd heat up this bath?"

Waite went into the hall and looked over the balcony rail. "Jimmy," he called down to the clerk, "could you bring Mr. Owen some more hot water?"

Back in the room, Waite took his seat. "Go on."

"They wanted me to give up my stills. Wanted me to be partners with 'em. I said what did that mean, that I'd do the work and they'd share in the takings, and they said yep, that's about what it meant."

"And?"

"And I told 'em no. Which is when they started coming after me."

"Were they the ones who tried to hang you?"

He nodded.

"I need names, Bit. And I need you to promise me you'll testify."

"I'll give you the names, Billy, but then I'm fixing to leave the county. I'm hoping you'll help me get something to wear—'less you want me dragging around your town dressed up like a wild woman. I'll tell you who they are, and for payment I want you to set me up. Train ticket, some pocket money."

"I could arrest you, Bit. Put you in jail."

The old man shook his head. "We both know you wouldn't do that, Billy."

He was right. "Who are they?"

He told the story of his hanging then, of three hooded fellows ambushing him at his still and opening fire on him. He shot back and got one in the leg but they had him pinned down behind his vats. They started shooting at it and whiskey began running out onto him. They called out and said they were fixing to throw a torch over in there, which would've ignited the whole place. So Bit surrendered. They beat him up some, then took his shoes.

As if to demonstrate this, he raised one of his awful yellow feet from the water.

"Go on," Waite said.

He related the failed hanging attempt, how he'd known he was a dead man when they'd taken off their hoods and let him see their faces. Last thing he remembered was being noosed aback his own mule and Lev James beating dust from the poor animal's rump, trying to get it to move out from under him and leave him swinging. "It must've moved, finally," he concluded. "For I don't recall no more."

"How'd you get away?"

"Here's the strange part," he said. "They was all corned on whiskey they'd stole from me—good batch, too—and I reckon cut me down 'fore I was all the way dead. Lucky it didn't break my neck. They put that youngest Burke boy to burying me. I come to my senses covered in mud and like to scared him to death. But it was him let me go."

"How come?"

"Cause I don't think he's one of 'em. I think he just does what they tell him to."

"But the older Burke boy . . . ?"

"Him? Hell, he was giggling his fool head off when Lev was trying to get the mule to buck me."

"You said they're fixing to try something. They're gone come after the courthouse. You know any more details about that?"

"After Arch Bedsole got killed, Tooch called a meeting at his store. Wanted ever man in the whole beat there. Said he had a revelation for us all. So I went. Gathering like that's always good for selling a few jugs. But it came pretty clear to everbody that he was talking about some high-minded stuff. Said the whole county government was corrupt and that he wanted to organize against 'em.

"Bunch of fellows left, and I left with 'em. I wasn't interested in joining no alliance nor nothing. Done worked my whole life by

270

myself, didn't see no need to change then." He looked at Waite. "Nor now. So I ain't gone help you track 'em, and I ain't going to court and pointing 'em out. I'm just telling you what I know so you'll be able to go up in there and shoot the guilty ones and let the rest of them folks get back to normal."

Waite looked over the names on his list. None surprising. "What about Floyd Norris?"

The door opened and the men watched the clerk carry in two steaming buckets, rags around the handles.

"Obliged," Bit said after the clerk had poured them in, steam fogging his spectacles. The clerk gave Waite a wearied look and left, the empty buckets clanking.

"Go on," Waite said.

"Floyd Norris never was part of 'em, far as I know. I imagine he signed their paper, but so did everbody. Fellow didn't sign, he'd hear about it."

Urgent footsteps up the stairs and both men looked at the door and then each other. Waite drew his sidearm and Bit ducked under the water, out of sight. The door opened. The clerk.

"Sheriff," breathlessly, "they've brought in Carlos McCorquodale. He's been shot!"

Waite burst out into the bright cold sunlight. A crowd had gathered around a blood-soaked horse with the boy lying across its saddle. Ardy Grant was sitting off to the side on the wooden walk, his hat off and his features vacant. His legs bloody and his pants in rags. Two or three men were standing by him asking him questions. Someone had handed him a canteen.

"They sicced their goddamn hounds on me," he said.

Waite and the doctor arrived at the same moment and several men took Carlos down off the horse's back and laid him flat on the dirt road. He'd been riddled with bullets. Waite counted the holes he could see, forehead, nose, belly, shoulder, kneecap. He stopped and looked up at the sky.

Someone led the horse to the side so it wouldn't get spooked and step on the boy. A woman turned away, sobbing. The doctor ordered everyone back and knelt over him, placing a pair of fingers to his throat. He then laid a hand flat on his chest. Oscar York stood across from him, his face as white as Waite had ever seen it, and it was to him the doctor said, "This boy's gone."

"Tell me," Waite said.

Ardy Grant sat across from him. He'd taken off his coat, vest, and gloves, and with steady fingers dribbled tobacco into a paper. He rolled the cigarette tightly and licked it, then put the whole thing into his mouth before lighting it.

Waite folded his arms. "Goddammit, Grant. Tell me your story before I put you behind bars."

"I done told the judge."

"Well, you're fixing to tell the sheriff."

He inhaled his cigarette and blew a shaft of smoke into the light. "Well, me and the boy was out in Mitcham Beat—"

"Doing what?"

The door opened and Oscar came in. Waite rose and scooted his chair over to his ashen-faced cousin, who took it and sat. The sheriff leaned on the edge of his desk. "Grant here was just fixing to tell me what happened."

"He's already told me," Oscar said. "He told me him and Carlos got ambushed by that Hell-at-the-Breech gang."

"Do you mind if I get the details, Oscar? I'd like to know what that boy was doing out there."

"I sent him," Oscar said.

"You?"

The judge nodded. He rubbed the bridge of his nose. "Wanted

272

Ardy here to show him the ropes. Toughen him up." He flipped a hand. His eyes were red-rimmed and raw. "But go on, Billy, and question Ardy. Sure. Why not. Why not waste more time so they can make another trip in and shoot me. Or you. Maybe they're planning a raid for Christmas."

"Oscar—"

"No, Billy." Oscar stood up. He pounded a fist on the desk. "You've already had your chance. Hell, chances. And all you've done is wait and drink your bourbon. The rest of us, we're organizing a meeting. I'm sending Ardy out to gather folks. We're fixing to organize a damn posse and ride out there and put an end to this mess. You can come if you want. I don't care one way or the other."

He and Grant left, the young man limping on his torn-up legs.

From his table in the hotel dining room, his coffee untouched on the cloth, Waite watched them ride in. They'd been coming in groups of two and three all morning, rifles over their laps, sidearms tied along their legs, landowners from Thomasville, Coffeeville, Fulton, Dickinson, Whatley, even Jackson. Some had ridden all night to be here. Main Street—muddied by exhausted, sweating horses— reminded Waite of Mobile, men congregating in groups and comparing pistols, black boys hurrying to keep the public trough filled.

Every so often he had been turning his sugar spoon in alignment with the minute hand of the large clock over the fireplace, which showed near one. The owner's wife came and traded his cold coffee for a fresh cup and said it was a shock there weren't more customers, dinner was their busiest time. "Don't posses get hungry, too?" she asked.

"I expect you'll get besieged after the judge is done with his talk," Waite said.

A block down the street, the courthouse yard had filled with men with guns and the fence around the building displayed lines of boys balancing on its top rails to see what was going on. Another group of men came from the south leading a pack of horses and a wagon arrived with an armed escort of several men. Rifles, Waite thought.

Finally it started calming down as Oscar pushed through the crowd and mounted the stile over the fence and raised his arms for quiet. Waite watched from his window, then went out to the porch where he could hear.

"We're going to put an end," Oscar was saying, "to something that should've ended a year ago. Nobody's blaming anybody—it started way out in the country, and nobody had any way of knowing it'd reach into town so fast, though some of us worried it would. But the thing I want you to know now is this: It ends, by God, tomorrow at dawn."

A righteous rumble of assent from the men. Waite knew some of them, good merchants all. Married men with wives and families. The livery owner there. Owners of the bank. A blacksmith.

"My young friend," Oscar was saying, motioning for Grant to come stand beside him, "was a lawman in Wyoming but he's from here. Some of y'all knew his momma, Bess Carter. A good, Christian woman. Ardy come home to see to Bess's estate a while back. Those of you who don't know him, I ask you to trust me when I say he's a good man. He's been out in Mitcham Beat doing some investigating for me—"

"Where's Billy?" somebody called.

"Drunk," somebody else said, and a laugh went up.

Oscar said, "He'll join us later, I expect."

The hotel owner's wife had come out and stood beside Waite; he could feel her watching him.

"Now I'll admit something to you all here," Oscar went on, his voice lower, "and I hope you'll forgive me for what I've done. I let my nephew, Carlos, go out to Mitcham Beat with Ardy here. The boy needed toughening up, I thought it would do him good. That's

274

something I'll have to live with the rest of my life, for while they were out there, those sons-of-bitches ambushed Ardy and Carlos, set their damn dogs on 'em, and you know the result. The doctor's already said that it was the bullets of at least three different guns that killed the boy."

How come Grant didn't get hit? Waite wondered. He buttoned his coat and stepped off the porch between a pair of horses, the woman still watching him. As he went down the street, away from the gathering mob, two fellows hurried toward him.

"Where's the meeting?" one asked.

"Follow the noise," Waite said.

His advantages over the mob: one, he knew the land better than Oscar did, though it was possible that Ardy Grant might know it better than Waite. Two, by himself, without dozens of men on horses, he could move swiftly, as he was now, low on King's back, gigging him with his spurs. Finally, while the mob had many targets, Waite had only one.

He figured the Bear Thicket was his only choice—going through Coffeeville was too wide a detour. Still, it seemed to take longer than ever to get there, the woodlands on either side dragging past, King's hooves drumming and mud issuing from underneath them as if man and mount were the point of a tornado dragging across the ground. Just past the covered bridge his hat blew off but he didn't go back for it, didn't even turn in the saddle to see it roll to a stop beside the road or sail past the bridge and whirl into the slow water below. He bent lower.

He'd been out of the thicket for a while when, from a hundred yards, he spotted the dead mule where it lay in the center of the road. He skidded King to a halt and sat watching for anything to move. The wind in his face brought the strong odor of blood and King stamped, nervous. Waite dismounted and led the horse off the road,

275

through the ditch and into the cover of trees where he whispered in his flexed ears and tied him to a cross limb. Drawing his rifle from its scabbard, he crept to the east, closer to the mule's carcass. He'd always believed his instincts and now they confided to him that no living man was about. Still, he went silently, lowering each foot to the bed of leaves as if Bedsole's entire gang was waiting, itchy to kill. He stopped.

There was a man lying in the leaves.

Waite dropped to his haunches and raised his rifle. He could see legs and a back. He watched the man's shoulders for movement but saw none. Dead? He edged forward.

Dead all right. Though his head was an unrecognizable, exploded mess, Waite knew him by his new shoes. Lev James. The sheriff approached him and looked carefully about. With his foot he rolled James over. He raised an eyebrow when he saw he'd been shot a number of other times, chest, shoulder, calf, half a finger missing from his right hand. His left fist was closed; Waite knelt and prized it open to discover a pebble. Curious.

He looked at the sky—soon buzzards would blacken it and descend on slow wings to squat in the trees with their curved necks and featherless heads. Then they'd flap to the ground and stand watching, waddling toward James and the mule, and in no time they'd have their heads inside the dead, pulling out long red ribbons of entrails and raising their beaks to swallow.

Waite stood. Had Lev James been with the gang when they ambushed Grant and Carlos? You'd have to assume not, else they'd have taken him back and buried him. Which meant somebody else had killed James. Grant was the logical candidate, but why hadn't he mentioned it? Waite held his rifle under his arm and dragged the dead man out of the woods and into the road, beside the mule, and left him there. Hopefully, if Oscar's mob came this route, the body would cause them to hesitate a bit and give him more time. Maybe make them question Grant's story.

He checked his watch—five o'clock. Night coming. He retrieved King and pulled himself into the stirrups and off they went, Waite glad to leave the dead behind, wondering how many more would die before the moon and sun changed places again.

Darkness was upon him. He rode quietly now, suddenly nervous at the thought of Bedsole's gang. Hell, count it a miracle you haven't tripped over half a dozen fellows in the bushes, lying in wait to shoot anybody not their brother.

He'd half expected to find Bedsole's overrun with horses, the gang there waiting. Yet the store, closed, seemed quiet, and save smoke and embers rising from the chimney, nothing moved about it. He approached over the field, on his hands and knees, through the picked cotton. This move would be tricky, he thought. Though there were no dogs to warn of his approach, he was going in on at least two of them, and Bedsole would have no trouble firing on sight.

Once he'd cleared the cotton he rested, his body covered in sweat, dirt, bramble, beggar's lice. He waited, rechecking his rifle and the pistol. The attic light he'd seen before was out.

Here we go, he thought, rising, striding over the road, up the steps. He looked through the glass door and saw only the boy, sitting on a stool by the stove, reading a book.

The door was unlocked, so he walked in, rifle held at his hip.

Macky looked up when the bell rang and closed the book.

"Tooch ain't here," he said.

"Where is he?"

"Over to War Haskew's."

"Then you and me just might live a little longer." He jerked the rifle toward the door. "Come on."

The boy obeyed, still holding the book, giving Waite a wide berth, and soon he was following Macky through the cotton, the rifle in the boy's back.

277

"Where we going?" he asked.

"Never mind. Just walk."

"You gone kill me?"

"No, boy, course I ain't. But there's others that might try to."

At the edge of the field, before they entered the woods, they heard a wagon. They knelt while Tooch Bedsole rode up and parked the wagon underneath the shed on the right side of the store and climbed down. He called for Mack. When he got no response he drew a pistol from his coat and went inside the store.

"Let's go," Waite whispered, and pulled the boy into the safe, dark trees.

Instead of killing King with more travel, he and the boy holed up in the loft of an old barn. Waite was wary of lighting a fire and so the skin on their faces grew tight in the chill air, and as the night deepened their fingertips and toes began to numb. Some small animal scratched around the barn and kept them on edge and Waite got up twice on his sore knees to frighten it off. Coon or possum, though he never saw it. At least he'd brought a couple of blankets.

The barn had much of its roof missing; overhead the sky darkened and disappeared, no moon to speak of, and they looked about in wonder as a languorous fog climbed between the boards and unfurled down through the holes in the ceiling, enclosing them in a cold vapor. Waite commented on it, quietly, but the boy said nothing, just gathered the blanket around his head, covering all but his eyes, and peered out from the cave he'd made. Across the loft Waite leaned his rifle against a crossbeam and periodically looked out the door to see if someone had followed them. He unholstered his sidearm and set it on the mat of hay beside his thigh. Below, the horse shifted in the stall, nickered, and was quiet.

*　　　*　　　*

Looking out, the sheriff would mutter things now and again. He unscrewed the lid of his canteen and drank a modest amount of water, then offered it to Mack.

Mack was thirsty but felt he should decline and did, no good reason he could think of. He looked across the barn at the walls, wide planks roughly fitted to each other. He knew where they were. Behind him through the boards were the remains of a burned cabin, its chimney rocks home to hurtling chimney sweeps sharp-winging in and out of the top and mingling with the smudges of bats dipping low.

It was Tooch Bedsole's place. The one he'd set fire to.

"You sure you don't want none of this?" the sheriff asked. "Gone be a long wait."

He shook his head, the dry blanket scratching on the board behind him. All the night seemed enhanced, he could feel its corners widening and its bottom and top closing. They sat listening to a barn owl and Mack wondered if they'd ousted it from its home in the rafters or eaves. You called baby owls owlets. He remembered that from one of Tooch's books.

"Boy," the sheriff said, "I ain't gone lie to you. There's a mob of 'em coming in the morning, and your buddies, all of 'em, will likely be shot or hanged. There's been a fellow up in here spying around, and he's give 'em names. I don't know which names or how he got 'em, or if they're even mixed up in it. But I got a feeling the innocent will suffer alongside the guilty come dawn."

They sat.

"I got a few names myself, boy. I don't figure you'll confirm 'em for me, but you don't have to. I trust the fellow that told me. You wanna know why I trust him?"

Mack shrugged and closed himself tighter in the blanket. He wished they'd go below and Waite would start a fire. His toes were frozen. If there were a fire he'd just put his feet right in it and let his shoes start to sizzle.

"I trust him because he's a fellow come back from the dead, and I don't figure a man who's tasted hell will bother with lying on earth."

This registered on Mack slowly. He looked up.

"That's right," Waite said, as if he'd read his mind. "Bet you didn't know Bit Owen was a old friend of mine, did you? That me and him was in the War together." He waved a hand. "Not that we knew each other back then. Just happened to wind up at the same place near the end, when everthing was going to hell. End of a war," he said. "You don't want to be on the losing side, that's for sure."

He fell quiet, gazing up at the sky through the broken roof. "Well," he said, "Bit, he give me names. Said Tooch Bedsole was your leader. Which I figured. Said War Haskew was in with him. Lev James. Kirk James. And those crazy Smiths. Massey Underwood. And yep, even your own big brother, which I hated to hear. But Bit told me he didn't think you were in it. Said he thought you were just working in the store. So I come out here to get you. Take you back in." He paused. "You mind if I ask you a question? Not that I figure you'll answer me. Hell. You ain't give me a answer this whole year. But I'll ask, just the same: *Why?*"

"Why?"

"Yeah. Why'd you let Bit go?"

Mack remembered the cabin remains behind him and realized that on their way here, he and Waite must have crossed the spot where Mack had shot Arch. Followed the selfsame route Arch had as he bled, the night he'd crawled all the way to Tooch's. All the way here. Such a long way to come, bleeding. To die in your cousin's arms.

"I wanted to even things up," Mack said.

Waite looked at him. "What's that mean?"

Mack's face was hidden within the folds of his blanket, and he began to talk, to tell a long story of a very dark night, where two boys played at being bandits, not with the intention to hurt or kill, just

280

wanting to get some money so they could visit a whore. A story of a man on a horse and an old pistol firing—almost of its own desire—and of the horse fleeing riderless into the night. The two boys standing side by side over a dead body, having crossed a ditch into a world edged in black, framed by a hood. The story took him a long time to tell, and by the time he was done the small animal was back, scratching at the wall.

Waite said, "You killed Arch Bedsole."

His memory raced back to the day he'd visited the boys at the widow's cabin, a year ago. Mack saying, "It wasn't me." Of his visit to Mack at the store and the boy hiding. He knew it was true. "Who else knows?"

"Just William."

"The widow don't know?"

"I don't believe so. I used to think Tooch did. That he was keeping me on at the store to kill me when he figured the time was right. But he never did do it. Then he let me in his alliance."

"You're a member?"

"I didn't kill nobody else, though."

Waite felt dead tired. "So you figured if you let Bit go, the scales would be in balance."

"I hoped."

"Well, maybe one set of scales is," Waite said. "But there's another set."

The blanket had felt, as Mack talked, like the hood of Hell-at-the-Breech. No one knew you, you were invisible, you could do or say anything in your heart and there would be no repercussions. His confession had flowed so easily from the darkness, like something freed from the deep, bouldered molars of gravity, something air-filled sucked up into the light from the bottom of a river. All this time when he had waited, expected, almost hoped to get caught, he'd begun to feel as though someone had dug a hole in his belly, shoveled out his insides as if trying to make a grave of him, as though the shell remaining was nothing more than a tunnel to channel cold air from that world to this. As if the boy who had killed Arch Bedsole had walked off that night and not returned, that what remained was a place marker where a boy should be.

But now the Macky Burke he had been so long ago seemed to reenter this cold, cowled body, to kick into its legs and shrug into its shoulders and reach into its arms like a coat, to fit his own head into its head and peer with his eyes from its eyes into a land, again, of the living, and he was living in it, glad now to flex his fingers and hear the minute, gravelly pops the bones made, glad to fill his lungs with fog.

He parted the blanket and pushed it down around his shoulders. He'd never again hide his face, he thought. If they led him handcuffed up the steps of a gallows, he would not allow them to douse him with a hood. He would take note of the bright earth as it was swept away. He would not have the last thing he saw be darkness.

The sheriff opened his eyes. They looked at each other. Waite felt betrayed. But he felt something else, too. As a child he had once stolen a silver dollar from the church collection plate. No one had seen him or caught him. He had the coin in his pocket even as the plate made its way down the row and to the next row behind his back and on down the row and to the one behind that all the way to the back of the church and into the hands of those who'd count it. And those men never knew as they dipped their fingers in and removed the money and stacked it that the plate was one coin light. He had gotten away cleanly. Yet almost immediately he'd felt the guilt. His conscience heavy as iron. At home he'd hidden the coin in a pair of socks. He'd tried to forget it all week. But sometimes he would withdraw it from the socks and turn it in his hand. He took it outside one afternoon to a pond and reared his arm back to throw it in. But he didn't. Come the next Sunday, he slipped the dollar back in the plate. It made a loud *clank* but nobody looked. His father and mother faced the pulpit, singing "Higher Ground." Yet because Waite hadn't been punished, he continued to suffer, and home later, the weight of his conscience a drowning thing, he'd gone tearfully to his father and told him the whole story. His father had smiled and said, "You'll not be punished, son, as I reckon you've suffered enough."

Waite looked at Mack Burke. A child's face. The night calling of the owl had continued and the boy's eyes were up, seeking the bird. Waite tried to imagine a judge—it would be Oscar—sentencing him. Hanging him. And Waite would be the one to pull the hood over his face and to catch him if his knees gave way. His would be the last face the boy saw and the boy's face would forever stay with Waite as had each one he'd hooded.

"I got to take you in," he said.

Macky nodded. "I know you do, Mr. Billy." He blinked. "You reckon they'll hang me?"

He shrugged, a lie. "Depends on the judge, I reckon."

"Judge York?"

"Depends."

They sat looking across at each other. Then Waite turned his gaze to the darkness outside. He had more questions and began phrasing them to himself. But when he looked back at Macky Burke, the boy had fallen asleep, his neck bent and head on his shoulder at an impossible angle like a baby's head would be and Waite understood that this was the best sleep he'd had since pulling the trigger of his dead daddy's pistol and killing a good man.

Waite didn't sleep, it seemed a thing he'd never do again.

*   *   *

283

When dawn came, hours later, he had to shake Macky awake, but within minutes they were up and walking, Waite glad to get some blood pumping through his legs and arms, which felt like pieces of wood. He'd considered going east and circumventing the beat altogether, but that would take days. He handcuffed the boy to dissuade any thoughts of escape and followed him with his rifle in one hand and King's rein in the other as they crept out of the woods. He'd never been so tired, raw-feeling around his eyes. The road was unsafe, he reckoned, in case Oscar sent out scouts or posted guards, so he and Mack doubled up on the horse and walked through woods when there were woods available and then loped over the naked fields as Waite eyed the horizon for any movement, glad now for the fog.

Finally they struck a patch of forest along a road and Waite knew they'd be covered better now, though the dewy woods were a chore to navigate with two of them on a surly horse. The fog hung from trees like bedsheets out to dry and now Waite longed for the sun to emerge and burn it away. The boy walked ahead of him and King followed behind, so ill-tempered that Waite worried he might take a notion to charge up and bite a hunk out of the back of his neck.

Old boy, he thought, I promise you that if we get out of here, I won't bring you back.

VII

William Burke and War Haskew spent the afternoon drinking whiskey while sitting on a pair of pine stumps along War's back acres, watching their breath race away on the brisk wind, discussing the recently come-of-age daughter of a farmer named Jed Finch. War claimed he'd gotten a finger halfway inside her, a fact William disputed as an outright lie. But since the topic had come up, they decided to meander over to visit Annie.

When they arrived, the dog didn't commence to barking as it normally did but neither took this as anything worrisome and climbed the steps. The fact that War would go first hadn't even been discussed, it was simply the way of things, as he was older and William's employer, so William sat on the edge of the porch. War tossed him the jug and rapped on the door with his rifle barrel. He rapped louder when she didn't answer. When she still didn't say anything, and her dog didn't either, they went inside looking for her.

Three hours later War drew his buckboard up along the front of Tooch's store.

He came out.

"Where the hell's Annie?" War called.

Tooch tilted his head. "Say what?"

"Annie. We just went over yonder fixing to get serviced, but she ain't there. Dog ain't neither."

They got down from the wagon and War tossed Tooch a sugar bag with eye and mouth holes cut in it.

"What the hell's this?" Tooch asked.

"We found it at Annie's," William said.

Tooch looked at it.

War said, "That ain't all. She'd shot at somebody, too. But the place was quiet as a damn graveyard."

Tooch glanced to the left, empty road, and to the right, the same. Over the cotton field just trees. "Looks like somebody's trying to make it look like we killed her."

"Where's Macky?" William asked.

Tooch folded the sugar bag. "I was gone ask y'all if y'all had seen him."

War and William looked at each other, then back at Tooch. "It's something happening," he said. "Let's get everbody together."

He sent a worried William after the Smiths in War's wagon and War after Lev and Kirk on the horse. It was well past dark when War and Kirk came riding up double, and even later when William returned with Huz and Buz in the back of the buckboard.

From the porch, Tooch asked, "Where's Lev?"

"Went to a auction in Coffeeville," Kirk said. "Ain't seen him since."

"We figured he'd of showed up here by now," War added.

Tooch removed his hat. "I think we can count him out," he said. "If they didn't shoot him they got him in jail."

William interrupted. "Did Macky get back?"

Tooch shook his head.

Inside, they stood along the front windows looking out into the darkness as a heavy fog began to accrue around the store, hooding it in white. Each man except Tooch held a rifle as if he expected some enemy to stitch itself together from the elements of night and fog and line up in the street, one for each of the six members of Hell-at-the-Breech, his double from some nether place, perhaps even wearing a hood to mask the ghoulish face beneath. No one spoke. No one voiced the possibility of coincidence or reasonable explanation. When a voice did come it was Tooch's.

"Two teams," he said. "War, you and Kirk and William go east and make the loop. Come on back round sunup. Huz, you and Buz go west toward town. Stay near the road. When you get to the bridge, turn around and come on back."

"What we looking for?" William asked.

Buz pointed outside and then tapped himself near his right eye.

Everyone looked at Huz. "He says we'll know it when we see it."

Tooch told them to get whatever they wanted to eat from the shelves. Said go back and stock up on ammo and, hell, get another pistol if they felt inspired to. This might be big, he said. Or it might be nothing. But be ready. Each man did as told, going into

Mack's room, selecting from the Colts in the drawer beneath the rack and stuffing their pockets with boxes of cartridges, William leaving the room last and pausing to notice his brother's neatly made bed.

On the porch Tooch bade them a somber farewell and watched them descend the steps in a line, then he went back inside, closing the door softly behind him. William, Kirk, and War waved to the Smith brothers who waved in return and the two teams went on foot in opposite directions, into the fog, into the darkness.

HOOVES,
AND THE
CREAK OF
GOOD
LEATHER

November 29 and 30, 1898

AT FIVE-THIRTY IN THE MORNING, the posse assembled at the First Methodist Church of Grove Hill. The men numbered forty-seven with fifty-two horses and ponies and half a dozen pack mules already laden. Many of the company wore heavy coats and pants and high riding boots.

Inside the church, standing below the pulpit, Oscar York wrote their names and the names of their wives, or mothers if they were young or unmarried, in his neat script in a numbered column on a legal pad. A half-dozen disappointed boys under the age of eighteen were congratulated for their sense of civic duty but sent home, a fight breaking out as they shuffled down the road. Ardy Grant went about checking each man's weapon, breeching shotguns or single-shot rifles and peering down the barrels and evaluating the actions of repeating rifles. At six-fifteen the group adjourned to the hotel for a quickly set-up breakfast with Oscar and all the rest removing their hats as the Methodist preacher offered a prayer for their guidance and safety. Their mercy. When they'd eaten and pulled their napkins from their collars and loaded their firearms, they posed for a photograph in front of the store, then mounted up and walked their horses and ponies down the street like a parade as boys and old men and women and children watched quietly.

Once out of town they pushed the horses to a lope. Among the group was a pair of white-bearded veterans surnamed Thompson, who'd dressed in their gray Confederate uniforms and wore swords along their legs. One had an arm missing, the sleeve pinned into the pocket of his coat. Both smoked apple-wood pipes. There was the lawyer Harry Drake in a grass-colored duck coat and railroad hat, the undertaker and his two lanky sons and the newspaper editor's assistant who planned to write a story about the events—he'd already begun to collect statements, jotting them down in his note-book.

It's just gone on too long. These doings. Them people have to know this is a civilized nation and there ain't no room for their kind of doings.

I don't know what to expect once we get out there. I heard they had a whole army of country fellows.

I wouldn't want to be them. Against us.

More than one of the members of the posse had asked about Sheriff Waite's whereabouts, but Oscar had only said, "He must have gone on in. As a scout."

"Won't we need him?"

"We'll likely meet up with him out in the wild. Besides—" He pointed to Ardy Grant. "There's your next sheriff, gentlemen. He's been out there already, and already he's engaged with the enemy. Today he'll prove his worth."

Grant sat on his horse, all eyes upon him. They noticed where blood had soaked through the wounds on his legs. The look etched upon his face one of a man who'd seen things he'd rather not report. "I'll do my best," he said, "but I'm honored myself, men, to be riding in the company of Judge York and Lieutenant Virgil Thompson and his brother, Lieutenant Claudius Thompson, who killed Yanks under the command of General Nathan Bedford Forrest in the War."

The brothers nodded.

"There is no little experience here," Claudius Thompson said. He filled the bowl of his brother's pipe with Old Settler tobacco and handed it to the one-armed man and then filled the bowl of his own.

Oscar and Ardy Grant set the pace in the lead, Grant recommending that the posse travel two by two in a well-spaced line, cavalry style. Behind them the Thompson brothers sat high on an identical pair of fine dappled geldings and behind them rode Drake alongside a quiet barber named Walters.

"Judge," Grant said as they slowed for a sharp bend in the road, "you might want to ride back yonder in the middle somewheres. You gone be the first one they shoot at."

In his leather saddle coat, riding gloves, and Stetson hat, Oscar York made quite a figure. He wore twin Colt revolvers he'd never fired and carried across his saddle his Winchester bolt action 30.06. His boots were newly shined and his chin freshly shaved. His horse had been groomed.

"No, by God," he said. "I'll lead this troop by example."

"Amen, Judge," said Claudius Thompson.

The posse galloped over the rutted road, horses cantering and men watchful of the banks of dead ivy and bushes looming on either side of them, but each rider kept his fear contained in his belly and made himself a smaller target in the saddle and pushed his horse a little harder. Presently they passed into a bank of fog and out again and into another. Chips of mud rising in the air and turning and falling. Dull pounding of the horses' hooves over the road. When the trees grew sparse and gave way to jagged fields of dead corn and cotton, each man breathed more easily.

Seven more horses met them within half an hour, men from Dickinson who'd ridden all night. They'd heard of the gathering posse and thought still more men might come the next day.

Oscar welcomed the new arrivals and they rode on again.

Within an hour they came upon the homestead of a farmer who'd sharecropped for McCorquodale, a Christian of decent reputation, and stopped in front of the house in a mounted semicircle two rows deep, some of the horses trampling a clothesline with a few shirts hanging, hens scattered and babbling underneath. Several men angled their rifles toward the door as the thin farmer with a crust of beard and filthy overalls and mismatched shoes stepped out with his hands raised.

Oscar stood in his stirrups with his gloved hands crossed on his pommel and announced their mission to the fellow and told him to fetch a hat and coat if he owned them, said if he had anything to ride he'd best saddle it up, too, and quick-like.

"I reckon I ought to stay here, sir," the farmer replied, twitching as a bare-legged child ran from inside the door and grabbed his knees from behind and stood peering out between them with dirty cheeks and sores on his face and arms. A thin woman came out and pulled the child back inside.

"Wrong," the judge said. He looked at the men to his left, his right, then back at the sharecropper. "You ain't got a choice, mister. You're being recruited to help us stamp out an evil plague that's eating the soul out of this very land. Land you plant and plow. Your own livelihood. You expect us to come in and do your dirty work? Those rascals out there must be stopped and by God you'll help us do it. If you refuse, the least that will happen to you is you'll never farm again in this county."

When they rode on, the new recruit, who said his landlord had taken his mule, sat aback a horse for the first time in his life. There'd been a brief discussion of whether or not to arm him and Ardy Grant mentioned the possibility that this fellow himself might be a gang member. You never knew. Briefly they joked about shooting or hanging him as the fellow whitened in the saddle, but Oscar said he'd vouch for him, knew him to be a decent enough character. Someone else suggested the farmer would serve them better by riding in front—if anyone shot from the cover of woods or from a house, let them kill their own. Wasn't the posse doing a service for these rural folk? Then let the rural folk work to protect it.

Four more farms yielded six more sharecroppers and four gaunt mules and so now behind a shield of nervous locals the train of men felt more solidly protected. Spirits were high and jokes abounded and flasks of whiskey were tossed from horse to horse.

Within two hours they'd arrived at the covered bridge that marked the western boundary of Mitcham Beat. Now the talking ceased and the men dismounted to piss or stretch their legs and let the horses rest. Some led theirs down to the edge of the creek for water but others stood looking anxiously at the trees across the wide green creek. The land known as the Bear Thicket.

Somebody said they ought to just set it afire and let it burn all the way to Bedsole's store. Set it afire and follow the flames in. Show them hell. Show them a damned breech.

Too wet, Ardy Grant pointed out.

Oscar had remained on his horse and sat with his breath billowing away from his mouth and the cold wind chapping his cheeks, his legs concealed by his coat. He had a telescope which he uncapped and extended and raised and peered through for a long time. He, Ardy Grant, and the Thompsons conferred about strategy, should they go through the thicket where the possibility of ambush was greater, or go via Coffeeville and risk their element of surprise. They agreed to go on through here, but to send the farmers in first. Oscar called for them to mount up and soon hooves thundered over the bridge.

The horses moved quickly underneath them, but the Bear Thicket seemed a hundred miles long. It felt as though they were riding through a canyon at night, dark inways into the woods on both sides like caves where shooters could lurk, each knothole a depraved grinning face, each jutting black limb a gun barrel. Each rider wary that he might be the one whose head or chest fell within the sights of the dead-eyed country scoundrels, scoundrels who'd shoot and then before their smoke dispersed disappear farther back into the woods only to reappear somewhere else to shoot again. Jokes had hushed and more than a time or two someone got jittery and fired into the cross-stitched woods only to flush a brown thrasher or finch. Oscar called a halt and had Ardy Grant pass a stern word back saying not to shoot unless you knew what the heck you were shooting at, that all this nervous firing would do was let the enemy know their position. Then they clamored on.

Waite and Macky sat resting at the edge of the woods at the top of a hollow, a picked cotton field alongside it. They could not see far and seemed to be the only living things about.

King nickered, spooked. His breath a mist. Waite rose from the stump he'd been sitting on and gazed down into the bowl of the hollow but saw nothing. The land below seemed clear of the annoying underbrush, just sloping ground plastered with wet leaves. Trees every few yards and fences of light brown vines strung between the trees and corded about themselves. Leading the horse, Waite got them moving again, descending to the bottom, veering farther from the road. He guessed they'd gone two miles thus far, each mile put behind them bettering their chances to get out alive. Even his back felt a little looser, and so it seemed particularly wry of fate to produce, just as they reached the bottom of the hollow, two men out of the fog.

The pair appeared less than thirty yards away, and for a long bizarre instant the sheriff thought his eyes were playing a joke on him—the men seemed to be the same man, or man and reflection in air: they wore identical overalls and straw hats, and the same brownish beards hung down their denim shirts like palls of Spanish moss. They raised identical single-shot rifles, too, both left-handed, and both sent a bullet past Waite's ears on either side of his head.

He and Macky dropped flat to the leaves and scrambled behind a mound of sand as the men dropped, too, but continued to rattle off shots, reloading and firing the single-shots at a shocking rate of speed. Waite fired a few rounds, then made himself stop, he couldn't afford to waste ammunition.

Then *King!* he thought, and realized the horse was gone, escaped in the shooting.

The woods had grown very quiet now, even the drip of dew seemed to have receded. Waite looked around. The fog was lifting— bad luck. With him against the two of them, he'd do better with more cover. He scrutinized the terrain before him, trying to spot something to shoot at, but all was quiet.

"Mack Burke!" came a voice from down the hollow. Closer than Waite had reckoned. "That you?"

"Don't answer," Waite whispered. He peered toward where the voice had come from but saw nothing, just the brown leaf-splotched ground and trees. Then he thought he saw movement. A gust of breath already vanishing, but he made out the tree from which it came. He sighted it and waited.

One of the fellows broke out running up the side of the hill. Waite aimed at him, but a second before he pulled the trigger the man dove behind a tree growing sideways out of the ground. Waite kept his sight trained where he'd been but then saw him again, several steps to the left—he was going for position, to get them in a cross fire.

They were in a fix, plain and simple. He shifted to lead the moving man but remained aware of his twin, who he assumed hadn't left his original tree. He caught sight of the second fellow again, now a good thirty feet farther uphill, and fired twice, hitting nothing but leaves and trees. Then the man vanished. Something pricked him on the cheek and he thought he'd been shot but it was only splinters of bark from a nearby hit. The first man had been smart and located Waite's position.

"You recognize 'em?" Waite whispered.

The boy lay peering out into the distance, pulling at his hand-cuffs. He nodded. "Huz and Buz Smith," he said.

"They part of Tooch's bunch?"

Macky nodded. Then he shook his head.

"Which is it, boy?"

"I don't know," he said.

Waite whispered for the boy to stay low, to not move, and rolled

297

himself between a log and the roots of a tree, his elbows in foul-smelling water. He felt it was a good strategic spot, unless they rushed him. Better, too, to put a little space between him and Macky. If they rushed them, Waite would get one of them, he was sure.

When the posse finally passed the end of the thicket and was riding along a fence line, it came upon a hill and the first riders over the other side saw the tiny leaning smudge of a shack on the landscape with smoke rising from its chimney like a line drawn into the sky. Oscar called for them to quicken and they did, quirting their nervous horses and kicking up mud as they descended on the homestead. A trio of hounds appeared and one was trampled, the others tumbling tail-tucked-away. No one gave an order but the finest horses came sliding into the yard first and men jumped off with drawn pistols and marched over the porch boards and the brother of the cobbler Wilkins kicked in the door. He came out dragging a short bald man by the seat of his britches and the blacksmith wound a rope about his bare feet and tied the other end to the pommel of his saddle.

The fellow screamed his innocence as he sat in the dirt. One of his arms was in a sling made from a diaper. Oscar raised a hand for him to quiet down and asked his name.

He stuttered it out. Butch Reed.

"Ardy," Oscar said, "you've been out here in this wilderness doing your detective work. What have you dug up about Butch Reed here?"

"He's a night rider," Grant replied, poking a chaw of tobacco into his mouth with a finger. When he had it secure he wiped the finger on his horse's neck and put his glove back on. "One of the worst ones. A member of Hell-at-the-Breech, all right."

"It's ah, ah, ah lie," Reed said, flapping his good arm.

Grant was off his horse in a flash, a knife from his belt at the man's throat. "You call me a liar again and you won't make your own hanging."

Oscar swung down and put a hand on Grant's shoulder. The young man pushed Reed to the ground.

"Are you a member of this lawless band?" Oscar asked him.

"I am nuh, nuh, nuh not, sir."

"Did you sign their paper?"

"I never signed no no no no no paper," he said.

"What of this, then?" Grant asked, taking from his coat a soiled piece of newsprint. He unfolded it slowly. "It says 'Butch Reed' right here."

The man's face grew even whiter.

"Well, I did sign," he confessed, "but they they they they they made me. They held guns on me and said if I didn't they'd burn my house and barn d-d-d-d-d-down and shoot me in the gut." Then crying he said they'd forced other fellows to sign, too. Made them slice open their hands and write it in blood. He said a lot of them out here were for the gang but some weren't. Some were just trying to raise a crop and feed their families.

"This day will be recalled as the day justice came through," Oscar said, turning. He climbed onto his horse. "And this gang and all its members will be stamped out. You, sir," he said to Reed, "have sealed your fate with your lie."

Grant remounted and they spurred their horses, Reed screaming as he was dragged, but soon his cries were lost in the pounding of hooves and only those in the rear of the posse who cared to look back saw the pregnant woman and a pair of young girls come onto the porch and watch them go.

They cut across a field looking for a good hanging tree but saw none and turned left onto a narrow wet trail between two more fields.

"I believe we took a wrong turn and wound up in Illinois," the lawyer Drake called.

They found a medium-size sweet gum dead center in a field, a child's swing dangling. A few grackles lifting from its upper limbs. The gum looked sturdy enough to hold the weight of a man, but when they knelt in the mud to noose Reed's neck they found him dead already, his skull caved in from a hoof. They pulled him into the sky anyway and left him swinging. A sign of things to come.

Someone shouted and pointed at one of the country fellows they'd drafted, galloping away on the horse they'd given him, kicking it viciously in the sides.

"He'll tell them we're coming," said Virgil Thompson.

"Ardy," Oscar said.

"Yes, sir."

He got down off his mount and pulled his rifle from its scabbard.

"Don't shoot," another of the farmers said. He hopped down from the mule he rode. "That was his cousin y'all just pulled up in that tree yonder."

As if he didn't hear, Grant pushed his hat off and knelt on one knee in the high dead bracken and cocked the rifle and aimed. He paused to wipe dew from his cheek and aimed again. The fleeing man seemed out of range. Then Grant shot. In the distance the farmer lurched and tumbled sideways off the horse. His legs came up once and then he was lost in the field. Two fellows were dispatched to retrieve the animal but ordered to leave the man where he lay. Then the posse pushed on.

Soon they'd left behind the flat terrain of field and were riding alongside yet another forest of pine trees on land that rose and fell. They rode through those pines and through more fields, coming upon a tiny cabin with a springhouse beside it and a fenced shed in the rear. A search found the cabin empty but there were warm coals in the fireplace, a pot of coffee half gone.

Beware, Oscar advised, they're around, and close. Keep your eyes on the trees. They left two men stationed at the cabin with instructions to capture anyone who returned, then the rest went on.

Half an hour later, at point, Ardy Grant saw a riderless horse loping across the field. He raised an arm and the great moving mass of men and horse came to a gradual stop, like a train slowing. As the horse drew near, Oscar said, "My god, that's Billy's."

Grant handed the judge his reins and dismounted, walking slowly toward the spooked horse where it stood sideways in the road, wall-eyed, its tail jerking. He spoke softly and raised a hand and sidled up to it, took its reins where they hung down and adjusted the bit. He stroked King's mane and fed him a carrot from his pocket and said more things. After a few moments he led the horse over to Oscar and said, "We have to assume they've killed the sheriff."

Oscar lowered his head. He raised it.

As men behind heard this news and passed it back through the posse, each rider straightened in his saddle. Some removed their hats. They looked at one another in silence, and then cursed or said they were doing the right thing, being here. They said it had to end, and end today. This wasn't any way to begin a new century.

Grant had pulled up onto his own mount and with Waite's in tow they began to ride hard again.

They came to a house and Grant rode right up on the porch and began firing through the windows. A woman screamed. A girl. The Thompson brothers had ridden around the side, tearing down a garden fence, and were waiting at the back door when the family spilled out. Claudius Thompson leveled his long pistol at the farmer who had shaving lotion on his cheeks and neck and shot him in the chest. His wife shrieked and flung herself down onto him. Several barefoot children scrabbled underneath the porch. One older boy, fourteen or fifteen, stood his ground and Virgil Thompson drew a gleaming shotgun from its sheath alongside his horse's withers. The boy backed up against the house. He shook his head. One-handed, Thompson breeched the shotgun and checked its loads. He snapped it closed, raised it one-armed, and shot the boy in the head.

Much of the posse had passed and was headed to the next farm on the horizon when Oscar got his horse, which had been spooked, to the back of the house. He looked at the dead man and boy and then at the Thompson brothers.

No one spoke.

The woman was still shrieking. She flung herself at Oscar's horse and he pushed at her. He said something nobody heard, then a gunshot came from inside the house and a bullet passed through the empty sleeve of Virgil Thompson. He and his brother both raised their pistols and fired into the window, exploding it in. They spurred their mounts around the house and paused at an angle from the windows.

"Send a man in," Claudius Thompson commanded.

Grant rolled off his horse and ran to the edge of the wall, pistol drawn. He crept alongside the house—grinning, Oscar saw—and at the corner turned and dashed to the front door. He kicked it open and went in firing. A moment later he came out.

"All's clear in here," he said.

They noticed smoke coming out the windows, and by the time they left to join the rest of the men, fire was licking out the front door and the children were crawling from under the house coughing.

Across the field more of the posse had shot a man a half-dozen times and shot several wiry blue dogs and corralled the man's wife and another woman into the pigpen. A light rain had begun to fall. One of the women held a squalling baby.

Oscar, now ashen-faced, called for a halt. He got down from his horse and seemed unsteady on his legs. He handed the reins to Drake. He looked at the dead man where he lay on his belly in the mud with nothing in his hand but a pair of pliers. He looked at the two women on their knees in the pigpen. The baby kept screaming.

"Somebody get them out of there," he said.

The barber slid his pistol into his pants and moved to obey but as he approached the pen the women shrank back, clutching each other, the baby between them.

"We must interrogate any man before he's dealt with," Oscar said. "I'll not have a massacre on my hands."

302

"You've got that already," Virgil Thompson said.

"But in war," Claudius Thompson added, "such is sometimes necessary."

Oscar looked at Grant. "Let me see your list, Ardy, and we'll determine if this man's name is on it. If it's not . . ."

He never finished. Someone was shooting to the east, perhaps half a mile distant.

Grant turned his horse that direction and whooped. Others followed. Oscar looked again at the women in the pen, both crying now, the baby splattered in mud.

"Oh my Lord," he said.

The road curved into trees. The posse followed it a quarter mile in. Gunshots were louder now, to the north. Grant selected three young men and told the others to spread out along the road in as long a line as they could, fifty feet apart.

"If we flush 'em out," he said, "shoot 'em."

The fog was gone but all Mack could discern were trees. Waite gazed out, from time to time he'd raise his rifle and shoot, then peer to see if he'd hit anything. There were other gunshots, too, coming from the west. Waite didn't seem to notice them.

"Mack!" Huz Smith called from down the hollow.

He wanted to answer.

"You okay, boy? He got you gagged?"

"Don't say nothing," Waite hissed.

Mack looked to the top of the hollow. He'd had a revelation. Telling Waite about his killing Arch had freed him from his guilt, but now here he was in custody with his hands bound, on the way to a hanging. At first that prospect had seemed a relief after a year's worry, but now as bullets flew overhead he knew the last thing in the world he wanted was to die—by bullet, rope, or anything else. He wanted to live. What if he'd told Tooch the truth, he wondered.

303

Tooch at worst would have killed him. Which was what the town folk were going to do. Yes, maybe Tooch would have killed him, but he might very well have had another angle. Tooch viewed things differently than most.

Mack began to wonder what might happen if Waite got shot here, now. If Mack's confession died with him.

Ardy Grant and his men spread out and crept into the trees, down the ridge and up another, toward the gunshots, which were louder, though sporadic. Grant said he thought it was two if not three weapons. With such wet leaves underfoot they could travel without noise and with their dark clothing they were hard to see. When the shooting stopped, they stopped, too. When it came again—*pop pop, pop*—they veered toward it and presently saw a fellow in overalls lying behind a log. He'd removed a straw hat and it lay beside his elbow in the leaves. Grant raised his rifle and laid the sights on the man's back and shot. The other men fired, too, and the country fellow jerked and then lay still. He jerked again and they fired more.

"Who's there?" Grant called once the echoes had faded, the smoke gone.

"Sheriff Billy Waite," came the reply. "And a prisoner."

"It's clear now, Sheriff," Grant called. "We've shot this sumbitch for you. It's me, Ardy Grant."

"There's another one behind me," Waite called.

Grant told two of the men to escort the sheriff and his prisoner back to the posse and the third to follow him—they were going after the other.

"We're running through," he yelled to Waite. "Don't shoot us, now."

*   *   *

304

Waite felt a mixture of relief and worry as he picked his way through the bramble and huckleberry bushes toward the road where he could already see the movement and color of men on horseback and hear low voices and the squeak of leather and horses nickering and blowing. He was out of one fix but here was another to negotiate, this one stickier because it involved friends. At least with enemies you knew where to aim.

Two other younger fellows, the newspaper editor's assistant, Parvin, and a surveyor called Brady, were dragging Huz Smith's body by the arms. Waite had relieved it of its rifle, a pair of pistols, and a bowie knife. Macky walked alongside Waite, still handcuffed, quiet as ever.

Waite helloed the road so the men, likely nervous, wouldn't open fire, and a voice hailed him in.

Several members of the posse dismounted as Waite and the two townsmen picked the long brittle wires of briar from their clothes and hair and brushed at their sleeves. Waite dislodged a brown thorn from his forearm. Macky looked terrified and didn't remove the flecks of briar and leaf still in his hair and attached to his clothes, causing Waite to remember the old folks saying how if you came across a fellow with leaves or twigs in his hair, he might well be a ghost.

Several men had gathered around Huz Smith's body. His shirt had come untucked and a shoe was missing.

Parvin and the surveyor were giving a report to Oscar and the others. This here one dead. Another on the run. The sheriff yonder rescued with his prisoner.

Waite wanted to find a place to sit down but didn't. He looked over the grim faces of the members of Oscar's posse, many of them men he knew, fellows he spoke to on the street or sat across from at church or transacted business with day to day—the undertaker there, a clerk there, there the pharmacist. Even the dentist. A dread had settled on Waite. This wasn't a posse of legally deputized lawmen; it was a lynch mob with an appetite.

Oscar came forward and he and Waite looked each other over, Waite's clothes torn and his face cut and dirty, his pants and boots wet and mud on his elbows. Oscar wore a worried look and Waite was surprised that he didn't seem to be enjoying the high drama of it all. Something must've happened.

"Oscar," he said, taking his cousin's gloved hand. "This is quite a party."

"I'm glad you're okay, Billy," Oscar said. "We found your horse a ways back and assumed the worst. He looks plumb rode to the bone."

"I'm glad you caught him. Me and him will both be relieved to get the hell out of this part of the county."

Oscar looked disappointed and cast a glance back at the Thompson brothers. Waite had long admired them, a pair who had reached the rank of lieutenant in the War, and were now co-owners of the bank.

"Hello, gentlemen," he said. "Glad you brought your sabers."

"Sheriff," Claudius said.

"Billy," said Virgil.

Oscar said, "We thought you'd join us, Billy. We need you here. Your experience."

Waite gazed past his cousin at the remainder of the men, some mounted, some not, some casting their eyes warily at the shadowed trees, and others glaring at the prisoner. A couple of them were approaching the boy, who stood quietly by a sloping bank of earth. He had his head down.

Harry Drake had worked himself closest to Macky and was talking quietly to him.

"Let me go see about this," Waite said, nodding to Oscar and the Thompson brothers and crossing the road to place his hand on Drake's shoulder.

"What's the good word, partner?" he said.

"I've never seen a dead man standing up," Drake said.

306

Waite noted the rifle the lawyer held. The pistol stuck in his waistband. "Well, he ain't dead yet," he said affably. "I'm fixing to take him on to town, leave y'all to your work. Truth is, he might need a good lawyer. You know one?"

"Billy," Virgil Thompson said behind him. "You know we can't let you take him."

He turned to face the old man and in doing so stepped casually between Drake and the prisoner.

"Osk," he said quietly, "this boy is arrested and in my custody. He's become my responsibility. I give him my word. Why don't you and your group go on and finish up whatever you've started here, but don't try to interfere with me carrying out my duty."

"Sheriff," Virgil Thompson said, "tell us his name."

He didn't. He looked at Oscar and tried to read his face. Something was troubling his cousin.

"Who is he, Billy?" Virgil Thompson repeated, almost gently.

"I'm damned if I'll tell you."

"Billy." Oscar leaned close to Waite's ear and whispered. "This has about got out of control. I don't know but that we've shot some innocent folk already."

"That's your doing, Osk. But if we let them shoot this boy, it'll be one more."

The bushes rattled down the road and three dozen guns went up.

"Hello in the posse," Ardy Grant yelled. "We're coming in."

He came out of the woods clutching his rifle, briars stuck to his sleeves. He batted them loose. Another young fellow followed on his heels. They trotted up the road swiping at beggar's lice on their sleeves.

"Morning, Sheriff," Grant said, stopping beside Oscar. He had a cut across his cheek and blood had dried in it.

Waite gave a curt nod.

"No need to thank us for getting you out of that spot back yonder," he said, looking around. "Appears you're in another one here."

"You get him?" someone asked Grant.

"Hell no. Fellow run like a goddamn chicken. We never really even seen him, just smelled him." He looked at the dead man. "Got that one there, though, didn't I?"

Grant noticed Macky behind Waite.

"Who we got here? Damn if it ain't Macky Burke, Toochie Bedsole's little house nigger."

Now a mumbling began among the riders, the name passing back among the craning necks. *Burke.* They began to line up across the road, getting their guns ready. Those still mounted were swinging down and joining the line which Waite knew with a lightness in his gut was a firing squad.

"Well," Grant said. "I appreciate y'all waiting for me to get here." He reached inside his coat and came out holding a revolver.

Waite had been scanning the faces of the posse, making eye contact with each man he knew. Most avoided looking at him, though, and were watching Grant. The young man walked over to the Thompson brothers and stood below them, talking quietly. Oscar seemed puzzled now, gazing at Macky Burke where he stood.

Waite felt inside his coat pocket for the handcuff key and reached calmly behind him and put it in Macky's hands.

Grant held the Thompson brothers' horses as they dismounted, then handed the reins to the fellow beside him. The three of them walked over in front of Waite.

"We thank you for bringing this one to us," Grant said, gesturing with his pistol for Waite to move aside. "We'll take him now."

"I can't let that happen, Grant," Waite said.

"The hell." Grant's eyes bugged. He raised his pistol and aimed past Waite's shoulder and shot, so near that for a moment Waite couldn't hear anything. Waite drew his own sidearm from its holster and put its barrel against Grant's stomach. Grant looked down. He understood what was going to happen and the skin tightened on his face, moving his ears back.

"Don't," he said, but Waite did.

Mack didn't hear it. There was an explosion, and he found himself facing halfway around from before. He tried to move his arm but couldn't and knew he'd been shot. In the left shoulder. He was afraid to look at it but did. It was bleeding, his entire arm numb. He couldn't feel the hand at the end of it but knew it still held the key. Somebody was moaning, he wondered if it was him. He sat down in the road.

Waite found himself gazing down as Grant lay in the sand holding his stomach. He coughed and retched. He looked up at Waite, his eyes confused, blood beginning to trail down from the corners of his mouth. He retched again, then fell back and rolled like somebody in holy ecstasy, arching his back and kicking himself toward the other side of the road where men moved aside in awkward silence to let him writhe. Some had pulled out their own pistols in case Grant wanted to take anybody with him. Most seemed to have forgotten Waite and the boy.

Waite had swung his pistol to cover the Thompson brothers should he need to shoot. They were watching Grant, who was cursing a steady stream—"Shit fuck hell goddamn shit"—now on his belly. When he rolled back over his entire shirtfront was red as a flag. He held another pistol, a derringer Waite had already seen him slip from his boot, and before Grant could raise it Waite shot again and saw Grant's left eye sucked into a black hole in his head.

He lay still.

Oscar stared down at him, the left half of his face painted now in blood. "Hell, Billy." He drew one of his twin revolvers as if in after-thought and held it canted toward the trees.

Waite forced his grip to slacken. Despite the heavy pistol his arm felt light, as if it might float up on its own.

The tension had eased and Waite remembered that the boy had been shot. He glanced behind him where Macky sat cross-legged, stunned. His shoulder bloody.

He looked at the line of men across the street and knew he had very little time to rein it all in.

"If anybody shoots this boy," Waite called, "you see what will happen. Even you, Virgil. Or you, Claudius. Harry. Oscar." He could remember no one else's names or he'd have gone through the whole list. All he could do was say, "You, you, you," pointing at each man.

Oscar knelt beside Grant and, careful not to get blood on his hands, went through his coat. He found what looked like a train ticket and stared at it for a long time.

"What you got there?" somebody asked him.

"Nothing," Oscar said. He continued to search his pockets until he withdrew the paper Grant had read from. He looked at it, then crumpled it in his fist.

"There's no names on this," he said.

"My Lord, Billy. What have I done?"

They'd moved off from the others.

"Killed some folks who might be innocent," Waite said.

"No," his cousin said, "the first fellow said he signed a paper. Ardy, he had that paper . . ."

"Osk," said Waite, "this is gone be a long time getting sorted out. Meantime you gotta put that in the back of your mind. Right now you've got to get control of this mob or it's gone get worse."

"You can do it," Oscar said. "They trust you. Me," he said, "well, they've lost respect for me. If I were them, I would have."

Waite knew he could do it. Could turn them around and head

310

them back to town. If he had to, he'd shoot somebody else to prove it.

But how many others were out there now, how many more members of Hell-at-the-Breech? With Lev James and one Smith dead, the others were liable to come into town madder than hell, seeking revenge, or they'd lie in wait along the road as they had with Anderson, and who knew who else they'd shoot. Might go after Waite or even Sue Alma.

"Okay," he said to Oscar. "I'm in charge, though. You'll do exactly as I say."

His cousin nodded. "I thank you, Billy."

"We're going to Bedsole's store. We're gone get Tooch Bedsole. And then we're going after some others. But it won't be done by no goddamn mob."

"Tell me what you want."

On the road, Waite had each man raise his right hand and he swore them in as deputies. He told them they'd fire only when he gave the order, or when they were fired upon. He told them the names of the men he knew were guilty and said that those men and those men alone would be dealt with. And he said again that if anybody touched the boy Macky Burke, he, Waite, would shoot that man.

Before they left, he saw that Macky's wound was tended to, it wasn't bad, little more than a chunk of meat shot out. Waite asked him if he felt okay and the boy said he reckoned he did.

"I thank you," he said.

"I wouldn't do that yet," Waite told him.

They mounted up, formed into lines, and began to ride east, toward Bedsole's.

War Haskew, Kirk James, and William Burke had spent a miserable night in the woods. Kirk had brought a jug which they'd resisted until they got so cold they tapped into it. After a while they found a dry spot and sat down to wait for daylight.

By the time the sun came up and burned off a little of the damned fog they were on the way to being drunk and they'd gotten a little fire going against all their better judgment. They were arguing about what to do. War Haskew said go back toward the store and find Tooch. Kirk said get the hell out. Just go. Every man for himself. William Burke was swayed to each argument until the next argument came.

The posse paused in a wide field surrounded by a pine thicket after two ponies collided and sent their riders flying. One of the ponies had broken its leg and had to be shot, and the rider of the other had dislocated his shoulder. While two fellows worked at getting it set, one of the lookouts shouted that someone was coming.

There were four of them, all armed, walking their mounts along the tree line, the lead man riding a fine roan with a white handkerchief tied on the barrel of his rifle. The lightest cold rain had begun to fall, beading on the shoulders of the men.

"They want a parley," Virgil Thompson said, pipe in his teeth.

Oscar uncapped and extended his telescope and peered through it, then handed it to Waite.

"That's Tom Hill out front," he said. The other men rode mules.

"Who's with him?"

"Can't tell."

Waite told everybody to stay put and rode out, meeting Hill, by himself, halfway over the field.

"Billy Waite," Hill said. "What the hell are y'all doing, riding like horsemen of the apocalypse, killing innocent folk?"

"There won't be no more people killed who don't need killing," Waite said. "I've took control now. Done deputized these fellows and we're gone cut this Hell-at-the-Breech gang's head off and stomp

312

on its neck. I know who's involved and who ain't." He drew his sidearm, aimed it at Hill's face. "Give me the names of them fellows with you."

Hill straightened in the saddle. He looked back at the three men who'd readied their shotguns, and held his hand up for them to wait. He said their names.

Waite lowered his pistol. "They ain't on our list. And you ain't either. So you fellows are invited to join us."

The justice gazed past Waite to where the posse stood like a pulsing black cloud of smoke.

"Join you?" Hill looked incredulous. "After what you've done to our beat?"

"Yeah," Waite said. "Either join us or oppose us."

When the posse rode toward Bedsole's store the rain had quit and their number was four stronger.

Mack rode alongside the sheriff on the outside of the mob, light-headed and handcuffed, but with the key in his right fist. The men around him rode with their rifles and shotguns unsheathed and all cast wary glances across the fields. He could tell from their quiet conversations that they expected to be fired upon from the trees, and he looked at the trees himself but worried that if any of Tooch's men tried such a tactic they'd lose. The fog along the ground resembled smoke, as if the world were smoldering in its heart.

Out of ammunition, Buz Smith climbed the slippery hollowside and peered at the store from the edge of the trees. Smoke from the chimney, nothing else. He hurried across the croquet court, its wickets pressed flat by weather, and went in the back door. Tooch was standing by the front, looking out. When he saw Buz alone he frowned.

"Where's your brother?"

Buz shrugged. He was soaking wet and cut in a dozen places. He took off his hat and went to the woodstove and held his palms out to get warm. He kept his rifle under his arm.

"What's the story?" Tooch asked.

Buz gestured in a way Tooch had seen a hundred times but it made no sense.

"What the hell you saying, Buz?"

The mute wiggled his fingers. He waved his arms. Tromped his feet. Ticked off numbers on his fingers.

"Did they get Huz?"

Buz nodded, then shrugged.

"You saying you don't know."

He nodded.

"Who was it?"

Shrug.

"How many?"

Shrug.

"Did you see the boy?"

Nod.

"Where?"

He pointed west.

This went on for a long time. Buz finally went to the mail desk and got paper and a pencil and drew a stick man with a star on his chest.

"Tom Hill? Justice of the peace?"

Shaking his head.

"Billy Waite?"

Nodding. He drew a smaller stick figure.

"Mack?"

Nodding. He drew two others, pointing at himself and then to one of the men.

"You and Huz?"

314

Yes. He drew them as they'd been in the woods and then drew three other men sneaking up behind them.

"Who were they?"

Shrug.

Tooch looked out the window again. "If it's three fellows I ain't worried. But if it's more. You think it's more?"

Shrug.

Tooch had laid out several pistols on the counter. He picked up a Winchester and checked its loads. He went to the window. He asked if Buz was hungry and he nodded. "Go on get something," Tooch said, pointing to a shelf. Buz went about cutting precise squares of cheese and laying them on several crackers he'd lined up along the counter by his pistol and several groups of cartridges he'd clumped into sixes. Tooch walked up and down the aisle.

"Where the hell's War and them?" he asked.

Buz shrugged, chewing.

"Didn't I say come back at dawn? It's on past dawn now, by a spell." He walked to the front.

In a few minutes he turned and walked to where he kept the mustache wax and got a tin of it and unscrewed the lid and reached a pair of fingers in and began to twist at the ends of his mustache. He climbed the ladder to where his room was and when he came down he wore a clean white shirt. He got a rag and some shoe polish from a shelf and set about polishing his boots by the window, watching the road more than his work. The clock had just struck ten when he looked up and down and then back up. When he saw how many men it was, he stood. He picked up a pistol from the counter and laid it back down. He looked at Buz Smith.

"Well," Tooch said.

Buz shook his head and pointed to the back.

"I won't run," Tooch said. "They ain't got nothing on us. If we run they know we're guilty and they'll catch us."

Buz waved good-bye and trotted down the aisle, grabbing up cartridges and pistols, and he went out the back door, still chewing.

The store appeared in the distance, and if the posse had expected an army of Tooch's disciples they saw only the store leaking smoke into the sky. Mack hoped Tooch had left, hoped they all had. He understood that his brother might be dead but turned his thoughts from this.

Waite whoaed King and turned him sideways in the road, a barrier between the store and the throng of men. He looked behind him as they wiped rain from their rifles and checked the loads in their sidearms. They rattled and clanked, the horses blew and neighed. Some of the men rolled up their sleeves, others pushed their hats back off their heads. The Thompson brothers sat unmoving and side by side like statues of soldiers that might flank the steps up to a regal building. Behind them the pharmacist seemed to be praying and others stared straight ahead. Oscar sat grimly in his flapping coat with his shoulders hunched. He looked at Waite as if they were boys again.

"You'll follow my lead," Waite called. He pulled his pistol from his side. "We won't have another massacre. If any damned one of you gets out of line in any way, I'll shoot him myself. Y'all got it?"

Mumbled assent.

"Come on, then," he said, turning King.

They galloped up in the mud and lined their horses in front of the porch. Every man aimed his gun at the storefront and some aimed pairs of pistols and men were creeping in the sheds on both sides and men were going around back. Tooch was surrounded. Mack hoped again that William was safe, that he would get the hell out of Mitcham Beat and go someplace else. He and the widow could meet up later and go west. See the flat land of the middle west and then climb the mountains and cross the desert to the ocean the widow had described, warm and forever.

For a moment he found himself beside Waite as they sat their horses in front of the store, waiting.

"Just be still," the sheriff said. "Don't look. This will be over soon."

With the men focusing on the store, Mack used his left thumb and forefinger to hold the key and tried to get its teeth into the slot.

Waite moved his horse to the front of the ranks and called for Tooch Bedsole and his men to come on out, hands in the air. He said surrender or we'll set fire to the store. He said they had ten seconds. Now nine. Eight. Already there were men lighting torches along the sides of the building, their pistols drawn.

Six seconds, Waite called.

For a long moment nothing happened. Each second crystallized in the air and passed.

Then the door opened and out came Tooch. A noise passed over the posse, breath held and let go and leather creaking, the jingle of spur and clack of metal.

Tooch carried no pistol and wore no coat so they could see he wasn't armed. Mack wondered why he would come out of the store like this. Why he hadn't run. Why he stood facing fifty and some upraised firearms with his arms folded. With an ease almost cordial he studied each face behind each barrel with his eyes glittering as if he meant to memorize the events of his own death. The participants. When he came to Waite he gave the shadow of a smile but when he looked at Mack it was with no more or less attention than he gave any other man.

The sheriff spurred his horse into the dirt between Tooch and the posse. "Tooch Bedsole," he said.

"My given name is Quincy," Tooch said.

"We know you're the ringleader of Hell-at-the-Breech," the sheriff said, "and that at your command such fellows as Lev James have acted. We know you've robbed and committed other crimes. We know that you're responsible for the deaths of Joe Anderson,

317

Ernest McCorquodale, and for the attempted murder of Bit Owen."

"Who?" Tooch raised an eyebrow at the name of Bit Owen, but he betrayed nothing else.

"Friend of mine," Waite said. "Got some cuts on his neck but he's in my custody with a hell of a story to tell."

Tooch's eyes narrowed as he cast them over the men before him and Mack thought of the other meeting so long ago and understood that Tooch had lost. He wondered how Tooch didn't seem to know this.

"Do you deny knowledge of the things I'm speaking about?" Waite asked.

"I do," Tooch said.

"You deny knowledge of the death of Joe Anderson?"

"Yes, I do."

"Deny knowledge of the death of Ernest McCorquodale?"

Tooch seemed at ease. He said, "I'm innocent of ever charge you brought up and of ever one you'll bring up. I'm a storeowner and a law-abiding citizen, nothing more. If lawless folks are at work, I don't know 'em. If Ernest McCorquodale's dead, I don't know one thing about it. He was a son-of-a-bitch that had enemies, he'd put many a family out. I expect any of these fellows who live out here would be happy about his going under. But I don't know nothing of it other than what you've said. Of Joe Anderson's death, I only know what I heard. And if you say 'Bit Owen' to me, all I can say back is 'Who?' "

A murmur went through the posse. He was proclaimed liar, killer, dead man.

"You ain't got to do nothing but ask any man in this beat," Tooch said. "They'll tell you my reputation. There's ain't one here who'll speak out against me. I see some out there now, among your number. I'm glad they're here to offer my defense."

He looked into the crowd, his eyes settling on Tom Hill.

318

"Our good Justice of the Peace," Tooch said. "Surely you'll take this man's word. Tell 'em, Tom. Tell 'em my reputation."

Hill sat on his horse. He'd removed the handkerchief from his rifle barrel and now used it to blow his nose. The members of the posse glanced at him but kept their weapons on Tooch.

"I can't proclaim your innocence," Hill said, "any more than I can your guilt. I'm only here trying to protect innocent folks so these murderous bastards won't kill no more children."

As if he didn't hear, Tooch looked to Jonesy Gray, enormous on his mule, his feet nearly dragging the ground. "Tell them, Jonesy. Did you ever see me commit a crime?"

Gray didn't answer but looked down at his hands. His cheeks were colored bright red in splotches.

Tooch turned to one of the farmers the posse had drafted. "Lou," he said. "Tell these men of my innocence."

That man lowered his head.

"You," Tooch said to another man, and another. None spoke for him.

Then, "Mack Burke," he called.

All eyes fell upon the boy.

"You've worked in this store along with me for more than a year. Tell these men, have you ever witnessed any unlawful acts here on these premises?"

Mack's ears blazed on the sides of his head. He felt sweat underneath his eyes.

"The boy condemns you with his silence," Waite said.

Then Mack cried, "No." His voice was high, a child's voice. "I ain't never seen him do nothing bad." Mack didn't know the reason he said it, and he would always wonder. Was it pity, guilt, loyalty— or was he simply offering Tooch, here at the end, the only thing he could, proof that the man still possessed the power to endear and ensnare?

Waite looked back over his shoulder, his lips pursed. Something

319

like wonderment softened the lines in his face and his eyebrows moved up his forehead.

Someone laughed, then another man, then all were laughing except Mack, Waite, and Tooch.

Then the moment had passed. Tooch was saying something else. He had moved his eyes past Mack. He was unbuttoning his shirt. He unbuttoned it and spread it open so his chest showed. Bare and flat. Small. Very white.

"You'll not dare shoot me," he said. "You men are here representing the law. You a justice of the peace. You a sheriff. And you have no evidence."

All the men were looking at Waite for instruction. Their rifles, shotguns, and pistols were ready. Mack saw that the sheriff now seemed very old and very tired. He and Mack, of them all, were the only two without a weapon pointed at the pale white torso of Tooch Bedsole.

Waite's horse began to back up, working its hips past the shoulders of two other horses.

Tooch was shaking his head. He raised a foot as if to step back.

"Fire," Waite said.

There came a sound as Mack had never heard, that of twenty then thirty then fifty guns shooting. The air seemed to bloom, to blaze with fire and cordite, the noise to come from inside his head.

Tooch outheld his hands as if to frighten a child but by then he was shaking in a kind of unnatural dance with his mouth opened and eyes wide and the hands out still, with one and then another finger disappearing and bright red circles in his palms and then he was suddenly yanked backward as if by a gust of wind. The air around him a red mist. His arms shaking. The glass windows exploding. His clothes jerked as if bats were trapped in them, pieces of paper from his pockets floating around him. He staggered back into the door, then stepped forward again, already dead, into a wall of bullets and went back yet again. Then he crumpled. Still they kept shooting.

Black holes appeared in the bottoms of his feet and scraps of paper turned in the smoke. The boards around him sparked as bullets hit nails. Wall of the store splintered and fragments of glass hung in their molding. Very bright blood began to spread in a circle around Tooch and he lay jerking only because bullets kept hitting him. Something sang past Mack's ear and he wondered if it was a ricochet.

They'd been walking along the road heading east, half a mile from the store, when the drumming of horses stopped them in their tracks. William dropped the empty jug. Without a sound they bounded for cover and had just slid down in the leaves when more horses than they'd ever seen thundered past. They saw Judge Oscar York, they saw the sheriff, and they saw—wearing a cold, startled look—Mack Burke.

"What the hell?" War Haskew said.

They filled the woods with their breathing as they batted their way through and at last, at the field's edge, over the picked cotton, beheld from a distance of nearly fifty yards Tooch from the waist up standing on the porch talking to the mob of riders.

"Your brother." War Haskew spat. "He's one of 'em."

"No, hell he ain't," William said. He pointed. "Look, he ain't even got a gun. He must be a prisoner."

"What ought we to do?" War Haskew said.

"Let's get the hell out of here," Kirk said. "Ain't no way in hell to outgun that mob."

"He'll talk his way out," War Haskew said.

"No," Kirk said. "Not this time he won't."

Then they saw a curious thing. Tooch began to unbutton his shirt.

Kirk said, "What the hell?" again, and they saw Tooch's lips move as he spoke words they couldn't hear.

Then the shooting began.

321

Tooch raised his hands and danced and fell back and hit the door and came forward again. They kept shooting.

"Goddamn," War Haskew shouted, and raised his rifle.

"No," Kirk said, but War had fired already.

In the distance Tooch had vanished, they couldn't see him over the horses and the men on the horses. William was firing, too, and yelling for War not to hit Mack but Kirk had already run.

"Cease fire!" Waite was yelling at stragglers—men who'd been late shooting, those with jammed rifles or those who'd needed gunfire to summon their nerve.

Another bullet whizzed past his ear. Waite looked across the field and saw the smoke.

"We're being shot at," he yelled, pointing. He tried to wheel King around but bumped into somebody's horse. He looked for the boy, but a shot hit the ground beside him with a thud. He tried to aim across the field but King turned again.

Now others in the posse had caught on and were turning their screaming horses. They were trying to reload, dropping bullets, a panic setting in. A man Waite didn't know chirped in pain and fell and lay gasping in the dirt, clutching his neck or shoulder. Tom Hill and his friends were riding off. Several others had drawn second or third guns and were shooting wildly in the air and at the trees and then the Thompsons were leading a charge over the field, Claudius firing his long pistol and Virgil the one-armed brother with his sword drawn and reins in his teeth.

Waite worked to get King settled. The shooting had stopped and the Thompson brothers paused at the edge of the woods to wait for reinforcements before they began the chase. His horse calm, Waite sought Oscar's eyes but his cousin was staring at Tooch Bedsole where he lay in a red muck.

The men with torches were lighting the building afire, though

Waite hadn't ordered it and flames were racing up the walls and smoke poured from the chimney in the back. Something popped inside the store and then a window burst out, fire eating its way up the boards and onto the roof.

Oscar dismounted and tried to pull his horse away, watching. He took his hat off. "My Lord," he said.

The last of the unhurt riders had recovered their mounts and most were crossing the road. The dentist was seeing to a man who'd been shot, yelling for him to hold still. Another—lying on his back, a wound in his neck—looked dead already, Waite didn't know his name. He walked to the edge of the field where riders were entering the woods and then looked back. To the east. The west. "Macky," he said.

William and War Haskew had shot their rifles empty before the men across the field realized they were being fired upon. Calmly, they reloaded.

"I ain't never shot this bad in my life," War Haskew remarked.

"What?" William said. He couldn't hear.

They raised their guns for another volley, War Haskew firing exclusively at Sheriff Waite as he looked their direction and pointed.

Now the mob's horses began to rear and buck. The man next to Waite fell. William had reloaded a third time and begun firing again when War Haskew took him gently by the shoulder.

"Let's get on out of here, buddy," he said. "They'll be coming."

"Do what?" William yelled.

Some of the men were pointing to their position where smoke from their firing hung thick. William waved wildly to scatter its rags from his face.

"If we don't go now," War Haskew yelled back, "we don't ever go!"

Men were already gathering for a charge, two old longhaired

soldiers halfway over the field. Bullets clipped leaves and hummed through the limbs. William looked for Mack but couldn't see him for the smoke. Maybe he'd got loose.

He and War Haskew turned and ran.

"Split up," War called.

William nodded and veered left down a gradual incline toward where he knew the woods grew thicker. His hat flew off. His feet smacked over the leaves. The ground dropped sharply like a step and he lost his footing and slid on his hands and knees in a froth of leaves to the bottom and landed running, thick arches of briar springing up, snatching at his clothes. He'd lost his pistol in the fall but didn't go back for it.

The trail tapered into nothing and he burst through a beard of Spanish moss, strings of which clung to him ferally, and he kept running, tiny barbs and thorns in his cheeks and neck and his right eye weeping blood and blurry from a whipped limb, a sharp pain in his side, cold tears tracking the dirt on his cheek. They'd lose the advantages of their horses in here, though, and if he got lucky he might be able to get to the Bear Thicket where you'd be crazy to go if you didn't have to. Running, ducking low limbs and dodging vines, he worked at reloading his rifle.

At the store, a few men remained in the road, some tending jammed weapons, others simply watching the fire, their hats clutched in their fists. A couple in the cotton field were chasing a spooked pony. Oscar had taken off his long coat. He removed his gloves with shaking hands and let them drop to the ground and pushed back his hat, his hair soaked with sweat.

Waite stuck to business. Kneeling, he sought a pulse in the wrist of the neck-shot man and, not finding one, removed the man's coat and covered him with it. He pinned the arms of the other shot man as the dentist bound a wound in his upper thigh.

"You're lucky," Waite told him as he struggled. "It missed the artery."

"Don't feel lucky," the man gritted through his teeth.

"Find him a bottle," Waite told Oscar, then he ordered two onlookers to the porch to drag Bedsole down, away from the flames. They wrapped bandannas around their faces against the thick boiling smoke and mounted the steps. Waite watched each take one of Bedsole's ankles and begin to pull, watched one man back-stagger to the ground as the leg he'd grabbed came loose at the knee. The man looked at the bare ragged calf in his hands like a stick of wood—the foot still socked and shoed—then flung it to the side and gaped at Waite. The other man let go the foot he held and bent; Waite thought he might be sick. Then he saw him grabbing at the blood-slick paper from Bedsole's pockets.

"It's banknotes," he called.

"You son-of-a-bitch," Waite said, climbing the steps himself and pushing the fellow off the porch. The man sprawled in the dirt, got up glaring at Waite, and mounted his horse and rode off after the others. Oscar ascended the steps and he and Waite squinted against the heat, staring at the body. Fingers and half-fingers were strewn about him and a piece of an ear lay by his head and his chest was collapsed in. He had no face, just a mass of bone and hair and gore. Chips of what must have been his brain. His remaining foot had four holes in the sole of its shoe. Blood was everywhere, they were standing in it, such a quantity as Waite had never seen, bright red lung blood and nearly black gut blood and all reds between. It had begun to bake and bubble from the heat, the odor causing Oscar to gag. He fumbled for his handkerchief and held it to his mouth.

Then shooting, from inside the store. Oscar leapt off the porch but Waite knew it was just the ammunition stock. He came down the steps unbuttoning his coat.

*　　*　　*

325

War Haskew ran with limbs snatching at his clothing. Bullets bit into trees to the left of him and to the right, made perfect circles through leaves he'd just passed. He saw an uprooted tree and slid down behind it and shot empty his magazine as fast as his arms and the lever would work. Whoever was chasing him took cover, and for a moment after he fired his last the woods were very quiet. Then he heard their horses. Saw a mane, a mouthful of teeth. He got up and ran again, fumbling for cartridges as he went. Something cracked, the stock of his rifle splintered. They were in front of him, too. He couldn't tell the men from the trees. His rifle was sticky. He looked at his hand, covered in blood. He unstuck it from the stock and held it up. Through the palm. He turned to the west, the direction he'd come from. Horses. Smoke. He heard more shots and leaves raised from the ground around him.

They found Kirk James hiding in a loblolly pine. He had a rifle and yelled if they'd let him climb down and stay alive he'd not fire at them. He said he wanted a trial. He said he was an American. He looked about them as twenty or so horses surrounded the bottom of the tree.

"I can take one or two of you with me," he called, aiming down. "I done picked you out," he said.

Several men were backing up, craning their necks, trying to get a good view. Someone said it was a coon hunt.

"Why ain't he shot at us?" a man asked.

"He ain't got his gun," another fellow reckoned. "Or he's out of lead."

They closed in.

Then Kirk shot. Claudius Thompson sat upright on his horse and looked stricken.

"Brother," Virgil said.

Claudius fell backward off the horse and lay dead.

326

"I told you," Kirk called.

Now the men below were kicking their horses and firing into the trees. Pine needles and branches falling around them. Above, Kirk closed one eye and licked his tongue out of his mouth and leveled his rifle on Virgil Thompson. Virgil Thompson fell.

A sound then like firecrackers and the air filling with smoke. More pine needles falling and limbs, then a rifle clattered down and landed barrel-first in the soft dirt and stayed upright. A shoe fell.

They used dogs to find William. They set them loose and watched them disappear into a dark alcove beneath a pine tree split in half by some long-ago wind. They sent in three young volunteers, all nineteen years of age, to follow him through vinework clever as wire and understory so thick their clothes soon hung shredded from their bleeding limbs. A few hundred yards into the chase, William shot one of the dogs when it got close. Then he shot the other. The three pursuers, now reduced to their knees and half blind from briar and branch, spotted him scrambling away on his knees. They shot and he shot back and they exchanged gunfire for half an hour from a distance of forty feet until both sides were empty. William knew he was lucky they never thought to spread out and cross-fire him. He thought if he could make the other side he might get out alive.

Ardy Grant woke, unable to move and only seeing from one eye, the other seeming to be gone. Above was a high white sky imposed with branches and pine needles that waved in a breeze. He heard buzzing. Faraway gunshots. He blinked as a fly crawled onto his eyeball. He tried to remember who'd shot him. Or why. He couldn't. Then he did: Sheriff Waite, for whom he felt nothing. He realized he wasn't afraid, and this relieved him. He had no sense of smell. He seemed to have no hands or fingers either. No feet. He was dimly aware of his teeth and felt very thirsty, that was all. He'd be okay, he thought. There would just be some waiting.

A shadow fell across his face and he opened his eye again. It could have been a minute or a day. It was somebody he didn't remember seeing before, a freckle-cheeked boy about ten years old and with yellow hair that looked like it'd been cut with a dull flintrock. He had a filthy face and there were two other boys with him. The first one bent and blew a fly out of Ardy's eye. Reached down and tapped his cheek.

"Can you feel this here?"

Ardy tried to say with his eye that he couldn't.

"They done killed you good," the boy said. He shook his head, though not sadly, and disappeared for a moment and said, as if from far away, "I'm jabbing my knife in your leg. Can you not feel it? Wait. This here one's going in real real deep. Up . . . to the handle almost. I expect that thing I'm hitting there is your bone."

He appeared again in Ardy's sphere of vision with a grin. Time seemed to have gone by, for now the sky was darker.

"Look," the blond boy said, dangling a bloody thing before Ardy's face. "This is your pecker. I sawed it off." He held it so it dripped blood in Ardy's eye, which closed of its own accord.

The next time he opened his eye he saw a faintly fuzzy field of stars. A dog appeared, sudden, breathy. It seemed to be licking his cheek.

Then a shout and torchlight and the blond boys were back, giggling. They were dragging him. Later they formed a circle around him and crept close, taking turns doing things to his body and describing the things they were doing. He understood what it meant to be a boy, for he'd been one himself a long time ago, and wished he were one of these boys here, now, with such a perfect victim as himself.

He'd forgotten his name and the next time he opened his eye he'd forgotten what it meant to be a boy and all of his memories were washed clear and he was nothing more than the skyful of stars he saw and face after grinning face streaked in blood as they appeared and made their strange sounds, and as the sky shrank and darkened at its edges his eye closed and opened and closed and the noise grew suddenly louder before it disappeared altogether.

Mack hid. He hid the evening through in the shell of a log he'd wallowed into. He knew that if he were to move too suddenly the whole casing would collapse about him in shingles and powder and the thousands of mites and ants hibernating in the log would be set loose in his hair and clothes and to a winter climate they'd never known. He tried to remember something but could think of nothing to focus on. Then he thought of the well. The one outside the widow's house. How it smelled of sulfur and the way the water was so cold. How he and William used to submerge their whole heads into it and come up blue-faced and gasping, their hair flat on their heads and eyes blinking. How breathless they'd been.

He opened his eyes to the familiar circle outside his log. He could see a long way, perhaps fifty yards. The log—he hadn't noticed what kind of tree it was when he'd forced his way in, scooping out wet, then drier, then dry rotted wood like fine yellow dirt—lay at the bottom of a hollow. It seemed to have fallen from somewhere higher and rolled to here. He imagined the ground shaking as it hit. He imagined the lightning or huge wind that had knocked it down, or the men who'd bent together on either end of their crosscut saw and pulled and pulled in a rhythmic tug-of-war as sweat flew from their chins and elbows while the blade ate its way in until they had to attack it with axes and cut on the other side and stop and peer up at the huge thing rising into higher clouds of forest; in spring or summer they wouldn't have been able to see the top and who could have said but they were hacking away at a joist that held up the very sky above.

329

In his mind it was him and William smiling at each other from the ends of the saw. Their faces red as blood as they pull the blade in deeper, the tree creaking and its high branches clicking and leaves murmuring. He slept.

When he woke it was night and he rose from the log with its crumbs and sections falling away from him. He shook himself and brushed grit from his eyes. His shoulder, stiff and sore, had stopped bleeding. He looked up at the stars through the trees and knew he was only a mile from home and began to trot.

When he whistled his low whistle the dog was up instantly and off the porch, over the yard and ecstatically licking his bloody face. She hadn't barked, yet the widow knew he was there as he'd known she would. Gradually, candles were snuffed in the windows, lamps blown out one at a time, the house darkening, and soon the door swung open and he could feel her standing there. He was at the end of a long journey that had begun with the three of them: killer, old woman, dog.

And baby now. She held it.

"Well?" she called.

With the dog at his thigh he hurried over the moonlit yard, ascended the steps, and looked down at her.

"Your face," she said. She saw his shoulder. "You're hurt."

"Granny," he whispered. "Tooch is dead. They shot him. They kept shooting him."

She lowered her head. "Child, I know it," she said. "Now get on in here."

Inside, she had him sit in a chair by the window while she put the baby in a crib made from stove wood and interwoven vines. She moved over the floor and poked about in a box, opening bottles and smelling them. She'd begun to make a potion when she stopped. She crossed the room in the darkness, so light on her feet the boards spoke nothing of her passing, and disappeared into her bedroom. When she returned she handed him a bottle of bonded whiskey. At

330

the look on his face, she said, "Among your biggest flaws, Macky Burke, is that things in the world continue to surprise you."

His chair received enough moonlight for her doctoring, her hands ministering to his shoulder first, then his cuts and scrapes, as he gulped from the bottle for the pain.

"They got Huz, too."

"Don't drink that all."

She dabbed the gash below his eye—he had no idea where he got it—with a poultice she'd made from eggs and something brown she'd crumbled up. It smelled like dog shit and burned.

"You know that, don't you. That they got Huz. And Tooch."

She nodded.

"They shot him a thousand times."

His eyes stung. Not for Tooch, or Huz, or anybody else, but for himself. For the loss of her fingers on his wounds. For the loss of the things she crumbled, for the loss of her biscuits, loss of her mystery. How long since she'd touched his face?

"Hush, boy," she said. "Leave the crying to that baby over yonder."

"I can't," he said, his shoulders shaking, "it's just another flaw, Granny."

"I reckon so." She wiped his tears away with her facecloth. "You're just eat up with 'em, ain't you?"

"Granny?"

"What?"

"Is William dead?"

She began putting things back in the box. "Not yet."

Later he wouldn't remember going to his old room and falling asleep, and hadn't planned to do so, but he woke some hours further in the night with a start, in his bed, which smelled exactly the same, of lye soap. Feather mattress, feather pillow. He was stiff, the skin around his trunk feeling as if it'd been pulled nearly off. When he moved, such pain flared in his shoulder he almost blacked out. It

331

passed soon enough, though, and with great care he sat up, hugging himself, and leaned to peer out into the black of the night. He raised the window and smelled the sulfur the wind carried.

His shoulder had loosened up, so he stood, rubbing his torso. Dizzy with the effort, he steadied himself against the wall until the feeling had passed, then willed his left leg to move, and the other to do likewise, and soon he'd made it into the front room, his eyes adjusting.

She sat without rocking in her rocking chair, looking outside, hands folded in her lap. The baby's breathing in the crib by her chair.

"A house cat," she said. "If you're ever of a mind to get me a present, I think I'd like a house cat."

"Granny," he told her, "if I live through the night, I'll get you a dozen house cats."

"Just the one, boy. Just the one."

"They'll be coming," he said.

"He'll come. I've been hoping he'll wait until the sun's up."

"I'd best go, then."

In the half dark, he couldn't see her expression. He limped across the room and stood next to her. Wanted to touch her face. Wanted her to touch him. Her hand came up then, as if independent of her will, and took his and pressed it against her cheek, the skin warm and as soft as a blanket made from cotton.

"Granny," he said. "I'm sorry for all that's happened."

"Hush, boy," she said, squeezing his fingers so hard it hurt. "Listen," she said. The dog began to bark.

"He ain't gone wait till light," she said.

William crawled through endless darkness. He shut his eyes to keep things from poking in them and when he'd stop to rest and open them the night seemed even darker than the darkness inside his head. He could hear behind him the men chasing him, though he knew they had run out of bullets, same as him. His thoughts were jumbled with past violence, buildings ablaze and gunshots, Joe Anderson's throat blooming red and how his shirt had darkened below his jaw. The colored family they'd pulled from their burning house and made watch as the fire raged. He shook his head to clear it and kept going in the direction that felt west.

Waite left King standing alone in the yard and swung down out of the saddle and stood waiting, light-headed from lack of sleep. The widow's dog came to the edge of the porch. It had been barking and now the bark faded to a low growl. The moon so bright overhead it threw shadows: the horse's, Waite's own bent length as he crossed the yard in slow steps. He levered a round into the rifle and heard a cartridge land in the grass, a live one, he knew—he'd already levered the rifle. He took a breath and walked up the steps, the dog slinking aside with its ears flat, head low, the growl a question now, his a familiar odor here. He tried the leather latch, unlocked, and opened the door. It was darker within the house than without and he stood waiting neither in nor out until the outline of the old woman rocking by the far window, holding a baby in her lap, was clear to him.

"Is he here?" he asked. He stepped inside.

"No, he ain't."

He closed the door quietly behind him. "I know he come here, Mrs. Gates, cause there wasn't no place else for him to go."

"He did come here," she said, rocking, "and I made him leave."

"Why would you do that?" He went along the wall. "That seems a little out of character for you."

"What do you know of character, Billy Waite?"

After a quick search of the house, he stopped by the hearth where he'd sat on his other visits when they'd talked inside. When the weather was cold. He eased himself down onto the stones. "Mrs.

Gates," he said, "my character's been called into question more since Arch Bedsole got shot than it ever has my whole life. I don't exactly know how that come about, but this whole mess has been a bad dream for me. For you, too, I know. It seems to me that we're the two innocents brought into this war."

"If you consider yourself innocent, then you're either almighty holy or almighty lost."

"Lost," he said. "I'd put a nickel on lost."

She looked at him. The baby coughed.

Because he could think of nothing to say or do, he laid the rifle over his knees and took a cigar from his side coat pocket and bit off the end and spat it into the fireplace behind him. He scratched a match over the stones and touched the match to the cigar until it flared. He held the match and in its light watched the widow as she rocked, her attention now on the baby. It started to squall and she sang quietly to it, a tune he didn't know. He wanted to talk to her but had no idea what to say. He reached behind him and ashed his cigar in the fireplace, though there wasn't enough yet to ash. The baby kept crying.

"You mind some light?" he asked.

She kept singing.

He found a stub of candle on a table and with the end of his cigar lit it. He carried the candle over to her and knelt before her, looking up into her blue eyes.

"I want you to tell me, Granny, if you know where that boy is. If you do, I promise you I'll take him safely to jail. I done been through too much to let that mob have him now." He didn't want to say this next thing, but he did. "He told me it was him that killed Arch Bedsole. So now I got to arrest him, just to ask him questions, try to sort all this out. It's gone be hell once I get back in the real world, where people expect answers for actions. There'll be folks down from Montgomery, too, I expect. The governor's office."

She said, "This here is the real world, Billy Waite. It's my real world. As real a world as I ever spent a night in."

The baby had quieted and he looked down, it was watching him.

"He's cute," Waite said.

"He's sick," the widow said, adjusting the blanket.

"It's cold in here," he said, standing. "You want me to bring in some firewood? I'll stoke us up a good one."

"I don't want a fire," she said.

The widow had told Mack how babies, in the womb, come to know their father's voices. She'd told him of occasions where babies turned—you could see the ripple of it below the skin of the mother's belly—when their fathers spoke. That in some cases, once the baby is out in the air, it will move its head toward its father at the first words he says. Now Mack thought of this as he fixed on the sheriff's voice, turning his head in the nest his arms made to hear the muffled words.

"Would you just let me be, Billy Waite?"

"You ain't cold?" his voice answered.

"I'm always cold," the widow's voice said.

"Just let me get us a good one going here."

Very slowly, Mack moved his head up. She'd had him climb into the fireplace and worm his way into the chimney, a thing that had seemed impossible but somehow had worked. A patch of night sky showed at the top, a place less black than everything else he could see, but an impossible distance away. He tried to picture how tall the chimney was, seen from outside, and couldn't.

"Do what?" Waite's muffled voice said.

"—Hell-at-the-Breech," she said.

He listened, here was the story the widow told.

How her two God-sent adopted sons William and Macky had, yes, killed Arch Bedsole in August of eighteen and ninety-seven. In a bungled robbery attempt. A child's foolish idea of fun. She knew of it through her own gift of knowing, knew the second Arch's life passed from his lips and nostrils into the strangely chilly air of August on that night so long ago. She'd sat straight up in bed. Felt a stabbing pain in her back, between her shoulder blades. Her boys were not under their covers, she said. They were nowhere in the house or around the house. Such a night filled with dark she couldn't see her own hand before her eyes, but still she lurched out with her cane and an oil lamp, to find what horror awaited her.

For she had already put together that it had been her boys who'd done the deed. She'd known they left at night, yes, they were boys. She herself had been young once. She remembered the first boy she'd set her hat for, she was fifteen, and how the two of them used to meet in a falling-apart barn on the outskirts of a town Waite wouldn't have heard of in Tennessee, used to stand smooching with a stall between them, for she'd been told that if their hips touched she would become with child. Oh, had it been so, she said, had that sweet boy possessed such magic hips that touching them to hers would have seeded her and they would have never seen this place, that the life she'd lived would have been another life entirely, even with her as the mother of a bastard, of a hundred bastards, but not the mother of killers.

"You see, Billy Waite," she said, "I thought they'd just gone out to see Annie, and I knew they didn't have the money she cost, so I figured they'd just outrun their lust, or swim it away dog-paddling over the river, or use Onan's solution. Never did I dream they'd try to become robbers, and that the man they'd try to rob would be Arch."

For she had heard them coming, she said, on their way home from the killing, and she'd doused her lamp and stood in the dark road so close to them she felt their wind as they passed, hearing enough of their talk to know one of them had become a murderer. Once they'd gone on out of hearing she relit the lamp and started her journey, finding at last a little blood on the road, and following its drops like a hunter trailing his deer, until finally she saw the light from the fire. It was the cabin where Tooch had been born and been living and it was on fire and in the light the fire gave she saw Arch Bedsole's bloody body lying dead and Tooch sitting on the ground holding the white-handled pistol Arch had always carried when he traveled.

She approached him. He didn't look up until her shadow blocked him from the fire.

Granny, he said, for he was one of hers, too.

Tooch, she said.

He said, You knew he was dead, didn't you?

Yes, Tooch. I did.

You always did know the strangest facts, Granny.

How was he killed?

He looked up at her. He said, I expect you know that already. Don't you?

He looked at her, then at the fire behind her. He said, I was inside reading one of them old encyclopedia books Arch got when he was little. He let me borry it. I was just setting there puzzling over some of them real big trees they got in California when I heard a noise outside. I blew out the lamp and got my rifle. When I went out, though, I couldn't see a thing. Did you ever see as black a night as this, Granny? So I went back in and lit the lamp again and come back out. That's when I seen him. Arch. He was coming through the yard. Bloody. I dropped the lamp, I guess, and run to him. Didn't see how the lamp had caught the porch on fire.

She watched him. He sat, his face orange in the firelight, his hair slick with sweat from the heat of it and blood already dry on his shirt. He gestured with the pistol.

By the time I thought to try and put out the fire it'd gone too far, he said. And Arch was dead. I could tell cause the fire lit him up. Showed the bubbles in his chest had done stopped popping. That's how come I knew him to be dead. I drug him over away from it and just been setting here wondering what to do.

"Did he say anything?" Waite asked.

"Yeah. He said something."

"What?"

You know that yourself, Granny, Tooch said. You know who killed him. Or you wouldn't be here.

That's not true, she said.

But it was.

"And the truth, Billy Waite, is this. I don't know if he said it was Macky that did the killing or if it was me that said it. And as I think of it more and more, which I find myself doing these days and nights, I find myself believing it was Tooch got me to say it, that when Arch got there he didn't have no idea who it was shot him and that Tooch Bedsole, black heart of his be cursed, tricked me into telling him what he didn't know. But there lay Arch Bedsole, dead. Shot twice. Once in the back, once in the chest."

What do you intend to do about my boys? she asked Tooch.

He thought for a long while. He kept throwing pieces of grass and leaves into the fire. Then he said, You know what.

I want to hear it from your mouth, Tooch.

No you don't.

Tooch.

Kill them, he said. It's my duty. I got to avenge my cousin.

You always hated him, she said.

Tooch stared at her. Yes, sir, he said. You always knew the strangest facts, Granny.

Part of the roof caved in. Something in the fire popped.

From her skirts she raised the pistol she'd always had. You won't kill my boys on this night, Tooch Bedsole, she said.

He looked up, into the barrel of the gun.

He stood slowly, the body of Arch lying between them. She held the pistol out, tried not to let it shake. Her finger touched the trigger.

338

All she had to do was pull it. Pull it and go home and get her boys, bring them back and have them toss Tooch's body into the fire. Hell could come early for him.

I can't let you kill my children, she said.

Granny, Tooch said, I'm one of your children, too. Ain't I? And this here dead cousin is another one. And so are most of the men and women who're starving in these cotton fields and hollows. We're all your children. You ain't gone shoot one of us, are you, Granny?

He raised his hand toward the pistol.

How you gone shoot me, Granny, who was orphaned, too, left by his own daddy and give to a sharecropper's life in the fields?

He stepped over the body. Stepped over it. She gasped at the callousness of the act, and as she did, his hand gently took the pistol from her. He uncocked it and ejected its cylinder and shook the cartridges out onto the ground where they glowed in the firelight. Then he handed the pistol back.

Kill them, he repeated. Myself. I ain't got much of a choice. Everbody loved Arch.

But why, Tooch? Why kill them? she pled. They're just young, stupid boys. It was a mistake. They meant to be robbers. They had no idea it was Arch they were trying to steal from. Why would you ruin not just two but three lives, for you'd ruin mine, too, you'd end it, just because of two stupid boys? They're all I've got, Tooch.

But his face was implacable in the light of the fire as it raged behind her and consumed the wood of the house and the skin of the deer on the walls and the wasp nests in the eaves and the dry mortar between the logs. The squat piece of wood used for a table and the R encyclopedia. Her back grew hot and she moved away from the fire with her dress smoking and continued to plead for her boys' lives, following him as he moved around the yard looking for things to throw in the fire. She offered him all the money she had, offered him her house, her old mule, her services in whatever capacity he would use. Were she younger she would have lifted her dress and offered herself.

339

To kill them would be such a waste, she begged, when they have so much to give.

What do they have to offer me? he asked.

The widow paused. A plan took shape in her mind. It appeared there fully formed, a gift she thought from the devil, she nearly swooned from the brilliant desperate weight of it.

Tooch, she said. Oh, oh, listen . . .

And she put forth the plan. The last words to flow from Arch's dying lips were that men from town ambushed and shot him *to keep him out of the election*. This would start a war, with the right man as its general. With the right man, the farmers in Mitcham Beat could be rallied, could be set to task to raise arms against their oppressors. A change could occur. . . .

For a long while Tooch was silent. The fire unfurled flags of smoke and ember into the night. He got up and went to the edge of the burning house and unfastened his pants and urinated into the flames in plain sight of her, urinated for a long time, steam rising around his feet, then shook himself off and came back fastening his pants. He looked down at her, she up at him.

Tell me more, he said.

They sat side by side, on a log Tooch dragged over, facing the fire. Arch lay behind them, eyes to the sky, as if seeing the future revealed.

"Together," she told Waite, "we talked all night. Together, we were conceiving Hell."

For a long time Waite sat. The baby had gone back to sleep and the only sound in the room was the creak of her rocking chair as she moved forward and back.

"How did Tooch get the store?" Waite asked at last.

"We used the Bible. Rebekah tricking Isaac. I was nursing Ed Bedsole as his time of dying came, and Ed was out of his mind. Tooch dressed in Arch's clothes and hat, and they looked enough alike, and sounded enough alike, that Ed signed everything Tooch set before him, he thought he was talking to Arch again. In a lawyer's office I lied, God forgive me, and said that Ed Bedsole had been of sound mind when he sold the store to Tooch. Tooch could've got all the Bedsole farms, too, but he didn't want nothing to do with cotton. All he wanted was that store."

For a long time there was nothing but silence. There was a murderer in a chimney and a woman telling all the dark things locked so long in her heart to keep the murderer alive.

"Billy," she said.

"What?"

"There's another thing."

He waited. Mack waited, too.

"When I got home it was near 'bout dawn. I found the boys in their beds. William was asleep and Macky was pretending to be. I wanted to see who'd done it so I looked at their guns. William's, the sixteen-gauge shotgun, hadn't been shot. It was Macky's pistol. I knew how many bullets he had in it. Bullets were so costly I knew of each one and had taught them thrift in the use of such things. He'd only shot one time."

Waite said, "Didn't you say Arch had been shot twice?"

"Yes. He was. Once through the back, from the back. That one came out the front. The other one was in his chest. From the front."

"What are you saying, Mrs. Gates?" Waite asked.

"This. The truth is, I think Arch wasn't shot the first time in such a way to kill him, for there wasn't so much blood after all. I think he was shot through the shoulder or side or some other place. I think he come up on Tooch and Tooch saw an opportunity and took it and shot his own cousin. And then I think he took that lantern and flung it at the house and stood watching it burn."

Mack imagined the widow, sitting motionless in her chair by the window, moonlight falling onto her deeply lined face, her eyes black holes under her glowing white hair, her tiny hands holding the baby that was sleeping in her lap. Then she said, "The reason I made my

Macky leave tonight, Billy Waite, is that I've come to hate him in the last year. Hate him for taking himself and his brother away from me. For the things he's made me do, lies he's made me say. The only way I've lived these last months is by lying and hating."

The baby stirred in her lap; it coughed. An arm raised out of the blanket and a tiny hand opened its tiny fingers. It seemed to be reaching for something and, not finding it, began to cry. The old woman ignored it and stared at Waite. Then she said, "I've said all I can say. Will you leave now, Sheriff?"

He had sat so long on the hearth he could barely move. The house had grown colder now and outside the earth had fallen quiet. He flexed his hands and stood, grimacing at the pain down his leg. He looked at the old woman and wondered if she were lying or telling the truth. Behind him a trickle of soot fell from the chimney.

He gazed into the mouth of the fireplace, not seeing her raise the pistol from the blanket on her lap. The baby's hand reached for it but she aimed it out farther.

Without looking at her, he walked to the door. "We'll keep searching for the boy. If he's got any sense, he's halfway to Louisiana right now. If he shows hisself, though, it may not go too good for him."

He turned back to her. If he noticed the pistol aimed at his heart, he didn't let on. "I'll bid you good night, Granny Gates." He spoke loudly, over the squalling baby. "I don't figure to be back out here bothering you again no time soon."

He opened the door and stepped out and closed it and stood gazing at the night. The dog watched him with its tail thumping the porch boards. Inside, the baby screamed. Carrying his rifle, he descended the steps and climbed aback his horse and spurred King downhill at a trot, passing the water trough which held within its framed water the moon's blank face. He looked up at it in its sky of stars, white vapor issued into the air with his every breath.

He rode past field after moonlit field and stopped at the burning store where the roof had collapsed but which still glowed and licked its fire at the sky. He sat watching, embers floating in the air like notes of music, Tooch Bedsole nothing but a pile of cinders shrinking on what remained of the porch. One of the fellows left behind to guard the place wandered over and asked Waite if he had a bottle. He said he didn't and the fellow walked off. Waite's face had begun to burn from the heat and King backed up of his own accord but still Waite watched. The chimney had been leaning all the while and with very little fanfare toppled sideways and scattered its glowing stones over wide and varying trajectories. The ground near the store had been dried by the heat and small fires sprang up in the grass around the stones that lay pulsing like fallen pieces of sky. One of the men went over and began stamping them out.

As if released from a spell, Waite rubbed the bridge of his nose and turned King and rode away. He passed beneath tunnels of dark trees, through ink-black fields, and passed the spot where Ardy Grant had been shot. The young man was gone from the road and for a moment Waite worried he might yet live but then he was dozing in the saddle and didn't start awake until the horse shied at the scent of blood from Lev James's dead mule. He passed burning houses where families or what was left of them lay in the yard, but he didn't stop to see if they were dead or merely sleeping.

The baby had quit its crying by the time Mack worked himself down the chimney and came out legs-first onto the hearth. He sat watching her rock the baby, she staring back at him. His shoulder now sore but manageable. There were things he wanted to tell the widow, yet he didn't speak. Nor did she. Then he sneezed, and sneezed again, and for a long time he couldn't stop sneezing until, for fear of setting the baby crying again, he got up and went into his old room. Covered in soot, he stood by the window where outside its glass lay the beginning of a world he would see and see soon. As soon as he would bend and raise the sash, slip through the shutters and into the night. He looked at the backs of his hands. He turned them over and looked at their palms, black, too. He would go in a moment, already a plan forming—work his way to the river, find the old canoe he and William used to paddle over to see Annie, wash the blackness off his skin and go through the yard and up the steps into her house, convince her to accompany him to Louisiana, where they'd get married, live, work, sleep, die.

In the next room the baby coughed. Careful of his shoulder, Mack slid up the glass. His fingers left ash marks on the shutters as he ducked through the window, but no other evidence betrayed his passing; even the dog failed to hear him where she lay sleeping on the porch.

William woke with his cheek against the ground. His teeth chattering. He heard scratching sounds close by and raised his head with a leaf stuck to his cheek like a leech and blood in the ever-deeper lines of his face and saw the three open-jawed men drawing near him like ghouls. One had a hatchet, another a knife. They were grinning.

He began to scrabble away and they thrashed after him. Soon he saw light dimly through the brush and at last he burst forth on the other side of the thicket and bailed off into the cold creek without looking at what lay waiting for him. The men on the opposite side— spaced fifty yards apart—whistled up and down the bank that here he came, and by the time he'd swum over they'd congregated and stood in wait. They dragged him ashore half naked and trembling and weak from blood loss and mummied him in about five pounds of rope. Then watched with wry humor as his three pursuers splashed from the thicket into the water. When the men had swum across, they went after William. They were kicking his crumpled, rope-cocooned form when the others pulled them off.

"Waite wants him alive," Oscar said. He had red-rimmed eyes

and wore a blanket around his shoulders and had been drinking all night. Two of the men lifted William and hung him over a horse.

When Waite arrived later in the morning they stood William up and leaned him against the wall inside the covered bridge, which they'd used as a barracks for the night. One of the boy's eyes was swollen shut from a boot kick, the other half of his face yellowed and blued and misshapen—somebody said he looked like an anvil—his dirt coating muddied by his own oozing blood. Waite said for Oscar and the rest to give the two of them a moment, and the men faded back.

"William Burke," he said once they were alone.

Hearing his name seemed to register on the boy. He raised his head. He tilted it like a puppy.

"Mr. Billy? Is that you? I can't see too good."

Teeth gone. His gums a bloody pulp.

"It's me, William."

"They gone hang me?"

"They are."

He lowered his head. "Reckon you ain't got no choice."

"No. You took up with the wrong bunch, boy."

"Tell the widow I'm sorry."

"She knows it."

"Where's Macky?"

Waite looked at the bridge's opening. The men lurking there skulked away.

"He's safe."

"He is?"

"Yeah. He'll be okay."

"I'm proud for him. He never did do nothing anyway. Not on purpose, no way. Rest of us, we, we—"

He seemed to forget what words to use and began to sink against the wall.

Waite walked out into the light feeling absolutely nothing and told Oscar they'd better go on hang him soon or there wouldn't be anything left to hang. Two men dragged him out by loose strands of rope. Waite said if they didn't want him to whip their asses they'd pick the boy up and carry him. They did. Waite didn't watch the rest.

He got his horse and adjusted the saddle and mounted up. Oscar was at his hip.

"Billy."

He offered up a bottle, just a slosh in the bottom.

Waite took the whiskey and finished it. He threw the empty bottle down the bank and spurred King on and left his cousin the judge standing in the shadow of the bridge. He pushed the horse to a gallop, the wind lifted his hair from his scalp. Within an hour the road had opened out, fields on both sides and the lightest sprinkle of cold rain.

He'd slowed to a walk when he rounded a bend in the road and encountered a curious sight: a buckboard wagon drawn by a pair of oxen with six stout black men walking alongside it and an old white-haired black man driving it. The wagon had a grand piano on it, festooned with rope and chain, but still each bump from the road chorded the piano's strings, a sound not music but something else, a thundering, roiling, muffled noise, the very voice of violence. He guided the horse around them without telling them that Lev James, the piano's new owner, was dead.

He knew that this war was over for him, but for the others, it would reach its smoke into the next century. Hell's breech had opened, and the closing, when it came, would come slowly. Years into the future the merchants of Grove Hill and Coffeeville would regard the trees and the shadows painted between the trees as places where ambushers would lie in wait, and for a time longer than Waite would live to see, the children of Mitcham Beat would be warned, *If you ever hear hooves, and the creak of good saddle leather, you'd better run hide, for the mob's come back.*

King, aware they were going toward Grove Hill, began to trot, the fields on both sides of them gray as the sky. As he rode, Waite hoped that Sue Alma would be home when he got there and would listen to all the things he had to say to her. That she'd have coffee on. He hoped Johnny-Earl would court, love, and marry the nurse who'd fixed his arm and that they would visit at Christmas. Before long he'd begun to nod in the saddle, his last waking thought a wish that the future would let him hold a baby boy named Billy Waite, who would grow to manhood and obey and endure the laws of man, who could survive the world the world was becoming.

ACKNOWLEDGMENTS

This novel owes a large debt of gratitude to the work of Harvey H. Jackson, III, who, in collaboration with Joyce White Burrage and James A. Cox, wrote *The Mitcham War of Clarke County, Alabama*. Thank you all—I appreciate your encouragement and support.

For help and advice on the manuscript in various stages, thanks to Monica Berlin, Barry Bradford, Robert Gatewood, William Gay, Hardy Jackson, Michael Knight, Jamie Kornegay, Roy Parvin, Sidney Thompson, and Tim Waller. At William Morrow, thanks to Lisa Gallagher, Michael Morrison, Jen Pooley, Sharyn Rosenblum, and Claire Wachtel, my editor. I also want to thank my agent and friend, Nat Sobel, for his continued faith and his careful reading of the manuscript. Thanks as well to the following institutions, whose generous financial support helped in the writing of this novel: The University of Mississippi, for the John and Renée Grisham Writer-in-Residency; The John Simon Guggenheim Memorial Foundation; Knox College; The MacDowell Colony; The Sewanee Writers' Conference; The University of the South, for the Tennessee Williams Fellowship in Fiction; and The Stadler Center for Poetry at Bucknell University, for the Philip Roth Residency in Creative Writing. Thanks also to Walt Darring, my first creative writing teacher. And to my parents, Gerald and Betty Franklin, I give thanks for a lifetime of support and love.

And finally, to my wife, Beth Ann, who read this manuscript many times, in many versions; who aimed her perfect poet's eye at each line; who listened and counseled; and who always believed, I can only say this: Thank you again, BA, for the things only you know. This book, and my happiness, would not exist without you. More than friends, now and forever.